necessary restorations

THE WALSH FAMILY

KATE CANTERBARY

VESPER PRESS

about necessary restorations

Sam Walsh is hanging on by a thread.

He works hard at concealing his chronic illnesses and represses the lingering pains of childhood, but he's running out of vices to distract him from his wounds.

Nothing feels good anymore. Not his prize-winning work preserving historic homes, not the family that refuses to give up on him even when he's at his most self-destructive. The only thing he wants is the conservatory-trained chaos he meets in a stalled elevator car.

She's the friend he never asked for and can't imagine living without. Then, she's more than a friend. She's everything.

Tiel Desai is not the same person she used to be.

She's finally found a place for herself in Boston, leaving the rejection and disappointment of her past behind. She keeps herself too busy to think about any of it, her days spent in grad school and with neurodivergent children in her music therapy practice, her nights devoted to the city's underground music scene.

She's learned how to get by—until Sam Walsh crashes into her world. He up-ends everything and takes spaces in her life she didn't know she had to give.

They find more in each other than they ever realized they were missing.

But finding it might not be enough to keep it—or each other.

CW: *History of emotional and physical abuse by a parent; parent illness; parent loss; estranged family member; chronic illness experienced by a main character; family abandonment experienced by a main character; infidelity in a main character's previous relationship; divorce experienced by a main character.*

Copyright

Editing provided by Julia Ganis of JuliaEdits. www.juliaedits.com

One

SAM

I NEVER THOUGHT I'd die in an elevator.

I always figured it would have something to do with my brother Riley leaving the gas stove on all night, killing us softly in our sleep.

Or gin. Chances were good that my liver was well on its way to pickled.

Or doorknobs. Touching those things was like licking the goddamn plague.

But this day was headed for the fires of hell, and it was all Shannon's fault.

"Hi, you've reached Shannon Walsh. Leave me a message and I'll get back to you soon."

Fucking voicemail. Again.

"I don't know where the fuck you are, Shan, but I've been waiting at the Commonwealth Avenue property for a goddamn hour. I thought we were trying to make a cash offer today, but I can't very well do that without you here."

Ending the call, I wet my lips and wiped the sweat from my brow. This heat wave was in its ninth day, and if I had even a lick of common sense, I would have hitched a ride to Cape Cod with my brother Matt and his wife Lauren for Labor Day weekend.

But no, I wanted to see the unit that just came available in the one-hundred-and-thirty-year-old French Revival hotel-turned-condo building in Boston's Back Bay. Specifically, I wanted my sister Shannon—the one who held the firm's purse strings—to buy that unit. I wanted to spend the long weekend drafting plans to demo it down to the studs and then restore the unit to its original beauty. I wanted to lose myself in lines and materials, things I could control.

And I wasn't up for third-wheeling it with the newlyweds.

I also wanted to be alone.

I could handle industry crowds and clients any day of the week and twice on Sundays, and I did it so fucking well they were willing to drop unreasonable amounts of money for my services. I was beginning to think I could finger-paint my designs and still collect six-figure commissions.

But I hated small talk. Bullshit conversations about weather or sports or politics held no appeal for me. I mostly stared at tits and asses until I was getting head in a coatroom or a drink thrown in my face.

And I was in a strange place these days. It was an odd in-betweenness; I wasn't sick but I certainly wasn't well. Not suicidal, but far from happy.

I'd been sliding further into this rut for months, and letting my work keep me too busy to notice. But while I was restoring everything I could get my hands on, the bottom was falling out on me. It was gradual, an evolution too small to notice without stepping back and examining from a distance. It was better this way. I didn't want anyone noticing.

So I was flying solo this Labor Day.

To me, alone didn't mean hunching over my drafting table all night, or skulking around the ancient Fort Point firehouse I called home.

No, alone meant drinking myself numb while some nameless young thing sucked the stress right out of me. There was nothing one hundred dollars pressed into the palm of the right maître d' and a good cocksucking couldn't soothe.

But let's be clear: blowjobs didn't *solve* problems.

If we were talking solutions, we were talking about my dick in someone's ass, and I didn't have the enthusiasm for that right now.

I needed a steady stream of gin, a blonde who knew her place was on her knees, and an otherwise interruption-free evening.

Go ahead: call me a manwhore.

Slut.

Player.

For all the disgust packed into those words, they were always tied with a fine, shiny thread of admiration. I did what everyone else wished they could, and I made it look good.

And I'd heard far worse. Someone always had some name to call me, and some of those names were hard to shake. For the better part of this year, I'd been replaying my last conversation with my father. The record was stuck on repeat in my mind, scratching and skipping back to the raw, awful parts.

My younger brother, Riley, had been leading a walk-through at a property in Bunker Hill—a string of decent row houses that my miserable bastard of a father, Angus, bought and dumped on us to restore—with Patrick, Matt, and me.

We were almost finished when Angus showed up, and I knew the minute he walked through the door that he was drunk. He'd been various shades of drunk since my mother died, and that day, he was cruel drunk.

And that was the day I refused to ignore his bullshit. I didn't want to walk away that time. It wasn't rolling off my back. I'd absorbed decades of his hatred, and that tank was long since overflowing.

He attacked everything that I was—my sexuality, my work, my relationship with my mother and my sister, Shannon—and told me I was a mistake. That I was too fucked-up to be alive. That I shouldn't have been born.

That was Angus's gift. He could hear every dark, twisted thought I had, and he knew how to sharpen them into daggers. Ten months later, I couldn't stop hearing those words.

I walked through the unit one last time, photographing what was left of the original design elements and noting restoration ideas. In the hallway joining the twin penthouse units, I texted Shannon to reiterate my annoyance. Then I hit up the manager at the new whiskey bar in the South End to reserve my preferred booth.

Tapping the corner of my phone to the elevator call button, I watched a woman emerge from the other unit. I stared at her, all summery and happy in her long yellow skirt and sleeveless magenta top, with a face like sunshine and a jingling ankle bracelet announcing her approach.

No one was allowed to look that pleased with life when it was too hot to exist.

"Hi," she said with a smile, her thumb beating a rhythm against the call button. Dark, shoulder-length hair fell across her face as she leaned forward. "This thing being slow again? It was slow last week, too. I guess that's part of the deal with old buildings, right?"

She was too much and too loud, and I dug in my pocket for some hand sanitizer. I'd come in contact with enough germs for one afternoon. I glanced up from her ankle and stopped attempting to extrapolate a good reason why any civilized person would wear a noisemaker, and shrugged.

She laughed, and said, "Okay then."

She started humming, and then shaking her ankle with the tune, and I looked for the stairwell. I couldn't stand in this hall with a chattering music box much longer, and sharing an elevator with her would require a sedative.

Despite my penchant for the high-end bar scene, I preferred quiet. Growing up with five siblings who made Attila the Hun's crew look like a chill group of guys who enjoyed churning their own butter meant I had to find that quiet for myself. Noise-canceling headphones, soundproofed insulation in my office, and enough space so that Riley and I could go weeks without seeing each other in the firehouse we shared.

Noticing a doorway at the far end of the hall, I gestured for her to step aside. A humid stairwell was a reasonable price to pay for serenity.

"Hey," she said, her hand grabbing my elbow. "It's here."

I met her eyes for the first time since she jangled into my personal space, and as much as I wanted to scowl at her invasion, her smile was too warm, her hazel eyes too bright. She was pretty in a way I couldn't comprehend—maybe it was her shortage of rail-thin, blue eyed blondeness, or the fact she wasn't made up, blown out, or put together, or that she wasn't simply looking at me but she was *seeing* me—and her smile transformed her whole face. Soon, I was smiling too.

Like a fucking lunatic.

Then I felt the first spasms of panic stirring my stomach, squeezing my lungs, making my skin too tight.

My instincts told me to walk away from Miss Music Box, pop some pills to cage the ugly green anxiety monster, and hike down eleven flights of stairs.

I always listened to my instincts. Beyond my siblings, they were the only things I could trust in this world.

But I stepped into that elevator anyway, gazing at her light eyes, and within ten seconds of the door closing, I was hurtling to my death.

"WHAT THE FUCK WAS THAT?"

I was hitting an octave above shrill, well inside screechy territory, but free falling in a blacked-out elevator didn't require perfect pitch.

"Hey. Are you okay?" I asked.

No response.

I wasn't on this roller coaster alone, right? That sweet, beautiful boy who gave me all kinds of lost puppy dog eyes couldn't have been a heat-wave-induced mirage.

The fall had tossed me against the side wall, and I was on my hands and knees, my shoulder throbbing. I knew I was going to feel that every time I lifted my bow or picked up my guitar for a week or two. Reaching out, I blindly patted the ground around me until my hand connected with a leg.

"All right, you better be alive," I said, my hand anchored on his thigh as I crawled closer. As far as thighs went, it was nice. Solid and strong, yet lean. "The only way this could get worse is if I'm trapped in here with a dead guy."

Dim lights flickered on overhead, and that had to be a good sign. We weren't slamming into the ground floor if there were emergency lights, and I was sticking with that logic.

"Oh, you are *adorable*. I should be concerned about whether you're seriously injured, but you are too freaking adorable for that right now." I laid my hand on his cheek. His eyelashes were long, longer than should be allowable for men, and thick and dark. His hair was the same way, but shot through with a touch of auburn, and it wasn't even close to fair.

Hell, this boy wasn't beautiful. He was gorgeous. The kind of gorgeous that modeled underwear in Times Square ads.

And he probably knew it, too.

They always did.

"Hey there, gumdrop, tell me you're alive," I said.

His eyes flickered open then narrowed, and he scrubbed a hand over his forehead. "Oh my fucking… What the…What the actual fuck just happened?"

His voice was surprisingly deep, a smooth strum of low bass chords.

It was *lethal*.

"Well," I sang, glancing around. "I think we're stuck in an elevator. And it's going to be fine. Look, emergency lights. Yay for emergency lights!"

He shifted to a sitting position, effectively knocking my hand from his thigh, and rubbed his eyes.

He'd been thrown clear across the elevator car yet he looked as though he just walked out of a J. Crew catalog photo shoot. He was tastefully rumpled in his preppy gingham check shirt and fancy loafers, and I half expected him to announce it was time for a yachting competition or polo tournament or something.

But that shit did it for me. I wanted to eat him with a spoon while he gave me a couple more smoldery, scowly glares.

That's right, honey. Tell me all about your purebred golden retrievers.

Static crackled from the intercom. "Hello? Anyone in there?"

"Hi, yeah, there are two of us—"

"Is this electrical or mechanical?" he asked, his palms pressed to his eyes.

"Power went out to the whole Back Bay," the voice from the intercom replied. "Must've been the heat wave. Rescue team is on its way, and we'll have you out of there in a jiff. Just, um, sit tight."

The good news: we weren't dead, and with any luck a fire-fighter would have to throw me over his shoulder and carry me to safety. Presuming this beautiful boy wasn't interested in the task.

The bad news: I was sweating like a beast. Not dewy, glis-tening girl sweat, either. I was starting to look like a defensive tackle at training camp. It wasn't until recently that I under-stood why my mother always had a handkerchief in her pocket; a lady had to keep herself tidy.

As much as I discarded my mother's—and grandmothers' and aunts'—commentary around all things lady-like, I couldn't disagree with them on a few points. To start, perspiration management was critical.

The other point was hair. I came from a long line of women who started sprouting dark upper lip peach fuzz right around the time they turned thirty, and I was no exception to that curse.

If anything, I was an overachieving early sprouter.

It wasn't even two weeks after my twenty-eighth birthday that I realized the shadow above my lip was a girlstache, and I'd been stemming the tide for the past year. As soon as I could afford laser hair removal, I was ditching the crème bleach and being done with that shit.

But the rest of it? The marrying a nice boy from the neigh-borhood, the house no more than three blocks from my parents' place in Jersey, the job at my family's restaurant? I was done with that shit, too.

I'd been done for a long time.

"Oh fuck," he murmured, and his head fell back against the

wall. He pressed his hand to his breastbone and I heard him counting under his breath.

"Yeah, I know. But this building is really good, I'm sure they're—"

"No," he grunted. He didn't look so hot anymore—still yummy, unwaveringly yummy—but more and more wrecked. He lifted a shaking hand in the direction of his leather messenger bag. "Can you reach in the front pocket and grab the case? Please."

I handed him the small kit, and when his fingers struggled to grip the zipper, I opened it for him. Syringes and vials of insulin sat in neatly ordered rows, and I glanced at him. Perhaps my excessive sweating wasn't the only bad news. "This is for a pump, right?"

"It's fine, just give it to me," he snapped. His eyes fell shut and his chest heaved as his breath came in short, shallow pants.

I crawled closer, climbing astride his lap while patting each of his pockets. Even with his face flushed and the muscles under his rolled up shirtsleeves twitching in distress, he was gorgeous. So perfect and so vulnerable.

"Really, don't touch it," he gasped. "Please don't. I can do it."

That was nowhere near accurate. His words were broken, at once slurred and frantic, and he couldn't align his fingers to snag the pump from my hand. My knowledge was limited, but the screen on his Walkman-sized device indicated his blood sugar was arcing high into dangerous territory, and we didn't have time for this debate.

"Twelve years as a band camp counselor and I know everything there is to know about operating one of these," I said. "Insulin pumps, inhalers, and EpiPens. I know them all. Can't start a fire in the woods, at least not on purpose, but I can work these."

"That's comforting," he muttered.

"Just breathe, pumpkin," I said.

His device was newer than the ones I encountered at camp,

sleeker. Humming while I inserted a new cartridge, I then watched the fluid move through the thin tubing that connected to his infusion site. The quarter-sized disc, I learned during last summer's mandatory health trainings, delivered insulin through a fine cannula that was placed under the skin. Another small disc, a wireless sensor, constantly measured tiny amounts of blood glucose and pinged readings back to the device.

The diabetic camper in my bunk had to rotate her sites around her abdomen every few days. She said it didn't hurt to insert them; if anything, it was less painful than frequent injections and the continuous glucose monitoring meant she didn't have to prick her fingers as much. I knew from the camp nurse that they could also be positioned on the thigh or upper arm, but the angry grimace on the underwear model's face told me he wasn't interested in questions about his regimen.

"What is that song?"

"Hmm? Oh, that. It's 'Anna Sun.' By Walk The Moon," I said. I snagged some tissues from my bag and mopped the sweat from his forehead and throat. "What else do you need?"

He shook his head, his hand flattened against his chest as he closed his eyes. "Just get off my leg and be quiet."

Shuffling to the side, I bit my lip and stared at his belt. It was navy with embroidered white whales, and it wasn't long before "Yellow Submarine" was buzzing through my head.

Here's the problem: I didn't know *how* to be quiet. Asking me for silence was like putting a giant cookie on the countertop, telling me not to eat it, and then leaving me alone with it.

I ate the goddamn cookie every time and I just couldn't help it.

Everything about me was noise and fidget and rhythm, and I couldn't function without.

So I tapped the chords on my wrist and stared at him. He was too pretty to be trapped in an elevator. I, on the other hand, attracted this brand of nonsense. This was par for my course, and wasn't it always the poor, lonely grad students in these situations? Never men who looked like they should be sending hounds off for a fox hunt—did people still do that sort of thing? —or debating the appropriate amount of time to age a cabernet.

"You didn't have to stop," he said. "With the song. Just talk less. For a few minutes."

With my iPhone in hand, I toggled to the right playlist and gave us each an earbud. He accepted it without question, and I figured averting a diabetic coma warranted this form of kinship.

For four and a half blissful minutes, I wasn't worried about elevator disasters. "More? Feeling better? Need anything else?" I asked. He nodded, his eyes still shut. "You want more, you're feeling better, and you need something, or—"

"It's fine," he snapped. "I'm fine. Play something else."

I shifted off my knees and settled beside him. We sat there, shoulder to shoulder, listening to LCD Soundsystem, Weezer, Taylor Swift, The Who, AFI, Van Morrison, Seven Mary Three, OneRepublic, The Smiths, Lupe Fiasco, and a handful of new bands for almost two hours.

So much for getting us out in a jiff.

The air was thick enough to chew, and I was way too close to experiencing one of my worst nightmares: smelling like a two-day-old Italian sub sandwich while in the company of other humans. As far as worst nightmares went, this wasn't on par with death by killer bees or finding a severed finger in a tub of hummus, but it was a real concern.

The underwear model wasn't faring much better in this heat. However, it was working out beautifully for me since he had ditched the gingham shirt, leaving him in just a gray tank and khakis. That, a ring on his thumb, a spendy-looking watch, two medical alert bracelets, a copper cuff, freckles, and the dark outline of tattoos on his shoulders.

Those freckles were just too fucking sweet. I wanted to touch everything and ask a dozen questions.

When the Neil Young song ended, I turned down the volume and said, "I'm Tiel, by the way."

He kept his eyes closed but the corners of his mouth tipped up. "Teal? Like the color?"

I got the 'isn't that a color?' routine a lot. Trust me, I gave my parents plenty of shit for that choice, and spent several adolescent years calling myself Renee. My mother could still produce homemade birthday cards I signed with my adopted name. I found it odd she bothered to keep them. In her book, I ranked just above the people who routinely let their dog poop in her front yard.

It wasn't until I was out of the house and fully myself that I stopped wanting to be a Hannah or Rachel or Emma. Or Renee.

My older sister, on the other hand, couldn't get enough of her name. She loved explaining that Agapi was the Greek word for divine love—at least that was her preferred translation. She liked it so much she tattooed her name on her own ass.

It was easy for her to embrace every ounce of her Greekness; she was my mother's clone. She had the wavy mocha hair, the perfect olive skin, the dark eyes, and the tall, slender figure.

In every way imaginable, I was Agapi's opposite. I was such an odd blend of both gene pools that I resembled neither of my parents. At first glance, I looked like the kid they adopted. Aside from inheriting my father's thick black hair and a slightly lighter shade of my mother's skin, my features were distinctly mine. Sometimes I wondered whether I'd feel differently about my family, my religions, my cultures if I'd ever felt like I belonged in any of them. To this day, I wasn't sure where I belonged, but at least now I knew who I was.

"No, not the color. T-I-E-L."

My name came with no cute translation.

"That's rather distinctive," he said, his eyes still closed and his smile spreading.

I shrugged and studied his short beard scruff. It was cute, and it softened the line of his jaw in a way that made fuzziness seem wholly sophisticated.

"Yeah," I said. "But I like that I can Google myself and not find anyone else out there with my exact, full name."

If I had to guess, this boy could grow one hell of a lumberjack beard in no time at all. It wouldn't go with the preppy look, but I got the impression he could pull off anything. Underwear models were gifted like that.

And wouldn't that be a sight? Skivvies, scruff, and smile.

"Okay, I'll bite. What's your full name?"

"Tiel Kalogeropoulos-Desai. But I dropped the Kalogeropoulos bit a long time ago. No one has time for all those vowels."

"That's amazing," he laughed. His breathing was a bit more regular, the pulse in his throat jumping a little less. Glancing at his device, I saw his glucose readings leveling off into safer ranges. "It's like the entire United Nations was crammed into one person."

"You know, muffin, instead of busting my balls, you could tell me *your* name. It seems like we're hanging together for a bit."

"Or dying together," he said, and then he laughed. "Sorry. I'm Sam. Samuel Aidan Walsh, if that's what we're doing."

"It's a pleasure to meet you, Sam, despite these," I glanced around the elevator, "circumstances."

He opened his eyes, all slate blue and serious, and he nodded toward the insulin pump and iPhone in my hands. "Thanks for sorting me out." I smiled, and he gave me a lopsided grin. "I'm sorry you had to see all that, Tiel."

And somehow, that was all it took. I was full-tilt smitten with this beautiful boy, from the inside out. I felt like a cartoon character with my heart swelling to ten times its normal size and thumping right out of my chest for all to see.

But before I allowed myself to think about that, the elevator shook, and metal-on-metal shrieked around us.

Everything went dark, and then we were falling.

Three

SAM

DEEP BREATH IN, *deep breath out. Deep breath in, deep breath out.*

Breathing means we're alive. Deep breath in, deep breath out. Just keep breathing.

"Hey there, folks," a voice boomed from the intercom. "Captain MacNamara here, Boston Fire Department. Is everyone still with me?"

At first, I didn't understand the words over Tiel's screams.

We were huddled together in the corner where we'd landed, Tiel's arms around my waist, our legs tangled, my hand holding her head to my chest. It was an involuntary reaction to the jolt, my personal space compulsions temporarily suspended, and neither of us were ready to let go yet.

"Shh. It's okay," I murmured against her hair, then spoke toward the intercom. "This situation appears to be getting worse, Captain."

"I know you've had one hell of a fall, and we're workin' on getting you out, but I'm going to need you to be patient with me."

"How much *more* patient?" I asked.

This building, despite all its Brutalistic splendor, was off my short-term investment list.

"We've got a lady trapped in the other car, and she's in labor. As long as everyone's all right in there, we're going to work on getting to her first."

Tiel looked up at me in the hazy darkness, giving me and my device a purposeful glance, but I shook my head. I had enough insulin to last me two days, and enough glucose tablets for the month. I was more concerned about sitting on the goddamn floor in a malfunctioning elevator. If anything, going into a diabetic coma would be preferable to picking up the flesh-eating bacteria that was certain to be crawling all over this death trap.

"Do you have an engineer looking at the mechanics?" I asked. "A power outage should stop an elevator, not cause it to free fall. Twice. This is a larger system failure, not just an electrical issue."

"I can assure you, sir, we've got our best guys on it." He cleared his throat. "Get comfortable. This is gonna take some time."

The intercom's connection clicked off, and Tiel shifted to face me, her lips pursed, eyes wide. "Okay then," she murmured. "Are you sure you're all right?"

"Yeah," I murmured. "I'm fine. You?"

She rolled her shoulders, wincing. "I've used a few of my nine lives today, but I'll survive. You seem to know a lot about elevators."

"My brother." I waved toward the doors. "He's a structural engineer. We work together. He babbles a lot."

"What do you do?"

"Architect," I said. "You?"

"Mmm, well, a bit of everything. I'm in grad school at Berklee, and teach a few undergrad classes. Give music lessons."

I returned my device to my pocket, and the movement

edged me away from Tiel. Gaining some space was necessary and appropriate and healthy, but without thinking, I shifted back immediately. I wanted to crawl into the opposite corner, wrap my arms around myself and breathe—alone—for several minutes, and I couldn't explain why I didn't. She'd already seen me fall apart. She knew about the thin tubing that snaked from my abdomen to the device in my pocket, and had a sense of how it worked. I could think of fewer than ten people on this planet with that much information about me.

"And don't forget about band camp," I said.

Grinning, she handed me an earbud and shuffled her playlist. We sat in the stifling heat, our backs to the wall and shoulders pressed together, enjoying the most random compilation of songs ever conceived. She hummed along with most, and sang with the others.

And it wasn't awkward.

It should have been awkward.

We were strangers in an admittedly perilous situation, but I was getting the sense Tiel was immune to the awkward.

Perhaps she was immune to me, and that was rather intriguing. No one was immune to me. Even my elderly office assistant, Theresa, would cheerily dissect the mess that was my calendar when I asked with a hot, lingering smile.

Nine songs slipped by, and my attention shifted from controlling my breathing to the pins and needles in my leg. When the emergency lights flashed on again, I rotated my foot tentatively, and groaned at the sensation coursing through my muscles.

"What's wrong?" she asked.

Squeezing my upper thigh, I hissed at the discomfort. "My leg's asleep."

Tiel shifted, baring a long swatch of inner thigh before righting her skirt and kneeling beside me. Black panties. Maybe navy.

Panties were my concern only when I was in the process of

tearing them off, and I was too busy keeping my crazy in check to acknowledge Tiel's panties. But I did find that expanse of skin fascinating.

She wrapped her hands around my leg and kneaded, gradually restoring the circulation. It was kind, and it seemed Tiel was unabashedly generous, but her hands were vigorously rubbing less than four inches from my cock. I didn't think she intended *that* type of blood flow.

"Hey," she said. "Look at that."

Oh, Jesus. Please don't call out the tent in my pants.

I opened my eyes, and glanced to my lap. She pointed to my left hand and her right, and the birthmarks just below our thumbs. They were fingerprint-sized and nearly the same coffee shade.

"Huh," I murmured.

"You're my freckle twin," she said. The pad of her thumb swept over my hand, touching the dark spot. "I've never met anyone with my exact same birthmark."

"And I've never been stuck in an elevator before. Seems like we're murdering statistics this afternoon."

In that position, I could see straight down her shirt and admire the full breasts gazing back at me.

Pink. A pink, lacy bra that made me wonder whether her nipples would be the same shade.

I could spot silicone from across a busy street, but these were as organic as they came. They were lovely, all golden and ripe, and bursting out of that lace. There was some sort of ripened fruit metaphor waiting to be made but I was too preoccupied to think that far ahead.

"Ahem." I glanced up to meet her bent eyebrow. "See something you like?"

The smile came to me easily, reflexively. "You have sensational tits."

I was familiar with only two reactions to that comment: insult and interest. Either I was being slapped across the face or dragged to a private corner, and years of experience taught me the odds always ran close to fifty-fifty.

Tiel's response was neither.

She sat back, howling with laughter until tears streamed down her cheeks and she hugged her sides. She bunched her skirt above her knees, exposing her legs and ankle bracelet. I stared at her golden skin, but I couldn't explain what I found so interesting.

"Normal people don't say shit like that," she said. "It's rude, Sam. *Rude*. And pervy. You're a perv. But thank you. It's nice to know they can still bring the boys to the yard."

She didn't take to any of my usual charms, but she didn't meet me with outrage or disinterest either. The challenge to find and test her boundaries spurred me forward.

"Please. You're a little pervy, too. You just gave my upper thigh a deep tissue massage like it was nothing, and beneath all that bullshit, you like me staring at your tits. You'd probably like sucking my cock, too."

"Do you hear yourself right now?" she asked. "Very rude. Very pervy."

I shrugged, working hard to disguise my growing fascination with her. "You like it."

Tiel rolled her eyes and busied herself with untangling the earbuds. "I'm not responding to that."

"Because you know I'm right."

I studied her, taking in her pouty lips, rounded curves, and toenails polished orange. I smiled and met her eyes. Who was this girl and why did I want to learn everything about her?

"Oh honey, your dimple game is fierce." She handed me an earbud. "Here. Put this in and stop being so pervy."

"Wait," I said, gesturing to her phone and pulling mine from my pocket. "Are you getting a signal?"

She shook her head. "No, I never get any reception in this building. I download everything. I don't trust the cloud with my tunes." She watched as I toggled through my phone's screens but couldn't find a connection. "Is someone going to be wondering where you are? Your girlfriend, or wife, or... someone else?"

"Uh, no." I laughed. "The only people who give a shit where I am at any point are my siblings, and they've all taken off for the long weekend. Some earlier than others. You?"

"No, not really." Her forehead crinkled and she looked back at me. "That's a little unpleasant, yeah? We could be in here for days, and no one would notice we're missing?"

"We could just as easily be out there," I started, gesturing to the elevator doors. "We could be out there for days, and no one would notice us either. People do an incredible job at ignoring each other."

She touched her hand to my thigh. "That's a really sad thing to say, Sam."

I didn't want my face to register the bitterness I felt, not right now, and I looked away.

Hours passed while we listened to music, and we tried to disregard the firefighters' shouts echoing through the elevator shaft as they worked to secure the cars.

It seemed like a reasonable path to follow. Better than imagining how many pieces my body would break into on impact.

I grew accustomed to Tiel's incessant humming and jingling, the way her fingers tapped along with the song. To say Tiel listened to a song was a gross understatement; the music moved through her, and it was overflowing onto me. If I saw her, out at a club or in line at a coffee shop, I'd roll my eyes. Her whole vibe—the bright clothes, ankle bracelets, and nonstop grooving with the beat—I had no patience for that shit. I didn't believe people could be that happy. But here, beside me, it was different. Tiel was authentic, and though I couldn't explain how, I liked it.

Eventually, a crew pried the doors open, and informed us we'd be squeezing through the narrow crevice as the car had stopped between floors on its last free fall.

"I'm gonna need you to hustle," the firefighter said.

Tiel and I turned to each other, and at once we said, "You first."

Rolling my eyes, I said, "Would you just fucking go?"

We quickly collected our things, but as we stood, the elevator wobbled and creaked. We held onto each other to keep our bearings, instinctively moving back to the corner.

The doors slammed shut and the car dropped, cutting us off from the rescue team.

"I am going to require a very large drink after this," Tiel cried, her voice losing its light cadence. "And then I'm never getting in another goddamn elevator again. I'll only take the stairs, and then I'm going to have an onion ass."

"'Onion ass'?" I asked. I glanced to my phone again, willing the service to return. I rarely gave Matt credit for much, but he would have managed the shit out of this situation, and thrown some solar panels on the roof while he was at it.

"Yes," she replied, squeezing my hand for emphasis. "An ass so round and tight that it makes guys cry."

Before I could check out her backside or respond, the doors opened.

"On my count, dive through the opening. Don't think, just do it," the firefighter ordered.

"PUT this in your body right now."

Tiel handed me a drink, and considering we were in a grad-student-infested part of Cambridge, I didn't bother asking about the brand of gin.

"Okay, but I'm warning you," I said with a smirk. "I will get ruder and pervier."

"Good," she yelled over the thumping music, and held up her vodka martini in salute. "I was beginning to think you were a nice boy."

Tiel pointed to the black eye I earned when shielding her from the impact of our elevator escape. It wasn't entirely chivalrous. I had been headed straight for that marble column regardless, and I happened to break her collision with it.

"Shit," she hissed after her first sip. "This drink is brinier than a ball sack!"

I leaned close, my lips hovering over her ear. "Normal people don't say things like that."

She looked up, her eyes locked on me while she drained her drink. "Okay, Freckle Twin, so we're not normal. There's no fun in normal anyway."

"Right," I laughed. Her sarcasm curled around me, shrouding us in a quiet world of our inside jokes bred from heat and apprehension, and the unexpected thrill of finding ourselves alive in the end. "Of course not."

She elbowed her way to the end of the bar and propped herself on a stool while I ordered another round. I opted to open a tab and handed my credit card to the busty bartender sporting a trio of lip rings. This wasn't a quick drink followed by bidding my partner in elevator captivity goodbye. Evidently, we weren't finished with our codependency yet.

I spent only a moment stressing over the objectively gross condition of this establishment. On a different night, I would have required a cocktail of pharmaceuticals to even walk through the doors of this joint without flying into obsessive-compulsive fits and there was no way I could have managed the wall-to-wall bodies. But tonight, something else was occupying my brain to the extent that I wasn't subject to all of my crazy.

I didn't know what it was, and thinking about my anxiety was also a fantastic way to invite it to return. Save for some bumps and bruises, we were alive, and I wanted to enjoy that.

With fresh drinks in hand, I settled beside Tiel.

"Can we just acknowledge that we survived some crazy shit today? I mean, *we* are the people who survived eight hours in a freaking elevator!"

"We are," I said, lifting my glass to hers. "We're the people who lived."

"That is perhaps the best reason to play Never Have I Ever."

"Oh God help me, you want to go there?" Tiel was random like that, and though I'd left the drinking games at the frat house, I was down for whatever she threw at me. "Is your objective to drink me under the table?"

"I'm sure you'd have plenty of fun under that table." She pressed her knee into my thigh, and it was like she was beating me at the game I'd invented. This was bold-faced flirting, and she was ready to outpace me. "You first."

I rubbed my brow with a chuckle. "Never had sex in an elevator."

Her eyes twinkled and she glanced around with a tight grin. "Somehow that surprises me," she murmured. "Never had sex in public."

She wanted my best offense, and I was giving it to her. Even if it ended with her slapping me and storming off. "But you'd like to."

We stared at each other for a minute until she offered a wiggle-shake-shrug.

"And you have?" Tiel asked.

I thought about shocking her, telling her that my hook-ups existed only in VIP lounge bathrooms, coatrooms, and the occasional private booth. But I held that card, sipped my drink without comment instead. I had a better play up my sleeve. "Never have I ever had sex in a bed."

"Oh come on! That's bullshit, everyone's had sex in a *bed*, Sam. Not even once? I don't believe you." I held up my hands, shrugging, and she shook her head. Shit, it was fun to see her stunned. "Explain that to me."

"Not much to explain. I don't date and I've never run out of women interested in blowing me. Beds are superfluous when there are private booths."

"So...what?" She gestured, trying to generate some meaning from the air between us. "You don't have regular, normal sex?"

I had an abundance of "normal" sex. I just hadn't bothered with any of it this summer. There was something pleasant and utterly detached about some good head, and the idea of much more didn't appeal to me. These days, I couldn't generate any excitement for getting out of my little bubble and touching people more than necessary, and fucking counted as more than necessary.

"I wouldn't say that. It just requires more work, and I'd rather relax while she finishes the job."

Tiel laughed and slapped my leg. "I can't believe you said that, you actually said those words. You're such a manwhore."

The music was loud, and even though we were sitting close together with Tiel's legs bracketed by mine, I had to lean toward her to speak. "You say that like it's a problem," I replied, eager to see the rise I got out of her. "This isn't about love or forever or any other bullshit notions. None of that exists. There are no illusions about what I'm looking for and we both know it ends when she swallows."

"Maybe not, but it's completely one-sided. She's servicing you, and you aren't even returning the favor."

It was fascinating that Tiel focused on all the fairness and none of the sluttiness, as if she didn't mind some highly casual sex as long as it ended favorably for everyone involved. Fascinating...but not the path I was pursuing tonight. I already knew too much about her for this to meet with the end I preferred.

"I didn't sign up to get her off. If she wanted that, she shouldn't have gotten on her knees," I said.

She shook her head quickly, and said, "So you only have oral sex? That seems..." She looked around the bar and waved her hand at me. "Unsatisfying? Inadequate?"

"No," I said, scratching my jaw. She didn't need to know an entire season had passed since I'd been inside a woman. "Not really. There's always anal. I get plenty of that when I'm in the mood."

She reared back and sent me a horrified glare. And there it was: her limit. "People are really into that these days, huh?" I shrugged and studied her cleavage. Her breasts were designed for fucking and licking and wasting entire days away. "You, sir, are operating in an entirely different league. That's wild."

"Yeah, and while we could debate this for hours, it's your turn."

"So you do understand reciprocity. Fascinating." She smirked. I didn't know what to do with a woman who both had the chops to spar with me and willingly elected to do so. "Never have I ever had a threesome."

So I kept pushing. "Again—but you'd like to."

"Is this some special gift you think you have? A random form of clairvoyance that you peddle to innocent, unsuspecting women?" she asked. She smacked my leg, keeping her hand on my thigh, but didn't notice that I evaded the question. "And no, that's not what I'm suggesting at all."

"It wouldn't be that difficult to guess what you *are* looking for," I said, my gaze moving over her body longer than necessary. This was entrapment. I was testing, baiting, willing her to kick me in the balls and tell me to fuck off, and I had no idea why I was doing it. "You want to make out with some girls and maybe get a little handsy, you want to get fucked somewhere not so private, you want two dicks in you at once, and you want to lie on a bed of rose petals and stare at the sky while someone eats your pussy. Throw in some kissing in the rain, and you're good."

I couldn't tell whether she was blushing from my words, the alcohol, the heat, or some combination of the three. She gulped her drink and slammed her empty glass on the bar before meeting my eyes.

"Do you enjoy poking at me with all these things you say? I

know you're trying to make me laugh, but you're being rude, you perv."

"Not poking. Just teasing you." I summoned the bartender for another round, appreciating her tits long enough to discern nipple rings under her t-shirt, and I felt every ounce of Tiel's censorious glare when I turned back to her. I was right up against her limits, and this time, the look in her eyes told me to ease back. "I think you'd like some teasing."

Tiel patted my leg twice and nodded. "It's your turn."

"Never have I ever been married. Not even close."

Tiel looked away while she piled her hair on top of her head, securing a messy knot with the band on her wrist. Her silence was a gust of arctic air, and I wanted to pull her hands from her hair and search her fingers for rings. I might be a manwhore but I did *not* talk to another man's wife about blowjobs and threesomes.

It didn't matter whether I was asking her to choke on my cock or not. And I wasn't—at least not right now—but it wasn't a line I'd willingly cross. "Are *you*…married?"

"Was." She looped stray wisps of hair through the band and focused on the fresh martini sitting in front of her.

"Okay. Your turn to explain that to me," I said.

She threw my words right back at me. "Not much to explain."

I gestured up and down her body, my head shaking. She was young and beautiful, spirited and fun. So much fun. I couldn't imagine generating the kind of enthusiasm that seemed to spring from Tiel without effort. "You couldn't have been married that long. What are you? Twenty-five? Twenty-four?"

She offered a serene smile, pressed her palm to her chest, and said, "Twenty-nine. But thank you, you've made my tender ego purr with satisfaction tonight."

"How are you older than me?" I stared at Tiel, her words feeling oddly provocative despite the intimate tenor of our conversation. "Maybe I'm morbid but I want to know what went wrong."

She frowned and looked out over the crowd. "You know when you're young, like eighteen, nineteen, twenty, and everything seems so fucking important? Like you're the center of the universe?"

I nodded. I spent those years acquainting myself with a significant quantity of pussy. My cock was the center of the universe then, and I couldn't say much had changed since. "I think so."

"So I went to New York City for college, to Juilliard—"

"You went to *Juilliard*?" I said. I studied her, watching as she rocked with the song blasting through the bar, and tried to meld the idea of a fiercely disciplined, world-class musician with the ballsy, boho chick in front of me.

Who exactly did I share that elevator with?

"Yeah, it's not a big deal." She waved the notion away as if to suggest anyone could wander into Juilliard. "Anyway...I met someone. A musical theatre nerd. A really gorgeous, attention-whoring musical theatre nerd who was being lured into more commercial settings. And in the infinite wisdom of nineteen-year-olds, we got married. Our parents went ballistic."

She laughed, shaking her head while she continued studying the crowd, drained her martini, and then untied her hair.

"It was fun for a little while, but it was just pretend. A scene he wanted to act out. It wasn't real," she said. "None of it's real when you're nineteen. And then he cheated on me. Apparently, he cheated a lot. And since we were poor college kids, neither of us could afford to move out of our studio apartment. So...we lived together, separated. I learned very quickly that I wasn't the center of the universe when I was sleeping on the sofa while my ex-husband fucked understudies."

At some point we'd stopped having a frisky conversation about bedpost notches, and it'd turned true and heavy. I scratched the back of my neck, my eyes wide as I digested her story. "I have to tell you, Tiel, I did not expect the jaded divorcee story from you."

"I'm not—"

"Oh, that was jaded," I said. "You're jaded, I'm jaded, we're all really fucking jaded."

I stared at her, studying her eyes, her mouth, her beaded chandelier earrings, the trio of amber necklaces around her throat, and then dropped my gaze to her chest. They truly were sensational tits.

"Ah, Samuel? Eyes up here, please."

I dragged my gaze from her breasts to her lips, and lifted my brows. "Yeah, you're not my type, but you have an incredible rack, and I'd like having those lips on my dick."

It sounded like my usual bullshit, but it was possibly the most honest, unfiltered thing I'd said all day.

She snorted, spraying vodka from her mouth and nose, and shook her head. "You need to shut that shit down. I'm not giving you a blowjob. Stop thinking about it."

I brushed the fluid from my shirt, but I'd been a sweaty, wrinkled mess for hours now. A little backwashed martini wasn't changing that. My eyes moved back to her breasts while she mopped the liquid from her face. "I probably won't, Sunshine."

She plucked my drink from my fingers and placed it on the bar, and grabbed my hand. It wasn't my style—no handshakes, no high-fives, not even fist bumps—but I let Tiel lace her fingers with mine anyway. I figured the adrenaline was still running high, and it was obscuring all my natural reactions. "Come on, perv. I want to dance."

I couldn't remember the last time I danced in a dingy bar, if ever. College was about reinventing myself, and I accomplished that with a full slate of frat parties and mixers masquerading as structured hook-up opportunities. After college, I replaced frat parties with Boston's most exclusive club scenes, and on most nights, I couldn't tell the two apart. It was all about shallow people trying to look good enough to fuck.

I didn't spend time trading innuendos with easygoing girls who didn't care how ridiculously enchanting they looked as they sang along. But here I was, watching as Tiel's yellow skirt tangled around her legs while she twisted and bounced with the music, her arms high over her head, and I could almost taste her inhibitions melting away. She didn't care whether her hair was disheveled or her mascara smudged, and it didn't matter to her whether anyone was watching or judging.

The opening chords of the next song rang through the bar, and Tiel searched the crowded dance floor, her eyes lighting when they landed on me.

"What are you doing over there?" Tiel yelled, pulling me toward her. She wrapped her arm around my waist and smiled up at me. Shit, she was pretty. "You have to sing with me. This tune demands it."

She was short—taller than Lauren and Shannon, but those two bordered on pocket-sized—and this angle gave me a priceless view down her shirt. It also meant that my cock was nestled against her belly, and her soft heat felt a little too magnificent for this situation.

Talking to her meant leaning down, moving further into her space, breathing in her sweet scent. As my nose brushed against her shoulder, I had the most overwhelming urge to lick her.

I'd never wanted to lick another human being in my life, and on most days, I wasn't comfortable touching anything that I hadn't personally sanitized.

But I really wanted to taste Tiel.

Instead, I brushed her hair away from her ear, dropped my hand to her waist, and asked, "What is this?"

"It's Bleachers," she said. "'I Wanna Get Better'."

Even as we leaned into each other, she continued moving, jumping with the beat. I followed her lead, and I tried to see what the world looked like from her eyes. She sang every word, her bright, happy eyes fixed on me while her expression morphed with the music as if she was telling me a secret story.

Some brittle, rough part of me spasmed, softening and rupturing by degrees as the words rang in my ears.

It was too much—this song, this day, this girl—and I wanted to surrender to all of it. Turn off the noise in my head, shut down the anxiety in my veins, and have one night free from my fucking issues.

But all that shit—it was the only thing I knew to be true. It was my filthy fucking security blanket, and I'd been dragging it around longer than I could remember. Somehow, somewhere in the haze of my masochistic workload and mindless fucking, that blanket turned into a gin-soaked noose, and it was tightening each day.

All I had to do was decide if I wanted to let it take me.

"You're not too pretty to sing with me, Sam," Tiel yelled. She scrunched her eyes shut, rocked her head with the rhythm, and tapped the drum beats against my back. If I hadn't been so close, I wouldn't have been able to distinguish her voice from the sound thumping around us.

When the chorus rolled through, I yelled the words with Tiel, and as I stared at her, I believed them.

Warmth spread through my chest and I laughed out loud. I *did* want to get better. I wanted every night, every day, every last ounce of my life to feel like this moment.

The song ended too soon and she dragged me toward the door. Though I wasn't ready for this night to end, I followed her to the alley.

"Hi," she whispered, her hands flat on my chest.

City noises surrounded us, and though it was long past midnight, it was disgustingly humid and only slightly cooler.

"Hi."

"We're friends now, right? After a near-death experience, we have to be. We'll tell stories about this for years," she said.

"Yeah."

"And sometimes friends kiss, right?"

Not understanding the meaning behind her words, I nodded like a fool. Tiel smiled, her hand shifting from my chest to wrap around the back of my neck. She urged me closer, and before any of this made sense to me, her lips were pressed to mine.

A moment of painful anxiety overtook me, and somehow I forced myself to focus on the way her body felt against mine, the taste of her mouth, the pressure of her tongue.

It was the first time I'd kissed a woman in five years. And there was so much more in my secret trove of nevers.

I didn't kiss, I didn't date, I didn't touch under clothes, I didn't let anyone touch me save for a particular appendage, I didn't fuck in beds, and I didn't undress.

Ever.

Ever.

Women liked to interpret it as my urgency to pull my cock out and get inside them, and it was good they invented that little story for themselves. Reality was less romantic.

Save for my siblings and medical professionals, no one had ever put eyes on my infusion set and it was safer that way. I couldn't handle anyone else seeing it, being horrified by it. Technology had improved over the past twenty years and it was smaller now, less conspicuous and revolting, but there was no getting around the fact I was never free from invasive medical equipment. It was just another piece of me that was better off hidden.

Fully dressed, stand-up sex also came with the benefit of distance. There was no intimacy to be derived from exposing nothing more than the required pieces, and doing it somewhere as impersonal as a coatroom. That kind of sex never tricked my mind into thinking any of it mattered to me, or that I could matter to someone.

And yet it was staggering to realize that, for all my manwhoring and working my ass off to avoid legitimate human contact, I had been missing out on something as simple and wonderful and fleeting as this.

Then she leaned back, and it was over.

"I just had to kiss you," she said with a shrug. "I couldn't not."

But I didn't want it to be over.

"There's a word for that. Basorexia. The uncontrollable urge to kiss," I said.

Tiel laughed and brushed her thumb over my lips. "I guess I'm feeling a little basorexic."

"Is that right?" She nodded, a shy smile teasing at the corner of her mouth. "Let me help you with that."

My lips brushed against hers, tentative and in absolute fear of screwing up this one moment when everything—fucking *everything*—seemed to fall into perfect alignment. I was free and normal and alive, and even if it only lasted for right now, I didn't want to lose one second of it.

"Just relax," she murmured. "We've already survived all the terrible things that could happen, right?"

Her tongue slipped into my mouth, as easy and sweet as a summer day, and I wanted to believe her.

"OH, MOTHERFUCKING HELL," I groaned. "I am too old for this shit."

I was offended—deeply, personally offended—by the sunlight. The universe should have known I required some fog and clouds this morning. It also should have supplied a bucket of Gatorade and ibuprofen, and left both within arm's reach.

"God help me, I cannot be responsible for my actions until I've had a bagel and a cappuccino." I groaned again, hoping the sun understood my dissatisfaction, and then I realized two very important things.

First, I wasn't in my bed.

Second, I wasn't alone.

"Hello there," I murmured.

"Why the fuck did we sleep on the floor?" Sam asked, his arms clutching my waist and his head resting on my belly. He looked up, surveying my apartment, and my bladder immediately rejoiced. He was groggy and disheveled, his eye a rainbow of bruises.

And he was shirtless.

Shirtless *and* tattooed.

Shirtless, tattooed, and wrapped around me like the best holiday garland ever invented.

"I think we had a little party," I murmured, gesturing toward the furniture shoved against the walls and the four empty wine bottles on the kitchen countertop. "And then passed out down here."

"That's right," he said. "They kicked us out of that shithole bar. I remember you saying it was too hot to dance in clothes anyway, and we had to get undressed." He hooked a glance over his shoulder at his black boxers. "Apparently, I agreed with that idea."

"And then we decided it was too hot to get off the floor." I draped an arm over my face and moaned, then studied his tattoos again. "Apparently, you agreed with that, too."

He seemed too well-bred for tattoos. Boys with fancy SUVs and gemstone cufflinks and watches that cost more than I earned in a year didn't get tattoos.

Two doves rested on his shoulder blade, a circle filled with repeating shapes on the other, and an intricate Celtic cross rose from his waist. There were others, smaller ones, on his sides, and another peeking out from his boxers.

These weren't spring break souvenirs or douchey faux-tribal bands. These were artful, significant designs that begged to be touched.

Explained.

I blinked away when he caught me staring.

"I'm never listening to you again," he said. "You're the one who dragged me into that damn elevator in the first place. If I'd taken the stairs, I would've had a decent gin and tonic, a respectable blowjob, and woken up in a bed like a civilized human being."

I felt his gaze land on my chest, a warm lick of attention, and I looked up to find him smiling at me. I didn't know what it was about this boy, but every time he smiled at me like that, all I could think was, *Oh shit.*

This wasn't dimple game. This was dimple war strategy.

I stared at him for a long moment, not sure whether I wanted to laugh or beat him with a broom. "Admit that dancing in your underwear is more fun."

"I will do nothing of the sort...but you...um," he stammered, angling his chin toward my chest. "You look good in that."

And yeah, like all the best hungover train wrecks in town, I was wearing nothing more than his tank and a pair of ratty blue panties. I smelled like stale wine, my morning breath could murder woodland creatures, and my thighs, in all their plump, unshaved glory, had been inches from Sam's face. He wouldn't be agreeing to much more alley kissing and friendly snuggle parties after this.

"Yeah, I really do need that cappuccino. I'm not fit for human interaction," I mumbled. I untangled myself from Sam's grip, slipped into the bathroom to put myself back in order, and prayed for the day when thinking about coffee would make it magically appear at my apartment.

After showering and changing into clean clothes, I felt a bit less like roadkill.

Just enough to know I practically threw myself at Sam last night, and then ordered him to strip down to skivvies and dance in my living room.

Classic post-traumatic response, right?

When I emerged, my apartment was back in order and Sam was programming his device. With his shirt hanging open, the ports on either side of his belly button were exposed. He didn't notice me watching him.

His black eye was matched only by a long, mottled bruise running down his side. I stepped forward, reaching out to feather my fingers over the contusion, but he closed his hand around my wrist and yanked me away.

"Don't," he warned.

"Sam, that bruise is putrid," I said, gesturing toward him while he pulled his shirt closed and buttoned quickly. He avoided my eyes. "Are you sure you don't have a broken rib or internal bleeding, or something? Is your infusion set okay?"

"Please, don't," he said, his voice strained and impatient. "I should go."

"No, no, no," I said. It was so much easier to talk while wearing fresh undies. "I made you sleep on the floor. The least I can do is get you some coffee and breakfast. I'm sure you need breakfast."

Sam looked around the apartment, as if he was trying to determine where he was. He eyed the ink sketch of a nude woman hanging above the fireplace, then looked back and forth between the two bedrooms on either side of the living room.

"Yeah, I should—"

"Stay. You should stay. I'll go grab coffee and bagels around the corner at Sweet Spoon. Today we can be the people who avoid all awkwardness after getting drunk and sleeping together but not *sleeping together*." I ran a hand through my damp hair and rolled my eyes. "Okay, wow. That sounded desperate. I'm not desperate. I just don't want to be awkward. Wow, yeah, I just *can't* stop talking, and I've made it *so* awkward." I took a deep breath and let my hands fall at my sides. "How do you take your coffee?"

Sam smiled—why did I have to feel that smile everywhere? Hot and tingly and wonderful—and he laughed. "I could just go with you."

"Yeah, that is a much simpler solution," I said.

We walked through my neighborhood in silence and waited in line with the early afternoon crowd while a remixed cover of No Doubt's "New" played around us.

There were no casual touches, no secretive glances, no easy cuddles, and I found myself edging closer to him to force an accidental embrace. I missed the affectionate freedom of intoxication.

It was ridiculous but I missed our stalled elevator, too.

"Are your rude comments reserved for boobs alone, or do

you ever branch out?" I asked. "What about inappropriate ass grabbing? Lewd gestures? Catcalling?"

Sam turned his attention away from the chalk-scrawled menu board, his eyes narrowed. He stared at me for a long moment, then a smirk pulled at his lips. He inclined his head toward the counter, urging me to step up without offering a response.

Once my iced cappuccino and bagel order was placed and the barista eyed Sam, he shuffled forward, his hands firmly stowed in his pockets. This was not the road to ass grabbing.

"Almond milk latte, iced, extra dry, no sweeteners."

"Seriously? You have a bad-ass cross tattooed on your back and you order an almond milk latte *extra dry*? Did you hear yourself?"

Sam handed his credit card to the barista and laughed. "I don't eat dairy. Or wheat. Or artificial sweeteners."

"What's left?"

He placed his hand on my back—finally—and steered me toward a dim, quiet corner of the café. "Plenty," he murmured before retreating to collect our drinks.

He made quite the picture: wrinkled khakis and shirt, hopelessly messy hair, heavy stubble, black eye. Somehow that didn't deter several customers from eying him up and down, and sending longing gazes in his direction as he returned to me.

I know how you feel.

Once the caffeine and carbs hit my veins, I was a happier woman, and again capable of speaking in complete, logical sentences.

"Feeling better?" Sam asked. Too hungry to stop eating and respond properly, I nodded. "Yeah. I can tell. So…random question. Can I ask you about your apartment?"

Mouth still full of bagel, I nodded again.

"Do you have a roommate?" He stirred his coffee, his brow wrinkled. "Also—what's the story with the art?"

"Mmhmm, yeah. About the art," I said. The drawings were

in every room, and though I was told it was odd to have so much nakedness in one small apartment, I did not care. "My great-grandmother, and she was a painter. She mostly painted ordinary things, like fruit, landscapes, children, but when she died, my father discovered this whole crate full of, well, you know…erotic art. And now I haul them around with me, wherever the wind takes me."

"Is that a way of saying you move frequently?"

I shook my head. "No. Not really. I go where I go. After I finished college, I didn't know what to do with myself. I knew I wanted a new city, so I moved here. I bounced around for a while, playing with a few different theatre companies, some bands, living in different parts of town, trying out the private music lesson thing, starting a grad program at Berklee." I finished that chunk of bagel and thought for a moment. "Eventually, the wind will take me somewhere else."

"And the roommate?"

"Oh, yeah," I laughed. "Miss Ellie Tsai. We met in college, in the strings program. She was T-si and I was D-si. Obvious love connection. She's on tour with a folksy pop band right now. She's the lead fiddle. Very important role."

"I can imagine," Sam said. "So you're a professor at Berklee?"

"Adjunct," I clarified, my mouth full. "*Adjunct* professor."

"What's the difference?" Sam asked.

"I teach more classes for a fraction of what tenured profs are paid. I'm obligated to assist the department chair and do all his grading. Plus research. Tons of research. Never-ending research. But that's the deal until I finish my doctorate." I redistributed the cream cheese to an even layer and took another bite. This wasn't the time to tell all of higher ed's dirty secrets. "I'm not convinced academia is for me. Like, forever. I don't like making forever plans. I'd rather see where life goes."

"I guess that's fair," Sam said. "What do you teach?"

We talked about my introductory music therapy courses, and the path I took into the discipline, which came after spending two years with a family who hired me to give their autistic daughter piano lessons. Lillian didn't speak much, and she struggled to interact with her family, but she loved music. We didn't have to talk to understand each other; the music spoke for us.

I didn't do anything miraculous or special with Lillian. I just taught her to control the notes, and she was the one who turned it into complex compositions. Her mother referred me to another family whose child experienced similar challenges, and soon I had more than my share of unique, incredible children who possessed my passion for music.

"So...After finishing work on a graduate degree in strings performance, I wanted to learn why music spoke to these children when nothing else could," I said.

"My sister's like that," he said. "She just kept finding new reasons to stay in grad school."

I stared at the table, debating whether I wanted another coffee or another bagel.

Most likely both.

"So you teach them violin? The kids, I mean. In your private lessons?"

Shrugging, I swirled my straw around the empty glass. "Sometimes. Sometimes piano. I'm working with a percussionist now, and there's one who wants to learn guitar."

"You can teach them all that?"

I nodded. "Most people who go to music school can play a few things. Not unusual."

Sam leaned back in his seat, crossed his legs, and folded his arms over his chest. The movements pulled his shirt open at the neck. He was slim yet strong—beautifully sculpted—and I wanted to taste the dips and curves of his shoulders.

"These kids, they're prodigies or something?"

I wanted to drag my teeth over his skin. Bite, lick, savor.

"Tiel?"

My tongue swiped over my lips, and I inhaled deeply. "Hmm?"

"I asked you whether these kids are prodigies, and then you zoned out on me," Sam said. "Are you okay?"

"Yeah, I'm great. I'm just..." I stared at my glass. "Nothing. I don't like calling anyone a prodigy. Some people can just play."

"And *you're* not a prodigy? You can 'just play' all those instruments?" he asked.

It was funny how the rest of the world offered a certain degree of reverence for children with boundless musical talent, yet my family saw it as a nuisance.

My parents seized on an opportunity to channel my hyper-activity and teach me some focus when I was five, but I knew they deeply regretted putting me into the area's early orchestra program. They never expected it would turn into an entity that defined my life.

Unless I was playing traditional Greek songs at the restaurant, I was an expensive, time-consuming annoyance, but not playing wasn't an option for me. It was the movement my heart and soul required, and once it became clear they didn't support that for me, I was willing to invent solutions to every obstacle.

My mother found my Rachmaninov and Prokofiev pieces "screechy." I took to practicing in the garage when I was seven, and cut the fingers off my mittens when winter rolled around. When my lessons and practice time were squeezed out by Greek school and church activities, I secretly woke up before sunrise to play. When I grew out of my three-quarter violin and my parents couldn't afford the full sized, I started babysitting to cover the expense. In high school, I saved my camp counseling salary for new bows, sheet music, and trips to see the New York Philharmonic at Lincoln Center.

I might have known—even when I was very young—that my violin was my ticket out. My talent and skill made me different, and it helped me leave.

"That term is kind of...hmm," I started. "Everyone has gifts and talents. Music is mine."

Sam opened his mouth to speak, but sneezed instead. Then he sneezed twice more. "Sorry," he said. "There might have been a little dairy milk in there." He pointed toward his half-empty latte and pulled a handkerchief from his back pocket.

"And that's why you're sneezing?"

He nodded. "I'm allergic to dairy. It'll pass in a minute."

"Wow," I said as he sneezed again. "That is unfortunate."

When the sneezing subsided, Sam pointed toward my empty cappuccino. "Would another one of those make you happy?"

"Very," I said, smiling when his hand brushed over my shoulder to grab my cup.

There was a gentleman hiding underneath that obnoxious player and he was too adorable for me. Just too freaking adorable. He could spend three months in the wilderness, come back looking like a mountain man, and I'd still want to nibble every inch of him.

"How much longer do you have in grad school?" he asked, placing a fresh cappuccino in front of me.

"Until I finish my dissertation, which is a small eternity. Still figuring those pieces out. I haven't exactly committed to a topic yet." I gestured to Sam, and his cup of tea. "You said you're an architect, right?"

"Right," he said. He produced a small bottle of hand sanitizer from his pocket and worked the liquid into his skin. It was methodical, and more than a little mesmerizing. "We specialize in sustainable preservation, which is basically the idea that the most ecologically sound option in building is to restore and improve existing buildings."

"That's cool," I said. "And you work with your brother?"

Sam laughed and scratched his chin for a moment. "I work with two older brothers, one older sister, and one younger brother. Third generation family firm, actually."

Multiple generations, three brothers, and a sister felt all too familiar.

I grew up stacking dishes and filling baskets of pita bread at my family's restaurant. It had been in business for over forty years, and all of my mother's brothers and sisters worked there, too.

Cooking, prepping, waiting tables, washing dishes, carrying deliveries—whatever it was, we did it. Me, my sister, and all nineteen of my cousins.

But I never belonged there.

It worked out well for Agapi. Manning the hostess station five nights a week was her dream job, and she met her husband on an emergency trip to the meat market when the restaurant was running low on provisions. It was amazing we hadn't added a butcher to the family until then.

"Third generation. That's impressive," I said.

Sam barked a laugh. "It's a fucking circus, and if we could hide a body in this town without getting involved with the mafia, we'd have killed each other by now."

Surprised, I looked up from my coffee to find Sam gazing at my chest again, and I'd never enjoyed gratuitous ogling quite so much. He was overt about it, but in a charming, curious way that I was finding increasingly tolerable.

"What are you doing today, perv?" I asked.

"I'd be interested in staring at your tits some more, and I wouldn't mind you sucking my dick like you promised."

"I told you to stop thinking about that," I said.

"And I told you I probably wouldn't," he said. "I haven't."

I didn't know what to do with his words. Was this flirting? Or friendly ball-busting? Or…something in between? What happened after a near-death experience, a drunken night, and a cuddlefest?

Ultimately, it didn't matter. I wanted to hang out with Sam, and I didn't care whether we were flirting or sparring or forging strange, new ground in the middle.

And that was the sweet little lie I was telling myself today.

"There are a couple festivals this weekend. A few bands I wanted to see. Let's be the random, mismatched people who don't look like they belong together."

"Speaking of which," he said. "What the fuck are you wearing?"

I glanced at my aqua shorts and ruffled red top. "What are you talking about? This is cute."

Exaggerated annoyance flashed across his face. "Let's start with the nine necklaces, and that one—" He gestured to the pendant just below my breasts. Of course he was staring at that. "Is that a fucking mermaid? You know what? It doesn't matter. Sure, all these colors and fabrics go together, but there's no losing you in a crowd, Sunshine."

"And that's why we need to hit some festivals," I said, stifling a laugh. He was adorable when he got fired up.

Sam frowned and leaned back in his chair, his arms crossed over his chest again. The closed-off, arrogant look worked for him. "Or I could go somewhere that's heard of Whitley Neill gin and takes the health codes seriously."

I pulled my lip between my teeth and moved my head with the My Chemical Romance tune, "Helena," as I considered his comment.

I couldn't compete with Sam's posh club scene and all the cocksucking, but I also knew he was at least eighty percent bluster. Probably more. He enjoyed getting a reaction from me, and for some reason, I liked giving it to him.

Sam reminded me of Ellie, but it wasn't until now that I understood that thread. Ellie and I found each other at freshmen orientation, our eyes meeting across a herd of orchestra dorks. We shared identical degrees of exasperation for self-aggrandizing professors, made a run from the team-building exercises at the same moment, and found ourselves chatting off to the side at every opportunity. We thought alike and had the same humor, our families were the pinnacles of weird, and we immediately understood everything about each other. And just that fast, she was my person.

It was like that with Sam, sort of. We were drawn together, magnet to metal. There was something inside him that I recognized, and maybe it was something inside me, too. I didn't know what it was or whether I wanted to find out, but quickly and without analysis, he was becoming one of my people.

"You can stare at my boobs all you want." I lifted a shoulder. "I could be talked into another drunken dance party."

He sat forward and folded his hands around my cup. "Where are we going and do you want more coffee before we leave?"

AFTER STOPPING AT HIS PLACE, Sam met me in the North End for St. Anthony's Feast, a gigantic Italian event with food, music, parades, and more food. Later, we made our way downtown to the Black Rose for an Irish folk festival. Sam passed on every snack I picked up along the way and looked mildly horrified when I offered, but he didn't mind admiring everything with breasts.

There was no escaping the obvious: Sam was a shameless flirt. I wasn't sure it was entirely intentional so much as it was an ingrained behavior like chewing with his mouth closed. I was gradually—grudgingly—realizing that his eyes automatically landed on boobs and bums.

Without a reminder, he'd speak directly to my cleavage.

I'd wanted to equate those habits with a lack of respect for women, but the more time I spent with him, the more I saw that argument teetering on unsteady legs. He held doors open for me and grabbed my hand when we crossed busy streets and insisted on paying for all four of my cappuccinos and said 'pardon me' every freaking time he blew his nose.

Sam talked about my boobs and asked for oral sex on the

hour, but that was his shallow, derpy way of enforcing the perimeter. It kept me—and everyone else—far enough away to miss the sweetheart under the surface.

He rolled his eyes when I said, "You haven't eaten all day." I pointed to the device tucked inside his pocket. I'd seen more than enough diabetic band campers to know regular meals were essential. It didn't make me an expert on the topic, but I didn't mind being the voice of snacking reason. "Let's sit down and get something."

"I'm fine." Sam glanced around, shaking his head as if he wouldn't be able to find anything palatable. "Don't worry about it."

His words were terse, and he was stewing in obvious distress, and I probably should have backed off. Reaching into his pocket, I glanced at the monitor. Being one of my people meant I didn't back off. "What's low for you?"

He offered a tight shrug and some under-the-breath swearing, looking uncomfortable, and murmured, "Around the fifties or sixties."

According to the screen, his blood-glucose was forty-one and falling. I gestured to it, meeting his eyes with a please-tell-me-you're-seeing-this stare. "Right. You don't like anything here." I waved at the stalls set up around Quincy Market and he shook his head. "Is there something you *do* like?"

Sliding the device into his pocket gave me an opportunity to get a little closer and run my hand down his back. I could feel all the muscular notches and grooves that I saw this morning, and reliving that memory was a bit sinful. The sin probably had something to do with my inability to stop rubbing him.

"There's a place near the Aquarium that isn't awful," he said. "But it's fine. Let's just stay here, and I'll get another beer."

"That seems like not a good idea," I said. "Let's go, Freckle Twin."

The city was bustling, and every corner revealed a new celebration, and this was how I loved Boston the most. It would never be New York, and the longer I lived here, the more I enjoyed that.

Sam led us to Rosemary and Sage, a sparklingly clean, shiny restaurant with big communal tables and floor-to-ceiling windows. It was mostly empty. I assessed the menu, quickly finding salad, more salad, and sandwiches filled with salads. Everything was organic and locally grown, with the origin attached to every ingredient.

Ward tomatoes. Apponagansett peppers. Langwater spinach and kale. Barden apples. Aquidneck cheeses.

"Do you see anything you'd like?" Sam asked. He sounded apprehensive.

"Yeah, I'm good with this." I nodded toward the menu. "I'm easy."

We ordered, and once a greens-and-berries smoothie was in his hands, the clouds left his eyes and he loosened up. He smiled, laughing to himself as if he suddenly remembered a hilarious moment. He met my furrowed eyebrow with a devious grin.

"So you're easy?" he said. "You could have mentioned that sooner."

"You're such a slutty beast," I murmured. "Drink your juice."

Our meals arrived—caprese panini for me, wheelbarrow of vegetables for Sam. I saw an armful of greens topped with asparagus, artichoke hearts, zucchini, peppers, carrots, celery, apples, beets, cranberries, radishes, cucumbers, mushrooms, seaweed, and bean sprouts. I didn't think it was possible to have an entire garden in one salad, but Sam proved me wrong. He went hard with the herb vinaigrette but picked a few stray red onions from the bowl and set them aside with a contemptuous glare.

If he looked at me the way he looked at those onions, I'd promptly shrivel up and die.

"Not a fan?" I pointed to his discard pile and he shook his head. "My family, they have a Greek restaurant in New Jersey.

I'm Greek, by the way. And Indian. Like the subcontinent, not the native peoples. Anyway. Everyone is conscripted into the workforce around the time they master walking and talking. For about two years, eighth and ninth grade, I think, I was stuck on pepper and onion prep. All I did, every afternoon, was chop. My entire life smelled like onions. The scent haunted me. Even when it was gone, I could still smell it. To this day, I can't look at onions without wanting to wash my hands with vanilla extract."

Sam wiped his hands on his napkin, laughing. "That sounds like child abuse."

"Finally," I cried. "Someone who sees it my way."

We ate and talked, covering everything from college to local politics to regional accents to my issues with the garbanzo bean, but we never discussed last night. I was *dying* to talk about it. I knew my flirt game was hardcore, but I didn't go around kissing dudes in bars. I didn't wake up with them, half naked, either.

I wanted to know whether we were laughing it off as 'oh my God, I can't believe we got that drunk and kissed' or giving each other the side eye like 'oh my God, we kissed and we want to do it again.'

I craved that kind of structure. I preferred to organize relationships into clear boxes and know all the boundaries up front, but in every other part of my existence, I let life happen and didn't worry too much about the details. If there was one thing I knew to be true it was that life would almost always go on.

After lingering at Rosemary and Sage, we traversed several neighborhoods, stopping at every event we encountered. We detoured to Whole Foods for an expertly selected bunch of grapes and ended up back in Cambridge that night, drinking beer, eating those grapes, and watching fireworks on the roof of my building. We sat shoulder to shoulder, gazing at the sky.

Sam turned to me and drummed his fingertips against my arm. "What's your name mean?"

I waited, watching the reflection of the fireworks in his eyes and hoping his fingers wouldn't stop. He didn't stray far from my side today, but he never touched me without an invitation.

I'd yank him toward the fresh cannolis, then he'd slide his hand down my back.

I'd grab his hand and twirl around, then he'd grip my hips.

I'd lean against him in a crowd, then he'd shift toward me.

I couldn't tell whether he was waiting for me to spell out my attraction to him, or he was very polite and very tolerant of my grabby hands but wasn't into me at all. I just needed some direction from him, and I knew I was going to be rubbing all over him until he asked me to stop.

"My mother took the Greek name Theola—which means something like friendly with gods or divinity or whatever—and twisted the soul out of it until she was left with Tiel. She's quite skilled at twisting the soul out of most things, actually." I tipped my beer back and edged closer to Sam, my head pillowed against his shoulder. "Everyone in my family has a monstrously Greek name. Like, they couldn't possibly exist without putting it out there, a giant fucking sign that screams 'Everything about me is defined by my lineage and I can't possibly have an identity unless it explicitly ties me to my ancestors.' And it's fine if that's who you are, but it's not me. I'm still stuck with a horrendously strange name, I know—"

"It's not. I like it. It suits you." He shook his head. "You're pure wild. You're something I'd find on an obscure trail in the middle of an ancient forest, in a special pocket of nature, and that's...amazing."

It shouldn't have mattered so much that he said those words, that he could sweep all of my not-quite-this-but-not-quite-that-either away. It gave me the odd sense that I wasn't a complete outlier and I might belong somewhere.

But that didn't mean Sam belonged with me. I wasn't sure where he belonged—aside from a Ralph Lauren ad—and it didn't seem like he knew either. "What's your story, Freckle Twin?"

He took a sip of his beer and eyed me over the bottle. "I'm fond of vegetables," he said. "You already know my gin preferences. I bought an old firehouse, and I spend most of my time fixing it up. I draw things and call it architecture. And I enjoy camping."

"How does one come to live in a firehouse?"

He reached for another bottle from the six pack, and popped it open with a churchkey. There was something to be said for a man who kept one of those on his key ring. "One sees the state refusing to add a two-hundred-year-old landmark to its historical sites, which basically opens it up for demolition. One then throws down some cash, moves in, and starts restoring it."

I wasn't sure what sparked more questions: the idea of living in a firehouse, the process of restoring that firehouse, or tossing money around. "Does it have a pole?"

"Of course," he said. "We've been renovating for almost four years now, and we haven't had the heart to remove the pole. I can't see why we would."

"'We'?"

"My brother Riley moved in about two years ago," Sam said. "The original agreement was that he'd only stay the summer, but he's handy and he likes projects. I keep him busy."

"So you have family around *all* the time?" My words came out too sharp and Sam shrugged, giving me a wary glance. "And camping? Like, outdoors? On the ground? Isn't that unpleasant?"

"I don't consider it unpleasant," he said. "I go to Maine a lot. Vermont, too. My sister, Erin, and I went up there last May. It's good to be alone, get away from things."

"So you're close with your sister."

I didn't intend for my tone to be so severe, nor did I intend my words to snap like an accusation, but they sprang from a sore spot.

"Not really. It was the first time I'd seen her in years. I don't hear from her much," he said. "She lives in Europe now. She's researching volcanoes, and it seems there are a number of them in Europe. I doubt she'll ever come back permanently."

"Wait, so…if your sister lives in Europe, you work with a different sister?" He murmured in agreement. "You're one of *six*?"

He released a dry, humorless laugh. "Yeah, we're the last of a dying breed of homegrown Irish-Catholic basketball teams."

"I didn't realize you were one of *them*."

He smiled, set his bottle down, and brushed his knuckles over my knee. "Indeed. My mother was from a little town in County Antrim. Northern Ireland, near Belfast. She wanted a huge family. She had a dining room table built to seat twenty, and I think she expected to fill half of it with kids."

"Six is damn close," I said. "Do your parents live around here?"

"My mother passed away when I was young," he said. "My father died last December."

"I'm so sorry," I said, the words rushing out in a gasp. I'd wanted to know whether he was beholden to a Sunday dinner routine, or often found himself with a list of chores, or was secretly a nice boy who took his mother to church every weekend. I never expected this. "Sam, I…I don't know what to say."

"There's nothing to say. It's a point of fact."

"That doesn't mean I'm not still sorry about your losses," I said. He shook his head, scowling as if it was ridiculous to express my sympathies. "Are you tight with your other sister?"

The way he rolled his eyes was so extraordinary, so exaggerated, so epic that I worried his eyeballs were going to pop out of their sockets. It came with a full body sneer that was positively adolescent, and he said, "Usually, yes. She stepped in and raised us when my mother died, and she's always been my biggest supporter. But Shannon and I aren't on the best terms right now."

Grabbing the keychain from his pocket—my hand found reasons to get in his pocket with frequency—I flipped open another beer. "You can't say that without expecting me to ask why," I said. "You're just baiting me."

"There's something going on with her," he said. "I think she's unhappy with herself and taking it out on the people around her, primarily me. Lauren—my brother's wife—is far too sweet to abuse. Andy—my oldest brother's girlfriend—won't put up with anyone's shit. Shannon hasn't spoken to Erin in years, and that issue is simply asinine. So all her angst is fired at me right now."

"Oh," I said, trying and failing to manage my reactions. "So there are *a lot* of women in your life."

"That's one way to interpret it," he said, frowning. "I'm not exactly hanging out in the women's shoe section at Nordstrom or getting advice on eye shadow, if that's what you're thinking. I mean, not usually."

I shook my head, attempting to brush aside Sam's response but I couldn't ignore the dread building in my chest. I didn't get along with families.

The fireworks eventually ended but we stayed there, watching the city lights. I couldn't usually manage this kind of quiet, but today had been the enjoyable type of draining. Yawning, I felt the humidity sapping the last of my energy.

"All right," he said. He pushed to his feet and collected the empty bottles and caps. "I should go."

"Do you like movies?"

Sam glanced at me, his brow furrowed as if it was a ridiculous question. "Yeah. Don't most people?"

"Some don't," I said. My ex-husband hated movies. If it wasn't performed live and on stage, he wasn't interested, and it was unbelievably comical how a fifteen-minute marriage was still dominating my thought process nine years later. "Stay. Watch a movie with me."

He squinted at me, repressing a smile. "Is that what friends would do?"

There was an opening and an out in that question, but

neither were quite right. Friends didn't kiss in alleys and wake up together, half-naked, but *more than friends* didn't exist for Sam. He was crystal clear about it last night, and I didn't need to hear that story twice.

But while I still didn't understand it, I was the magnet to his metal and I was opting for something over nothing.

"Friends do whatever the hell they want," I said. "Obviously, you need a friend to guide you and teach you some of the non-rules. You're very lucky to have me."

"As a *friend*?"

"Of *course*," I said, my voice overly cheerful to hide my lie. "What else would we be?"

He gazed down at me, pausing as he considered this. There were any number of things we could be together: tennis partners, duet singers, international jewel thieves, the top-ranked music reviewers for *The Phoenix*, but I didn't suggest any of that. It was too easy to slip lovers into that list.

He extended his hand, and when my palm connected with his, he pulled me tight to his chest. "All right, my friend. You pick the film."

He was on the sofa, his limbs tangled with mine, and asleep within the first half hour of *Stepbrothers*. I laid there, listening to the movie and feeling every inch of his beautiful body pressed against me and narrating every filthy fantasy I could imagine as his chest rose and fell.

What if I snuggled into him, my bum tucking against his shorts and the form-fitting boxers just beneath? Would he pull my hips tighter against him, grind into me, harden on contact?

What if I reached out and stroked him? Or traced his tattoos again, following the dark lines down the path of his body? Would he melt into my touch, or pull away?

Friends could kiss and friends could have mostly-clothed sleepovers, but friends couldn't grab dicks.

As I fell asleep, I nestled into his chest and laced my fingers with his.

Just like friends.

We did it all over again the next day. This time, we broke past the city limits and headed west to Lenox and the Tanglewood Jazz Festival. The event was paired with a gourmet food and wine tasting, and I was happily astonished to see Sam talking with chefs and sampling the goods.

Late in the afternoon, the wine was getting to my head and it was still hot and cloyingly humid, and we went in search of a quiet patch of lawn to relax. I'd always loved lying on the cool grass and listening to the earth. It was almost as if I could hear a rhythm, a heartbeat, that quiet symphony for those who chose to listen.

"So what kind of porn do you watch?"

I turned my head to glare at him, not amused by his interruption to my earth-music listening. "Rude and pervy, Sam."

"We've established that," he said, his fingers smoothing my tangled necklaces and coming awfully fucking close to my boobs. "What do you watch? Or is that not something friends talk about?"

He'd been doing that all damn day. Every comment circled back to friends, as if he was hammering home a crisp reminder. Even though we woke up wrapped around each other, it was obvious he wasn't interested in anything more than slick comments about my best features, pointing out opportunities for me to blow him, and casual touches. Plus a few sweet kisses.

And I was fine with it.

Maybe *fine* wasn't the right word because I wasn't completely fine.

"I don't watch much porn," I said, turning my face to the sun with a long exhale. I was clammy and tired, and the early pinches of a too-many-types-of-wine-in-one-day headache were crawling along my skull. "Although I'm certain you'll be telling me all about your preferences any minute and I can't wait to hear that."

"Of course you watch porn. Everyone does," he said. His fingers connected with mine, curling together.

I rolled to my side, leaning on my elbow to meet his eyes. "I don't, though. It's way too creepy to be sexy. I truly dislike all the hairless guys with their shaved balls. You have to agree that's weird, like some bald, plasticized version of perfection that has no actual connection to the way people have sex. There's just no....hmm. I don't know what I'm trying to say," I said. "I need it to feel significant, and I want it to be real and flawed."

Sam smirked, and I knew there was a dirty, sarcastic quip ready on his tongue, but he dropped his gaze to my tangerine sundress and the boobs that were most definitely hanging out at this angle. "Why?" he asked.

"Because it should," I said, and that was the logic I preferred. "Even when it's casual it should mean something. Life is too short to waste on things that aren't important enough to be *real*."

Sam's hand slipped through my hair and settled on the nape of my neck, and he stared at me, his eyes crinkled as if he was processing something complex. He pulled me toward him and I flattened my palm on his chest, registering the steady beat of his heart before our lips connected.

It was light and quick, passing before his flavor seeped into my senses, and I wanted a little more.

Sam was like that song you couldn't get out of your head. That beat you kept on repeat because it awakened your cells and sent rhythm rippling through your muscles as if it were the only song you were ever intended to hear.

The one written with only you in mind.

I could close my eyes and move with the music, but I wasn't going to let myself believe I was the only one enjoying the song.

Even if I wanted a lot more.

Five

SAM

I CAME to a stop on the empty lane, and stared out the window at the sunny knoll for a few minutes before leaving my Range Rover. With a heavy sigh, I climbed out of the car and collected the chrysanthemums and gardening supplies from the trunk.

The walk was short, and it was one I'd be able to do blindfolded.

My first task was always raking. Leaves from the ancient oak tree nearby were already tinted with red and gold, and I'd have much more to rake in the coming weeks.

Then I turned to pruning the pale pink rosebushes. I never felt ready to speak until things were neat and tended.

With several deep breaths to slow the pounding in my veins, I dropped to my knees and arranged the chrysanthemums around the tombstone.

"Hi, Mom," I said. "It's a beautiful day. Sunny, with a nice breeze. I brought you some new flowers for the fall. I can't believe summer is almost over. I don't even know where the time goes anymore."

I brushed some dust from the engraving that read *Abigael Ailis Walsh* and continued. "I went to some festivals and

concerts, and I know, I don't usually go to things like that, but…
it was different for me. It was good."

I uncapped my water bottle and wet my handkerchief, then
wiped dust from the second engraving on the stone: *Kerry Aibh-
linn Walsh*. A single date was attached to her name, a beginning
and an end within itself, and for as many times as I visited this
cemetery, I couldn't help but relive the day they died.

I was lucky today. The memory didn't have me choking back
vomit or steal the breath from my lungs; it only left me with the
sense that my skin was two sizes too small.

Sometimes I wondered whether the memories were real. I
was five years old when I held my mother's hand as she died,
and though it all seemed blindingly vivid, it only came back to
me in jagged clips of high-speed film. I remembered the
screaming and the blood and the icy cold of her hand in mine,
and I remembered nodding when she said, "You're going to be
all right, Samuel. You're going to be all right without me."

There was more, I was sure of it. I knew Patrick or Matthew
would be able to fill in the holes, but even after twenty-three
years, I could barely manage these memories.

"I met someone. A girl—Tiel." I looked to the ground, the
trees, the tombstones, the sky, hoping to locate the words I
needed because I couldn't find them within myself. "I think I'm
a little lost, Mom. I knew it before I met Tiel, but it really hit me
this weekend. Tiel loves everything. *Everything.* She loves music
and food and people, and I'm not sure I love anything. I don't
think I know how to."

Packing up my supplies, I glanced at the tombstone again.
"I've never *wanted* to love anything. I'm not sure that I can. But I
was with her, touching her and feeling happy—or something
that felt close enough to happy—and I wanted to feel that way
all the time."

I readjusted the chrysanthemums and stood. "Same time
next week, Mom." I ran my hand over the curved top of the
stone, not yet prepared to say goodbye. "You'd like her," I said.

"There's something about her that feels...I don't know. It's ridiculous, but it's like I'm okay—for once in my life—when I'm around her. I don't know how, and maybe I'm hallucinating, but she does something to me."

"IT IS bizarre to be doing this on a Tuesday," Shannon said as she settled into her seat at the conference room table, cell phone, latte, and laptop in hand.

"It would be less bizarre if you were on time," Patrick muttered.

"I'm five minutes late. Does that warrant a debate?" Shannon asked. "Or are we going to start the meeting?"

He rolled his eyes and exchanged an impatient expression with Matt. "All right, people. Shannon's here, so we can start."

"Thank you, Patrick," she said. "How was everyone's long weekends?"

And this was how it went every Monday. The six of us—Shannon, Patrick, Matt, Riley, me, and our newest addition, Andy Asani—hiked up to the attic conference room, shared updates on our work, and argued about everything. It was the loudest portion of my week. We were genetically incapable of having a discussion without yelling; every conversation existed on the same level as a barroom brawl.

"We went to a seafood festival in New Hampshire," Andy said, nodding toward Patrick.

It had been over three months since we realized they'd been seeing each other all winter, and I still didn't understand their relationship. I couldn't date a woman and work with her all day.

Then again, I didn't know the first thing about *dating* women.

"You went to a *seafood* festival?" Riley asked.

"He ate the fish," she said, jerking her thumb at Patrick. "I drank the beer."

They exchanged a quick high-five before he said, "I was bartending down in Rhody. Newport kicks ass on long weekends."

Patrick glanced at me, frowning, then turned to Riley. "Are we not paying you enough?"

"I was filling in for a buddy, and I just like it," he shrugged. "But if you're looking to unload some cash, I won't stop you."

"And what about you, Sammy?" Shannon asked.

I glared at her, waiting for her to realize she stood me up at Commonwealth, didn't return my calls, and ignored every single one of my fucking texts this weekend. She went right on typing and sipping her coffee.

"My weekend was sensational, Shannon. I went to six different music festivals in four states, got drunk at the Feast of St. Anthony, passed out in Cambridge, and almost died in a goddamn elevator crash. Where the fuck were you on Friday and why the fuck weren't you answering your phone?"

No one moved for a full minute, and then Riley said, "Did you get to the Thomas Point Beach Bluegrass show? I heard that was good this year."

"Is that a metaphor for something? Or are you talking about an actual elevator?" Patrick asked.

"Yeah. What do you mean, you almost died?" Matt said.

"The power went out in the Back Bay, and I was trapped in an elevator at the Comm Ave. property for eight hours," I said.

"The same elevator that slammed into the basement of that building?" Matt asked. "The one I read about, with the massive system failure compounded by the outage?"

"Same fucking one," I said. "So I'd love to know, Shannon. How was your weekend?"

"Did you go somewhere?" Patrick asked her. "You didn't mention anything...I thought you were staying in town."

"That's because I don't need you to approve my weekend

plans, Patrick," she said. "I don't have to tell you where I'm going, or what I'm doing, or who I'm with."

"But it would be good if you tell me, so I don't wait around at a property and get stuck in a fucking elevator," I replied.

"Jesus Christ, Sam, I'm sorry! I lost track of things, okay? I'm sorry." She slammed her coffee cup down and crossed her arms over her chest. "I went away with some friends, and I forgot about the appointment at Comm Ave., and—"

"The only person you spend time with who isn't presently accounted for in this room is my wife," Matt said. "And she was with me, on the Cape."

I turned to Matt. "Do you ever get tired of saying it with that sanctimonious tone? 'My wife'?"

He shot me a smug grin. "Never."

"But you're okay, yeah?" Riley asked. He pointed to the yellowing bruise on my face. "Is this from the elevator or blacking out in Cambridge?"

"Elevator," I said.

Waking up in Tiel's apartment left its marks, but they weren't bruises.

"Why didn't you call one of us?" Andy asked, angling her pen at Riley, Patrick, and Matt.

I lifted a shoulder and mumbled a response into my coffee cup.

"All right," Patrick murmured. "Let's get back on track here. Sam's alive. Shannon can't manage her appointments. Moving on."

We reviewed the active projects, as well as the ones we were considering. I didn't mention the Commonwealth property; I wasn't convinced I wanted to see the inside of that building ever again.

"Sam…" Shannon held up her hand while she paged through her notebook. "I can't go with you to the ASNE event in November."

The Architectural Society of New England's annual banquet

didn't matter to me, and if Shannon hadn't insisted that I attend and personally collect my awards each year, I wouldn't go. But she claimed it was great networking—even though none of those people agreed with our approach to preservation—and she made a point of attending, and befriending everyone in the room.

"And where will you be?" I asked.

She continued turning the pages, stopping occasionally to rearrange the sticky notes and mark reminders on her daily checklists, and murmured, "It's personal. If you need me to find someone to go and hold your hand, I will, but don't pout over it."

I snapped my laptop shut and stood, sending the chair careening into the brick wall behind me. "You're being a dick, Shannon," I called as I stormed down the stairs.

They'd talk; they always did. Either it was my outbursts or my obsessive tendencies or my whoring, but regardless of the topic, they'd hide the sharp objects and nominate someone to check on me.

Back in the comfort of my office, I set out my projects for the day. After an hour of hectic, unfocused work, I was prepared to storm into Shannon's office and put my issues on the table.

I was halfway down the stairs when my phone chimed. I'd snapped a picture of Tiel reclining on the grass this past weekend, and seeing it on my screen had me stopping mid-step.

"Hello?"

"Hey," she said. "There's an AC/DC cover band performing tonight. They're acoustic, and I think there's a banjo involved, but I hear good things. You should come with me."

I laughed and hustled down the stairs, bypassing Shannon's floor and heading outside, onto Derne Street. "Should I?"

"Yes, you should. You need more banjo in your life. In fact, the shortage of banjo in your life is a rather dire situation."

I hiked to the top of the street and watched the Beacon Hill traffic. I didn't have a creative reason to decline the invitation, and I was struggling to concoct one. I was comfortable being the guy with the booked calendar, but it dawned on me that Tiel didn't give a damn about any of my bullshit posturing.

"All right, Sunshine, but I need to put my head down and get some shit done."

"Wise decision. I'll text you the address," she said.

I jogged down the street and up to my office, closed the door, and dug into my projects with newfound urgency. Hours passed without my notice as I plowed through designs, emails, client calls, and some scheduling conversations with my preferred contractors.

A knock sounded at my door, and I pulled my glasses down my nose before looking up from my drafting program. Shannon stood outside and dangled a bottle of pale yellow juice between her fingers.

"I come bearing gifts," she said. "You have to be hungry."

Glancing at the clock, I realized it was nearly four in the afternoon, and I'd been working on this design straight through since eleven. I was hungry.

I nodded and stood, stretching to work the kinks out of my neck and back. She was careful to shut the door quietly, knowing I hated the way everyone else slammed everything around here.

Did they not remember the hell we went through to restore this building? Or the shit we took from Angus when we bought it? This brownstone was a labor of love, one that owned actual blood, sweat, and tears from each of us. The least we could do was handle the doors with a bit more care. I wasn't going to be the one repairing those hinges.

"I wanted to apologize about Friday. There's nothing else I can say other than I'm sorry." She set the bottle on my desk along with a bag of raw pistachios, and sat. "Carrots, honey, lemon, and celery. Andy said you were loving all things carrot."

Andy was my partner in juice crimes. She was the only one

who appreciated a decent cold-pressed juice in this office, and she often spoiled me with some of her homemade creations.

One glance at the label on the bottle and I knew Shannon dropped at least ten dollars on this juice. She probably sent her assistant, Tom, to get it from the Kendall Square café, but it was the thought that counted.

"Thank you," I said. A glance at my glucose monitor showed I was damn close to setting off the low blood sugar alarms, so I dug into the juice first. "I was going to stop for lunch soon."

"You can't be skipping meals. I'm going to have Tom start placing a lunch order for you every day. You're going to get yourself sick," she said.

I hadn't been taking care of myself, not the way I should. But Shannon didn't need to know that.

"Save the nutrition lecture for another day, Shannon."

"Fine." She paused, took a breath, and continued on. "I'm sorry about the ASNE event. It's the only event I'll miss this season."

I thought about her comment while I plowed through a handful of pistachios, and realized it was ridiculous for my big sister to escort me to these events.

"Actually, skip them all," I said. "I'm sure you have better things to do."

For as long as I could remember, she had been the ranking female figure in my life. I could dump my problems on her and she'd sort them out, gathering them and placing them in an order that made sense. I'd spend all day winding up issues in my head, letting them build and strengthen until they were little cyclones, and she'd walk every single one of them back.

My role was equally well-established. I helped her select reasonable clothing—her taste was atrocious, and left to her own devices, she'd wander the streets in cable knit ponchos and purple culottes—and managed her online dating profiles. We ate brunch together most Sundays, then spent the afternoon hitting open houses throughout the city.

My siblings claimed Shannon coddled me, and that I dispro-
portionately sided with her in business, but we shared a bond
they'd never understand. We were both exiled, refugees from
our own father.

He detested all of us, but Shannon and I took the lion's share
of his wrath.

Angus kicked her out before she finished high school. He
invented reasons to hate her, but most of all, it was because she
was our mother in every way possible, and he was set on
destroying every memory. It was easier to tear Shannon down
than live with the reminder of Mom. He did the same thing to
Erin, but he also liked beating the shit out of her.

He evicted me the summer before college. He was convinced
of my homosexuality—despite my earnest efforts at losing my
virginity to a woman—and wouldn't tolerate that kind of sin
any longer. He clung to the gay piece as the focal point of my
expulsion, but in all reality, he abhorred everything about me.

For nearly a decade, Shannon and I learned to live with his
torment and abuse, shielding each other from the worst. But
over the summer, things started changing.

She seemed distant and distracted, and became aggressively
defensive when I called her on it. We'd never kept much of
anything from each other, but now we were relative strangers.

She peered at me, her expression turning sour. "Is this about
Angus?"

"What? No. No, this has nothing to do with him, and if it's
the same to you, I'd rather we not continue bringing him up."

That fucker was good and dead, and we needed to stop
resurrecting his memory every twenty minutes.

"That sounds like it's definitely about Angus."

"Shan, stop trying to psychoanalyze everything I say. I have
a shit ton of designs to finish today, and I need to get my ass on
the treadmill tonight, and then I'm going out. Thank you for
lunch, but unless there's something else, we're finished with this
conversation."

She tapped her finger to her lips and sat quietly while I emptied the bag of pistachios and drained the juice. She was probably watching to confirm that I was, in fact, eating.

"There's one more thing. Something I hope will make you happy."

There was that word again: happy. But Shannon couldn't give me happiness any more than she could trap lightning in a jar.

She grabbed the framed snapshot from my desk, the one from the Boston Marathon finish line two years ago. She was in the middle, her red hair tucked under a Walsh Associates baseball cap, with Patrick and Matt on one side, and Riley and me on the other. Arms linked over shoulders, we leaned together, smiling. We looked completely typical, and from that image alone, no one would know we were tainted by neglect, abuse, and loss.

But...maybe it was possible to feel as lighthearted as we looked.

"Am I supposed to guess, or are you planning to say something?" I asked.

"It's a good thing you're cute, Sam. Otherwise I'd slap you upside the head for this shitty attitude." She shook her head, replaced the frame, and flipped open her tablet. "I renewed your driver's license for you. It will show up in a week or two. Oh, and I adjusted the automatic order for your replacement parts. When I went through the supplies at your place last week, it seemed like you were running low on infusion sets and insulin cartridges, but had enough skin preps and test strips for an eternity. Just let me know if you want more or less, or something different."

I brushed the pistachio shells into my waste basket and stared at her. "Where were you this weekend?"

"I went away with friends." Shannon could negotiate the spots off a Dalmatian but she couldn't tell bold-faced lies, and the red tint creeping across her cheeks gave it all away.

"Where?" I asked.

She threaded a lock of hair between her fingers and studied it, avoiding my eyes. "Nantucket. I took the ferry from Woods Hole on Friday."

"Who did you go with? What did you do?"

She shrugged and continued inspecting her hair. "Simone and Danielle, and it was a regular girls' weekend. Beach, brunch, booze. What else would we do?"

I waited, watching while a hot blush consumed her cheeks and neck. She didn't do girls' weekends with her law school friends, and she hated listening to Simone humble-bragging about the high-profile divorces she handled. "Why aren't you sunburned?"

"Sunscreen," she answered simply, but it was a bullshit answer. Shannon's skin was incredibly fair, and she couldn't go to the beach or pool without collecting a thick patch of freckles and some painful burns.

"Why don't you cut the shit," I said. "What is the purpose of this exercise, Shan? Does it not seem ridiculous that you're keeping something from me? From all of us? And you do notice that you're making a bigger deal out of it by lying about going to Nantucket, right?"

"Since you have a busy afternoon, I'd rather get down to the reason I came in here," she said. "We were approached last month by a real estate agent who was representing a very private client. Since the agent was absurdly vague about her client's interests, Patrick and I decided not to engage."

"Okay," I said, annoyed that she was deflecting again. I went to the small refrigerator behind my desk to refill my water glass, and offered some to Shannon.

"No, thanks. The agent came back, saying the client really, really wanted to work with us. It seems the client saw the *Boston Globe* spread on the future of green restoration." She gestured to where the freshly framed newspaper feature showcasing one of my projects leaned against the wall, waiting to be hung. "And the client insisted on working with you."

"I don't have much free time, Shannon," I said. I slid my four-page call sheet filled with requests for consultation across the desk. "And no offense, but I don't have a lot of patience for dealing with agents."

Shannon wore a lot of hats around here, and licensed real estate agent was one of them. She was also our legal counsel and chief financial officer, and while she spoke the language fluently, she was the only non-architect in the bunch. She seemed to like that form of schizophrenia.

"Well, it gets better." She toggled through a few screens on her tablet, then turned it toward me. "Turns out the client is Eddie Turlan, from The Vials." She pointed to a picture of the punk band popular in the eighties. "He and his wife are huge environmentalists now, and they want a complete green rehab and restore, and they want a big publicity splash, too. They purchased this brownstone in the South End." She swiped through another screen and zoomed in on the location. "It was built in 1899, and until the Turlans bought it, the property had been owned by the *same family*. It was renovated in the twenties, and then again in the sixties, but it hasn't been touched since then. In fact, it's been vacant since the late eighties."

She switched the map to street view, and I stared at the red brick house. This property saw three centuries with a common lineage, and everything about it screamed virgin canvas. There'd be shag carpets and vinyl wallpaper to remove, and probably some room-flow dynamics to resolve, but it didn't bear the weight of changing hands, and that was a rare delight.

"They want you to design it, and they offered to go well beyond your standard fees." She toggled to another screen, and handed the tablet to me. "Here's the most recent communication from the agent."

I skimmed the email, noting the budget the Turlans were comfortable with—it was astronomical—and some of their design preferences, and handed it back to Shannon. "I still don't have time."

Shannon nodded, and the devious grin on her face told me she already cooked up a plan. "You could make time if Riley moved off Matt's projects and started working with you." I began to protest, and she held up her hand. "I think you've argued with me enough today. Just listen. He's come a long, long way in the past eight months, and you have to admit that."

I sighed, knowing she was right.

He still couldn't zip his pants with any regularity, but he could be trusted to manage a couple of projects.

"I was also thinking this could be a phenomenal opportunity to partner with the roof garden girl," she said. "If there's ever been a property that needs a roof garden, it's this one."

I reached for the tablet, and paged back to the aerial map. Again, Shannon was right. Even with a quick glance, it was obvious this property would be perfect for all my favorite green features and my favorite sustainable landscape architect.

"What's the timeline with all this?" I asked.

Shannon nodded, her fingers drumming against the arms of the chair. It reminded me of Tiel and her non-stop fidgeting. Somehow, Tiel's noise was nothing like the noise my siblings created.

"They'd like to know as soon as possible. They close on the property in forty-five days or so, and want to start construction immediately. I promised them we'd follow up by Friday."

I ran my hand over my desk, savoring the applewood's gorgeous grain. I came across the felled tree while camping in Vermont last fall. I didn't know what I'd do with it at the time, but it gradually took shape while I worked it in my shop. This desk, the attic conference table, and most of the furniture in the Walsh Associates office came from my workshop at one point or another.

"I'll call Magnolia and find out whether she has any flexi-bility in her schedule," I said. She'd been bugging me to involve her in a project start to finish, to better understand the entire lifespan of a restoration rather than the narrow elements where she was typically involved. I respected her commitment to continuously learning and improving, and this property seemed like a good opportunity. It also meant I'd be able to think through problems with her, and she was amazing in those situations. She asked all the right questions and poked holes in my theories, and I loved that. "I need Riley freed up in the next couple of weeks, and I want the blueprints pulled from City Hall by noon tomorrow. Get your errand boy, Tom, on that one."

Shannon clapped her hands together and said, "Yes! I knew you'd be all over this. There's just one more thing." I groaned and she held out her hands. "Actually, two things. One: why can't we just call her Roof Garden Girl? I really prefer that to Magnolia. I mean, please. Who names a child Magnolia? It requires her to be a landscape architect, or own a flower shop. And two: there's a strict non-disclosure agreement attached to this client. You can't go tweeting about working on Eddie Turlan's house."

I rolled my eyes. "I don't tweet, and you'll need to talk to Magnolia about that. I don't think we know her well enough to give her a nickname yet."

The nicknames dated back to childhood when Riley couldn't pronounce any of our names correctly, always cramming them into garbled amalgamations like Mattrick and Sherin and Sammew. Somehow it was easier for him to say Optimus Prime than Patrick, and over time, we each earned our identifiers.

Despite my attempts to adopt Iron Man as mine, my siblings thought Tony Stark was more fitting.

"But you'd like to know her a little better, right?" Shannon asked. "You'd like to get on a nickname basis."

"You're reading into this rather far, Shannon."

She smiled, collected her things to leave, and paused in the doorway. Of course, she was the Black Widow, and as she stood there in the fitted plum dress I selected last April, sky-high heels, and piercing stare, she looked every bit the part.

"I really do want you to be happy, Sam. We all know the past year has been difficult for you, but we can't help if you don't let us."

Sipping my water, I tried to construct a response that acknowledged her concern without revealing how deep into my private Quechee Gorge I had dropped. She'd been waiting—realistically, it was my whole damn family that had been waiting—for me to fall apart since that miserable bastard died last year, but I wasn't giving them the satisfaction of being right.

They'd been there for me my entire life, and I appreciated that to no end. But I needed to do this on my own, and if this weekend with Tiel was any indication, it was worth finding the path out. I got there once; I could get there again.

"I know," I said. "I'm trying."

Six

TIEL

I SLEPT late on Wednesday mornings. My classes didn't start until noon, I didn't have any regular sessions with my little buddies, and I never reserved practice time in the studio. I always capitalized on this scheduling gift by going out Tuesday evenings. I should have used those hours for catching up on grading or research, or some form of exercise, but after a night spent trolling the underground music scene, sleep always won out.

Irritable didn't begin to encapsulate my reaction when my phone buzzed across my side table before eight. Cracking an eyelid enough to visualize the screen, I found Eleanorah Tsai's face smiling back at me.

"Please tell me this is an emergency," I growled.

"Can sweaters be an emergency? Because I need you to send me some," she laughed. "I packed two and I had no idea that Ottawa in September was like New York in February. Oh, and maybe some socks, too." I made a vague sound of agreement and she continued. "Yes, the weekend *was* fantastic, I'm so glad you asked. We played our asses off on Saturday and Sunday, and then we did the tourist thing at Niagara Falls, and I'm shocked to admit the tourist thing was really cool but it totally was. Then we spent all day yesterday on the bus to Ottawa, and ran into a hockey team at the hotel. Never would have guessed Canadian hockey players and bearded pop-folk boys could be best friends for life after draining a keg."

"BFFLs," I said, shifting to sit back against the headboard. "Gotta love them."

"And how did you spend your holiday weekend?"

"I have a crazy story for you," I said. "It's a story with many parts and several strange events."

"Please do not start at the end, go back to the beginning, and then periodically return to the end," she said. "That shit gets annoying unless it's intentionally ironic."

Laughing, I told her about the elevator and Sam, our kiss in the alley behind Sligo's Pub, the festivals we visited, the movies we watched, and last night's AC/DC cover band. He was the only person in a suit—three-piece or otherwise—and he spent a full ten minutes explaining the purpose of pocket squares to the bartender, but he enjoyed himself.

It was possible he enjoyed staring at the bartender's boobs more than the tunes.

"He probably thinks I'm turning into a stalker or something, because I wouldn't leave him alone all weekend and then I dragged him out last night."

"Hmm," Ellie murmured. "Do I sense that you *like* this prepster?"

"He's really freaking adorable and he's witty, and he needs to have some fun," I said. "So yeah, I *do* like him."

"I feel like you need a sociologist to observe this," Ellie said. "So what are you going to do?"

There was no pretending that I wasn't smitten with Sam, and at the very least, there was a curious friendship between us. But more than that, I was determined to figure him out, to understand why I was so drawn to him, to get past the player and find out why he was working so hard to keep people at a distance.

"Gogol Bordello is playing at Brighton Music Hall next weekend," I said. "I bet he's never heard of Gypsy punk..."

"Now there's a dissertation topic," she said. "The impact of live music on prepster reformation. I'd read that."

"Huh," I said, my lip caught between my teeth. "That would be interesting."

I DECIDED THAT, if I was going to dominate all of Sam's free time, I should at least see to his education in the fine arts. It was hard to believe that someone who knew this town inside and out was learning about an entirely new world from me, a relative newcomer. His knowledge of the area's music scene was paltry at best, and he'd only been to a handful of painfully mainstream arena shows before meeting me.

It was shameful.

Before the month of September ended, I introduced him to all my hidden (and not-so-hidden) favorites: The Sinclair, Café 939, Wally's, Great Scott, Paradise, Lansdowne Pub, and Toad.

It wasn't contrived, this whole hanging-out-with-Sam-thing. Not exactly. I was always on the hunt for live shows, and though he engaged in an ample amount of grousing, he was a willing participant. When he wasn't busy layering on the hand sanitizer or condescending all over the beverage options, he was rocking out with the rest of us. Feigning an adequate amount of snotty disinterest was how he kept his Cool Kid card.

We had fun together, and we enjoyed some tunes in the process. Keeping my eyes open for something new to broaden and deepen Sam's exposure was part of my daily routine now, and that was how I ended up scrolling through show listings instead of grading a waist-high stack of papers.

My tastes were about as varied as they came, a collage of genres, artists, time periods, and my strategy with Sam was all about exposing him to a broad range of performances. There was some old-school funk, blues, low-key punk, and an assortment of my favorite new trend—rockish-pop-alt-folk.

The indie scene made more sense to me with its small-stage simplicity. The venues were tiny, carved into bars and pubs.

There was an incredible steel-drum band playing at a divey joint downtown, and even though I'd probably have to sacrifice my studio time to crank these papers out tomorrow, this was an event Sam could not miss.

He didn't answer when I called, which meant he was in a meeting or tied up with one of his properties, or his phone was muted. Quiet was his preferred speed for most things, and it wasn't unusual for him to spend the entire day with his phone set to silent. It turned tracking him down into a game of hide and seek.

Tiel: what r u wearing
Tiel: it's important

I waited, staring at the pin-eaten bulletin board on the wall opposite my desk in the office I shared with four other adjuncts. It was a bland memorial to doctoral student life, with its outdated calls for research study participants, roommate requests, and jazz bands and string quartets advertising their availability for weddings, all ringed by a halo of well-loved delivery menus.

My essay-grading guilt won out when I couldn't justify gazing at walls and liking everything in my newsfeed much longer, and dug in for another round. On the whole, I enjoyed teaching, and grading wasn't bad either—I liked getting new perspectives on music therapy from students—but the volume of it stoked my natural tendency to procrastinate.

I blew through eleven papers before an incoming text sounded. Ringtones and other phone chirps usually annoyed me, but I'd discovered one that was like an old-fashioned bike bell and couldn't help smiling every time I heard it.

Sam: I'll ask those questions, thank you.

Tiel: No but srsly. Must see reggae. No 3 piece suits allowed

Sam: What did the English language ever do to you? And may I add: with the autocorrect features on your phone, you have no excuse to use loose combinations of letters.

Tiel: Do you yell at kids to get off your lawn too?

Sam: You bet your ass I do, and that brings me back to the matter at hand:

Sam: What are you wearing?

Tiel: 8 pm curtain. Want to get food first?

Sam: You're terrible at this

Tiel: ….what?

Sam: What. Are. You. Wearing.

I gave my cobalt blue dress an ambivalent glimpse. It was cute but didn't rise to the level of semi-sexting. Knowing that Sam ran hot and cold, toggling between being highly suggestive and tattooing "Just Friends" across his chest, I seized this burst of hot and snapped a neck-down selfie. The lighting was horrible and the faded chartreuse walls were the most noticeable element of the photograph, but I sent it anyway.

Reminding myself to keep it light and fun was complex. I wanted to analyze all these signals, dissecting his comments, smiles, touches into their microscopic parts and ascribing motivation to each, and I wanted a better title than friends.

But I wasn't doing any of that. This hazy, ambiguous place was the best I was going to get from Sam, and even after a matter of weeks, I wasn't walking away. We had a history of sorts, a bond formed under intense circumstances, and we *were* friends. I was also a little hooked on him.

Part of me knew I was getting the Sam Walsh Treatment: the panty-dropping smiles, the smoldery scowls, the well-honed lines. I knew the better portion of women in this town were probably familiar with it, too.

Yet…there were moments when I couldn't climb past my

doubt. Glances that lasted a beat too long. Kisses that spoke of more than drunken affection. Lingering touches that screamed "I will fuck you so hard you won't remember your first name."

And it was that doubt that kept me clinging to the threads he offered. I understood enough about Sam to know he didn't have romantic relationships; he didn't even do a full night with one woman. Asking him for more or giving him an ultimatum would freeze out friendship. While I wasn't content with the friend zone, I wasn't willing to lose it either. I'd survive on boob-gazing, casual kisses, and as much touching as I could get away with.

And flirty texts.

Sam: What the fuck are you wearing?

Sam: Just…fuck

Tiel: Yeah, I know, I probably have too many bracelets for you or this color is too bright or whatever. I don't want to hear your complaints. I like this.

Sam: I was not looking at the bracelets.

Tiel: Ok….?

Sam: You are fucking gorgeous

Sam: This picture is going to get a substantial amount of use

Sam: Are you alone right now? I'd like to discuss this

The empty desks surrounding mine were piled with books and papers, and boxes filled with yet more books and papers. My officemates and I saw each other in fly-by moments, and sometimes not at all.

The door was open, and the photocopier in the outer office was cranking a big order, but otherwise the floor was quiet. Most day classes ended by four thirty, and evening sessions didn't start until six. There was another half hour of solitude.

Tiel: Yes

Sam: Do I have your full attention?

Tiel: Don't you always?

Sam: Definitely not but I'm going to tell you a story anyway

Sam: Here's what I'd do with you: I'd move the dress off your shoulders, pull it down, and suck your nipples

Sam: And when they were wet and hard, I'd bite them

Sam: Then I'd slide my cock between your tits, hold them tight around me while I fucked you

Sam: And I'd watch my cock hit your neck and your chin and your mouth

Sam: And I'd come on your tits, shooting all over those hot nipples

I stared at the screen, my eyes widening with each message. Anticipation was rising in my body, and I felt it each time I squeezed my thighs together and heaved a hungry sigh. I could imagine the look of concentration that would settle on Sam's face while he fucked my breasts. The way he'd focus on executing perfect, precise movements. How he'd deliver equal amounts of his orgasm to each breast.

It looked so good in my head, but...I didn't want the performance. The filthy meticulousness of it all. I wanted him chaotic and wild and too fucking lost in the moment to remember whether he was coming on my nipples or my mouth or everywhere because the only things that mattered were the lightning we created and him marking me in some indelible way.

And I didn't want the version he shared with anyone before or anyone after.

Tiel: Um, ok perv.

"Tiel."

"What?" My head jerked up, and a blush colored my cheeks when my eyes landed on my colleague, Kyle Milhouse. I was flustered and marginally embarrassed that I'd been having this exchange at work, and concerned that my face was painted with I've-been-naughty guilt. The only person I'd ever sent dirty texts to was Ellie, and those were all dick jokes.

"Hi," I said, too loud, too bright, too peppy. "What can I do for you?"

He leaned against the filing cabinet, one ankle crossed over the other. Kyle was an assistant professor in the music therapy department, and had extensive experience in private and clinical settings, although much of his work was with adults. He was smart and could quote more research off the top of his head than seemed healthy, but he was as boring as a box of paper clips. "One of my students came across an interesting case, and you were my first thought."

"Yes, of course," I said, gulping down my shallow, lusty breaths. The bike bell tone chimed, and the sound traveled over my electrified skin and down my spine, and I was too fucking aroused to be talking to this professor. It was all I could do to keep from wiggling in my squeaky chair to relieve the pressure between my legs. My phone kept singing, and Kyle cleared his throat as I mumbled my apologies and flipped it to silent. He waited, staring, while I blinked at him, and a solid minute must have passed before I fished a notepad from my drawer. "Go right ahead."

He nodded, pleased yet obviously miffed I wasted an ounce of his time. "Seven-year-old female, presents with selective mutism and extreme social anxiety. She was referred to the interpersonal skills group that Quaranto is running, but that was not appropriate for the subject's range of needs. The one thing the subject would share with Quaranto was her interest in a particular musician." He flipped through his leather-bound journal, tracing a finger over the notes before looking up. "A band. One Direction."

Kyle said the words as if they were another language, an upward inflection tagged onto the end to embed his removal from this little girl's preferences. That kind of snobbery was rampant in music school, so much so that I barely noticed it anymore.

"There's an opportunity to publish in here." He set a file on top of my meager pile of graded essays, patting it twice like he was psyching it up to run the four-hundred meter dash. "You're due to get another paper out."

Kyle added some passing comments about clarifying my dissertation work and getting in on a research byline that would add some depth to my candidacy if I was hoping for tenure-track opportunities in the future. All the cheerful topics I knew and loved.

When he left, I blew out a heated breath that I'd been holding high in my ribs since Sam's texts. My response was meant to rattle him, to give him shit about his incredibly hot reaction to the clichéd "what are you wearing" line. He could do better, of that I was certain, and I was comfortable telling him as much.

Sam: I beg your pardon?
Sam: Feeling a little hot and bothered? Do you need a minute to handle things?
Sam: Let me know how it goes. I like details. I also like to watch.
Sam: Pictures are always welcome
Sam: Did you say you wanted to catch a show tonight? Should I meet you somewhere or pick you up?
Sam: Yeah, you did mention a reggae show. Splendid. Interested in dinner?
Sam: Are we good?
Tiel: Do you text all your friends about coming on their nipples?
Tiel: Or is it more like the same story and slightly different (always happy for you) endings?
Tiel: Although it all comes (lol) down to your skill in fluid placement

Sam: You're fucking hilarious

Sam: And when I text with my friend Nick, I can guarantee none of those conversations pertain to me coming anywhere near him. This was all for you, my friend

Tiel: For Nick's sake, that's probably good. Pick me up at 730

Sam: Wear that dress. I want to stare at your tits, friend

Tiel: Anything you want, friend.

Sam: Wait – does that include coming on your tits?

Tiel: Would friends do that?

Sam: No. FRIENDS would not do that.

Sam: Are we still friends?

Tiel: Always

I tossed my phone to the desk and flopped back in my chair, unsatisfied and irritable, and in desperate need of some extensive alone time with my vibrator.

Seven

SAM

IT WAS one of the chilliest October weekends of the year, and I showed up at Tiel's door with Thai food. She mentioned something about a recital earlier that morning and wanting to stay in tonight, and I was happy to oblige. We'd gone out most nights this week, and I was too freaking tired for much more than yam wunsen kung and a beer. I couldn't even get it up for a sharp outfit, opting instead for jeans, a Cornell hoodie, and a long sleeved t-shirt. I managed some rainbow argyle socks, but only because they were on top of the pile.

I heard her violin's squeal and hum from all the way down the hall, and though I had to think for a minute, I realized she was playing an old Rise Against song. I only knew it because she'd been singing parts of it for weeks, and now I couldn't get it out of my head either.

The sound rose with smooth fury, and I listened, just leaning against her door. When she stopped, I waited, hoping I'd hear it again.

Instead, I got a text asking where I was with the red curry and pad kee mao.

"Sorry," I said when she opened the door. "I was enjoying the show."

She glanced at the bow in her hand and shrugged. "Yeah, it is not where I want it yet. We're not posting that one anytime soon," she sighed.

Like a creepy dick, I Googled her last month. I didn't know what compelled me to do it, but I was sitting in my office one afternoon, talking myself off the ledge from another futile argument with Shannon, and decided to look up Miss Desai. It was that, or start another filthy text conversation and I couldn't walk around construction sites with an erection. Again. That was begging for trouble.

I expected to find her course syllabus, maybe a bio on the college website, and the standard social media fare.

I found a YouTube channel with two dozen clips, each boasting more than a half million hits. She played popular songs—Fall Out Boy, Tom Petty, Paramore, Muse, The Shins, Britney Spears, Hot Chelle Rae, The Who—and they were the most fucking incredible things I'd ever heard.

I watched every video, some more than once.

If I was anywhere near as talented as Tiel, I'd tell people about it every day. I'd tattoo the fucking URL on my forehead and announce it every time I walked into a room. It took some strategic questioning—and shots, shots always worked on Tiel —but she divulged the whole story.

It started with her posting a clip of a Panic! At the Disco track for critical feedback, hoping to get some advice on how to blend the sounds the ways she wanted them. Instead, she got requests for more songs.

Tiel kept improving the Panic! At the Disco tune, but posted others from her early morning studio sessions. She'd even started recording multiple tracks, each with her playing different instruments, and layering them into one like her own self-contained quartet. She rolled her eyes when I suggested she was an internet celebrity and the only virtuoso I'd ever met.

Being famous wasn't her concern; she did it for the music.

Once inside her apartment, she rehashed her morning with

one of her kid friends, and how his parents arranged a small recital at their JCC, but he wasn't interested in playing. After some warm ups, he came around, but she sat beside him on the piano bench the entire time.

"That sounds like torture," I said, unpacking the boxes on her coffee table. I gave the particle board structure a baleful glare and mentally cataloged the wood in my workshop. I could build better shit while I was sleepwalking. She needed some furniture that hadn't been passed around grad school apartments for the past six presidencies.

"It's not," she said. She popped open two beers and carried them to the table. "If you don't push every now and then, you don't grow."

She talked about the tonality problems she was having with the Rise Against song, and while I didn't understand half of what she was saying, I liked listening to her while we ate. There were bridges and chord progressions hampering her progress, and her ongoing struggle to feel as competent with the cello as she did with the violin. She was honest about her weaknesses, and rarely hid behind them by overcompensating the way I did.

Intellect was always my cover. I'd yet to encounter a situation beyond high school where my vocabulary, my expertise, my extensive reading didn't protect me. Smart was intimidating, and it kept people from noticing anything beyond big words, off-handed references to literary texts, and endless amounts of sustainable preservation research at the ready.

Clothes were my second line of defense. If I was swagged up, no one noticed the bulge from my glucose monitor. An eye-catching tie, a fancy pocket square, some trendy color combinations. They were the ideal distraction, and I was careful to cut slits in my pockets to allow the tubing to thread beneath my clothes and through to my device without risking exposure.

It wasn't entirely self-preservation, though. I enjoyed shopping, and when I started pulling in respectable money, I liked building out my wardrobe with designer suits. It was true what they said about looking the part.

She pushed the empty container away and reached over, fingering the medical alert bracelets on my wrist and turning them over to read the engravings. She was quiet, and I hoped she wasn't noticing how my pulse popped into warp speed when her fingers brushed over my skin.

It didn't matter how many times in the past two months she reached for me. I still wasn't used to it, but not because I couldn't handle her touching me; it was because I *could*, and that realization was still mind-blowing.

"How long have you been diabetic?"

"Since always," I said.

"And this one?" She lifted the other bracelet. "You're allergic to *all* antibiotics?"

"Pretty much. I prefer natural remedies anyway. You'd never believe what you can cure with some apple cider vinegar." She gave me a sidelong glance clearly intended to communicate her distrust of my witch doctoring.

We settled in to watch a movie—*The Social Network*; her choice—and I kicked off my shoes, and draped her legs over my lap.

Within minutes of the movie starting, Tiel was talking. She *always* did this. She'd ask where she knew an actor from; I'd spend ten minutes searching IMDb. She'd want to know whether a specific song was on the official soundtrack; I'd pull it up on Amazon. She'd realize she'd chattered through the first half of the film and was confused; I'd recap it for her. She'd see an actress with great tits and hypothesize whether I'd fuck her or why I wasn't fucking someone like her in a coatroom at that moment; I'd ignore that entire commentary.

"You remind me of Mark Zuckerberg," she said, glancing at my jeans and hoodie. "Your style is obviously very different." She gestured to my feet. "I mean, those are some snazzy socks, young man, but you're smart and really cerebral, and more socially awkward than most turtles."

"Thanks?" I muttered.

"Don't look so offended," Tiel said.

She pulled me toward her until we were lying together on the sofa, her back against my chest and her ass to my crotch. I held my breath for a long moment, terrified that she'd feel the infusion site and glucose sensor under my shirt. They were on either side of my abdomen, and if she leaned in at a particular angle, she couldn't miss them.

"You're far more likable," she said, patting my thigh.

"Well that's good," I said, a breath rushing out with my words. "Because I doubt you'll find Zuckerberg wandering the streets of Cambridge these days, and he's definitely not bringing you Thai food and beer, Sunshine."

I studied her while she watched the movie, and ran my fingers through her thick, glossy hair. She kept it short, about shoulder-length, and it was a bone-straight curtain of sleek ebony. There was no explaining my attraction to her ear or the tiny constellation of studs trailing up her lobe, but I loved the silky skin just behind it.

I usually waited for a sign from her, some indication that she wanted a bit more than friendly cuddles, but she was busy analyzing the evolution of Justin Timberlake's music since his boy band days.

I didn't want to wait for that sign tonight. I wanted to touch her and taste her without invitation, but I'd backed myself into this goddamn *friends* corner with Tiel, and that meant I'd lost my balls and what was left of my mind.

In the process, I'd also lost my taste for slutting it up and hadn't enjoyed anonymous sex since August. I just couldn't convince myself to want that anymore, and none of it made sense to me.

My world was gradually shifting and reshaping itself, and all

I knew was that I felt different, but different in ways I couldn't verbalize. There was the obvious—fewer blowjobs, less gin, more underground concerts, many more movie nights—but it was so much more. Part of me wanted to assign a name and some order to all this. A bigger part of me knew I wasn't rolling around rock bottom anymore, and for that victory alone I should focus on savoring the sweet woman in my arms and the quiet peace we'd found in this absurd friends-but-more-than-friends construct.

To be fair, I might have built the corner I was backed into, but I never stopped asking Tiel whether it was what she wanted.

Would friends *do that?*

Are we still friends?

Just friends, right? That's what you want?

The door was open for her to say no, *hell no*.

"Keep doing that," Tiel murmured, leaning into my hand. "You haven't said anything nice about my boobs all night. They're feeling neglected."

My fingers tangled in her hair, and I brushed my lips over that hidden spot between her hairline and the shell of her ear. It would be the perfect location for a tiny tattoo.

A little something only I knew.

"You're wearing that pink bra," I said against her hair. "The comfortable one you claim you've had forever. The one you took off through your sleeve a few weeks ago. It makes your tits look so soft and full, and fucking edible."

And *fuck me*, I wanted to tear her clothes off and drag my tongue around the heavy underside of her breasts, sucking and licking and biting until I had to feel with my hands, my cock, my entire being. I wanted to spend hours there, tasting her, mapping her curves, discovering what made her moan and arch.

There was so much to learn, yet buried deep inside that desire was the realization that I wanted something *different* with Tiel, something too fucking complex to start unless I knew what

I was doing. The friendship we'd forged was significant, and I wouldn't destroy that by running in dick first. Sofa-cuddling and sporadic sexting paled in comparison to the hungry knot of affection that was growing in my chest, doubling and tripling and fucking exploding with every touch, kiss, glance.

And if I didn't find a path out of the friend corner soon, my balls would be blowing up like the Fourth of July.

DUN-DUN-DUN-DUN.

"It's all he'll play," Beth whispered. "It's been almost four hours, and he hasn't stopped."

Dun-dun-dun-dun-dun-da.

She crossed her arms under her breasts, her nails worrying her linen sleeves. Everything about her was tight: her ballerina-rigid posture, the sock bun high on her head, the way her hands gripped her elbows.

She was girding herself for battle.

I didn't usually see Lucas on Fridays, but when Beth called this morning, I set aside my preparation for the classes I was teaching next week.

Peering around the doorway, I watched Lucas's narrow shoulders rising and falling as his slim, pale fingers slammed against the piano's keys. He played with the velocity of a classi-cally trained pianist who knew the notes nearly as well as Beethoven himself.

"He's *in* it," I murmured.

"What does that mean?" she asked, her expression slightly horrified.

I gestured to the piano and the seven-year-old seated at the bench, but knew Beth wouldn't understand my meaning. "He's in that headspace where the only thing that makes sense is the music."

Her frown deepened. "It's been hours. He's going to be hungry and tired."

"Give us some time. We'll be fine."

Warily, Beth retreated. Hovering was her way, and if there was one thing I learned from seeing Lucas three times per week for the past year, it was that Beth would lie down in traffic for her kid. She'd fight and argue and nag for him, and she wouldn't stop until he had the very best of everything: doctors, therapists, dietary consultants, teachers.

I wasn't sure where I fit into that particular ecosystem, but jamming with Lucas was almost as entertaining as performing a live show. According to Beth, he loved music as a baby, and long before he received an official autism spectrum diagnosis, she found that music was the only thing that truly soothed him.

I studied him for several minutes, listening as he worked through the Fifth Symphony's first movement. It wasn't a typical repertoire piece for violinists, but I knew it well.

Miss Michaels, my middle school orchestra teacher, loved Beethoven. She tried her damnedest to get a bunch of kids from suburban New Jersey to play the Ninth Symphony without sounding like a dying trash compactor, and for that I'd always admire her.

I never felt like I didn't belong in that classroom. It didn't matter to anyone whether I was the weird girl who couldn't sit still. In that classroom, everything made sense.

If it weren't for Miss Michaels, I'd probably still be in New Jersey. She convinced me to apply for a private conservatory high school, and then persuaded my parents to let me attend when the admissions letter arrived. She spent months helping me practice for my Juilliard audition, and though my family was minimally pleased when I was accepted, it was Miss

Michaels who said, "You have no idea how special you really are, do you?"

When Lucas started the movement again, I secured my violin in place and joined at the strings cue after the first eight notes. He turned when he heard me, his fingers moving as if independent entities, and a slight smile broke across his face. Shifting closer, I positioned myself in his line of sight as we played.

He wasn't comfortable with eye contact, but he did like watching my fingers.

We worked through the piece twice more, and then I showed Lucas how to gradually change the tempo—the *molto ritardando* motif—and we played that for another hour.

As we approached the final notes of the movement, his fingers stilled over the keys. He glanced at me and nodded, then hopped off the bench and left the room.

That was how our sessions typically ended.

I tucked away my instrument—I called her Jezebel because she'd seen it all—and Beth intercepted me before I could leave.

"Can I just hug you?" she asked as she wrapped her arms around me. She was oddly strong for such a skinny woman, and I squeaked at the force of her embrace. "I don't know how you do it, Tiel."

I wanted to tell her and all the families I worked with that I wasn't doing anything remarkable. We were messing around with the algorithms of music and manipulating the notes to bring order to the chaos in our worlds, and I enjoyed it as much as these kids.

But they didn't understand it the way we did. It wasn't just sound; it was our operating system.

My new friend, Seraphina, was the exact same way. She didn't talk, and spent our first session crouching in a corner, her head tucked against her chest as she drew her finger back and forth over her knee. The repetitive motion gave her a constant to focus on while the texture of her jeans against her finger gradually dulled to soothing pressure. These were the little mechanisms our brains invented to deal with stressful situations.

I played some One Direction songs on my guitar while she tried to melt into that corner, but after the fourth song, I noticed her glancing at me. Sometimes interest was enough to suspend fear, even for brief moments.

I wasn't in much of a hurry, so instead of heading directly for the T station, I stopped in Copley Square and settled on the grass. I loved these crisp, sunny late October days, and I wanted to soak it all up before wintery slush became the norm.

With my sunglasses in place, I lay back, watched the clouds, and hummed U2's 'Staring at the Sun.' It was amazing to me how, in the middle of a bustling city, I could always find moments of tranquility. My cloud-gazing gradually descended into napping until my phone vibrated beside me. Glancing at the name on the screen, I considered letting it go to voicemail.

But that just meant I'd need to call him later.

"Hi, Dad," I said.

"Hello, Tiel!" he said. "I didn't expect you'd answer."

Yeah, that pretty much summarized my relationship with my family. But he should have understood. He knew what it was like to be an outsider in this family, to surrender so much of himself in order to assimilate.

Then again, it wasn't as though I'd surrendered anything.

My parents met when he was in college, and he interned at the accounting firm down the street from the restaurant. It was sweet, really, and if I removed it from the context of them being terribly disinterested in me as their child, I could admire the beauty of their story.

My mother usually covered the day shifts and spent the evenings looking after her nieces and nephews so the rest of my family could work the dinner rush. That was the order of things: life revolved around the restaurant. Instead of getting lunch to go, he started sitting at the counter and talking to my mother while she worked. They married less than a year later, and Dad had been managing the restaurant's finances ever since. Her parents weren't thrilled about her marrying a non-Greek, non-Christian guy, but considering they let him handle all the money, I assumed they made peace with it.

But that didn't mean our home wasn't a tidy melding of cultures. We were first and foremost Greek, and when the opportunity suited the situation, we were also Indian. The only outward sign of mixed ethnicity was my strange name.

Looking in from the outside, no one would guess that my father grew up in a traditional Hindu home. He embraced my mother's culture, customs, and faith. His Hinduism was like sprinkles on the sundae: an extra, a bonus, an if-we-have-room.

"Yeah, I'm sorry about that," I said. "I've been a little...disorganized recently."

"You should consider purchasing a day planner," he said. "You're well?"

I wasn't starting a discussion about the nine million things I managed on a regular basis or whether "disorganized" was code for "I didn't want to talk to you."

"Very well. Things are good. How are things there?"

"We had the christening for Melina's new baby this morning, and it was beautiful. There's a party tonight," he added.

I pulled my lip between my teeth and hummed. I didn't even know my cousin had been pregnant, let alone given birth. That was the price I paid for taking a gigantic, purposeful step away from my family, and *shit*, every time I heard stories about births and weddings and joyful, together moments, I doubted my decisions. Being the outsider hurt, and it wasn't like breaking up with a significant other or growing apart from friends. It was cutting that blood-thick kinship and feeling like a traitor every day, and accepting that the pain was good. Healthy. Necessary.

"But I'm calling about Diwali," he said.

He didn't have to say anything else; the question was implied.

When I was younger, we'd go to certain Hindu celebrations in the region. Diwali for the new year, Holi to welcome springtime, Navratri in the fall, and others when the dates worked with our other commitments.

Agapi never expressed much interest in my father's culture, preferring instead to spend her time helping at the restaurant and getting involved with our neighborhood church and its Greek Orthodox Youth Association. These celebrations became the special thing we did together, just me and Dad.

But family was complicated.

My parents were mortified when I got married, and insisted I come home immediately because—*obviously*—New York City was a bad influence on me. That, and music was an absurd waste of time, and I'd never succeed, and I should be more like my sister and work at the restaurant before I ended up addicted to drugs or pregnant or homeless, or all of the above.

I didn't return home, and we didn't speak for nearly three years.

I was dead to them, or that was what I was left to believe. Not a single word from my parents, my sister, or anyone in my extended family. No birthday cards, no calls on Christmas, not even an email when my great aunt Iris died. Nothing.

Then I received a letter from my father with an invitation to a Diwali party. I was divorced, sharing a two-bedroom apartment with five other band geeks outside of Boston, and working no fewer than eight jobs, but I spent the last few dollars in my bank account for the train fare to Newark.

I needed to believe they hadn't abandoned me entirely.

It was good to see him again but it was strained, loaded down with layers of disapproval. I wasn't first chair in the Boston Symphony Orchestra—or any orchestra, for that matter —and, from his perspective, this music endeavor was an apparent failure. According to my father, it was time to put this all behind me. He even offered to let me perform in the restaurant on Saturday evenings.

Maybe it was pride or maybe it was my diehard belief that a Greek restaurant in Jersey would never be *my* home, but I hugged him goodbye and knew part of me was actually, really, truly dead to them.

Since then, I'd been home twice: Agapi's wedding and my grandfather's funeral.

He made a point of calling me at least once a month, and though the conversations became less tense, none of this got any easier.

"I wish I could, Dad," I said. I ran my fingers through the brittle grass and sighed. "Really. But I can't get away that week. I have midterms to grade, and one of my little friends, Lillian, is having a piano recital."

"That sounds like something that's important to you," he said. "There will always be another Diwali."

When we disconnected, I toggled through my phone to find tonight's live music listings. Talking to my father stole my energy and the pounding delight of a concert was the only thing to refill my tank. I tagged several intriguing shows and sent a text to Sam.

Tiel: Let's go out tonight. Too many good shows to miss.
Sam: I wish I could. Business dinner with the landscape architect on my next big project.
Tiel: I wouldn't think you'd be a fan of business dinners
Sam: Eh. I'm not but I am a fan of this architect.
Tiel: Ok. I'll be at the Roxy if you finish early or whatever.

The only thing that message was missing was a starry-eyed emoticon to go along with my aggressively casual tone. My preference was spending every night with Sam, and I think that inclination went all the way back to our first night together. There wasn't a point when I wanted it to end.

Sam: Do you…miss me?

Tiel: Of course not but you still don't know the difference between folk and funk, and that's a crisis

Sam: I think you miss me and want me to tell you some dirty stories

I really, really did. On both counts.

Tiel: I've always been a captive audience

Sam: Unfortunately for you, I have to present a proposal but believe me when I say I'd rather talk about your tits than a 3 million dollar renovation

Tiel: I'll find a way to survive without

Needing more coffee, I headed down the street to the café I favored in this neighborhood. I was happiest with a cappuccino in my hand, and a steady stream of caffeine was my only real luxury. It wasn't like I could afford many more luxuries; playing music and going to grad school were damn expensive, and it looked as though I'd be paying for my education for several decades. That fact gave me periodic flashes of panic, and it proved I didn't have a plan for dealing with life yet.

When I came down from those bouts of hysteria, I reminded myself I preferred the unplanned life. I knew there'd always be special kids who needed my help, and I could figure it all out as I went along. There was no need to carve a future into stone or declare myself, forever and always, for any particular path. I craved the freedom to wander: travel the world, get a different degree, learn another family of instruments, join the circus, or whatever.

That didn't mean I was blowing off my dissertation. I liked academia enough, but I wasn't sure I was willing to kill myself for a tenure-track professorship. It was an enormous commitment, and I worried that I'd drift away from the things I loved: working with kids, and playing and sharing my music.

But there was a convenience associated with the never-ending story of my doctorate. My schedule gave me the flexibility to work one-on-one with kids, and spend the summer with a noisy crew of geeks at band camp, and the fluidity of my research allowed me the space to study and explore.

When I stepped away from all that and looked at it from a squinty side view, I knew I was also building a life free from expectations. No real obligations or responsibilities of any kind. I couldn't disappoint anyone if I didn't commit to anything, and no one could reject me if I didn't stick around long enough to be rejected.

Most days I told myself I was unfettered by materialism or career-obsession, and that was a joyous gift in this world, but I knew it was so much deeper than that.

I could handle any amount of criticism of my work—the music, the therapeutic sessions, the teaching—but I couldn't deal with rejection. It was less devastating to walk away from relationships, to be the one who stopped calling or broke it off with vague clichés about focusing on myself or not looking for anything serious right now.

I slept better when I wasn't worried whether I was good enough for anyone else. I chose not to worry about the future, and the possibility that I'd end up sad and lonely and wishing I'd done it all differently.

With my iced cappuccino, I wandered through stylish shops on Newbury Street. As I ran my fingers over a display of vibrant ties, it occurred to me that Sam hid from rejection, too. The cavalier attitude, the consumerist approach to sex, the distance he required.

Perhaps that was what I recognized in him: the bitter taste of abandonment, the one that never fully dissipated.

That was how I knew him.

"ALL RIGHT, just a few more things on my list," Shannon said.

Those exact words had passed her lips twice already, and I was tempted to clarify her definition of *few*. I was tired and irritable, and after lifting weights for two hours in the middle of the night, my arms protested every time I reached for my coffee.

I loved Shannon, I really did, but there were moments when I was convinced she just liked hearing herself speak. It was phenomenal that she managed all the non-architectural elements of the business by herself, but that didn't mean I needed to hear about it every goddamn week.

Shannon turned toward Patrick. "Do you want to talk through the Wellesley issues?"

He rolled his eyes, murmuring something to himself while he shook his head at his laptop screen.

"I'll take this," Andy said. "We've updated the energy systems and done a fair amount of restoration on the interior, but there's quite a bit more that should be done. I would argue that, given the age and craftsmanship, we should be talking about more extensive preservation. I see this as a project we'll carry for a longer term."

When that quiet bomb detonated, the temperature in the

room dropped. Everyone sat back in their chairs, eyes were averted, and silence lingered.

I knew it was just a house, but I also knew this house was much more than four walls, a roof, and some dirt.

It was true what they said about never being able to go home, and not just because my father told me never to step foot on his land again when I was eighteen. If, by some fantastical turn of events, I found myself at Wellesley—the shorthand we used to refer to our childhood home—it wouldn't be the same place that spawned my fondest memories and worst nightmares.

I alternately loved it and hated it, wanted to keep it in our family for eternity and wanted it burned to the ground, thought about visiting and promised myself I'd never pass through those doors again.

Shannon cleared her throat, a sure sign for everyone's attention. She said, "The real question, at least from my perspective, is whether we want to carry the property for another calendar year. Knowing that we can't close out Angus's estate until the house is sold. Any additional work means we're leaving the estate open longer. We're also paying property taxes on the house."

Angus and his fucking will.

It wasn't bad enough that the bastard took three full weeks to die after his stroke, but he needed to leave us with an obstacle course of a will, too. He wanted his money given to certain people (his non-existent future grandchildren, of course) and spent on specific things (restoring that godforsaken house), and even in death, he wanted to maintain his public appearance with contributions to all the right institutions (Cornell, the regional hospital).

"And what are the implications of that?" Patrick asked.

Shannon shrugged. "It's mostly a pain in the ass for me. But—"

"Do we have to talk about this?" I asked. Every time

Shannon brought it up, I could hear my blood rushing through my head like a water cannon, and I had to talk myself out of imploding on the spot. Angus owned enough real estate in my head already. "Can't you just let Andy keep working and not bring it up?"

"Shouldn't we figure out how we're paying for this?" Matt asked.

"I've only used a quarter of the budget," Andy said.

I glared across the table at her, and hated her frugality.

"Sam's right," Patrick said. "As long as there isn't a specific objection to extending the work, Andy and I can figure it out later. And we have an hour of agenda topics to get through in fifteen minutes."

The project updates were quick, and focusing on my properties brightened my mood. I'd always been able to fall into my designs and block out the world, and right now I was hoping for that relief from the Turlan restoration.

Shannon recapped the non-disclosure agreement terms, and reminded everyone to keep quiet on that front. "And," she said, "Roof Garden Girl officially agreed to work on this project with Sam. If this goes well, I think we should talk about developing a more formal partnership with her."

"If I never hear about another roof garden, I'll be a happier person," Patrick said.

"I'm sure you'd find something else to bitch about," Matt said while Andy laughed into her tea.

"I think everyone's heard this by now," Shannon said. *If everyone knows, you don't need to repeat it.* "To support some of Sam's work so that he can dedicate the time necessary to this, Riley is finished with Matt's projects starting today."

Riley tapped his coffee cup against mine and offered a crooked smile. "I feel like the village donkey. Everyone's getting a ride."

IF SOMEONE HAD TOLD me two months ago that I'd be stepping into a dusty attic in Allston for some bluesy piano on a rainy November night, I'd have told her she was crazy.

It wasn't as if my original plans were much better. I'd been thinking about finally building the chairs I'd promised Riley for his new office, and maybe making some vegetable soup. It wasn't winter until I made vegetable soup.

But Tiel called, and she insisted I couldn't continue living without seeing this pianist.

So, regardless of my day from hell and whether I needed to be alone with my snarly mood and beat the shit out of something, I went to her anyway. In all deference to honesty, I rarely denied her anything.

Much to my displeasure, Shannon and I had ended up arguing over inconsequential details relating to the Turlan project's PR schedule, and I was now an hour late meeting Tiel. My attitude was out of control and I was more interested in hitting the treadmill than learning to appreciate niche music. The drive was a nightmare, and I was prepared to leave after a quick drink and a long hug.

We spent an inordinate amount of time together these days. The city's music subculture kept us hopping from venue to venue, and though I didn't share her investment in the scene, I couldn't help but get Tiel's enthusiasm all over me like a bad case of chicken pox.

When we weren't chasing down shows, we were watching movies at her apartment. There was no lamer approach to the weekend, but I was fucking addicted to our movie nights. The films themselves had nothing to do with my obsession; they were the gateway drug.

It started out with us falling asleep on her sofa over Labor Day weekend, but as the weeks and months passed, movies became the front for sneaky snuggling.

We'd start out on opposite ends of the sectional, the picture of platonic. Gradually we moved toward each other, and the reasons were seemingly legitimate: ottoman placement, popcorn distribution, air conditioner proximity when it was hot, quilt sharing now that it was cold, cowering during scary moments. It always transitioned to us lying together, and that was where the boundaries evaporated.

I mean, where the fuck was I supposed to put my hands when she was curled up next to me? Once my arm was around her shoulder, it was all too easy for it to slide down and rest on her hip.

God, those hips were sinful. The flare from her waist to hip was a perfect hourglass, and whenever my hand rested in that spot, I had to talk myself out of pulling back her clothes and running my teeth along her skin. It was bad enough that I found myself in that position on a weekly basis, but her fucking wiggling was endless. It was like receiving a goddamn lap dance without all the glitter and skank.

From there, it was a quick journey to her belly, and that was my favorite spot.

It sounded a little fetishy even to me, but I adored splaying my fingers out over her tummy. I'd always preferred waifish women, but I revered Tiel's curves. Maybe it was her boundless confidence or complete comfort with her body. I wouldn't want her any other way.

And I loved touching her. If it were socially acceptable to fuse my hands to her body at all hours of the day, I'd do it and I wouldn't apologize for a damn minute. She was soft and beautiful, and I felt an unusually spectacular comfort when I was pressed against her. I could be content with a layer of clothing between us but it came with a dose of agony. I wanted to feel her skin under mine, and that was the greatest shock to my system of all.

The kissing was another issue. Since the elevator incident, I shared more kisses with Tiel than I had with all previous women combined. To her, the opportunities were limitless, and she seized plenty of them. It was always playful and sweet, and if she ever noticed the aroused state she left me in, she didn't mention it.

And we were still friends.

Friends who kissed, friends who slept together on sofas, friends who woke up tangled in each other as if it were their last embrace.

Friends. Profusely affectionate friends.

She was seated at a small table in an alcove framed with an angled dormer window. She could have looked like a damn fool with her eyes closed and head rocking with the melody, but that was what made Tiel irresistible. She was real, and real in a way I didn't think was possible.

There was no space in her life for self-consciousness, and she didn't see any reason to modify herself. She didn't say the right things and she didn't manage her reactions to suit anyone. She wore whatever the hell she wanted to wear—usually the wildest colors in the crayon box and many more necklaces, bracelets, and anklets than any one person should wear at a given time—and she laughed off my critique of her attire.

My approval was irrelevant to her, and that was fucking amazing.

I slipped into the seat across from her and tapped my fingers against the back of her hand. Her eyes opened, hazy and slow, the way she would first thing in the morning. To be clear, she was a bear first thing in the morning, but she was also terribly cute.

"You made it," she said, her face breaking into a bright smile. "I was getting worried."

"You are exceptionally devoted to the music scene," I said, casting a glance around the space. "Now, I really need you to blow me for this one, Sunshine. I can't remember the last time I went to Allston by choice."

"Wouldn't you just love that," she said.

"In fact, I would. I've been in the market for a decent blowjob all week."

In truth, I'd skipped out on my usual scene for weeks. Although no one inquired about the change in my routines, I was armed with some defensible arguments.

I was exhausted—Tiel *had* been running my ass all over town, and she didn't tolerate anything less than total participation when live music was involved.

I was getting in control of my health—hence the soup.

I was behind on my woodworking projects—Riley was sitting on milk crates and Tiel's coffee table was a shit show.

The reality was less clear to me. I didn't want to go out alone anymore. I'd grown accustomed to her quirky chatter and complete inability to filter herself when flustered. I didn't know how to entertain myself if I wasn't making gratuitous comments about her breasts or listening to her babble.

On the rare nights that I did venture beyond the firehouse, I couldn't force myself to tolerate the club crowd unless I was with Riley. Even then, I stayed firmly in wingman territory. I couldn't replicate her frisky take on the world with any of the vapid, thigh-gapped party princesses, and no one could hold my attention quite like Tiel.

"That should be easy," she said. "Considering your asking price is so low."

Tiel frequently editorialized on the topic of my sex life. I let most of her commentary slide without discussion as I wasn't about to defend, rationalize, or apologize, but I picked up a sore note in her voice tonight.

I massaged her wrist, knowing she spent most of her day in the studio and that often left everything from neck to finger aching. "Your tits are a work of art. Da Vinci himself couldn't have sculpted a better pair."

Tiel sent me a skeptical glare while the waiter took my order. When he was out of earshot, she said, "Does that shit really work for you? Do real women actually beg for the privilege of sucking your dick as a result of those comments?"

I leaned forward, my elbows propped on the table while I

rubbed my eyes. I loved debating with her, but I couldn't do it tonight. I was tired and I hadn't eaten more than some walnuts since morning, and as much as I craved time with Tiel, I didn't want to be listening to sad piano music. I wanted to be in her little apartment with my head in her lap while she talked over entire movies and I wanted to feel her, skin-to-skin, and know her in every way I could.

"I really don't want to go there with you tonight. Is there a specific question you're asking, or are you just busting my balls right now?"

She didn't say anything while the waiter returned with our drinks. I studied the space again, recognizing that this wasn't Tiel's usual scene. She liked fast-paced shows that kept her bouncing with the music, and a vibrant, hip crowd that embraced every subculture under the sun. This seemed too sedentary and sleepy for her.

"You know I got married young," she eventually said. "And that it didn't work out. I was nineteen, and I never stopped to realize that my life was going to change. I mean, you don't get married and live in separate dorm rooms." She laughed, her fingers running through her dark hair. "There was a lot to figure out. Before I knew it, we were ending things."

I didn't know what to say. I watched her eyes, those expressive hazel eyes, and waited for more.

"I had to grow up really quickly," she said. "Too fast. And not just because I got married. Sometimes, I look back and I think, wow. I never had a chance to be a kid."

This was how Tiel got her thoughts out: she started at one point, veered off in a different direction, doubled back, traveled in another direction, and reached the end point in a circuitous, disorganized way, but it made sense in the end. My brain preferred a more linear approach, but there was something captivating about her thought process. Something about getting lost with her.

"I understand," I said. "I've never been divorced, but I know all about growing up too soon."

"I know. I think I can see it in you," she said. "Isn't that why you're willing to accept quick, emotionless sex from women who expect nothing from you? Isn't it your way of repossessing some youthful irresponsibility?"

I should have known she wasn't following the path I expected, but nothing could have prepared me for a discussion of her divorce to end with my sluttiness. I'd never thought of it that way, and I wasn't especially comfortable with that extrapolation. At the same time, I didn't see a reason to unpack her assumptions.

"And you're suggesting there's an issue with that?"

"Let me ask you something." She scooted her chair closer and folded her arms on the table. "Think about the last time you hooked up."

I couldn't remember the last time. I knew it was before meeting Tiel, but I couldn't surface any memory of the location, the person, or the act. A cute strawberry blonde came to mind, but she was earlier in the summer and she only stuck out because I *never* went for redheads.

I knew I sampled an artisanal gin that night, and it was exceedingly herbaceous for my preferences. I had a lengthy conversation with the bartender about that bottle of gin, but I couldn't recall anything about the woman who got on her knees for me.

"Shit," I murmured.

Tiel lifted her glass and rolled the base on her coaster, leaving a series of overlapping circles from the condensation. She chewed her lip for a moment, and frowned at her drink before meeting my eyes. "I think I have you figured out," she said.

I made a show of looking at my watch. "And it's only been what? Eight? Nine weeks since you forced me into that elevator? Certainly there's a prize for nailing me down inside two months."

She smirked, and I could tell I was getting her riled up. "I bet your standard operating procedure is incredible."

"You're damn right it is," I muttered.

"Of course," she laughed. "You have all the right moves and flawless execution. I'm sure you can accomplish more in ten minutes, in a random closet no less, than most men aspire to on their best nights."

I gestured over my shoulder, motioning toward the restrooms. "Would you like me to demonstrate? You pick the closet."

"Your skills are legend, Samuel," she said. "But that's the issue. Sex isn't about skill. It's passion, and you can't fake that." She brushed her hair away from her face, shrugging. "I know some musicians who can shred every single piece of music put in front of them, but they have no passion for the sound and you can hear it. It's technically perfect, but it's so fucking soulless that you never want to listen to that piece ever again."

This was her way. She'd ask one seemingly simple question, pull one thread, and take me apart. The topics varied, but every time it came back to peeling away the layers of self-preservation I'd painted on over the years. She knew how to strip me down and see me without any of that protective veneer, and in a sense, it reminded me of Angus. She heard all the outlandish thoughts rambling around my head, but instead of decimating me the way he did, she took those loose, frayed threads and pulled me back together.

"Most people think passion lives in some thundering monster, a primordial entity that calls all the shots from deep inside your brain, but it's not," she said, growing animated. "It's details. It's the way itsy bitsy sounds bend around each other and create magic. It's pressing your mouth to someone's neck because you can't imagine living another minute without feeling her skin on your lips. Fingertips digging into hips until they bruised. Reaching for someone in the night. Knowing her taste in your soul but never feeling fulfilled. Awakening all the beasts you've kept hidden inside, and letting them grow and breathe because she wants to know them. That's passion."

I stared at her, convinced I was observing something filthy and exquisite, and I couldn't find a single thing to say.

I was suddenly uncomfortable, too warm and too confined in this small space. I tugged my sleeves down, then ditched the cufflinks and rolled my shirt to my elbows. It wasn't enough, and though it was a delicate Italian silk that didn't take well to folding, I unknotted my tie and shoved it in my pocket. None of it cooled the obnoxious tension clawing at me.

At first, I couldn't comprehend my visceral reaction to her comments. Tiel and I talked about sex all the time. It was mostly my conjecture about her mouth relative to my dick, and it was all good fun.

"But you can't really get any of that in a hook-up, can you? Sure, itches scratched, biological urges met, whatever." She threw her hands up as if regular, hearty orgasms weren't elemental to the sanity of men everywhere. "But you never learn what that person likes and craves. You don't even know what *you* crave, and it doesn't matter how well you perform when there's no soul. No passion."

She held out her hands, the evidence presented.

There were no quick comebacks in my arsenal, and honestly, my dick was too busy getting strangled by my trousers to form a rational response.

"Why are we talking about me? I'm great. Let's talk about you, Tiel. When was the last time *you* had sex?"

She raised her glass halfway to her mouth then stopped, and set it on the coaster. "It was July."

"Was it any good?"

Our eyes locked, and I noticed a blush creeping across her cheeks as we continued staring at each other. "It was fine."

"'Fine' seems like an awfully low bar," I said. "You're comfortable with that?"

She glanced out the window, her gaze distant while her fingers tapped the tabletop with the piano's rhythm. "Actually, it *was* good. We weren't...hmm." She balanced her chin on her fist and paused. "We just weren't the right fit."

I shifted in my seat, and the movement jostled the table and sent liquid sloshing out of my glass. I hadn't touched my drink, and now it was dripping off the table's ledge and staining the knee of my trousers. I brushed it away and shook off my hands, more frazzled than I was before, and gulped down my gin and tonic.

I didn't want to talk about her having sex with some shabby guy. Some loser who didn't understand her, who couldn't handle her idiosyncrasies. But I couldn't stop.

"Why not?" I asked.

Tiel tore her attention from the narrow stage, but didn't respond immediately. "I go for the passion, and that's not an easy find. Being with someone is a lot more than inserting one thing into another."

"There's nothing wrong with a little insertion," I muttered.

Tiel shook her head and smiled. "Nothing at all. Sometimes insertion is good, but it's the harder pieces that don't come together."

"Without the harder pieces," I said, "the insertion won't be especially satisfying."

I gestured to the bartender with my empty glass. The last thing I needed right now was another drink, but if this conversation was any indication, I was long past making wise choices.

"You know that's not what I'm talking about," she said.

Of course I knew. Just like I knew the punk-ass bitch she was banging in July wasn't good enough for her.

She watched me while I checked my phone and sipped my drink, and eventually turned her attention back to the stage when I didn't respond.

I didn't trust myself to say anything. She was dragging me back to the land of the living, one strange concert at a time. She was holding my whole fucking universe together with her convoluted dissection of my existence and more sofa snuggling than I'd ever dreamed of, and I couldn't fuck any of that up with my jealousy.

My waning interest in *friends*.

My industrial-strength blue balls.

So I didn't mention how much I hated thinking about any man touching her. I didn't point out that anyone who left her with a 'fine' memory of sex hadn't earned the privilege of knowing her intimately. I didn't tell her she deserved someone who treasured her.

I didn't say anything because I couldn't offer her much better.

Ten

TIEL

Tiel: Hey. U want 2 c some tunes 2nite? Done w grading now

SAM'S SCHEDULE was packed this week, and I hadn't seen him since we parted ways on Lansdowne Street in the early hours of Sunday morning. I dragged him out to see Reel Big Fish and Less Than Jake at The House of Blues, and after the concert, we kissed against the Fenway Park gates.

It was much like being back in junior high. Tons of kissing, tons of awkwardness, and massive apprehension about when— the real question was *if*—we'd get to the other bases.

Though it shouldn't have, it surprised me. I wanted more than he did, and I had to keep reminding myself that. He liked our little routine, and though I wasn't sure when—we did spend a good chunk of time together—I was certain he was getting some action on the side. I couldn't substantiate that with anything more than an odd sense, and I made more than enough critical comments about his sex life. If I was wrong, he would have corrected me by now.

Shaking my head, I tapped Ellie's number and hoped she wasn't in rehearsal. Thankfully, she answered on the second ring. "Explain to me why I should hang out with the preppy player who loves all this ambiguity."

"I take it this fascinating experiment is still going on," she said. "And maybe you shouldn't?"

"But he's so adorable and funny and the swoons. So many swoons." I knew there were two Sams: the womanizer with the smooth, panty-dropping smile that mowed down everyone in his path, and the sweet, beautiful boy who thought so much more than he spoke. I saw both, and when I looked closely, I could convince myself that they were one and the same.

"But he's an asshole…?"

I could almost see her face twisting into a confused grimace, and I laughed. "He's not."

"Okay. Explain these straight girl problems to me," she said. "Us lesbians are far less complicated."

"Do you have a few minutes?"

"Yeah, we're still riding Wilma," she chuckled. "This girl gives as good as she gets."

I sighed. "Do you think the band could get a new bus for the next leg of the tour, or maybe give Wilma a new name?"

"That's unlikely," she said. "We're rather fond of Wilma. We get on our old lady every chance we get."

"That was funny for the first three months of the tour," I laughed. "I don't know what he wants, and I don't think he knows either. We hang out all the time, and he's always talking about my boobs and that's great, but it's so freaking confusing when it stops with snuggletime. And for all I know, he's got a rotating cast of slampieces and he's just using me for the soft stuff."

"Mmhmm, that is a conundrum," she said. "You can tell him what you want."

"Yeah, I do not see that working out well."

"That's dumb." I started to interrupt, but Ellie continued. "No. Seriously. That's dumb. Put on your big girl panties and act like a boss. Tell him you want the snuggletime to become snugglefucking, and if that's too much for his delicate man-psyche, tell him to piss off."

"Ell, I don't want to tell him to piss off. He's cute and a total freak but in the most precious ways. He always gets me coffee, even if it's ten o'clock at night, and he hasn't judged me for that in weeks. He carries a cloth handkerchief and uses obscure words—"

"Don't besmirch the use of obscure words, even in jest," she said. "That's perspicacity, young lady."

"And he sneezes more than anyone I've ever met, and has some seriously gorgeous tattoos. He knows how to have a really good time, even when he's the most overdressed guy at Sligo's Pub and orders his gin with diced cucumbers."

"Does Sligo's dice cucumbers now?"

"No," I said. "Never. But he asks every time."

"God bless him," she said. "But listen—big girl panties. End of story. Unless you've failed to mention that he has crazy eyes or baby arms or something, because those would be legit no-go situations."

Sam's naked back and shoulders flashed through my mind, and though that memory was crystal clear, the memory wasn't enough. I wanted to feel those chiseled muscles and trace his tattoos, and I wanted him over me, under me, everywhere.

Falling asleep together on the sofa wasn't cutting it anymore.

"We're at the venue now, my dear. I gotta get to sound check," Ellie said. "Let me know how it goes with the prepster."

We said our goodbyes, and when I ended the call, I saw a new message waiting for me.

Sam: Perhaps you could translate that for me as I do not understand alpha-numeric gibberish.

Tiel: Dude, you act like you're a 92 year old technophobe sometimes

Within seconds of sending the message, my phone was vibrating with an incoming call.

"Being twenty-eight has no bearing on whether I tolerate the bastardization of the written word via text-speak," Sam said without introduction. "You know I can't decipher that shit."

"You need some tunes, my friend. Meet me upstairs at The Middle East at eight and—"

"What I need, *friend*, is a break from unwashed grad students who think they can get away with plaid-on-plaid, and I can't choke down much more bottom-shelf gin."

I liked arguing with him. It was futile and amusing, and it always revealed more of the nerd hiding beneath the pretty face. "You could avoid that problem altogether by drinking more beer."

"Or," he said slowly, "*you* could meet *me* at Verdigris in the South End at eight. That is, of course, if you can handle my side of town."

Smiling, I dragged my fingers through my hair. *Big girl panties*, I reminded myself. "I think the real question is whether you and your side of town can handle me."

I SPENT extra time flat-ironing my hair into a sleek, smooth bob, and had to constantly remind myself to keep my hands out of it. Fingering the short, flowy black and white geometric print dress I borrowed from Ellie's closet instead, I surveyed the industrial space of Verdigris. The gleaming dance floor was packed with bodies and pulsing techno music pounded from every corner.

This wasn't my crowd. I didn't know anything about people who went out with the purpose of being seen. I went out because my soul required live music for its survival. Trendy clubs, fancy dresses, artificially generated music—I didn't see the appeal.

"I didn't think you were coming."

Pivoting, I found Sam gazing at me. In dark trousers, a light purple Oxford shirt open at the collar, and suit coat, he was all player tonight.

Sam stepped forward and reached for me, then stopped abruptly and shoved his hands in his pockets. He looked utterly confused—and that was the Sam I knew. He was always caught up in complicating his own thoughts.

He needed to worry less and enjoy life more. I could handle his quirks—the picky eating, the refusal to touch anything he deemed unclean, the subsequent hand sanitizing—but I couldn't understand how he spent so much time deliberating his every step. He took the expression 'look before you leap' to monstrous heights. I knew he'd be happier if he let some of that shit go.

Maybe then snuggletime would turn into snugglefucking.

I could hear the wheels turning in his head when I leaned into his kiss or demanded that he offer his chest as my pillow, and those wheels never turned him in the direction of his hand under my shirt or my ass bent over the bed.

I closed the distance between us and wrapped my arms around his shoulders. "But aren't you happy to see me now, Freckle Twin?"

I felt his laugh on my temple, and held onto him a little longer. I pressed my face to his neck and inhaled, and as peculiar as it sounded, he smelled like wood.

Perhaps it was more peculiar that I savored that woodiness.

"Of course," he murmured. "The VIP lounge is down the hallway."

"Not yet." Shifting back, I met his eyes. "Who are we going to be tonight?"

He smiled, and it immediately lifted the darkness hovering around his eyes. His sadness wasn't hard to see, a wound not quite healed. I didn't know who hurt him or when it happened, but I knew some days were harder than others. He didn't brood, but carried a heavy load and sometimes it was plain to see. "I haven't decided yet."

Leaning close, I asked, "Want to know what I think?" He nodded and his hand skimmed down my back, landing low on my waist. Right where I needed him. There was no point playing coy when all I wanted was more Sam, and right now, I was ready to make some demands. "I think we should have some drinks and some dances. Then we'll get the hell out of here and I'll let you get pervy on me at The Middle East. And then we go back to my place and see what happens."

"You want that?" he whispered.

"Don't you?"

"Yeah," he said, his breath rushing out over my cheek. "I do."

Grabbing his hand, I towed him to the bar. Despite the crush of people vying for the bartender's attention, Sam caught his eye immediately. We knew this routine well—drinks, music, storytelling—and we laughed through the first two rounds while catching each other up on life since the weekend.

His updates often centered on his work projects, but his siblings made frequent appearances. They were different from my family, and their business was nothing like the restaurant, but I couldn't understand how he put up with their insane involvement in his life.

The whole idea made me itchy.

He knew I wasn't especially tight with my family, but I spared him the gory details of it all. Instead, he asked about my courses, studio time, and sessions with my little friends. He said it was strange that I called so many people friends. I didn't share that concern.

Tonight, he was pumped about a new renovation he was starting on Monday, and when he mentioned it was Eddie Turlan's new house, I slapped both hands over my mouth to keep from screaming.

It was a pee-your-pants-at-a-swanky-club kind of moment for me.

"I could play all The Vials' songs by the time I was ten," I said. "Have you ever heard punk rock violin?"

"No," he said with a smile. "But I'm not supposed to say anything about it. Pretend you didn't hear that. They have an extensive non-disclosure agreement."

"Because they don't want people like me creeping on their new house," I said.

"That, and they're hoping to bundle the restoration with a special anniversary release of an old acoustic performance in Paris. They figure they can get some architecture and design magazine coverage, and cross-promote."

"The Vials, acoustic in Paris?" I repeated. "I must have it. Do you know I'd listen to a recording of a garbage disposal if it was acoustic in Paris?"

"I do now," Sam laughed.

An endless string of runway-ready women passed by our table, each one gifting Sam with their standard-issue Fuck Me hair-flipping then glaring at me as if I was the garden gnome he was forced to tote around for the evening.

He was accustomed to this. He enjoyed it, too.

And I hated pretty much everything about that.

"How many hearts have you broken this week?" I asked.

Sam sent me a bitter expression. "I don't break hearts. I don't go anywhere near hearts."

I knew that was his take on reality, and I knew he liked an appropriate amount of distance between himself and the world. I existed in a strange little pocket of his life, and I was only there because I kept bullying my way in.

"Hearts broken, cherries popped. Same thing," I said.

"Not doing any of that either."

"Maybe not intentionally." I wiggled my empty glass at him.

I knew I was poking the beehive, and Sam did not like it. But I needed to know whether he was still trolling the club scene for hook-ups, even if it hurt to hear the truth. Even if it meant I wasn't going to get what I wanted.

He picked it up and signaled to the bartender for another. "No one gets their heart broken over a hook-up," he said.

"So you've never been with the same chick twice?"

He shrugged in that tight, impatient manner he acquired when the conversation veered a little too far beyond his comfort zone. "When would I even have time? I'm scouring the city with you and the rest of the band geeks every goddamn night."

"In other words, you can't remember." He rolled his eyes and pivoted toward the bar, again motioning for my refill. "And we prefer to be called orch dorks, thank you."

With his attention directed away, I was free to gaze at him. He was in his element here, of that I was certain. This was his territory. He wasn't standing back, waiting for me to give him some backstory on the band or venue, pointing out the best corner for sound and service, or introducing him to friends. He looked like a king gazing out over his court.

"You should give out wristbands or hand stamps so the women who've serviced you can find each other in a crowd. They'd probably form a support group," I said. "At least a hashtag."

He turned back, slowly dragging his eyes from the bar to me. He didn't seem altogether pleased with my comments. "A *hashtag*?"

I was uncomfortable here, and it was showing in my words. I felt out of place, as if I'd stumbled into the cool kids' club and they were waiting for me to leave so they could get back to their regularly scheduled minion crushing.

"There's enough of them. A couple hundred, right? You can't be into four digits without getting seriously chafed. Do you have a balm for that?"

Sam stared at me, cool and still while I struggled to restrain all of my fidgeting. "Why are you asking?"

"I know you. I know what you like." I gestured toward the artificially busty brunette who was lingering near our table. My boobs at least had the decency to be somewhat uneven, and they'd never know *that* level of perky. "Maybe you'd rather be with someone else."

He glanced at the brunette, offered an incendiary smile then a quick head shake, an obvious "you are flawless but not tonight" command, and bent toward me, his arm braced on the edge of the table. "Do I need to remind you that your tits are incredible? Or that you're absolutely fucking gorgeous?"

His hair looked darker under the club lights, but fine threads of auburn still shone through. It was brilliantly styled but I wanted my fingers in there. I wanted the imperfect Sam, the one who didn't offer fake, overly animated smiles for every minor celebrity who stopped by the table for a bro-hug. The one who didn't shave on the weekends, and wore ancient sweatshirts and jeans with thick, retro glasses to watch movies at my apartment.

"That isn't a definitive statement."

"It's quite definitive," he said. "And I don't think you know everything, Sunshine."

"Then maybe you should teach me something."

His eyes widened and lingered on my lips. "Maybe you should tell me what you'd like to learn."

I opened my mouth but the words stuck together in a choked groan. I wanted to know what his tattoos meant and what his tongue would do to me. I wanted to taste him, all of him, and I wanted to memorize the way he looked when he pushed inside me and when he orgasmed. I wanted to feel his weight on me, and I wanted to see his lips form the dirtiest words imaginable.

I wanted it *all*.

But I wanted a lot more than one night with him, and that wasn't part of his protocol.

"I'm getting shots," I announced, yelling despite the narrow distance between us.

"No," he said, cringing. "I don't want to wake up on the floor again."

"That hasn't happened in a long time." I brought my hands to either side of his face. "But I'll take better care of you tonight."

Sam grabbed my elbows and held me in place. "Is that a promise?"

He brought his lips to mine, and I expected a quick, innocent kiss, but the moment we met, it changed.

A quiet growl sounded from his chest and his arms locked around my waist, and I couldn't resist the slide of his mouth over mine.

There was something subtle and dangerous about Sam, like a jaguar sizing up its prey. He was polished and refined, but beneath it lived a fierce, chaotic current. The primal gentleman. For the first time, I realized he could absolutely destroy me if I let him.

When we broke apart, I exhaled a breathy laugh, and Sam said, "Yeah, I'm going to get those shots now."

Some tequila, some dancing, and a lot of overly auto-tuned techno music later, I was ready to leave the posh side of Boston nightlife. I gave it a try; it just wasn't my scene, and I wasn't convinced it was Sam's scene either. He liked being there, being seen with the right people, but this wasn't him.

Eventually we hopped a cab downtown only to discover the act I wanted to see was sold out. Rather than wandering around Massachusetts Avenue to find another show in the area, Sam insisted we head to the next on my list of top choices.

The cab swerved to avoid some pedestrians spilling onto the street near Boylston, and the force sent me sliding across the seat and careening into Sam.

"You just keep crashing into my life, don't you?" he murmured.

"Trying to get rid of me?" I asked, my hands braced on his chest.

"I don't think I should," he murmured.

"Then don't," I said.

We arrived at the absurdly small venue in Porter Square just as the headlining act went on, and we found a spot near the front. I twirled away from Sam at one point, and started dancing with a group of rockabilly chicks. Now *these* were my people.

He smiled and nodded, and I saw him retreat to the bar. I assumed he was going to flirt with the bartender, but he never took his eyes off me. I liked him watching. I knew it was creepy to say that, but I sensed him staring at me and it was glorious.

The band kicked off a slow tune, and the blonde to my left pulled me close to sway with the song. It was a perfect, mellow moment until I spotted Sam on the other side of the venue. His eyes were locked on me, and I'd never felt such a hot, intense gaze. His suit coat was gone and shirtsleeves rolled up, and right then, I wanted his hands on my body.

I wanted it enough to get a little silly.

I went up on my tiptoes and kissed the blonde with the Veronica Lake hair. It felt crazy and exhilarating and so, so smooth, and the adrenaline coursing through my veins drowned out the band. Her tongue rolled against mine, and her hand moved up to glide over my breast and down to my ass. She sucked on my bottom lip, and it was an overwhelming, slightly mischievous experience.

"You're pretty," she whispered, and squeezed my shoulders with a tight hug. "Do you want to meet my boyfriend? I think he'd like you."

I didn't know how to react to that, and there was a laugh forming in my throat, but a hand closed around my arm, and Sam was tearing me away from her. I crashed into the hard wall of his chest, my fingers digging into his biceps to keep me steady as the crowd around us rocked with the music.

"What was that?" he asked, his lips brushing over my ear.

"You have to ask?" I said. His arms were wrapped around me, pressing me flush against his body, and though it was exactly what I wanted, I wanted more.

"I have an idea," he chuckled. He ran his hand through my hair, then tucked it over my ears. "But I want to hear you say it."

"You were right. I wanted to kiss a girl," I said. "The opportunity presented itself."

"Did you like it?" I traced the placket on his shirt and nodded. "Would you like to do it again?"

It was too loud to follow this conversation in the middle of a live show, and I was a heartbeat away from shoving my hands down his pants. I dragged him down a dark hallway, but he didn't let me take control for long. He spun me around and pushed me against the wall, his body layered over mine.

"Is that what *you* want?" I asked.

He laughed, a rueful smile on his face, and followed the line of my collarbones with his finger. Sam dipped his head to my chest and kissed the path he had drawn, then moved up, over my throat and chin. When he finally reached my mouth, I pulled him closer.

"That wasn't the question, Tiel. You said you enjoyed it. Maybe you want to find that chick and ask her to lick your pussy on a bed of rose petals. That would just leave double penetration and some public indecency."

"You'd love that," I said. I dug my fingers through his hair, destroying the precise styling. I stretched up on my toes and teased my lips over his. "You could watch and—"

He surged against me, flattening me, and claimed my mouth. "Watch? I don't get to participate?"

"Such a pervy boy," I groaned.

"And you love it," he said, his lips on my neck. His hands skimmed up and down my sides, his fingertips brushing my breasts slightly yet just enough to leave my nipples tight and wanting. "Don't you?"

I grabbed his hands and pulled them away from my body. "Why wouldn't I?"

"How many questions can you answer with another question?" Frowning, he placed my hands on his belt and fisted my dress at my hips, edging it up as he wedged his thigh between my legs. "Don't ever apologize for what you want."

Sam's hand slid beneath my dress to cup my ass, and he squeezed, tucking me against him until my panties were pressed to his trousers. He lifted his head and sent me the darkest, most sensual smile I'd ever seen.

"Oh would you stop with the smolders?" I said. "I've already bought it. You don't need to keep selling."

He laughed and rolled his pelvis against me, and I felt the thick hardness of him through our clothes.

Oh, holy fucktarts.

"What is that supposed to mean?"

"Can we be the friends who kiss and have dance parties and watch *Pulp Fiction* in bed?" I asked. "And…maybe more?"

"*Friends* do all that?"

I shrugged, hoping he'd embrace my definition. There weren't enough words in the English language to properly encapsulate the types of friends a person could have, and there wasn't a word to describe Sam and me.

Believe me: I *wanted* a word. A name, some structure, clear boundaries.

Sam smiled and pulled me against him. "What about *Reservoir Dogs*?"

We stared at each other, no more than a few inches between us, and this moment was fluttering like a hummingbird, fast and frantic. We weren't hanging out because we survived an elevator hostage crisis and felt some strange kinship. We weren't drunk-flirting. Whatever this was, it was evolving. "Maybe tomorrow night."

I pushed away from the wall, clutched Sam's hand between both of mine, and marched toward the back room. I'd been to this venue enough to know it would be empty at this hour. It was dark and adequately private, and this was what he liked. It wasn't as posh as Verdigris, but it would get the job done. I didn't need to think; I knew exactly what I intended to do.

Sam was saying something as we entered the room, but I covered his mouth with my hand.

"Shh," I said.

I dropped to my knees and fumbled with his belt, but his hands came around my wrists, stopping me. "No, Tiel. *No*." Waves of discomfort rolled off his body, and if the tight bunch of his shoulders was any indication, he was slowly dying from mortification. He gasped, "I have to get out of here."

He released my hands and bolted from the room.

I gulped down my embarrassment and blinked away the tears in my eyes. Easing back until I was crouched against the wall, I swallowed the pathetic whimper that threatened. "Okay," I announced to the room. "So, that was awful."

Any guy with a steady stream of girls sucking his dick should have been able to manage a graceful brush off, and I'd seen Sam send out plenty of disinterested vibes to women all night.

I just hadn't noticed they were being aimed at me.

Eleven

SAM

THERE WERE TOO many things happening at once.

I couldn't breathe, the music was actually preventing me from hearing my thoughts, my cock was throbbing, and I was a fucking asshole.

Somewhere between a chick sticking her tongue down Tiel's throat and now, I managed to tell her I didn't want her. I hadn't said those exact words, but the sentiment was clear.

The truth was, I *didn't* want Tiel sucking me off in the back of a grungy bar. I also wasn't interested in a claustrophobia-induced panic attack from a room that resembled the season premiere of *Hoarders*. I was at least ninety percent certain I was getting E. coli from the air alone. Was it actually painted black or just that filthy?

This hadn't happened in years. Small spaces didn't send me over the edge the way they used to. It was one of the few victories I could claim in this battle. I mean, I survived that elevator fiasco. Mostly.

Bending at the waist, I anchored my hands on my knees and sucked in the crisp night air. I knew it was near freezing but the adrenaline was pumping too fast for the cold to register against my skin.

It wasn't the cramped room, not entirely, but the jet engine roar inside my head wasn't letting me put any of those fragments into a logical order.

"What is this all about? What's wrong here?" She chuckled, and it wasn't a joyful sound. "And this is what I do to men."

Motherfucking shit almighty, why did she have to see this? I needed to stop falling the fuck apart while Tiel watched.

She fetched my glucose monitor from my pocket—not without grazing my cock, of course—and studied it, humming. "This seems low. Maybe you should eat something."

Instead of answering, I stayed focused on breathing, and unearthed some of the old visualization techniques the school psychologist was so keen on teaching me. Beaches, lakes, woods, mountains. Think about those wide open spaces, the sounds of nature.

And Tiel.

She was rubbing my back, her hand moving in measured circles, strokes, and pats. When I was calm enough to notice, I knew without a doubt there was a song in her head.

"What are you playing?" I asked, my voice raspy. I'd trade my own blood for a gallon of water at this point.

She shoved her hands into her pockets and took an exaggerated step back. "The Fugees. 'Guantanamera.' Aaaaand now that you're not dying on the sidewalk, it's time for me to go."

"Tiel, listen to me," I said. I pulled her back to my chest and kissed her neck. "I fucked up this whole thing, and I want to explain, but I can barely think right now."

"No, we're fine," she said, forcing a hollow laugh. "Nothing to explain." She ran her hand through her hair and pushed away from me with another fake laugh. "I'm just really drunk and being stupid, and I shouldn't have done any of this. I was totally wrong. I'm so sorry."

She wasn't drunk and she wasn't stupid, but I couldn't begin to form those words. I heard her shoes against the pavement, and I was alone with the noise in my head and my anxiety and the bone-chilling cold.

I didn't know how to explain why I pushed her away. Where would I even start?

I couldn't tell her that being with her made me feel sane for the first time in months.

Or that I felt rusty, broken pieces of myself healing every time I kissed her.

Or that she was beautiful and genuine in ways that stunned me.

Or that I wanted to bury myself in her for days, but I needed *her* more than I needed pussy.

Or that I was terrified I'd fucked it all up with her tonight, and I'd lost the only person who wasn't genetically required to tolerate me.

I couldn't tell her any of that, and instead of making it worse by going after her, I guzzled some water at the bar, collected my coat, and called a cab. There was nothing I could do to take back what I'd said or erase the snap of pain that had crossed her face when I said it.

I hated myself on the cab ride home. Every few minutes I opened my mouth to direct the driver back to Cambridge, but I knew I was the last person Tiel wanted to see at her door.

I spent the rest of the weekend closed up in my workshop at the firehouse, starting and then discarding one project after another. I had salvaged enough wood from my last camping trip to replace all the kitchen countertops and finally dig in to my crazy tree ring tile idea, but I kept thinking about Tiel.

None of this felt right, but how the fuck was I supposed to know what constituted *right*?

By strict definition, I'd never had a proper relationship. I'd fucked my way through entire sorority houses but the closest I'd ever come to a girlfriend was a sweet Theta who only called me after unfulfilling sex with her meathead boyfriend.

He didn't eat pussy, and I didn't know any better.

At different points in my life, there had been women who qualified as fuck buddies, but none of those relationships grew into anything substantial or long-term.

Besides, once women looked past the pretty face and got to know me, they realized I was the grand master of assholes and more damaged than the Titanic's hull. No one wanted to stick around for that. I'd also stopped being a generous lover before the close of my first year of college.

When I was young and naïve, I wanted to learn everything about sex and I wanted to be fantastic at it all. It was the no-credit class I added to my freshman course load.

As with most things, I learned quickly. It turned out I was also the nice guy, the one who ate pussy well and could always be counted on for an easy fuck after a long night party-ing. I knew how to pick an above-average winter formal dress, too.

What I didn't know were the boundaries between sex and emotion, but they quickly became obvious. More specifically, I got my heart thrashed—repeatedly—and I felt worse than shit on a stick each time.

The nice guy business wasn't helping me on my quest to get good at sex. If anything, the nice guy was the enemy. I shifted gears, and got into the business of fucking a lot of girls and not giving a shit about their feelings.

Or their orgasms.

After that, it was easier to stop connecting with people.

Outside of my siblings and their significant others, I didn't have relationships. The only friends I could identify were Magnolia and Matt's marathon training friend, Nick. He was an honorary brother, and he earned that distinction by pulling the plug after Angus had been in a coma for three weeks and showed no signs of resurrection. There were other reasons—he was an amusing guy and decent doctor—but sending Angus on his way sealed the deal for me.

I couldn't risk getting thrashed again, so I retreated, pulling further and further into myself. I was comfortable there, safe, protected from ever truly experiencing anything.

And then Tiel fucked it all up and I was hyperventilating on a godforsaken sidewalk in Cambridge.

I decided to start thin-slicing the acacia for my tile project, and forced myself to stop worrying about Tiel. Unfortunately, none of my projects held my attention, and after a close call involving fingers and a circular saw, I hit the treadmill.

Outdoor jogging wasn't for me. Matt and Patrick loved their dawn patrol runs, but city pollution and pollen usually disqualified me from those events. I managed to get my shit in order to run the Boston Marathon with them each spring, and then I retreated to the convenience of my home gym and state-of-the-art air filtration system.

As I powered up the surround sound and the opening wails of Tiel's rendition of "Seven Nation Army" filled the basement, I relaxed, and felt better for the first time since she walked away on Friday night.

"ISN'T GIGI SUPPOSED to be here now?" Riley asked. He glanced up and down the quiet street while loosening his tie. He'd further bastardized Magnolia's unofficial nickname—Roof Garden Girl—into RGG, and was now taking it one step further with Gigi.

If it were up to Riley—also known as RISD, after his alma mater, Rhode Island School of Design—no one would go by their given names. No one would wear ties or socks, or zip their pants, or get out of bed before noon either.

"Magnolia said she'd be here after her last consult, but she was coming from Westford." I shrugged and returned to the designs on my iPad. "It's only four-fifteen. Give her a couple of minutes."

Riley and I were an unlikely pair, but we tolerated each

other well. Living together was easy, and despite his fondness for wrinkled, coffee-stained clothes and cheap beer, I liked having him around.

He ran his palm over the curved stone surrounding the bay window, following it to the edge of the structure and down. He brushed away dust to reveal the mason's original cornerstone.

It was the little things—the cornerstones, the ninety-year-old newspapers found in attics, the floorboards stamped with the lumberyard's brand—that reminded me I was a tiny blip in time.

I always wondered about the people who came before me, the hands that built this home and all the others I worked to preserve. I hated thinking their artistry could be demolished and replaced with glass and steel and concrete.

Some things were worth saving.

"Shannon says you're into Gigi," he said.

"Shannon likes inventing things to talk about," I murmured.

"What is your problem with her right now? You bitched about her all summer, and you're only marginally better now."

I continued studying my designs. I didn't want to dump my stupid little feelings all over the fucking sidewalk. I'd done enough of that already.

"You spent the summer drunk," I said. "I'm not sure how you had time to notice anything."

"I spent the summer drunk because all you do is mope around with a goddamn raincloud over your head." Riley grabbed the iPad from my hands. "You've been pissing and moaning about Shannon since Matt and Lauren's wedding. Listen, I know everyone got into some crazy shit that night, but there's no reason she's not allowed to let her freak flag fly. Is your problem that she hooked up or—"

"Would you shut up? You're being—"

"Hey, Sam! Sorry I'm late," Magnolia called. She walked toward us in a dark pink dress and knee-high rubber boots, her dark hair flowing over her shoulders in long mahogany waves, and an enormous smile on her face. "Somehow there is more traffic getting into the city in the afternoon than there is getting out."

She pulled me in for a tight hug and clapped her hand on my back. There was nothing half-assed about this woman; she couldn't even give a weak handshake if she tried.

"Hi, I'm Magnolia Santillian." She shifted the emerald bag on her shoulder and extended her hand toward Riley.

"Riley Walsh," he said. "Can I call you Gigi?"

Her smile curled into a confused smirk. "What now?"

"Ignore him," I said. "Let's get inside."

The interior was amazing, and I hadn't stopped raving about it since my first visit in late September. The wide-plank hardwood needed attention, and most of the walls showed evidence of water damage, and where we should have found floor joists between the third and fourth floors, we found a hole stretching the length of the house. Aside from those issues, it was a perfectly undisturbed brownstone.

We walked through each room, presenting the plans, photographing, noting things I missed the first time around. We debated techniques for two hours, and reveled in the freedom of a near-limitless budget.

The demolition would be quick, and by my estimate, we could start late next week. We were only looking at pulling up some linoleum in the kitchen, treating some lead paint issues, blowing out the god-awful green tiling in the bathrooms, replacing drywall in most rooms, and reconstructing the joists.

It was late when we wrapped up at the Turlan property, and considering I managed fewer than two hours of sleep last night, I wasn't interested in going back to the office today. I wanted the hottest shower in the universe, kale and kabocha squash soup, and a nice blend of anxiety meds and sleeping pills to drown it all out for the night.

Full belly, empty head.

My phone vibrated with a text, and I dug it out of my pocket immediately. When I saw it was a message from Shannon reminding me that I owed her designs for a charity auction—some stupid shit where I drew up plans for an outrageously elaborate and expensive home, and though people always bid on the auction, they never went through with building the damn house—I nearly smashed it on the sidewalk.

I hadn't heard from Tiel in three days, and it was the longest I'd ever gone without talking to her. Sure, we'd only been hanging out for a little more than two months, but we had a rhythm. We were friends, or something like that, and we talked at least once a day. Add to that her complete bastardization of the English language via texts, and I heard from her on the hour.

Now that I was captain of my own douche ship, she didn't want anything to do with me. I couldn't blame her. I wasn't what anyone would call decent, healthy, worthwhile. I didn't care about people the same way Riley did, and I didn't want to fix things for others the way Matt did. I stared at tits and asses, and I rejected a gorgeous, kindhearted woman without explanation, and the sidewalk panic attack was the cherry on top.

I didn't deserve a nice girl.

We were inching through traffic when Riley turned to me and asked, "Where did you meet Gigi?"

That nickname was annoying but acknowledging that would only lead to its permanence. He was a stubborn brat like that. "At an event last year," I said. "Some design magazine was sponsoring a spec house in Newburyport, I think, and she was there. We started talking about the sustainability features, and how they were completely wrong for the house. It looked cool in the magazine but it was ridiculous in practice."

"And that's when you decided she was going to have your babies?"

I choked out a laugh and glanced over at Riley. He looked completely serious. "No, not at all. She's very nice, and I appreciate the way she thinks about preservation and landscape architecture. I like talking through design problems with her, and I've referred many clients to her, but…no."

"Dude," he sighed. "That was not what I saw."

"What is it you think you saw?" I asked.

Riley shifted to face me but I kept my eyes on the road ahead. "First, she hugged the shit out of you."

"That's how she greets everyone," I said.

"I didn't get a hug," he said. "Second, you two touch each other all the fucking time. Every time you opened your mouth, she was right there with her hand on your arm and all, 'Oh yes, Sam, I *love* that idea! That *is* brilliant, Sam! Put your sperm inside me, Sam!'"

"That's how she is." He gave me an exaggerated look, and I said, "You can get out here. I'm sure you can walk home."

"Let me remind you—she didn't touch me once." Riley plucked his water bottle from the cup holder. "I mean, she is hot in that 'I'm the boss of your cock' kind of way, and I can see how she'd find my dominant aura in conflict with that."

I thought about Magnolia, and her bright smiles and shiny hair. She was one of my favorite thought partners, and could always be counted on for local industry gossip, but I wasn't attracted to her.

Not at all.

These were the rare moments—the ones where I was forced to remind myself that not being attracted to one woman didn't mean I wasn't attracted to women in general—that resurrected my father's words.

Abomination.

Filth.

Queer.

He started calling me gay before I finished kindergarten, and then I was too young to make sense of it. I only knew it was wrong in his eyes.

That *I* was wrong.

Shannon always told me to ignore him, but it was more difficult when kids at school started saying the same things. I was eight when I comprehended what everyone was saying to me, and it was overwhelming.

I believed I was gay for years. It wasn't until I stayed after school to watch Matt's track and field practice one day—it was a thin excuse to avoid riding the bus alone, which always led to someone kicking the shit out of me—that I understood I wasn't.

Instead of lurking near Matt, I watched the cheerleading squad and found myself in the uncomfortable position of concealing a short-lived erection and the messy aftermath.

I spent years trying to determine whether it was possible to be gay and find women attractive. This was a major point of confusion and stress, and though I'd always thought I kept it well hidden, Matt took up the topic the day he left for college.

He was two years older but I'd skipped a grade, and was starting my senior year of high school. I wanted to get out of the house as soon as possible, and I would have been able to finish high school in three years if I hadn't caught pneumonia and spent four weeks in the hospital the previous winter.

I was young for college, and in plenty of ways, I was immature, too, but anything would have been better than living with Angus.

We never talked about the kids who tormented me or the names they called me, but Matt knew that year would be difficult. He was aware I'd get my ass handed to me more times than I could count when he wasn't around to intervene.

"Here's what you need to do. You need to put on about thirty pounds of muscle and you need to start running. I know it's hard with your asthma, but you can start slow. Take Riley with you. He needs to stay out of trouble, and if you let him believe he's training you for a half marathon, he won't have nearly as much time to smoke weed in the attic."

I had been reading *The Count of Monte Cristo* for the ninth time—all twelve hundred pages of it—and set it on my bed. "Okay…"

"And then you need to get laid. In my opinion, you stare at tits too much to be gay, but I'm not about to tell you who you are. Fuck who you want to fuck—consenting adults only, please —and don't apologize for it. Not to yourself, not to me, and definitely not to Angus."

I did what he said, and though getting my ass into shape was one of the most physically grueling things I'd ever done, he was right. That wasn't to say my graduating class suddenly became my best friends or stopped making jokes about me enjoying the boys' locker room too much, but I found my confidence, and with it, I learned to stop giving a shit.

When I went to Cornell the following year, that confidence spawned a reinvention. I left all of the old Sam—the pale, skinny, sick kid who peed his pants during a fire drill in the first grade—behind, and tried on a new version of myself.

"Listen, maybe you aren't into her," Riley said as I pulled into the fire engine bay and came to a stop behind the old pickup I used for camping trips. "Whatever. But she's into you, and she thinks it's mutual."

"Riley, you're blowing this out of proportion," I said. "She's a friendly person. She'd invite you to her parents' house for Sunday dinner if you asked. She'd offer you her extra ticket to next weekend's Patriots game if she had one—she might, so speak up if you're interested. She's authentically nice, and it's hard for us to recognize that because we're a far cry from well-adjusted adults."

"Don't say I didn't warn you, dude," he said.

We retreated to our separate corners of the firehouse, and I spent an hour on the treadmill in my basement gym. I hoped to burn off the sickly feeling that I'd been carrying since Tiel walked out on Friday night.

It didn't work, and I was too irritable to wander around the house much longer.

My workshop held no appeal either, and after a shower, I headed to Alibi at The Liberty Hotel.

The converted jail was one of my favorite preservation projects of late. Not only was it the coolest fucking idea I'd ever heard—unfortunately, it hadn't been my idea—but it was the best spot to see the most fascinating people.

Actresses in town shooting the latest movie, athletes showing off their championship swagger, bankers and CEOs who needed to talk about how much they're worth, the few remaining old Boston socialites.

And me.

I didn't have any Hollywood producers in my phone book, but I folded right in each time. It helped that I knew the architects who worked on The Liberty's restoration and could speak fluently about the process of transforming it from a decommissioned jail to high-end hotel.

Everyone loved that shit.

I was self-aware enough to acknowledge that seeing and being seen offered a degree of validation that I craved. Any kid who was systematically relegated to humiliating daily taunts or dismissed by pretty girls would relish an evening spent chatting with the Celtics' point guard.

To the best of my knowledge, none of the dickheads I knew from school enjoyed anything like this.

Mondays were slow nights, and I watched a group of guys who seemed to be reciting scenes from *Swingers* while I nursed my drink. Women approached, and some were bold enough to sit beside me and attempt a conversation. It should have been enough to pull me out of my head tonight, but it wasn't.

My funk, my gorge, my black hole…whatever it was, I was falling further.

Most women moved on when I didn't reciprocate their interest, but one didn't get the hint. I could have excused myself; I did have an early meeting back at the Turlan property.

Instead, she rattled on about her work (ignored that part), her friends (bitches—all of them—but she'd find one for a threesome if I wanted), her Twitter followers (quite a few, apparently), and I just wanted her to shut the fuck up.

It got as far as letting her pull my cock out in the coat check room before my skin was crawling, and it wasn't from an impending anxiety attack.

Isn't that why you're willing to accept quick, emotionless sex from women who expect nothing from you? Isn't it your way of repossessing some youthful irresponsibility?

It was Tiel. I couldn't stomach the idea of anyone else touching me.

Without a word, I zipped up and all but ran home.

Once my front door was closed behind me, I dropped to the ground and pulled out my phone. It wasn't drunkenness or depression. The polished concrete just seemed like the best spot to hate myself.

I scrolled through my texts and missed calls, hoping I'd see something from Tiel. There was nothing, and though I didn't know what time it was, it felt like the right time to call her. This needed fixing, and if she tore my beating heart out of my chest and sliced it like pastrami, at least I wouldn't have to live with the regret of not trying.

I started thinking about how to explain what happened on Friday when I realized she was talking to me.

"Sam, I can hear you breathing. If this is a butt dial at one in the morning, I'm going to be epically pissed. You know I have studio time at six every Tuesday."

"You're fun," I laughed. "You're my Sunshine."

"You're drunk."

Was I? No. Not as much as I should be. "Quite hardly," I said. "You really are fun, Tiel. I enjoy your company."

"Uh-huh."

"When are we going out again?" I heard her yawn and glanced to my watch. It *was* after one in the morning. "We can go to another filthy music house if that's what you want, but I think you'd like The Liberty. You'd find it adequately strange."

"Sam," she sighed. It was a long, elaborate sound, and it landed somewhere between annoyed and fire-breathing. "Do you remember Friday night?"

"I do," I said slowly. "I think I might have been an asshole."

Tiel laughed, and as it rang in my ear, I realized I was smiling.

"You were just being yourself, honey. Don't beat yourself up about it," she said.

"That was the sweetest insult I've ever heard," I chuckled. "I'd take your abuse any day. But seriously, when are we going out next? I'm beginning to tolerate hillbilly music, but I'd listen to anything if it meant I could kiss you again."

"Hillbilly music," she repeated, her voice bubbling with laughter.

"Can I tell you a secret?"

"How drunk are you?" she said.

I wasn't acknowledging the drunk comment. I didn't care if she thought alcohol was greasing the words. "I'm in a weird place right now, like a funk. It reminds me of the last time I was camping near the bottom of Quechee Gorge in Vermont except I'm stuck there, in the canyon. But when I'm with you, I don't feel stuck."

"Oh, Sam—"

"Don't do that, Tiel. Yell at me for being a dick, give me shit for ordering cucumbers in my gin, but don't talk to me like I'm a three-legged dog." I slid farther down, pillowing an arm under my head as I stared at the ductwork on the ceiling. "I want to see you."

"I don't think that's good for me," she said.

"Come out with me on Friday," I said. "I'm getting an award for something. We can do that, and then go wherever you want. I want to see you."

"I don't know, Sam. I want to see you too, but…"

"There's nothing to deliberate," I said. "I'm a lonely perv without you."

She sighed, and I realized I should have gone after her. I should have followed her home and explained the web of crazy in my head, all of it, and if I had done that, I wouldn't be sprawled on the cold concrete floor right now, alone.

"What's the award for?" she asked.

"I built something and people liked it," I said. "I'm pretty great like that."

Tiel burst out laughing, and I let the sound unravel all my twisted misery. With each of her gasping breaths, I felt lighter, freer, and if it was possible, happier.

"I'm going to tell you what I'm thinking from now on," I said. I heard the slur in my voice but hoped she didn't notice. This was honesty, not inebriation. "All the time. Total honesty. If I'd said what I was thinking last week, I wouldn't have hurt you and you wouldn't be mad at me now. I don't always say what I want to say."

"Oh, I know that," she laughed. "You have entire conversations with yourself that no one else is invited to."

I closed my eyes, smiled, and convinced myself to just fucking say it. "I'm picking you up at seven on Friday. Wear something that gives me a decent view of your tits. I need to keep myself entertained around these crusty old architects, and there's nothing on this planet I enjoy more than your breasts. You have no idea how much I want to taste them. I had the first wet dream I've had in years this week, and it was because of those tits. I didn't even mind waking up in a fucking puddle."

"What the fuck are you doing on the floor? And who are you talking to? You know I can fucking hear you all the way upstairs, right?" I turned my head and saw Riley standing over me. He grabbed my elbow and hauled me up. "Get your ass into bed, son. We have a meeting *with clients* at eight."

"Is that Riley?" Tiel giggled. "Are you in trouble?"

"You have five minutes to be asleep or I'm taking your phone," Riley said as he pushed me in the direction of my room.

"I'd rather be sleeping with you." I groaned and shuffled

toward my bed. "Actually, I'd rather fuck you *then* sleep with you."

"Now I know you're really drunk," she mumbled.

"The world makes sense when you let me hold you, and I can only imagine holding you naked would bear similar, if not better, results." Tiel didn't respond, and I checked my battery before saying, "Was that the wrong thing?"

"No," she said. "No. Keep saying exactly what you're thinking. I'll see you on Friday."

"Tiel?" She yawned in response. "Thanks for sorting me out. Again."

"Of course, Sam. Always. Sleep well."

I fell face-first onto my bed, and slept until the alarm on my glucose monitor started vibrating against my hip before dawn. I couldn't keep doing this to myself. Drinking, not eating, exercising like crazy. My body had no idea what was going on from one minute to the next, and it showed in these violent blood sugar swings.

One of these mornings, I wasn't going to wake up.

Nauseous, numb, cold-sweat shivering, head throbbing, and mouth drier than Death Valley, I blindly scrolled through this morning's *Boston Globe* while choking down some glucose tablets and promising myself I wouldn't let this happen again. I hated these hypoglycemic fogs with a passion, and it took my body hours to truly recover.

The highlight, by far, was a text from Tiel.

Tiel: In case you forgot, you called me last night. I suspect you were very drunk and will be very hungover when you read this.
Sam: I didn't forget. I'll pick you up at 7 on Friday. I'm spending the night with you and we're watching *The Boondock Saints*.
Sam: (Thank you for writing in actual words. My retinas would bleed if I had to read text speak)
Tiel: You're welcome but you're rude. RUDE.
Sam: Because I said I'm staying with you?

Tiel: No. You can always stay with me but how do you know I want to watch that movie? Maybe I want to watch *Pitch Perfect*.
Sam: We'll watch whatever you want. Just let me take your clothes off and spend the night with you.

If I could hold on to her, I'd be okay.

Twelve

I HELD a black sheath dress over my body and inspected myself in the mirror. I'd worn that one to an audition. Too boring, and not particularly forgiving when it came to my hips.

"And then the venue crew misplaced the good Strat and all the fiddles," Ellie said. "Needless to say, we spent a bloody hour going through the vans, calling the last venue, and basically losing our fucking minds. And they were backstage the entire time. I've never been so ready to punch someone in the throat as I was at that moment."

I grabbed a purple sweater dress and rubbed the fabric between my fingers. Too heavy. I'd be a greasy sweatball before we left the apartment.

"Maybe I shouldn't go," I murmured.

Sam and I talked throughout the week and continued texting each other first thing in the mornings, and while he frequently referenced wanting to get naked and spend the night with me, I needed more time to sort this out. I was still bruised over last Friday, and that rejection didn't dissolve because he got drunk and unloaded everything on his mind.

"Oh, lawd. I don't understand why we've had this exact conversation every day this week. He called. He apologized. He was a typical Neanderthal man. Get dressed and go to the damn event!" She swore under her breath. "You're still into him, yeah?"

I dumped three gray dresses—more audition and formal performance wear—on the bed. They would work for the occasion, or at least from the limited information I was able to extract from Sam, but I hated them with the fire of a thousand suns.

Throw in some black tights and I was my grandmother on her way to Friday evening mass.

"He's the right combination of cool and nerdy," I said. "He's secretly precious."

I flung two maxi dresses on the bed—too summery, and with a thin layer of icy snow on the ground, it definitely wasn't summer anymore—and a floaty pink thing I wore to a rustic wedding last spring. Too fairy princess.

"You like hanging out with him?"

I stared at a red dress edged with white cherries. Too quirky.

"Yeah," I said.

This was the first time in months that we hadn't gone out during the week, and it was odd not seeing him. Even with his commitment to stream of consciousness honesty, talking or texting wasn't the same as being *with* him. I thought about inviting him out on several occasions, but tonight was different from our usual music, drinks, and movies routine.

This ventured into date territory, and I didn't want to muddy those waters with a mid-week hop for some R&B in Roxbury.

I threw four more dresses to the bed, all printed with random objects—pineapples, cats, bicycles, dragonflies—and sighed. They were perfect for teaching music therapy classes, or sessions with my little buddies, but they weren't even close to appropriate for an Official Work Event.

"Stop analyzing. Don't be that analyzer girl," she said. "We don't like Analyzer Girl because she spends her whole life reading into everything guys say when she should be kicking ass."

I glanced at my near-empty closet. Maybe I could get by with jeans and an Abbey Road t-shirt.

"I'm not being Analyzer Girl, really. I'm not. I want Sam like fat kids want cake—and I was a fat kid so I know—but he's a player who didn't want to play with me. There's really no other way for me to interpret that one," I said. "How many guys do you know who turn down a BJ?"

"I can think of a ton of reasons why he'd turn down a beej in the back room at Hermit Crab," Ellie said. "But I'm a little shocked you'd be game for something like that. Think about it. At best you're friends with limited benefits. At worst, you're weirdos who occasionally have sofa sleepovers."

I held up and then discarded another dress. "He said it himself. He's been in a funk. I'm funkified enough to get him out of it, and when I do, he'll add me to his discard pile."

I settled onto an empty corner of the bed and polished off the iced cappuccino I picked up on my way home from my lesson with Seraphina. She wasn't talking yet, but now she looked at me and occasionally offered a nod to indicate she wanted to play 'More Than This' again. And again. And again.

"Hey, Analyzer Girl? Can you put Tiel back on? You're annoying." She said something to one of her bandmates and laughed. "Do you need my permission to cancel on him? If you honestly don't want to go, say it. I'll call and tell him you moved to Copenhagen."

"I want to go," I said. "I just can't find anything to wear."

I wasn't giving voice to the thoughts pinging through my mind: was he still hooking up every night? Was he fucking club girls only to call me five minutes later and ask about my day?

I wanted to be that girl who could roll with rooftop kisses and sex-free sleepovers and then some, and considering I initiated it all, I should have been able to handle it. But I wasn't built that way.

Not anymore. Maybe not ever.

"What about that navyish dress? The lacy one?"

Frowning, I thumbed through the closet one more time until landing on the sleeveless flared skirt dress. The sapphire color seemed mature without being boring, and the eyelet embroidery pattern was cute and eclectic.

"Yeah," I murmured. "Maybe."

"I have to run. It's chow time and these boys are under the impression their beards entitle them to more food. But listen, whatever you're working yourself up about? Use your words. Tell him what you want and what you don't want. Big girl panties."

I turned up my Taylor Swift playlist and packed the dresses back into my closet, then set to finding shoes. Ellie mentioned her beige heels, but I didn't understand why anyone would wear beige. I wasn't designed for heels, either. I wobbled too much, and never managed the elegant strut of women who knew their way around some stilettos.

The dress paired perfectly with a fuchsia cardigan, and the flat iron brought some order to my hair while a crème treatment tended to my girlstache. Thankfully, the fine whiskers weren't multiplying in length or quantity, but like clockwork, they switched back to black within a couple weeks of bleaching. I was nearly finished with my eyeliner when I heard a knock.

He was facing down the hallway and adjusting his cuffs when I opened the door, and he pivoted, giving me a slow motion view of his charcoal gray three-piece suit.

Oh, holy Moses.

I'd heard the phrase *suit porn* before but never saw the interest until Sam Walsh. It helped that he was standing in my doorway with a lopsided grin, and I knew what he hid under all those fine fabrics.

I mean, mostly. There were a few lingering mysteries that I was, ahem, *curious* about.

"Hi," he said. His eyes moved over me, and his smile fell into a scowl. "Are you wearing that to piss me off?"

I looked down at my dress and gold ballet flats, and back up at Sam. There was often commentary about my clothing, but it was playful, not scowly. "What?"

"How is this any fun for me?" He gestured to the lace that covered my chest and shoulders. "What did I do that took your tits away from me?"

"You ran screaming from me like I was a fucking zombie trying to suck your brains out through your dick," I said. I crossed my arms over my chest, annoyed that I'd spent an hour rummaging through every scrap of clothing in this apartment only to meet with his dissatisfaction. As far as I was concerned, he'd lost the right to cleavage-viewing. "And when you finally called me, it was one o'clock in the morning."

Sam stepped inside and closed the door behind him, his eyes rolling when he turned to me. "No. That's not what happened. Not even close."

He rubbed his brow, and his cufflinks caught my attention. They looked like real emeralds, and somehow they matched his pink paisley tie and silver pocket square beautifully.

"Then tell me what happened," I said.

He shoved his hands in his pockets with a sigh before meeting my eyes. "I didn't want you sucking me off in some back room like any of those...you know what? It doesn't matter what I did before. Blowjobs are a lot like cheeseburgers. Just because I can get one anywhere doesn't mean that's what I want."

"Since when do you eat cheeseburgers?"

Yeah, I liked to focus on the core issues like that.

"I don't. That's not the point, Tiel."

He laughed and held out his hand to me, but I didn't budge. I could let go, I could forgive and forget, but it took me a little longer to get there than most. My sister always said I held grudges, though I didn't see it that way. My feelings just moved at their own speed, some faster than others.

"I know your name. You're not one of them. You're different. I don't want it to be like it was before...before you."

"Oh..." I hadn't considered that option.

"I'm sorry about everything. I'm a douche waffle," he said.

I was softening. I could feel it in the way my arms refused to stay rigid across my chest and my mouth wiggled into a smile. "I'm not familiar with douche waffles."

"That's a technical term. Riley taught me that. It's reserved for epically poor decision-making." He moved closer and ran his fingers down my arm to my hand. "Please? I can't stand being close but not touching you."

I felt his breath on my cheek and ducked my head, looking to his well-polished wingtips. "So you weren't horrified by *me*?"

He bent down and traced my jaw and lips with his thumb, his brow furrowed. "Sometimes I don't know which direction you're going. I don't know what you're thinking," he whispered. His hand dropped to my hip, and those blue eyes of his were all demanding and precious. "And I need a minute to catch up."

He was right. I was all over the place, a non-linear ball of zigzagging shades of gray. I was hyper and hard to follow, and there was barely enough space in my head for the random thoughts living there.

I laced my fingers with his and nodded. "You're forgiven, but you have to know it's very rude to reject a girl when she's getting on her knees. Regardless of your feelings for cheese-burgers."

"Won't happen again." Sam tucked my hair over my ear and pressed his lips to my neck. He was warm and wet, and elec-tricity pulsed through my body, and an all-at-once rush. "Even though I don't have a clear shot at your tits, you look fucking gorgeous."

I melted into him, forgoing all the confusion and stinging anger I'd been clutching since I left him last weekend. I used to brush off his comments about my appearance as his version of player charm, but there was a thorniness in his words that cut into my skin and told me he believed it. "You look…wow. Who dressed you?"

He shifted to face me. "I dress myself. Since when do I need someone to coordinate a shirt and tie for me?"

"I realize you are exceedingly competent, Samuel," I said, my hand sliding along the buttons of his vest. "Who are we tonight?"

"We're the beautiful people who smile and nod while regulation-loving industry pedants tell us what it was like before all the modern trends ruined things for them," he said. "And I'd like to be the person who kisses you just because you're next to me."

"And where does *Pitch Perfect* figure into that plan?"

He squeezed my hip and chuckled. "Get the award, have a drink, then we're getting the hell out of there." His finger skimmed the edge of my sleeve, and I was ready to rip the dress off and climb all over him. "Hour, tops. What we do when we get back here…well, that's up to us."

The event was held at a historic mansion in Winchester, and I'd never seen such an ornate house before. It was filled with antiques and artwork, and I was too terrified that I'd set off a chain reaction of shattered vases and ripped draperies to touch anything. I was truly concerned that, at any moment, I could hiccup and destroy a priceless tapestry.

We stayed a bit longer than an hour, and it gave me an opportunity to see a new side to Sam: the architect. He spoke passionately about preserving old homes, but the enthusiasm he had for sustainability was irresistible. People sought him out to hear his perspectives on green design elements, and though most peppered him with endless questions about technicalities, and others just wanted to argue with him, it didn't take long for them to share some degree of his excitement.

I didn't know it was possible to have such an engaging

conversation about things like adaptive reuse and conservative disassembly, but he proved me wrong. That level of brilliance was intoxicating, and the longer I watched him being the Sam I knew—not the shallow club rat—the more I wanted to put my hands all over him. Knowing tonight was The Night only amplified my wants, and everything he said back at my apartment was heating, humming, swirling around us now.

There was something in the cadence of Sam's voice that filled me with sudsy tingles when he introduced me to his colleagues, referring to me as an accomplished violinist and college professor. I tagged the adjunct part on every time, but it didn't seem to make much difference to these folks.

It was even more surprising that his colleagues regarded me with a measure of respect I hadn't experienced in years. They weren't looking at me like I was a bohemian musician, either. I'd always been the nanny, the piano teacher, the band geek, Agapi's sister. I'd never heard someone speak about me with so much pride. For a moment, I wasn't out of place, even in this grand mansion and surrounded by these smart people.

I loved it, but it was overwhelming. There were more than a few moments when I thought about telling some dirty jokes or busting out my breakdancing moves to remind everyone that I wasn't terribly serious or professorial.

Sam collected his award, briefly thanked the audience, and I was acutely aware that the sexiest man in the room had his arm around my waist. I leaned into him, letting that magnetism claim me. "Let's take a walk," he said, inclining his head toward the hallway.

Our fingers tangled together, we followed the hallway to a winding staircase and quietly explored the second floor. He stopped to study a design carved into a window frame, his thumb moving over the shapes with fascination.

"Are you getting a major architect boner right now?"

Sam glanced at me, his smile turned all the way up to feral. "You're welcome to find out."

"Maybe later." I waved at the wide hallway, and asked, "So what makes this place special? Why does it turn you on?"

His eyes closed and he shook with a soundless laugh, pulling me back against his chest. "This," he started, his chin nestled against my shoulder and his arms wrapped around my torso, "is in the Greek Revival and Regency styles. It has brilliant stained glass, and all the proper period features, but what really interests me is restoration detail. See this?"

He led me toward an open doorway, and pointed to the jamb. Thin inlaid brass swirls traversed the narrow space, and I realized I never would have stopped to look at a doorjamb before, but that was exactly what he noticed.

"That's what makes it special. A local college bought this property about twenty-five years ago when there was lots of free money for historic properties, and they could have gutted the place. It was a wreck, abandoned and falling apart. This property was waiting for a bulldozer to end it all." He lifted his shoulders. "I like that they saw something worth saving."

We were talking about this building, but we weren't. This was Sam, and as I repeated his words in my head, I pivoted and squeezed him in a tight hug. Maybe I was trying to put the pieces back together, or prevent new cracks from forming. I only knew I wasn't letting that bulldozer anywhere near him.

He kissed my forehead, and stepped into the room. It was dark, and though it seemed intentionally closed off for the event, Sam gripped my hand and pulled me inside. Pointing toward the built-in bookshelves, he said, "I've been here before. Meetings. Events. Random bullshit. And I've been thinking about this room all week."

It appeared to be a typical study with dark wood as far as the eye could see, dusty old books, and heavy furniture. "Because it's nice and manly?"

"No," he whispered, backing me against the shelves. "Because I wanted you right here."

He bowed his head toward me, and at first, he was all tentative, tight kisses. His hand slid up my arm and over my shoulder, stopping to cradle my neck while his other hand moved down my back. My fingers shifted to his hair, tugging just a bit. He groaned into my mouth, a mix of acute pain and intense relief, and everything fell into place.

He didn't roam my body in search of more intriguing parts and he didn't shift suggestively to get my hands on his intriguing parts. He just kissed me as if it was the most important thing he could do right now. As if *I* was the most important thing.

"How much longer do you think we can do this?" he asked.

"I don't think anyone else is coming up here, so…"

"No." His lips passed over my cheek and temple, stopping there while his hand slipped under my dress. "How much longer can we pretend this is enough?"

His mouth crashed onto mine, and he took me. He wasn't waiting on me to call the shots or establish the limits, and I let him take me. Sam hooked his hand under my knee, and brought my leg to his waist. Off balance, I teetered, and reached for the bookshelves.

"No," he murmured, prying my fingers from the wood and placing them on his shoulders. "I want your hands on me. I want you for me, always."

His fingertips were light and gentle as they skimmed up my leg and traced the edge of my panties. He teased me with these wispy touches, following the fabric without inching closer to where I was growing wet and impatient.

"I can't pretend, Tiel," he sighed. "I can't pretend that I'm not falling for you."

I pulled him closer, feeling his erection against my thigh and swallowing his groan with a kiss. "Then don't," I said. He growled against my lips, and I bunched my dress around my waist. "Don't ever pretend."

Entire lifetimes passed in his eyes, and he stared at me,

silent. Fear skittered in my gut, reminding me that he could change his mind any moment.

"You promised," I whispered, "to tell me what you're thinking."

"These panties, these sweet lacy things? I want to rip them off. I want to keep them in my pocket all night, and I'll be the only one who knows your pussy is bare." The hand gripping my backside moved down, and he cupped me, the heel of his palm grinding against my clit. "And once those panties are off, I'll make you come quick and hard, right here. Then, I want to be inside you for hours. Maybe days. Maybe forever."

"Sam," I moaned into his shirt. I couldn't decide whether I was appalled or impressed by how quickly I felt the heat flooding my center. I always required so much to get there—foreplay, lube, wine, toys, more foreplay, more lube, yet more wine—but I was there now.

He kissed my jaw, slow and tender, and whispered, "Is that what you want, my *friend*?"

"We can be very *special* friends," I said.

Sam laughed against my shoulder. "You say that, and it's the filthiest thing I've ever heard." He gripped the lace between my legs. "Say it again."

"Friends," I sighed, and the tear of fabric seemed to fill the room. I was a mess, flushed and wet, and shocked by my reaction to Sam. The air was cool against my skin, but I barely noticed it over my desperate desire for his touch.

I knew he preferred quick—in and out, hit it and quit it, one and done—and I expected him to unzip and make it happen. Instead, his fingers trailed back and forth over my exposed skin, never dipping inside, never offering more than light pressure to my clit. It was calm and measured, so much more civilized than I expected from him.

And I was going to fucking explode. I was right there, a breath from coming with the gentlest touch, and when I wasn't lust-drunk, I was going to examine how Sam managed to accomplish that. I didn't believe I'd ever get off with a guy. Orgasms were rare for me, and always the product of a vibrator.

"Do you want me inside you, Tiel?"

I was soaked and aching, and I'd long since lost control of the sounds I was moaning into Sam's suit coat. Anyone in my position would have said yes. Anyone with sense would have said yes.

But I shook my head against his head. "No."

In my heart—and a few other spots—I wanted him. I'd wanted him since that very first moment.

But my head wasn't ready to get on board, and I hated that. I hated that a fifteen-minute marriage could leave its watermark on every relationship since, and I hated how doubt always outgunned lust.

Or whatever this was.

He tipped his chin up, sucked in a breath, and froze. His hand moved to my outer thigh and he leaned away from me. "Oh, I'm...I'm sorry."

I brought his hand between my legs, rocking hard against his palm while he studied me, confused. I was coming apart the second he touched me, and I bit my cry into his shoulder while the weight of my orgasm moved through my muscles. My hand shifted from his chest down to his belt, and then lower, until I was gliding over his erection. Sam's eyes closed, and his head fell back on a groan. "Do you have any other friends? The kind you kiss?"

God, I fucking hated thinking about everything before *right this second*. I wanted to redefine it all, own his firsts and seconds and everything after that. But I didn't want to be a jealous, possessive bitch who needed to be held back every time I remembered that Sam had a life before meeting me.

My fingers curled around him, squeezing, and I startled at his sharp hiss. He grabbed my wrist and held me in place. "I don't want to kiss anyone else, Tiel."

His fingers shifted around mine, guiding me. "What about your *friends*? At the clubs? You don't *kiss* them?"

Sucking in a breath, Sam shook his head. He moved my hand faster, harder, and he whispered, "No more club friends. No club friends in *months*."

If I hadn't been rubbing his cock, I would have twirled around in celebration. "You could have mentioned that earlier in the week."

"I'm an intensely flawed human. Unzip me," he growled. "*Now*. I just want to feel your skin on me." I was shocked by the authority in his deep voice, and—ever the gentleman—he must have noticed it on my face when he added, "Please."

The simple task of unfastening a belt and drawing down a zipper was shockingly complex when an erection was involved. Once I freed him from his boxers, I let my thumb rub his head and stared at him. I thought I knew what a decent cock looked like, but Sam put them all to shame.

I started stroking, slow at first, but then he covered my hand with his and showed me what he needed. It was strange and filthy to watch both hands moving over him, but it was perfect, as if it was intended to be this way and everyone had been doing it wrong all this time. The little noises he made—the hums and sighs, and pants and moans—they wove through my nerves, stitching themselves into my skin.

His fingers dug hard into my shoulder, demanding that I feel his sweet agony, and when he groaned "Oh *fuck*, Tiel," I was finished. This boy was mine, and I'd never stop being his.

He came with a shout, growling my name against my neck and dragging his teeth over my skin. He leaned into me, pressing me against the hard edges of the shelf as he spilled into my hand, through my fingers, onto the skirt of my dress. "You're trying to make my mind explode," he said. "You've never done a single thing that I expected."

"Let's not change that," I said. "You need a little chaos."

Dropping his head to my shoulder, he said, "I think that shook some brain cells loose," he said.

I rubbed his fluid between my fingers, and along his shaft until he swore and hissed. "Something tells me you'll be just fine without them."

He produced a handkerchief from his pocket and wiped my hand clean in a quick movement, but this dress was paying a visit to the dry cleaner. The lace patterns meant the stain wasn't egregious, but anyone who looked closely would notice. After gingerly folding the fabric—he didn't say it, but I knew he needed a fix of hand sanitizer—he tucked it in his pocket. "Did you…?" he asked.

"I didn't think you cared."

He fisted the shreds of panties, drew them down my legs, and stuffed them into his suit coat. As promised. "I do, because if you didn't come," he growled, "I'm shoving these panties in your mouth to keep you quiet and fucking you right here. Now *tell me*."

Suddenly shy yet insanely aroused, I nodded against his chest.

"Good. I promise to pay more attention next time."

"Will that be soon?"

Sam laughed and smoothed my skirt into place. "We're leaving *now*."

I couldn't control the fiery blush as Sam guided me downstairs and through the crowd. It seemed like there was a giant sign over my head, announcing to the world that my underwear was in this man's pocket and it was there because he fucking *ripped* it off me while he ordered me around.

And I liked it. God, I couldn't explain *why* I liked it, and a fraction of me didn't want to like it, but fuck…I wanted to obey his every command.

We were almost to the door when I heard a voice call to him. "Hey, Sam!"

Turning, I was confronted with one of the most beautiful

women I'd ever seen. Tall, slim, more hair than I'd ever know what to do with, and she was walking straight toward us.

Sam turned to me, his eyes wide and a little panicked, and he squeezed my hip. "Allow me to apologize for this in advance."

Thirteen

SAM

PANTIES WERE POWERFUL. Seeing them, touching them, ripping them. But none of that quite met the level of knowing they were nestled inside my pocket and Tiel was bare under that skirt. The skirt I came all over.

Almost powerful enough for me to tell Andy I'd talk to her on Monday and take my girl home for the night.

She smiled at Tiel, and flashed a confused glance in my direction. "Hi," she said. "I'm Andy Asani."

Tiel shook her hand, and I saw all the questions and doubt behind her eyes. In that instant, I wanted to start over with her, and never mention any of my whorish history because now it was living and breathing between us like a goddamn parasite. I couldn't even try to evolve because I'd sold her on the asshole version of me, and shoved it in her face every chance I got.

I made it this way, and I knew that. I was the one drooling over every pair of tits that entered my line of sight even though Tiel's were the only that interested me.

I was the one who insisted on all the comments about casual sex, as if I needed her to know I was hot shit in my stupid little universe.

I was the one who didn't mention I hadn't thought about

anything casual sex since she dragged me into an alley and breathed new life into me with her kiss.

"Andy, this is Tiel Desai." To Andy's credit, she didn't show an ounce of shock over seeing me with a date. If there was one thing I could count on Andy for, it was equanimity. "Andy is an architect. She works at the firm with me and she's with…" When Patrick rounded the corner with a bottle of beer in one hand and a martini glass in the other, he skittered to a stop and stared at us. He wasn't as reliable with the equanimity. "Patrick."

He smiled at Tiel, his eyes darting between her face and where my hand was wrapped around her hip. If she mutated into Mystique right then and there, it probably wouldn't have surprised him more than seeing me with a woman.

"Patrick," Andy said, collecting her drink from his hand. "This is Tiel. She's here *with Sam*."

I scratched the back of my neck and sighed. My dick was still wet from coming in her hand, and my body still wanted to consume her, but I also wanted to show her off. I needed to prove that someone as intelligent and stunning as Tiel would want me, even if me and my bucketful of crazy weren't close to worthy of her.

"Tiel. Hi," he said. He turned to Andy. "Am I supposed to know what's going on here?"

Shaking her head, she sipped her drink and jabbed her elbow into his ribs. "No, honey, you're fine," she laughed.

Patrick and I stared at each other, his brow furrowed, and I counted the seconds in my head, just waiting for the right moment to get the fuck out of here. But he wasn't having it. "Is there anyone I should talk to?"

There were fucking *panties* in my pocket. These were not the conditions for a business discussion.

I waved down the hall, impatient. "Larson and DeCosta are under the impression they own the Andover planning and zoning boards, and Ciccannessi suggested he's tearing down some abandoned Cape Annes in Newton next year and building condos. Seems like a tragic idea to me, but that's Shannon's domain, and she's busy with her disappearing act every other weekend."

"Shannon doesn't have to be the only person who handles shit, and this is the only time she's been away since Labor Day weekend. And we're here," he said, nodding toward Andy. "We can handle it."

"Right, because the two of you are so fucking chatty," I said.

"Do you have time to restore some Queen Annes? We can take them off Ciccannessi's hands right now," Patrick said. "I'm the last person who wants to see another condo built, but as far as I can tell, you have enough projects for the next forty-seven years."

"Matt might have some time coming up," Andy said.

Tiel's fingers moved down my back and under my suit coat, closing around my shirt. That was when I realized she hadn't said a word since I had her backed against those bookshelves. She had no clue what was going on.

"Tiel's a conservatory-trained violinist," I said. "And a professor at Berklee."

"Adjunct," she said.

Patrick frowned, not understanding the sudden shift in topic, but Andy—thank God for Andy, because Patrick was a socially inept wildebeest—knew where I was going. "What do you teach?"

"Music therapy." I wanted her to elaborate, to talk about the kids she worked with and places she'd performed and her online viewership, but then I caught the icy glare she was shooting at Andy. She held it another moment, then glanced at me and said, "You're busy here. I'm going to head home."

"No, you're not," I said. "If you're going anywhere, I'm going with you."

Her eyes darted to my chest, knowing her panties were

stowed in my interior pocket. "Don't worry," she said. "You can catch up with me later."

She waved to Patrick and Andy, and hurried through the vestibule. There was no way in hell I was letting this turn into a repeat of last weekend. "I don't care what you do about Ciccannessi," I said. "I'm with Tiel tonight."

"Just you wait a second," Andy said, holding up her palm. "What the hell does that mean? What the hell is going on? Who *is* that and why does she hate me?"

"I'll explain on Monday," I said, and jogged through the door and down the gravel driveway to where she was weaving through cars and small snow banks. I caught up to her, but she didn't seem interested in acknowledging me. "I clearly recall telling you not to go anywhere. Get your sweet ass in the car so I can take you home."

She shook her head and continued down the path. "Go back inside. Do your thing. Buy your houses or whatever."

"I didn't fuck her," I said, and Tiel froze. "I know you're thinking it, but you're wrong. She's with my brother."

"But you've thought about it," she said.

"No, actually, I haven't once thought about it. My brother is in sick, crazy love with her," I said. "I know you think I'm a depraved dog and I'll fuck anything that moves, but I'm not. You're the only woman I've touched since the elevator."

She hooked a glance over her shoulder. "Really?"

It was mostly true. All this fucking honesty was more difficult than I anticipated. "Okay, this girl grabbed my dick when I was out last Monday, but nothing happened."

"Oh my God," she groaned, and continued down the driveway. "I knew it. Why do you have to be such a damn whore?"

I followed, and caught her around the waist before she reached the main road. "I don't want any of that to matter anymore." I kissed her neck and earlobe, and she slowly relaxed into me. "I want to take you home. I want to undress you. I want to kiss every inch of you. Twice. I want you in *my bed*, and I want to be inside you."

She covered my hands with hers and nodded. "So, what? You're finished with hook-ups? You're just over it?"

"You're too hilarious and gorgeous for me to want anything else," I said, and I meant it.

"Stop it with the smooth lines," she laughed. "I don't buy it. That shit doesn't work on me, player."

"Then don't buy it, but know this—I have a pocketful of my own jizz right now, but since I'm fucking obsessed with you, it didn't even cross my mind to make you handle that situation. If I wanted a hook-up, I'd have you on your knees licking it off."

"Aww," she cooed, and shifted in my arms. "There's the perv I know and love."

"Never left," I said, and kissed her. "Can I take you home now?"

"To watch *Pitch Perfect*, right?"

There was a time in my life when I understood women, and that period ended when I met Tiel. I didn't know whether this was a trick question or a new form of foreplay, so I nodded and guided her up the driveway. I'd untangle this when I had her behind closed doors. "Of course, Sunshine."

I started talking the minute the car started, and didn't stop the entire ride to her apartment. There was a furious energy burning inside me, and unloading every random thought was the only way to keep from sliding my hand under her skirt or dragging hers to my crotch.

I recounted my frustration with several architects, bemoaning their guideline-driven rigidity and refusal to consider the possibility that old techniques might not be the best techniques. I commented on everything from the host's bowtie to the excessively large cheese spread, and passed some judgment on the early use of poinsettias and holly as decoration at the mansion.

If she only knew the power wielded by those panties.

The best parking spot was more than half a block from her apartment, but she insisted she didn't want me dropping her off at the door. As we walked in silence, our hands linked, heavy, wet snow started falling. I held out my palm and watched the flakes dissolve against my skin.

"It isn't quite the same as rain," Tiel said. "But maybe you can kiss me in it anyway."

Part of me wished she'd forget everything I'd said that sweaty night in September, but another part of me was thrilled I was the one checking off that list. I stopped and she pirouetted —she was so fucking cute when she did that—right into my arms. When my lips met hers, it was a moment that seemed to stretch on and on.

Until snow started gathering on my head, and dripped all over us.

We made it back to her apartment before getting entirely soaked. We stared at each other for a moment, shaking out of our coats, damp and breathless, not knowing what came next.

There was the *should come next*, the *want to come next*, and a slightly different avenue altogether.

And I only knew the different avenue. Every breath was new territory for me, and I was a dissociative blur of stress. I didn't know what the fuck I was doing here, how bed sex worked, how I'd navigate the infusion set situated on either sides of my belly button, or whether this was devolving into another friendly movie night. But my desire was winning, shoving all that shit into the background.

"You're wet," Tiel announced, fingering my collar. She pulled me into the tiny pink-and-maroon-tiled bathroom that screamed of the 1960s, pushed me against the sink, and rubbed a towel over my hair.

I lifted an eyebrow as she buffed my chest. I wasn't particularly wet there, but that wasn't her concern. "Don't want you to catch a cold," she murmured.

My thumb pressed her lips closed, and I said, "There are

moments when I look at you, and I can't even comprehend how beautiful you are. You really are pure wild."

Then my mouth was on Tiel, devouring her, opening her until she was sighing for more.

"Thank you," I murmured against her jaw. "For tonight. You were incredible."

Her hands moved down my vest, touching and unbuttoning as she went, and she offered a quick kiss that transitioned into my tie wrapped around her fist and my tongue in her mouth. "Anytime," she panted.

"Really? You'd do that again?"

"Of course," she whispered. "That champagne was far better than the piss I drank on New Year's Eve."

I passed the towel over her shoulders and arms, then tossed it to the ground. Even though Tiel—and *only* Tiel—had seen my infusion set before, I hated having that apparatus on display. She caught sight of it the morning after the notorious elevator incident, and a few other times when I stayed the night, but never stared at the glucose sensor or insulin port.

I could temporarily detach the tubing that connected the insulin port to the pump so that I wasn't chained to the device, but I couldn't yank the infusion set out. She was going to see them and feel them against her skin, and the case could be made for keeping a shirt on. But I didn't want anything between us tonight, and *holy fucking shit*, there were entire quadrants of my brain going into lockdown over that notion.

Without breaking her heavy gaze, I unbuttoned my shirt, dropped it, and yanked my gray tank over my head.

"I have a couple more events over this month and next." I pulled Tiel toward me, locking her between my legs, and I was thanking every higher power that I could name because she didn't even glance at my abdomen. "I understand if you hated it. They are the most insufferable assholes I've ever met, and they seem to think it's fine to slap some spackle on two-hundred-year-old plaster and call it restoration." I sighed against her lips, my eyes closed. "I'll go alone if you really hated it."

"Oh no," she laughed. "Did you even notice the number of cougars you had drooling all over you? Someone has to block and defend."

I dragged my lips over the slope of her neck, and pressed my tank between her breasts. "Want to watch that movie now?" I asked. She giggled, nodding, but this wasn't our typical routine. We weren't going to the sofa and we'd be lucky if we saw more than the opening credits. "Put this on." Her fingers closed around the shirt, and I kissed the tender spot beneath her earlobe while I unzipped her dress.

I stepped back, my hand on my belt buckle, watching Tiel while she clutched my shirt. Conflict was painted all over her face, and despite what happened at the mansion, we were crossing new lines. We'd spent more than two months kissing and snuggling, and the prospect of taking her to bed—an actual *bed*—loomed so much larger than it had earlier tonight. If she dropped that dress, there weren't many things that could stop me from licking her entire body, and that redrew all the boundaries.

"Turn around."

My brow quirked as I fought back a smile. "I ripped off your panties two hours ago. You didn't ask me to turn around for that."

"That was the champagne's prerogative. Not mine." I didn't exactly remember it that way, but I wasn't going to argue with her. "Turn around."

I complied, but she didn't account for the bathroom mirror giving me a glorious view of her body or the way she studied the ink on my back once her dress and bra were off. I sighed when her fingers moved over the intricate designs, loving her touch more than I could ever explain.

"This is so beautiful, Sam."

As I turned, she caught sight of a fishhook inked on the

underside of my arm and rubbed her thumb against it. My eyes swept over her breasts, barely restrained by the tank, and I drew her closer.

Her thumb passed back and forth over my bicep, at first tracing on the simple shape and then pressing her mouth against it. "I wanted to taste it," she said. "I wanted to feel it under my tongue."

My fingers skimmed up her face and into her hair, my gaze shifting to her mouth. She rose up on her toes to kiss me, and her lips were slow as they moved against me, her tongue gentle, and it brought forth a slight moan that I couldn't stop. It was one precious kiss, but it seemed bigger than a loud, thrashing orgasm.

"Let me tell you what I'm thinking," I said, my lips returning to her neck. "We'll watch the movie after. We're going to be lucky if I last three minutes once I get inside you because, let's face it, I've been thinking about this for two months."

"No, you haven't," she laughed. She traced the Celtic knot wreath on my shoulder, then followed it with her tongue and teeth, and I was dangerously close to coming all over her again. "You say that to undersell yourself and look like a champ when you over-deliver. Your lines don't work on me, sir."

I dragged my fingers up the backs of her thighs until her entire body shivered, and another version of me would have fucked her here. It would have been quick and hard, and it would be good for us both, but it was too easy to fall back on my old tactics. It scared the shit out of me, but I was undressed and taking this woman to bed tonight.

"You wore a pink skirt when we went to House of Blues last month, and in the right light, it was see-through. You were wearing dark panties with light stripes, and I didn't spend the night with you because I had to go home and jerk off four times."

"*Four* times?" she asked. "Stop making shit up."

"You still doubt me." I brought her hand to the erection that was drilling into her stomach. "If you don't want this, say it and we'll forget the whole night. I'll leave. We'll go back to seeing shows and watching movies because you're my best friend and I'll do *anything* for you, but know that I'd very much enjoy fucking you—" I thrust into her hand. "Right now."

Her hand moved over me, and I gave her a quick nod of encouragement followed by a groan that must have originated in my toes when her fist curled around me. "Don't." She shook her head and pushed my trousers down to my ankles. "Don't leave me."

I marched her out of the bathroom and down the hall to her bedroom, her adorable ass peeking out from under my shirt, and *fuck fuck fuck*, that was a look I wanted to remember. Hurriedly, I disconnected the tubing from my infusion set as best I could and dropped the device on her bedside table.

"Sam?"

I couldn't keep my hands off her, and they were everywhere from her legs to her belly to her breasts, and as much as that shirt turned me on, it needed to go. It was cute while it lasted. "Yes, Sunshine?"

"If I let you in," she said, climbing onto her bed as I followed. "Promise not to break anything."

She was caged beneath me, her hand firm on my cock while I inched the shirt up her sides, but she was suddenly so much more delicate than I'd ever noticed.

"It's a deal," I whispered. "Just don't break me either, okay?"

A smile spread across her face, and she inched my boxers down. "Show me where I can touch you."

I was ready with a sarcastic response, but then I understood what she was asking. The beauty of quick and dirty stand-up sex was that I never needed to fully undress. All these years and I'd survived without taking off all my clothes, never once baring the freakish medical equipment that was never far from my side. Not until Tiel got me drunk and we danced around her apartment. And now.

There was an urge coursing through my veins to get up, grab my clothes, and get the fuck out, but not enough to actually do it. The tension between wanting Tiel and wanting to protect myself was overwhelming, but the suffocating stress was fading just enough to focus on the woman beneath me. Guiding her hand to the disc on my belly, I said, "This is the blood sugar sensor."

She nodded, her expression neutral as her finger circled the flat, hard plastic surrounded by a thin adhesive shield that kept it in place. I moved her hand to my other side, another protected disc. "And the pump port is over here today."

"Does it hurt?"

"No, but..." I hesitated.

"It's okay, Sam." Tiel offered a patient smile, and pulled the shirt over her head and there was nothing, nothing between us anymore. All the filthy things I wanted to say to her, the practiced ways I wanted to touch her, all of it drifted away and instinct took over.

Before this moment, I had no idea what it meant to be aroused. My dick got hard plenty, but I'd never felt a longing in my core, my marrow, until Tiel was naked beneath me. She was lush and curved in all the right places, and those tits—there was a reason I'd been enamored with them from the start—filled my hands in the most sumptuous way.

She wasn't just stunning and sexy, she was fun. She giggled when my stubbly chin scraped between her breasts, down her belly, and between her thighs, and it was the most amazing, lighthearted sound in the world. This wasn't rough, anonymous sex simply for the purpose of scratching the itch. This was real, and just like all things Tiel, that realness called into question everything I once believed about myself.

"You're gonna have to hold still," I said, my lips grazing between her pelvic bones.

"And if I don't?" she asked, rising up on her elbows. "What happens then?" There was a challenge in her eyes, a sparkle that made tearing some panties look like amateur hour. "Will you punish me?"

My eyes dropped to her bald apex. I didn't have much practical experience with kink, but God help me, I was ready to learn. "Yes," I said. "And you'll like it."

The last time I licked a pussy, I was just old enough to vote. The memory wasn't especially vivid—none of them were—but I knew it wasn't especially good pussy. The instant my tongue reached Tiel's wet center, it was like savoring something I hadn't known I was craving.

She tasted like heaven itself, and for once, I wasn't concerned with how quickly this would end.

I wanted it to last, and that was an arresting realization. I wasn't busy mentally walking through my projects or selecting which excuse I'd use to zip up.

Her incessant wiggling *was* a concern, and without much thought, my hand swung out and connected with her upper thigh. She gasped, and it was a long, stuttering noise that packed entire sentences into a single sound. In that second, I was half-convinced she was going to kick my ass to the curb.

But when I looked up, I found her eyes wide and a lusty smile stretched across her face. She fucking *loved* that. "Oh, you little perv," I said.

I grabbed her legs but she was too quick, and she crawled away, giggling. "You're not allowed to growl at me like that," she said.

I chased her into the pile of pillows at the head of the bed, her chest flattened against the headboard. I roped my arm around her waist, pulling her hips toward me. "Why not?"

"Because it makes me want to do irrational things," she said, yelping as my hand cracked against her ass. "And this is already pretty irrational."

Placing her hands on the headboard and widening her stance, I kissed up her spine and over her shoulders, finally turning her head toward me and landing on her mouth. "The only irrational choice would be not doing exactly what I tell you to." I tapped her hands. "Do not let go."

Making good on my promise, I explored every inch of Tiel. She squirmed when my tongue moved over the pounding pulse in her throat, the dimples low on her back, that sharp curve of her waist. By the time I situated myself between her legs and started biting the soft, soft skin there, she was vibrating.

"Condoms," she panted. "Drawer. Sooner rather than later."

I'd never once taken orders from a woman while we were going at it. I'd acknowledged requests for *more, this, that, harder, faster, slower*, but even when I was a full-time, card-carrying nice guy, I was the fucking boss.

"Sweetheart," I said, licking the arousal from her slit. "I will get there in good time. Don't you worry about that."

Despite her resistance, I inched lower and lapped at her. Her sweet little clit just begged for my attention, and the sounds she made the second my tongue connected with it were the most erotic things I'd ever heard. She possessed a new level of porn star moaning, and that shit was intoxicating. A few more well-timed cries, and this party would be ending quickly.

"No-*oooo*," she wailed. "Get there now."

I was the fucking boss, but God, I would do anything to make her happy.

Levering up on my knees, I bracketed my legs on either side of her, my cock sliding along the cleft of her ass. I took her tits in my hands, squeezing them and twisting her nipples until she bucked against me, screeching my name while my teeth sank into her shoulder. "Your neighbors are going to know who I am," I said, my hand sliding up to cup her jaw. I tilted her face toward me. "Is that what you want?"

She licked her lips, and yeah, I really wanted her mouth on my cock but that would be off the table until she stopped worrying about my slutty history. "I can't be quiet," she whispered.

Nodding, I strummed her clit with one hand and brought

the other down on her ass. It would be enough to keep her throbbing while I stepped away. I hated leaving her for even a second, and walking away from her while she was on her knees at the headboard tested all of my control. I found what I needed, took some cleansing breaths, and returned to the bed quickly. With the condom rolled down, I leaned into her, my lips on the back of her neck, my cock teasing her swollen tissues. "Tell me again that you want this."

"I need you inside me," she groaned.

I felt lightheaded, besieged with the power she was placing in my hands. I pushed into her, and when she let out a deep moan, I shoved those torn panties in her mouth before it unfurled into the screaming wail I felt shuddering beneath her skin. "Give me fucking *everything*," I said. "I want it all."

The tight coil between her shoulders loosened, and she dropped her head between her outstretched arms. Again, I was expecting a knee to the groin and a door slammed in my face, but she sighed, humming when I was fully seated inside her. My hands layered over hers on the headboard. I brought my mouth to that precious spot behind her ear for a minute, just tasting while I moved in her.

"You are delicious," I murmured. "Your skin, your mouth, your pussy. But you know what I want to taste now?"

I rocked forward, cursing under my breath as her muscles clamped around me. She shook her head and curled her fingers through mine.

"I want to know how you taste when you come," I whispered. "And I'm going to fuck you now because I intend to find out."

Soon the headboard was slamming against the wall, and regardless of whether the neighbors knew my name, they knew exactly what was going on here. Tiel ground into me, her hips snapping to meet my thrusts, and the hushed cries from behind that balled-up fabric elevated every ounce of desire in my body.

I was gutted—torn in two and split the fuck open—and I

recognized my long-held fears decimated and discarded on the ground around us.

I lasted far longer than I expected, and part of it was the awe of exploring the boundaries with Tiel. My handprint on her ass, the panties in her mouth, the sassy, defiant way she followed my orders—she shut down my stress and only allowed me to think about my cock and her pussy and the warm place inside me that she owned.

Her shrieks intensified, and I drew her hands from the headboard and brought them to her breasts. Watching her pinching her nipples harder than I expected she'd enjoy had me pounding into her until she was quivering in my arms. I whispered, "Oh, you are so ready. So ready."

Tiel nodded, her eyes squeezed shut. My balls were full and heavy, and I was well overdue to empty myself into her. Bringing my hand between her legs, I circled her clit while I gradually pulled out and then drove into her. I lingered on that tender spot, the one that felt impossibly deep and absolutely fucking *mine*, and I stayed there as everything in her shuddered and sighed.

Her head and hands fell forward, clutching the few pillows remaining, and those beautiful rolling spasms unleashed my orgasm. The explosion immobilized me for several seconds— maybe it was minutes, I couldn't tell—leaving my brain superbly numb. I couldn't hear anything over the fire hose of blood pumping through my body, but I pulled out, tied off the condom, and flipped Tiel on her back.

She barely noticed me settling between her legs but when my tongue swiped her pussy, her eyes popped open and she fucking *screamed*. I took one last taste before crawling up her body, gently running my hands over her hips, belly, breasts before tossing those panties aside and laying my lips over hers.

There was nothing else that needed saying, and we lay there in a rumpled pile of blankets and pillows, kissing and clinging to each other.

It was magnificent.

We stayed there in that euphoric haze until my hands started twitching—my favorite low blood sugar symptom, right behind the temporary loss of my peripheral vision. In all reality, I was thrilled to get this much time with Tiel before crashing, I just hated rolling away from her. I reconnected my device and wasn't shocked to see an abysmally low reading. "Do you have any juice?"

"Mmmhmm," she sighed. "Fridge. Like always."

I'd never asked Tiel to stock organic juices or unroasted nuts, but one week in late September I noticed them there. She was concerned in quiet ways, and it never bothered me when she'd peek at my device and tell me to eat.

I made it to the kitchen, downed an entire carton of orange juice, and breathed through the instinctive panic that set in every time I got this low. Once my calves didn't feel quite as frozen anymore, I grabbed a jar of almonds and some water, and shuffled back to Tiel's room.

She was exactly where I left her, naked and glowing brighter than the moon. She glanced over, smiling, and asked, "Are you okay?"

I reorganized the pillows and linens, and crawled to her side. "Just needed a snack."

Tiel curled into me, and laid her head on my shoulder. "I believe you promised we'd watch *Pitch Perfect*."

Munching a handful of almonds, I smiled at her. "And you should know by now that if I say I'm going to do something…" I said. I grabbed the remote and toggled through her DVR stockpile to her reigning favorite, then dropped a quick kiss on her lips. "I do it."

"THE CASTAVECHIAS WENT to Scotland over the summer," Patrick said. "They visited castles."

Riley frowned and nudged Matt's shoulder. "Why is that an issue?"

"They'd like to redesign," Andy said. "Again."

On most Monday mornings, that news would have annoyed the shit out of me. But today? Today I was as cheerful as a fucking ladybug in July. It probably owed something to some incredible bed sex—who knew rolling over to a warm, soft, willing woman at all hours of the night could be so fantastic?—but it was more than that. I felt lighter, healthier, happier.

I was falling in love.

"Are they being charged the dicking-around fee? What is this? Version nineteen?" Matt asked.

"Yes," Andy said. "But the bigger problem is that we're already halfway through a Dutch Colonial restoration. The project shouldn't become a Scottish castle, and..." She met Patrick's eyes with a shrug.

"And they want us to go to Scotland with them." Patrick waved his hand dismissively. "Something about recovering stones and floorboards."

"They want us to go this weekend," Andy said.

"Wait. Does that mean you're actually going along with this? You're stuffing a medieval castle into a Dutch Colonial?" I asked. "Does no one care about concept anymore?"

"It's like a turducken," Riley said.

Matt pressed his fist to his mouth in a poor attempt at concealing his laughter, and while I should have found some humor in Riley's commentary, I couldn't. I was too stunned at the idea Patrick would bow to anyone like this.

"We wouldn't do that," Patrick said. "We can work with floorboards and stones, but we won't be digging any moats."

"So you're going to Scotland," I said. "This weekend."

"Possibly." Patrick shared a smile with Andy that didn't feel entirely appropriate, considering it was Monday morning and four people were watching. They were always doing that— looking at each other and saying things with infinitesimal shrugs and furrowed brows and quick smiles. They could prob-ably go an entire month without speaking to each other and not miss a beat.

Riley leaned to me, asking, "What are the odds they come back married?"

It was amusing to watch a blush climb up Patrick's neck and across his face, and it was even better seeing him and Andy exchanging tense glances while they pretended to be engrossed in their screens.

I handed over a twenty. "I'll take that bet, and my money is on no," I said, my eyes on Andy. "Princess Jasmine looks like she's about to castrate you and Optimus might hold you down while she does it."

"Yeah, Riley," Shannon said. "Not everyone needs to get married fourteen minutes after they meet."

Matt leaned forward, his arms folded on the table, and he glanced at Riley and me. "Did she just insult me?"

"Sam, why don't you tell us about Tiel?" Andy sat back with

a smug grin and gestured around the table. "I know everyone would love to hear about her."

I wavered between wanting to tell them everything about Tiel, and hiding her away and protecting her from their breed of friendly. I wanted to prove to them that I was capable of keeping something good in my life, even after everything we'd been through, but I was also greedy. Sharing her with my family meant just that—sharing—and they were grabby little bastards. It would be only a matter of time until Lauren and Andy adopted her into their yoga-and-farmers'-market routine on Saturday mornings, or Shannon's Thursday night drunken pedicure outings.

I wasn't interested in surrendering that time to them.

Not when I could have Tiel surrendering to me.

"Or maybe we should talk about Thanksgiving, Shannon. What's the plan?" I asked.

"I'm not going to be in town for Thanksgiving. I have reservations at a spa in New Mexico, and considering the shit you all put me through on a daily basis, I don't want to hear any whining about it either," Shannon said. "I'll order everything from the farm like I usually do, and I can have Tom pick it up, but I won't be the one reheating it. You're grown men. Figure it out for yourselves."

"So I'm hearing two things," Matt said. He pointed to Shannon. "One, it's really shitty that you're just now mentioning this a week before Thanksgiving. Lauren and I will have Thanksgiving at our place, and fuck you very much for waiting until Sam brought it up. It's not like you've hosted for the past fifteen damn years or anything."

"See? The newlyweds want to do it. Let them trot out their new crystal and china. Crisis averted." She shook her head and kept her eyes on her screen.

Matt pointed to me. "Two, I think we'd all like to hear about Tiel."

Patrick said to Matt, "You're going to love this story. You would have enjoyed seeing this firsthand."

"What were you even doing at that event?" I asked him. "If you were going to be there, I certainly didn't have to."

"You were getting a fucking award, so yes, you did have to be there," Patrick said. "And stop evading."

I rolled my shoulders and sighed. They had me cornered. "I'm seeing someone," I said. I was aiming for casual although I'm certain it came off as defensive. "Her name is Tiel."

"And she's a *college professor* and a *violinist*," Andy added. "She's *very* pretty and wasn't even wearing hooker heels. And I'll go out on a limb and say they've known each other for a while."

Riley kicked me under the table. "Is this the same chick you drunk dialed last week?"

"Oh. *Oh*," Matt said, frowning at me. "So we're talking about a real girl? An appropriate, adult, professional woman?"

I ignored Riley and glared at Matt. I knew he was not referring to age. "She's a couple months older than me."

"She didn't look anything like his usual syphilitic crew," Patrick said to Matt and Riley.

Shannon looked up from her screen, the first hint she was listening. "And how long has this been taking place?"

I shrugged. "A little more than two months."

"Is that why you've been so pleasant recently? I assumed it was some new meds or a colonic or a fucking juice cleanse or something, but this is great news," Matt said. "Good for you."

"Oh no, no, no. We don't do secret affairs in this office. Not after the shit these two"—Shannon pointed to Patrick and Andy —"pulled last spring."

"I wouldn't say there's been any secret." I swirled my coffee cup and glanced to Shannon. I didn't want to argue with her today. Not after my girl woke me up with some tremendous morning sex, and holy shit, where had *that* been all my life? So rather than reminding Shannon that she hadn't talked to me about anything outside the realms of my projects and my eating habits in months, and we hadn't been out together since the summer, I folded my hands in my lap and smiled.

Last winter I'd told this group we were too fucked-up for anything normal, but I was starting to believe that was a choice I could make. Happiness, too. I didn't have to dig myself out of a hole; I just had to decide I could and should have whatever the fuck I wanted.

Right now, I wanted Tiel.

So she liked being spanked and gagged and God only knew what else, and most importantly, she liked when *I* did those things to her. We were both within throwing range of thirty and yet we'd discovered all manner of new bridges to cross together, and that swelled in my chest like a rebel yell. I was fucking delirious for her.

"You're saying this is a legitimate thing," Shannon said. "Dating and the whole normal relationship? Seriously?"

Was that what we'd been doing? All those nights out, the kissing, the touching, the texting each other 'good night' and 'good morning' as if the continued rotation of the earth depended on it—was that *dating*?

Shit. That *was* dating. We'd been dating, sort of, all this time and it took me until this weekend to get my hands on her tits.

"Yeah, Shan. Pretty much."

"The universe must really fucking hate me if *you're* in a healthy relationship," she murmured. "Just wait, RISD will be next, and I'll start hoarding cats and learning how to knit because what else is there to do with my time? Soon enough, you'll all have kids but you won't let me near them because all I'll want to do is smell their little heads and make them promise not to let you assholes put Auntie Shannon in a home."

"We already discussed this," Andy said. "No one is letting you start a cat colony. Cool it with the end of days talk, or I'm cutting off your caffeine supply."

"Bring her to Thanksgiving," Matt said.

"Yeah," Andy said. "Maybe she'll like Lauren more than she liked me."

"You can't hold that against her," I said. "She's the friendliest person I know. We did not expect to run into you two. We were on our way out and Patrick was his usual jovial self, and she wasn't wearing any—" I stopped myself before that thought went any further.

I'd never spared them an intimate detail in the past. If anything, I enjoyed the shock value of announcing I'd fucked another nameless, faceless woman in some questionably private location. But not now.

If Tiel was walking around bare-assed because I shredded her panties, we were the only two who needed to know about it.

"Oh shit, son," Riley yelled. He clapped me on the back before rolling away from the table, laughing. "I need to meet this girl. Anyone who goes commando at an Arch Society gathering is a keeper."

"She didn't—no, I mean, I ripped her—fuck," I groaned. "Never mind."

"I've never had that much fun at any event put on by the Arch Society," Matt said. "I might start attending more frequently."

"Definitely a keeper. At the very least, she should come drinking on Black Friday," Andy said. "We'll see if she still hates me then."

"As entertaining as this has been, we have a business to run and far more important things to discuss this morning," Patrick said. "And it's already eight thirty. All of you—shut the fuck up unless I tell you otherwise."

STANDING in the center of the Turlan's kitchen, I glanced from one wall to another. The flow was all wrong and it wasn't built to accommodate modern appliances—hence the refrigerator in the mudroom. The original design relegated cooking to the shadows, closing it off from the other living spaces with several small, choppy sections: the butler's pantry, the dry goods pantry, the laundry, the galley. Bringing order to this room was my current puzzle, the one I'd been poring over all damn week, and I was getting it right this morning. I was convinced I'd make sense of it all if I stared long enough.

"What is this?" Riley asked, gesturing to a small pass-through between the interior and exterior. That, along with a grimy white tile backsplash, was revealed with the top layer of drywall removed. "Other than a respite from the cold for squirrels?"

"Milk door," I murmured. "It's where the milk bottles were delivered, and the empties returned."

Riley shifted his weight and flipped through his notebook. That was one of his new things: keeping track of shit. I was actually impressed with how well he was doing. He snapped a picture and scribbled some notes, and though it was troubling he'd never encountered a milk door, I was more concerned with the kitchen. I was determined to preserve as much of the 1890s materials as possible, and there was no reason to demolish anything when it only required restoration. The cabinetry was in remarkable shape considering its age, and once we repaired the hardware and removed the flaking paint, it would be as good as anything new.

"All right," I said, my arms outstretched as I held the plan in my mind. "We're opening up that wall. The lower cabinets stay, and the uppers form this side of the island. Move that block"—I gestured behind me—"to the opposite end, and that's the space for the refrigerator. Then blow out the dry goods pantry, and we have some clean, parallel flow lines." I glanced to Riley, and the pencil frozen over his notebook. "Did you get all that?"

"Um..." He flipped to a new page and started sketching.

"Could you repeat the part about the walls? Which ones are we changing?"

I went through each section of the kitchen again, and tagged every cabinet with blue painter's tape and a notation about its new home. I trusted Riley, but I also knew he was likely to lose that notebook.

"You two are comedy." Pivoting, I saw Magnolia in the door-way. "Listening to you bitching and snapping at each other on a dreary Friday morning is better than candy."

"Gigi," Riley called, his deep voice booming.

She approached, immediately leaning in for a hug and brushing her lips over my cheek, and though I'd defended this exact behavior a couple of days ago, it felt different now. The embrace she offered Riley was quick, and then she shifted toward me, smiling.

"What about the backsplash? Tearing that out too?" she asked. It was covered in a thick layer of glue and decades of dirt, but there was something pristine under it all.

"No, that just needs some attention," I said, purposefully stepping away. "It can be cleaned up, and it will look better and last longer than anything we could replace it with."

She peered at the tile, nodding. "Sounds good. What else are we looking at today?"

"There's a plumbing issue, a fireplace issue, and a flooring issue. Take your pick," Riley said.

"I love plumbing," she said, shooting a wink in my direction. "I always like getting my hands on the pipes."

I led the way to the second floor, taking two steps at a time while Magnolia and Riley recounted last night's football game. They were both New England sports fanatics, yet held very different views on players, coaches, and game strategy.

"Here's the issue," I said, interrupting their playoff predic-tion debate. "The pipes throughout the property need to be replaced; we knew that. At every other junction, we have rotted or missing floors and it's very easy to install new supply lines.

But we have immaculate penny-drop tile in here, and we're not disturbing it."

"Now we're trying to find a magician plumber," Riley said.

"Yeah," she said, squatting to trace the black-and-white tile pattern. "You'd never match these, not unless you found a box in the attic or something. These were custom."

"I want to go in through the first floor ceiling," I said, ignoring Riley's shuddering groan behind me. This wasn't his preferred plan. "It's a standard flat ceiling, and cutting into it is the only way to retrofit the plumbing and preserve these floors. I don't care if it's a pain in the ass or really fucking expensive; it's the best solution."

Magnolia leaned back on her haunches, her lips pursed as she considered this. "I never would have thought of ripping out a ceiling to save a floor, however..." She wrapped her hand around my forearm to pull herself up, but she didn't retreat. "It sounds like your best bet. What's left? Fireplaces and flooring?"

"It's fine," I stammered, backing out into the hallway. "The fireplaces just need servicing, and maybe some new flashing before we get a heavy snowstorm."

Magnolia paced the hallway, her fingers running over the bird's-eye oak walls. "Flooring?"

"The genius here wants to cannibalize the planks from one room to make up for the ones we're missing in the dining room and main parlor," Riley said.

She sidled up beside me, elbowing my bicep. "Which room?"

"Fourth floor. The maid's room," I said. She was close, well into my personal space with her body angled toward mine in a manner that spoke of intimacy and heat. I didn't know how I'd missed this before but I was seeing it now. "We can't replicate the original flooring on the first floor, and I'd rather repurpose the wood upstairs and replace it with a near-match, unless you see an alternative."

We traipsed all over the property, examining the floors, debating solutions, and eventually prying a plank from the fourth floor to confirm that it matched. Magnolia was always nearby, her fingers brushing mine as we climbed the stairs, her hand on my shoulder for balance when she studied a delicate sconce, her body crowded against mine to inspect a section of wood.

"I have some appointments on the North Shore this afternoon, but I'm going to be back in town around seven." Magnolia lifted her brows, the question obvious in her eyes. "Up for dinner? Drinks?"

Oh, holy fuck.

Riley was right. She might not be planning the wedding, but at the minimum, she was under the impression we were flirting. And I *did* like her—not in the "I'm tearing your panties off now" way, but as a friend and colleague, the "let me pick your brain about some design challenges" way.

"Not tonight," I said. I should have mentioned that I was seeing someone but I was more concerned with finishing this visit. Soon enough, she'd notice I wasn't reciprocating, and there was no sense making it awkward for her.

Magnolia accepted this without discussion, and departed after another hug and cheek-kiss. When I glanced up from shuffling the bluelines into their proper order of disciplines, Riley was leaning against the kitchen sink, a smug grin stretched across his face.

"Believe me now?" he asked. "About Gigi?"

He played the part of the barely-reformed stoner man-child, but the kid was insightful. He understood people and situations, and he knew how to boil it all down to its most essential pieces. He didn't put much of this wisdom to good use, of course.

"Don't we have other properties to see today? If you have time to be pompous, I'm not giving you enough work."

"In other words," he said under his breath. "Yes, you are aware that she's already named your children and decided where you'll live out your golden years."

"And what?" I asked, my arm flailing in his direction. "It would have killed you to jump in and help me out?"

"Sure, I could have done that." He shrugged and reshuffled the bluelines. "But ask yourself this—why didn't *you*? Not ready to let Gigi off the hook?"

"She was never *on* the hook," I yelled.

I wasn't doing that. No, that was like having my finger on the self-destruct button, and pressing it just to see what happened. I'd been finding creative ways to destroy myself for years, but I wasn't there anymore. Well, not in the past eleven days. Longer if we excused the momentary lapse in judgment at Alibi.

"You're blind if you think the girl who wants to *handle some pipe* isn't on your hook," he said.

"She's a nice girl and I don't want to embarrass her." I grabbed the designs from him, again placing them in the correct order. I didn't know what the hell he was thinking, putting the civil page above hazmat, or mechanical behind electrical. "Do me a favor next time and intercept," I said.

My day couldn't end fast enough. I needed to go to Tiel and get lost in her, and fuck away every shadow that developed around the edges.

Nothing I did made the time move more quickly. I raced through my late afternoon meetings and delegated some walk-throughs to Riley with the hope he wouldn't fuck things up, and worked myself into a good fit of fury while I inched through traffic on the Longfellow Bridge.

The only benefit to this misery was I had plenty of time to plan what I intended to do when I reached Tiel's apartment.

Unfortunately, I forgot all of it when she opened the door.

"Hey," she said. Grinning, she looked me up and down as she leaned against the door. I knew my hair was a fucking disaster from dragging my hands through it in traffic, my tie and collar were wrenched open, my glasses were off kilter, and I probably looked a little wild.

I felt a little wild.

I stepped toward her and said, "I have been thinking about you. All. Day."

"Sounds unproductive." She gave me a displeased look but moved closer. Her fingers walked down my tie, stopping to study the tiny blue shells against the pink background. She played at being unhurried but her wide, eager eyes gave it all away.

"Get over here," I said. Her hands were in my hair and my lips were on her before the words were out of my mouth, and somehow I managed to kick the door shut behind us in the process. "Bedroom."

"Sofa," she murmured against my lips. Her hand wrapped around my tie, she yanked me into the living room. She was a little fireball, all rowdy and starved for this brand of affection.

"Bedroom," I growled, steering her toward the hallway.

"It's like nine feet away," she said. "Sofa's right here."

"I will be fucking you in the bedroom," I said. "I will also be spanking the shit out of you in there, so unless you'd like to sit on the sofa alone, I recommend you take your sweet ass down that hallway."

Tiel released my tie and broke out of my hold. I was certain this was the moment she'd be punching me in the face for being a prick, but she bit her bottom lip, gave me a wicked grin, and scampered down the hall while tossing her clothes off behind her.

Then I realized she wanted me like this, raw and demanding and prowling for her, and in that place I knew I wasn't keeping anyone on the hook. I was all in for this girl, and every time her body bowed under my hands, I started to believe she was all in for me, too.

SOME ORGASMS WERE like fender benders. Quick, generally harmless, forgettable.

Others were more like backing into a bus. More damage, more memories.

And a select few were like a fucking train wreck. Blacked out, body-splitting. They turned you inside out and back again.

As I lay face down on my bed, Sam's hand caressing my tender backside, I knew I'd never been so still before. There were tunes in my head—always—but I wasn't fidgeting, nodding, tapping, fiddling, swaying. Just my breath, in and out, and the occasional shuddering aftershock from that train-wreck orgasm.

"What are you doing next week?" he asked.

Chewing my lip, I tried to remember my schedule. It wasn't as easy as it sounded. Without calling up the calendar on my phone, I wasn't sure where I was supposed to be at any point in time. Too many details.

"Oh, next week is the holiday. Yeah. The college closes at one on Wednesday, but of course I'm teaching at noon. I've been going back and forth on whether I let those poor souls off easy and cancel class."

"And then?" he asked. "The rest of the week?"

"Um, I don't know." I wanted to melt into the mattress and sleep for at least four hundred years.

Ellie and I used to host a big Thanksgiving dinner and invite stray students from Berklee. We both knew how much it sucked to be too poor—or, in my case, too disowned—to get home for the holidays, and we didn't want anyone feeling that way.

It wasn't anything elaborate, given that neither of us grew up in homes where we celebrated the Norman Rockwell version of Thanksgiving. My family thought turkey was best accompanied by pastitsio, souvlaki with tzatziki, and rice-stuffed grape leaves, and on more than a few occasions, substituted lamb for turkey altogether. Nonetheless, Ellie and I DVR'd every holiday episode on the Food Network, watched them repeatedly, and cobbled together some semblance of dinner for our guests.

This year, we passed the torch to a married couple who joined the faculty before Ellie went on tour. That was a big improvement over wrangling a raw turkey into submission.

"Studio time. Grading papers. Nothing special," I yawned.

"My brother and his wife—"

He paused, glancing at me purposefully, and I swore he did it to let the word 'wife' simmer between us. Either he wanted me to know he hadn't touched this lady, or he really liked that terminology. Couldn't be sure.

"They're having a thing at their place. You could come with me, if you wanted." Sam grabbed the satiny duvet from where it was bunched on the edge of the mattress, and pulled it over us. "Shannon won't be there, though. Apparently she's going to a spa in the Southwest which seems really fucking strange, even for her."

Snuggling closer to Sam, I ran my fingers through his chest hair, and pressed my ear against his heart. "I probably should have said something a long time ago," I sighed. "But I don't do families."

"That's good to know," he said. "I'm only interested in you

doing me, and the more I think about it, I would actually break my brothers' arms if they got anywhere near you."

"Charming, perv. Real charming."

"Don't even pretend you don't love me," he said, slapping my backside.

It was a playful snap, but exactly what I needed. There was some relief associated with his hand cracking across my skin, a calm pleasure I'd never tapped into before. I didn't understand why I liked half the things he did to me, but I didn't care.

"So what do you mean, you don't do families?"

"I can't—" Edgy impatience started swirling in my stomach, and I dragged my hands through my hair. I pushed away from Sam and grabbed his tank, pulling it over my head. "I'm not good with it all. I'm not the girl you bring home to meet the parents."

I knew my mistake the second those words slipped off my tongue but before I could backtrack, Sam said, "You don't have to worry about that with me."

He'd shared details of his mother's death over the past months, and it was obvious it left a huge, gaping, ugly scar on him, but he'd never talked about his father. Anytime I asked, Sam responded with, "He's dead" and wouldn't elaborate.

"I'm sorry. It's just…" I folded my legs beneath me, staring at Sam from the other end of the bed. He looked so cozy and precious against my pillows, like he belonged there. "I'm terrible with families. A walking disaster."

"That's ridiculous. You're the person who seduces random people in elevators," he said, pointing to himself. "You can convince otherwise polite, chaste men to get drunk and dance with you." Another exaggerated gesture toward himself. "You know the life story of every barista in town. You persuade non-verbal children to play the piano, and play it well. You have more followers on your YouTube channel than the population of Wyoming. You aren't terrible with anyone."

"You wanted to be seduced," I whispered. "It just took you two months to realize it."

"You can bet your ass I wanted you seducing me," he said. "Now get over here and tell me the real reason you don't want to meet my deranged family."

Sam tended toward slim, with long, lean muscles, but it never escaped my notice that he was strong, especially when he was dragging me across the bed like I was a doll. I kind of loved it.

Trapped beneath him with my hands pinned over my head, there was no easy out, and at this point, there was no reason to avoid his questions. "I'm not like you, Sam. I don't understand big, involved families. I can't even begin to explain my own."

"Sunshine, I don't understand them either. It's more like love and tolerate," he laughed.

"Well, that's kind of the problem," I said. "They've never tolerated me. Everything I do—moving away from home, going to Juilliard, getting married, getting divorced, being a 'lowlife' as my mother likes to put it—mortifies them. I'm a giant embarrassment, and unless I'm moving back to Jersey and waiting tables, they don't want anything to do with me. I see them maybe once a year, and it's only for funerals or weddings. I just don't fit in with families."

With my wrists locked in Sam's grip, I couldn't wipe the tears off my cheeks. I hadn't cried about this in ages, but being there—vulnerable and exposed and completely safe—brought it all back to the surface.

"And what happens when you call them on that shit?" he asked, his thumb brushing my tears away.

An incredulous laugh burst from my throat. "That's not how my family operates," I said. "There's plenty of the big, fat Greek family stereotype to go around, but we don't have thoughtful conversations about feelings. They tell me they don't approve, they make a lot of pained, pinched faces at me, and I do my own thing. That's how it goes."

His brows furrowed and he gave me a confused grimace. "You've never said 'Mom, Dad, I'm really fucking talented and successful, and if you have a problem, that's tough shit'?"

It was strange how he seemed much more comfortable vocalizing himself with his family than with me, and somehow the reverse was true for me. "No, Sam, not really." I shrugged, my attention turning to the beautiful definition in his shoulders and biceps. "We sort of had that conversation when I decided to go to Juilliard and they weren't digging that plan. They said it wouldn't work out, that I wasn't good enough for that level of study, that I was on my own. They didn't see why I couldn't go to the local college like everyone else. In their eyes, leaving was disrespectful to my family."

"Oh that's nothing," Sam said, and my eyes flashed to him, stunned. "My father hated me until his final breath. I probably deserved some of that because the last thing I said to him was that the rapey demons in the eternal fires of hell were going to have a blast with him."

"You're too pretty to hate," I said, aiming for some levity.

"While that is true," he said, "it didn't stop him from kicking me out of the house when I was seventeen because—according to him—I was a disgusting homosexual who shouldn't have been born. If society was still roasting witches at the stake, I'm confident he would have put a dress on me, claimed I cast a spell on our dog, and moved me to the front of the line. He also found great pleasure in blaming me and my siblings for my mother's death which is absolutely fucking illogical but he never trafficked in reality."

Okay. So that was why Sam didn't like talking about his father.

Fair enough.

"Families are really fucking complicated," he said. "And that's exactly why you should spend some time with mine. They're the loudest motherfuckers I've ever met, and we give each other a lot of shit, but they're already Team Tiel." I gave him a skeptical look but he continued. "All I heard about this week was how much they wanted to meet you."

"Have they met many of your other *friends*?"

"Don't do that," he said, his voice heavy with warning. "You know damn well they haven't, just like you know *friend* isn't even close to the right word for you."

"Then what is?"

I still needed structure and definition. There was evidence suggesting that we were in a committed relationship but I required the words and I wanted them plain and clear, like the ink on his skin.

He shifted, bringing his knees to my hips and squeezing me tight. Leaning down, he pushed the tank aside and pulled my nipple into his mouth and oh, sweet jellybeans of joy, he could whip me into needy, breathless heat in no time at all. If the hard cock nudging my belly button was any indication, I wouldn't be waiting long.

"All I want to call you is mine," he said against my breast. "You're mine, and I'm yours."

"HEY," I said around my straw. I was mastering the art of walking, drinking, and talking today, all while lugging both my violin and viola down Boylston Street. This was as close to an aerobic workout as I got. "The prepster wants me to meet his family. Explain to me why this won't end in all sorts of disaster."

Ellie groaned into the phone. "Lady, why are you calling me before dawn? This is obscene and you need to learn a thing or two about time zones."

"I need your wisdom and guidance," I said.

I heard the rustling of sheets and several irritable groans before she said, "All right. Lay it on me."

Sipping my iced cappuccino, I darted across Hemenway Street. While the college was technically closed today, I knew the studio spaces would be accessible and I was desperate to get in some practice time. I needed to figure things out, and music helped me do that.

"Like I said, Sam invited me to meet his family. Today. For Thanksgiving."

Ellie coughed and I heard her guzzling a drink. "And why is that a problem?"

"Because families hate me," I yelled. "He's The Beatles and I'm The Doors."

"While that is a lovely comparison, I think it's worth reminding yourself that your family is simply different. They're butthurt about a lot of shit, and their reactions are extreme. Most families don't operate that way, and plenty are very nice."

"That doesn't account for Dillon's family," I said. "They couldn't stand me."

"Ah, the one who shall not be named," she sighed. "They're also anomalous. If we want to trot down memory lane, let me say this—they were too busy setting him up to be the next Michael Bublé to let anything get in his way. That was about him, not you. Lightning doesn't strike the same spot three times."

"Okay, yeah, but..." I slurped the remains of my coffee and immediately wanted another. "But I'm not 'meet the family' girl. It's too, I don't know, involved."

"You're also not 'freak out over little things' girl. What is this really about?" she asked.

"I don't know. I'm not into big families, and Sam's family is as big as they come."

Ellie snorted. "That's a lame non-excuse. You don't give a fuck about what anyone thinks...unless you actually care whether they like you. Or maybe," she said, "the prepster cares whether they like you, and you care about the prepster."

My stomach rumbled as I let myself into the studio, and I knew I should have grabbed a bagel with that coffee. "Well," I said, hedging, "that might be part of it."

"Can I also mention that your interpretation of the variations between The Beatles and The Doors is based upon extensive analysis, and not necessarily the view shared by the majority? At their core, those are essentially both male-dominated, tradi-tion-averse pop bands that capitalized on the late sixties social climate that embraced anything countercultural. Really," she said, and I knew I was in for a patented Ellie Tsai random analogy, "they're peanut butter and almond butter. Very different taste but same philosophy and application."

"That's helpful, Eleanorah. Really helpful," I grumbled.

"Make one of those filo dough pumpkin pies that everyone loves—the one with the spice that I like—then have a drink, don't let the prepster leave your side, and make them love you. Bring your awesome sauce and you're good." I grumbled, not sharing her confidence, and she continued. "The sex is respectable?"

"Yes," I said, and it came out too quick, too certain for Ellie to miss the emphatic tenor of my voice.

She laughed. "Then meet his family. Just don't get drunk and puke all over them. That would not be a good start."

"Shut up," I said. "I'm going into the studio. You go back to sleep."

HERE'S the problem with me: I knew how to roll with all the punches and I was exceedingly confident in most areas—put an instrument in my hands, and I'd rock your socks off—but my wobbly spots were about as strong as gravy.

When I was in that wobble, I wasn't quite myself. I retreated, reverted, and put all of my personality in my back pocket. I was sweaty-nervous and sarcastic—not witty sarcastic, either; sharp, cutting sarcastic—and I couldn't climb far enough out of my shell to have painless, civil conversations with anyone.

I landed in that wobble every time I went home to New Jersey, and now, standing beside Sam, pie in hand, in the elevator headed toward his brother's loft.

I'd pushed this off all day, first devoting the entire morning to the studio and then mixing up some gingery pumpkin pies. I didn't ignore Sam's texts throughout the day, not entirely, but I didn't offer any indication that I was looking forward to this exercise. I'd spent a ridiculous amount of time selecting the navy-and-poppies dress with the wide, red sash and dark leggings, and I even considered wearing heels for a split second. That was how I knew I'd really fallen in deep.

His hand traveled from my waist down my hip and under the hem of my dress. "Have I told you how gorgeous you are today?"

I let out a tense laugh and shook my head. "I don't believe you have."

"Well then," he said, squeezing my ass. "You are completely fucking gorgeous, and these leggings are making me incapable of speaking coherently. I'm going to enjoy peeling those off later."

Bunching the tail of his shirt in my hand, I drew Sam closer to me. "Don't abandon me, okay?"

The elevator doors opened, but we didn't move. "I'm not going anywhere if you're not," he said.

Sam's brother and sister-in-law lived in one of the most posh waterfront buildings in town, and their loft was an eclectic blend of modern and vintage. It didn't make a ton of sense, but it was awesome. I loved the funky velvet settee in front of the sleek marble fireplace, and the colorful artwork flanking the long wall of ocean-side windows.

We found everyone gathered around a long table off the kitchen, take-out cartons and wine bottles spread between them. I counted six heads—one more than I expected—but saw the threads of resemblance between them quickly.

Talk about good-looking men.

They weren't carbon copies of each other, but I knew they belonged together. Tall and strong with glints of auburn in their hair. Sam was shorter, leaner, but he was definitely one of them.

They were laughing hysterically and didn't notice us until Sam cleared his throat.

A little blonde popped up from her seat and scrambled over to us. "Hi," she squealed. "You must be Tiel. I'm Lauren, and I'm so happy to meet you. Come on, sit down."

Lauren cooed over the pie I handed her, squeezing my shoulders and insisting I didn't need to bring anything but that she adored every variety of Thanksgiving dessert. She steered me toward a seat and loaded up my glass with white wine.

"So you've met Patrick and Andy," she said, gesturing to the opposite end of the table.

I glanced at them, forcing a smile. Andy was one of those ageless women who could be anywhere between twenty-two and forty-four, and would look that pristine her entire life. Sure, she might earn some silver hairs along the way, but she'd always be beautiful and unshakably cool.

"This is Matthew." Lauren dropped her hands on his shoulders. "He belongs to me." He tugged her onto his lap while she giggled, but that didn't stop the introductions. "That's Riley," she said, pointing to the man on my left. "And Nick."

"I've met you before," Nick said, rising to shake my hand from across the table. "Where have I met you?"

"I have no idea," I said.

Don't be awful, I reminded myself. *Talk normal. Smile.*

I'd remember eyes like those. Nick was darker than Sam's siblings, but he was equally drool-worthy. It was rather laughable how many attractive men were packed around this one table.

Smile. Stop glaring at them.

"It'll come to me," Nick said.

"I thought you weren't with us today," Sam said from the kitchen.

Nick grabbed a container and stuck his fork inside. "Technically, I'm on call," he said. "Until midnight. Then, you know, it's time to rage. Or whatever people who have lives do these days."

"And by *rage*, you mean you'll be hanging out at the hospital?" Sam said. Nick laughed and grunted in agreement. Sam returned with a glass of water, and settled beside me with his hand on my thigh. "Is this tapas?"

"Yes," Matt said, nodding resolutely. "With the Black Widow

in New Mexico, no one reminded Tom to pick up the turkey. So, we called Toro last night."

"Who's Tom?" I asked. I knew all about the nicknames—Shannon as the Black Widow, Patrick as Optimus Prime, Matt as Juggernaut, Lauren as Miss Honey, Riley as RISD, and Andy as Princess Jasmine—but hadn't wormed Sam's out of him yet. I was hoping it wasn't Tom.

"Shannon's assistant," he said. "Has anyone determined whether she's actually in New Mexico?"

"We are not talking about this. She's entitled to a little space," Lauren said. "Instead of dragging all that drama out like a prize pig at the county fair, why don't you two tell us how you met?"

"It certainly wasn't the way Sam usually meets women," I said, and *shit*, I sounded so antagonistic. He turned to me, his eyes searching my face for some explanation. Everyone else laughed and it was obvious they were comfortable busting each other's balls, but I saw how much my comment hurt him.

"We met over Labor Day weekend," Sam said, his gaze focused on me. "Tiel introduced me to bluegrass, and a few other things."

"Andy said you're a professor," Lauren prompted.

They were harmless, well-intentioned questions, but I hated them. I didn't want to be fodder for their rumor mill. I'd seen enough of it with my mother and aunts. They criticized everything about the women my uncles and male cousins brought to family dinners. Either they didn't help in the kitchen enough or they had too many new ideas about roasting lamb, or they were too nice, and that was clearly an indication they were fake bitches. It was always something.

"Adjunct," I said. "I teach music therapy classes at Berklee."
Don't be a bitch. Say more than the utter minimum.

"That sounds fascinating," she said. "I'd love to pick your brain some day. I run an independent school, and getting a music program going is one of my priorities for next year."

"Like, your own little Barbie dream school?"

For real: stop being a bitch.

To her credit, Lauren laughed off my comment as if it was the best thing she'd heard all night, but Sam continued staring me, his eyes narrowed as he tried to understand my freakish behavior.

"What's wrong?" he whispered.

"Nothing." I shook my head, and his expression turned doubtful.

"Is this area home for you? Do you have any pets? What's your last name? Have you ever seen *Dexter*? What's your position on the Celtics' best year, and full disclosure, Pierce, Allen, and Garnett outshine Bird, Parish, and McHale any day of the week," Riley asked. "Come on, we need details. This boy's turned into a steel trap."

Nick snapped his fingers and pumped his fist in the air. "You did the seminar on the comparison of music therapy and pharmacological sedation using chloral hydrate in pediatric EEG captures."

"What were you doing there?"

Just don't be bitchy. These are nice people. Don't be bitchy.

I thought back to that presentation at the children's hospital. I'd only stumbled into that research because one of my buddies couldn't stomach the drugs used to put him under for certain tests, and I was convinced he didn't need them in the first place.

"I cut brains," he said. "You know, for medical purposes. I had eight first-year pediatric neuro-surgical interns with me." He shrugged and looked at his palm, tapping his finger there as if he was counting something. "I don't let them sedate toddlers anymore unless they've already tried and failed non-pharma measures, and I can only think of a few cases."

"I'm glad it's working," I said.

I dedicated two years of my life to that project. I should be able to punch up the enthusiasm for real-world application.

Nick asked, "You're at Berklee?" I nodded. Nodding prevented more douchery from spilling out of my mouth.

"What else are you working on? I have plenty of residents who need to publish, and enslaving them brings a lot of joy to my life."

"Well," I murmured.

Don't. Be. Bitchy.

My current research could be summarized on a small sticky note, and there was no way in hell I was getting in front of the dissertation defense committee this year.

I wanted to leave so desperately. Just get up and *go*. Nick meant well, that was plain to see, but I required more breathing room than this family allowed. They were all so *much*. "I've been applying some new therapeutic approaches with children on the autism spectrum. Too early to draw any correlations."

"All right," Patrick said. He leaned forward and gestured toward me with his wineglass. "You're obviously very intelligent. What the hell do you see in the runt?"

At first, I didn't understand who Patrick was referring to, but then I heard Sam chuckling beside me. *The runt.*

"Don't answer that," Andy said, shaking her head. "What he meant to say was Lauren and I go to an incredible winter farmers' market on Saturdays, and you should come with us this weekend."

Please stop. I don't belong anywhere near your little sister-wives group.

"Yeah, you have to come to yoga. Even if you hate yoga, this chick will make you love it," Lauren added, pointing to Andy.

"Is that a requirement here?" I asked. "Compulsory vegetable shopping? Let me guess—matching Lululemon workout clothes, too? Is that the price of admission to the clubhouse?"

The table fell silent, and they couldn't excuse that one as caustic humor. I was officially standing in epic, flaming bitch territory. They both stared at me, frowning, and then turned to each other with puzzled expressions. Sam edged my wineglass closer to me, a clear signal to drink up and shut up.

"When are you going to tell us about Scotland?" he asked,

jutting his chin toward Patrick and Andy.

"You won. They're not married," Riley groaned.

"It was cold and wet and Scottish," Patrick said. "Otherwise unremarkable, considering we spent the whole time digging up rocks."

"You have an impressive ability to not enjoy things," Matt said.

"Yeah, it's mostly derived from living with you for the past three decades," Patrick replied. "But I will say this—Scotland had decent scotch, and quite the healthy supply of it."

The discussion moved into a review of their overseas journey, and the locations everyone wanted to visit. Nick talked about his interest in a Doctors Without Borders trip, and Matt mentioned his sister, Erin, and her extensive research travels, but Sam stayed quiet.

It was a nice reprieve from their prying questions, and I was able to sit back and breathe. I was horrified by the snarky things I'd said to Andy or Lauren, and I couldn't bring myself to make eye contact with them. In this mood, I'd inadvertently maim them with my scowly faces.

They picked at the remaining tapas but soon turned their interest to dessert. Lauren attempted to distribute slices of pie, but the guys overrode her, and dug in with spoons. Knowing Sam's preference for cleanliness—and his flippant comfort with discarding anything that didn't look 'right'—I expected him to recoil when the dishes came our way. Instead, he took a small bite from an untouched corner, and whispered to me, "I don't know what you put in there, but I'm a fan."

"That's high praise considering you primarily eat raw nuts and greens," I said.

He offered a chastened grin, and said, "I know what I like."

Riley growled, a sound vaguely similar to the one I'd heard from Sam on many occasions, but from Riley it was cartoon comical. The top four buttons of his shirt gaped open, and he slipped his hand inside to scratch his sternum. He looked around the table and said, "I feel like doing something irresponsible tonight." His gaze landed on Nick. "Come on, Acevedo. Let's have an adventure."

"You should know," Matt laughed. "Riley's version of irresponsible adventure involves waking up in the bed of a truck on its way to Canada or getting his nipples pierced by a random guy in an alley."

Riley rubbed his chest, frowning. "Those hurt, man. I still have scars, physical *and* emotional."

"He's also been permanently barred from Howl At The Moon," Patrick added. "Something about getting naked and dancing on a piano."

"As if that wasn't standard fare," Riley muttered. "And if we're airing all the dirty secrets, why don't we talk about the party after Matt and Miss Honey's wedding?"

"Nope." Nick shook his head, his gaze never wandering from his glass. "Let me stop you right there."

"Why?" Matt asked. He looked between Sam, Riley, and Nick. "What happened?"

Riley stared at Nick, smirking. A silent exchange of severe expressions, raised eyebrows, and head shakes occurred while the group watched, then finally Riley laughed. "Nothing," he said, spooning another bite of pumpkin pie. "Acevedo knows how to have a good time. Not surprising for the good doctor."

I was missing a ton of subtext here, but from the looks of it, I wasn't the only one. Matt and Lauren were reminiscing in hushed tones about their nuptials while Patrick leaned toward Andy, brushed her hair from her shoulder, and whispered something against her ear. Everyone seemed genuinely nice— or, nice in the 'we're family so we talk a lot of shit' way—and amusing, but it was impossible to keep up with it all. There was so much history simmering between these people, entire lifetimes that I'd never fully understand.

Nick and Riley started planning their night out, and I could not have given Sam more insistent glances if my eyeballs popped out of my skull and pounded on his chest. I'd been outrageously impolite and I wasn't comfortable being grilled by his family, and I just wanted to leave.

We eventually made it out of their loft, but not without a carousel of hugs and swapped phone numbers, and the same incessant request to spend more time getting to know me.

"Are you okay?" Sam asked once the elevator doors closed. He pulled me tight to his chest, his forehead crinkled with confusion. "You did *not* seem okay in there."

I edged away from him, positioning myself on the opposite side of the elevator. "I'm not on board with this, Sam. I told you. I don't do families."

He leaned against the elevator wall, his arms crossed. "You know why they asked so many questions? They're trying to figure out why a smart, beautiful woman has given me more than ten minutes of her attention. They can't fathom someone like you wanting to hang around someone like me."

"Meaning what?" I yelled. "You could have anyone you wanted. You could find a pretty girl who spoke French and wore pearls, and knew how to pick out bottles of Chianti."

"Uh-huh," he murmured. "That's not the consensus from that group, and in case you haven't noticed, Chianti, French, and pearls are not high on my priority list."

The doors opened and I moved through the lobby and to the street quickly. It was the type of cold weather that immediately resulted in a runny nose, and I was probably walking in the wrong direction, but I just needed to get away from it all. The wintery air bit my skin but the shock was a refreshing calm on my system.

I was being irrational, and I knew it. But I required breathing space, freedom, independence.

I wasn't part of anyone's tribe.

My friends were abundant and I had deep, caring relationships with many, but Ellie was the only person I truly trusted. Not once in the past eleven years had she ever turned me away when I needed her, and there'd never been a whisper of doubt that we accepted each other, baggage and all, implicitly.

Everyone else in my life—all the people who I should have been able to rely on—had given me reasons to walk away, and not a single reason to return.

And Sam...I wanted to carve out a special spot for him, and there were so many moments when I believed he deserved one, too. But I couldn't let that lightning strike again. I couldn't let myself be abandoned, and it was too soon to know anything for certain.

"I don't do families that are all up in each other's business. I see my family for deaths and weddings because they can't respect boundaries. If yoga and farmers' markets are part of the deal, I can't."

"Would you wait a godforsaken second, Tiel?" Sam jogged to catch up, coming to a full stop in front of me with his hands braced on my arms. "Yoga and farmers' markets aren't part of the deal," he said. "The only deal is that we like hanging out together, and sometimes we do that naked."

I blew out a breath and shook my head. I was in desperate need of a tissue and the wind was blowing my hair in nine different directions, and somewhere beneath my wobbly spot, I knew I was hurting Sam.

I didn't want that. That player veneer ran thin, and underneath it, he had his own wobbly spots, too. He was sensitive and sweet, and he needed someone to love all over him the way he deserved.

Sniffling, I said, "Maybe we could go back to my place now."

He produced a handkerchief from his pocket and waited while I blew my nose. "My place," he said.

"We're closer to mine," I said, nodding in Cambridge's general direction.

"Equidistant," he said. "My place."

I'd never visited Sam's house, but he always had a renovation story to tell. Part of me expected him to be living in a full-blown construction site with tarps and jackhammers and wet paint. "But we can make almond milk mudslides at my place. Then we can turn the tunes up and dance in our underwear."

He brought his thumb to my face, tracing my cheeks, nose, and mouth before laying a kiss on my lips. "That does sound like a better idea."

One of my favorite Cat Stevens songs was playing when we got in his car, and he let me discuss the intricacies of the music while we headed to my apartment. I needed to shake off my nervous energy, and Sam indulged, asking questions and letting me talk the entire time.

I was halfway through blending the modified mudslides when Sam placed his hands on my hips, his palms circling over my clothes. There was a hot insistence in his touch, and he soon dipped beneath my dress and inside my leggings.

"Don't move," he ordered.

His body shifted, and he dropped to his knees behind me. True to his word, he peeled my leggings down, one aching inch at a time. His mouth moved over my exposed skin, kissing and licking, and when my clothes were bunched at my ankles, he pushed my legs apart. He drove his fingers inside me, stroking and thrumming my clit until I was bent over the countertop and begging.

And then Sam's fingers were gone, abandoning me seconds before I came, and I was ready to scream.

Springing up, I rounded on him, my eyes as furious as I felt, and he just smiled. "Did that not go the way you wanted?"

"Rude!" I yelled. "Very rude!"

I was wet—not simply aroused—and I sensed my fluid coating my thighs. It was almost embarrassing, and I was some-what convinced I'd find a puddle on the floor very soon.

"Maybe." He grabbed a handful of my dress and yanked me against his chest. "You've had a rough night," he said, and I nodded. "It's going to get a little rougher."

My default reaction to overwhelming situations was laughter, and when those words washed over me, I dissolved into giggles despite his dark, severe tone.

"Oh, Sunshine," Sam hissed, slipping his fingers into my mouth. I tasted myself on him, and I wanted to be revolted but I was too fucking turned on to care. His eyes darkened as I sucked, his groan hoarse and exactly as desperate as I felt. "I am going to own you tonight."

He pushed me against the refrigerator and freed me from my leggings and panties. Ducking under my dress, his tongue swirled over my clit and it only took a few well-placed licks to prime my body for explosion.

And once again, he stopped a minute too soon. Wailing, I beat my fists against the refrigerator. This was torture, and he knew it.

"Saaaaaaammm," I moaned.

He offered a knowing grin and placed feathery kisses on my thighs and pelvic bone and just barely between my legs. "Do not doubt that I'll gag you."

"I'll finish this myself," I said, but the threat sounded whiny and petulant.

He chuckled, his warm breath tickling my leg, and he continued teasing. He didn't believe me.

Unable to see past the screeching urge for release ringing through my body, I bunched my dress at my waist and brought my hand to my center. I'd barely grazed my clit when Sam's hand curled around my wrist and pinned it to my side.

"Don't you dare," he said. He stood, leaning into me while I squirmed, angling for his hard length where I needed it. "*I'll* make you come. Only me, and only when I'm ready."

"You're such a dick," I yelled, burrowing into his shoulder.

"And you love it." He dragged his scruffy chin across my chest, inflaming my nerves and drawing out a shiver that didn't seem to stop. "How long should I make you wait?"

I shook my head, whimpering, "No more."

"Should I fuck you right here?" Sam asked. He lifted my

hands above my head and speared his hips against me, and the impact sent vibrations rippling through my body. "Or against the counter? Your ass looked fucking edible bent over like that."

He traced the line of my arm, over my breast and belly, and brushed my folds. It was a delicate touch, like he was stroking something incomprehensibly fragile, and desire sparked in my veins until I was trembling.

It was an agonizing, throbbing need, but Sam didn't stop. His body trapped me there, his chest flush with mine, his grip tight on my wrists, and I could feel the drumbeat of his heart pounding in time with mine. He whispered filthy things about how much he loved touching me and teasing me, and how he wanted my arousal dripping all over his wrist, and that my pussy belonged to him.

I hated hearing those words—my ladybits were my own, thank you—but I craved them, too. It was primal and animalistic, and if my hands were free, I would have closed my fist around his cock and said the exact same thing.

I took tremendous pride in belonging only to myself, but right now, with my body heaving in spectacularly painful need, I wanted to be Sam's. He could claim my pussy, my orgasms, my everything.

"Do I need to restrain you?" he asked, and even the scrape of his teeth on my earlobe was too much stimulation.

"Sam," I rasped. "*Please*."

He released me, but I didn't have long to miss the weight of his body. He led me into the bedroom, yanking the rest of my clothes off in the process. His were quick to follow, and then he was over me, his palm splayed between my breasts, pressing hard.

He pushed into me, slow and deliberate, and he kept me anchored in place while he stroked all the way in, his hips snug against mine, and then all the way out. I didn't think it was possible for him to torture me any more than he had, but this —*this* was the most licentious torture imaginable.

Eventually, he shifted his hand down my body until the heel of his palm rested over my mound. When I edged up to meet his thrusts, that pressure sent hot, crackling snaps of electricity through me.

"Oh, fuck, Sam," I cried, my shoulders digging into the mattress for more leverage.

"You want to come for me, sweetheart?" he asked, as if I'd been holding out on him. I made some hysterical, mewling sound and he smiled, nodding. His jaw locked, his strokes deepening, slamming into me as I arched my back.

I knew the minute he came because his face always took on the same expression of serene suffering, and he'd groan my name, low and gravelly, like a secret prayer. I let myself believe that moment belonged to me, that his body couldn't possibly react that way to anyone else.

Just as I was pulled under by that warm, soothing orgasm, he ground his palm against me, and that wave morphed into a fucking tsunami. Every muscle twitched and sighed, the spasms rolling through me as if they'd never stop, and tears streamed down my face.

I'd never cried during sex before, and I wasn't sure why I was crying now. Sam folded me into his arms, and his fingers tangled in my hair while my quiet tears fell. He didn't say anything, and he didn't need to. He held me, inviting me to be vulnerable and raw without judgment. And that was when I knew, when I heard it.

I love you.

I love you.

I love you.

I wanted to say it, scream it, sigh it into his skin. I wanted him to know he was *ruining* me for other men, and that when I stripped away everything, I couldn't imagine any other men in my life. And it wasn't even about the sex; it was him.

But…we were nowhere near those types of declarations. We were still floating in ambiguous oblivion; we might be having

sex and meeting the family, but we had assigned no name or
structure to this.

"How did you know," I started, clearing the lump in my
throat. "How did you know I needed that?"

He thumbed the trail of moisture from my face and smiled,
shrugging. "I wish I could explain." He laughed and pressed a
kiss to my lips. "I just know what to do when I touch you."

Ruined. I was so fucking *ruined*.

Patting his chest, I nodded toward his glucose monitor. That
activity was longer than I realized, and he hadn't eaten anything
for hours. "You should get a snack."

He kissed my forehead. "Are you going to be all right for a
few minutes?" I nodded while he reconnected his pump. He
gave it a foul expression as it registered his levels. "Okay. You
get under the covers and decide what we're watching tonight."

Sam returned quickly, one hand loaded with Turkish apri-
cots, the other gripping a bottle of mango juice, and a jar of
pistachios in the crook of his elbow. I snuggled up to him while
he ate, knowing he needed to focus on himself right now. After
ten minutes, he blew out a breath, and I asked, "Better?" He
murmured in agreement. "Side note. Why do they call you 'the
runt'?"

"Is it not obvious?" he laughed.

"No," I said. "In fact, from where I'm sitting…" I hooked a
finger around the band of his boxers and peeked below. "I'd say
quite the opposite."

He pressed his hands to his eyes, rubbing. "You're such a
perv," he laughed. "Since you didn't notice, I'm four or five
inches shorter than my brothers, and they have a good twenty,
maybe thirty pounds on me. Did you see Riley? Hell, most days
I wonder whether I should be getting that kid tested for
steroids. He's huge."

"Yeah," I said, burrowing farther into his chest and dragging
my nails over his stomach. "I don't think I'd want you any other
way."

Seventeen

SAM

"KNOCK, KNOCK." Glancing up, I found Shannon leaning against my office door. "Have a minute to spare?"

Beyond Monday morning's meeting and some quick public relations conversations, I hadn't spoken to Shannon all week. She spared us the details of her spa weekend, and since she did look rejuvenated, I didn't press the issue of her whereabouts.

"Sure," I said, setting aside the notes I'd received from Matt on the Turlan property's structural updates.

"I was going to place a lunch order," she said, her voice intentionally casual. "Did you want anything?"

"I'm good," I said. I gestured toward the lidded container of Waldorf salad. "What's up?"

"Just a few things. Your dry cleaning was dropped off this morning, and it's in the back seat of your car. I checked in with your endocrinologist's office, and your next appointment is next Monday afternoon. They'll have you do some blood work too, so I blocked that time on your calendar. I sorted out your expenses from last month, and assigned costs to clients as best as I could determine. I'll need you to look it over, but that will be quick. And I had Tom arrange your travel to that conference in January, the one in Arizona." Shannon sat down and crossed her legs, focusing on the dozen or so thin bracelets on her wrist. "I was really bummed that I didn't get to meet Tiel. Everyone said she was…intriguing."

She laced her fingers together and gave me a quick look, and she knew what she was doing. She thought she could hide that landmine in the middle of her spiel and then act surprised when I flew off the fucking handle.

I'd never seen Tiel be so aggressive and hostile before—I didn't think she had it in her—though I'd also forced her into that situation. I knew about her family and all the shit back home, and I should have known it wasn't going to work out the way I anticipated. It fucking killed me to know that Tiel only had herself to lean on, and I harbored this quiet hope that she'd meet my family and never want to leave.

"Tiel *is* intriguing," I said. "I've never met anyone with so many accomplishments, and I have to practically beat them out of her. It's refreshing to meet people who don't view themselves as gifts to this planet."

"And some people are attorneys, Sam." Shannon looked away and I noticed her struggling to repress a furious scowl.

"So it wasn't rose petals and rainbows," I said, exasperated. "I seem to remember you going all corporate commando the first time Matt brought Lauren here."

"That was because Riley was being a juvenile delinquent." She rolled her eyes and dismissed my comment with a wave. "Look. I've heard several times that dinner was tense, and your guest was a hard pill to swallow. I'd just like to hear about it from you." She lifted her shoulder and brushed some lint from her lilac skirt. "Are you trying to prove a point, or going through some kind of angry girl phase?"

Okay, so I was ready to fly off that handle now. "Has it occurred to you that *we* are a bit intense, and not everyone handles this tribe the same way?"

"No, not really." She scooted the chair closer and folded her arms on my desk. "It has occurred to me that you might be having some difficulties coping with stress. We've been talking about the estate and the work at Wellesley a lot, and I know those are triggers for you. I don't think adding a toxic relationship with this girl is going to help you, and maybe it's time to get an appointment with Dr. Robertsen."

My fucking psychiatrist. The guy who convinced me I didn't need to wash my hands forty-nine times a day and kept my medicine cabinet stocked with the best psychotropic drugs he could prescribe.

"Shannon, I'm going to say this once." I pressed my palms flat on my desk and counted to twenty-six before standing. "Get the fuck out of my office."

When I pointed to the door, I noticed Riley standing there. "Hey. We're walking properties this afternoon, right?" He consulted his notebook—I was shocked he hadn't yet left it in a contractor's toolbox or on the subway—and said, "Yeah, you wanted to check out the Turlan basement now that the power washing is finished. We also have five others to see."

I gathered my things and glanced to Shannon. She hadn't moved, and I was certain this was only bolstering her belief that I needed some shock therapy. I stormed through the office and down to the basement garage, and Riley rambled on about last night's football game while I fumed. The afternoon traffic didn't help my mood, and I was tempted to turn back around and finish that conversation with Shannon.

She was entitled to an opinion. She was even entitled to voice her opinion. But she had no right to decide my relationship with Tiel was toxic when it was probably the healthiest thing I'd ever done.

"I get that you're busy being pissed right now," Riley said. "But it would be good to know what you're looking for this afternoon, otherwise I don't know what to show you."

"She's just happier when I'm a fucked-up mess, isn't she?" I said. We were parked outside the Bay Village remodel I'd handed off to Riley, but I wasn't ready to get out yet. "She doesn't actually want to fix problems, she just wants to make herself feel important."

"I'm going out on a limb and saying that's an exaggeration."

I glared at him. "Do you think I have a toxic relationship and require psychiatric intervention?"

He rolled his eyes and tucked his notebook back into his bag. "There's nothing wrong with getting help. It's not a sign of weakness, you testy little bitch." He shook his head, his fingers running through his hair. It was getting long, but he managed a decent man-bun. "Tiel's a cool cat. It'll all blow over." He jerked his thumb to the house. "Can we go inside now?"

"Why are you in such a fucking hurry?" I asked as I grabbed my coat and materials.

"I've been working on intercepting your dear friend Magnolia, and we're going to the Bruins game tonight," he said, bouncing on the sidewalk. "Did you know she's a triplet?"

I didn't have the patience for this conversation. Digging my phone from my pocket, my annoyance skyrocketed when I saw a text from Shannon.

Shannon: Please consider it. I'm worried about you.

"Yeah," I said, glaring at my screen. "Two brothers."

"I know," he groaned. "It would have been interesting if they were chicks, but at least she has some season tickets to exploit."

"You do that," I murmured, typing out a response.

Sam: Take your own advice.
Sam: And by the way – thanks for all your unconditional support.

Eighteen

SAM

WHEN TIEL OPENED THE DOOR, the internal debate started.

"You're wearing that to piss me off," I growled. That 1950s-style cocktail dress put those tits on display and I couldn't decide whether I could handle anyone else's appreciative eyes on her. I knew it was immature and territorial, but those reactions were instinctual, and I struggled to manage them.

"What is your problem now?" She glanced down at her black dress and pink flats, and fuck, she was stunning. Not many women could wear that dress without looking overly stylized, or as if they were headed to a costume party, but Tiel made it work.

Taking her into my arms, I kissed my way from her ear to the valley between her breasts. "My problem," I murmured, "is that you are going to give all these old preservation guys massive boners. There are going to be fatal heart attacks left and right. That's just negligent, Tiel."

Laughing, she yanked me up. "Seems like a good way to go."

"Good? Fucking fantastic. I'd like to die thinking about your tits, and my version of heaven is living between them." My hands skimmed up her sides and down her back. I knew I needed to attend the Preservation Society of Greater Boston's holiday party and say nice things to boring people, but I was more interested in burying myself in her until Monday morning. "What are you wearing under this?"

"You can find out later," she said. "We're already late."

"We're not missing anything," I murmured.

Dropping to my knees, I burrowed under the poufy layers of her dress while she giggled and shrieked. This was what I craved about Tiel—her playfulness, her desire to find joy in every moment of life, her willingness to get rid of anything that didn't make her happy—and so much more.

"I will be ripping these off at some point tonight," I said from under her skirts. It was too tempting to stay there, my finger sliding over her silky panties and feeling her heat up close. I pressed my lips to her mound, basking in her scent, and left a trail of bites and kisses down her thigh. I leaned back and smiled up at her, pleased with the rapid rise and fall of her chest and the blush riding her cheeks. "You wore those because you knew I'd want to tear them off."

"Yeah," she nodded. "That might have entered my thought process."

"Oh, that's my perv," I said, enveloping her in a hug. "You are so fucking gorgeous."

On the ride to the downtown venue, Tiel recounted her conversation with her best friend, Ellie, about a mishap on tour. She was so animated and free, and I hoped to hell she didn't lose it all when we arrived at the event. I hadn't mentioned that Matt and Patrick would be there, or that they'd be bringing Andy and Lauren, and it was a risky gamble. It could backfire horribly, or she'd get out of her own head long enough to show them the person I adored.

The silver lining in all of this was Shannon drawing the short straw and getting stuck at a different event across town with Riley. In the two weeks since she'd barged into my office, I hadn't discussed anything more than business with Shannon. To her credit, she hadn't revisited her comments or found back-handed ways to renew her argument.

Tiel inclined her head toward me when we entered the historic home. "You know, when we're together, we're way cooler than everyone else."

Chuckling, I said, "I'd like to think so."

Her full skirt didn't let me rest my hand on her ass the way I wanted to, but it gave me the opportunity to wrap my arm around her waist and hold her close. We mingled for two hours, and it soon became obvious that everyone was more interested in chatting with Tiel than me. Despite her issues with my family, she nailed the small talk, and my colleagues couldn't get enough of her.

She was the right balance of art for the purists, quirk for the wonks, and kind, babbling charm for the introverts. She possessed a natural quality that put people at ease and drew them out, and I knew that was what she was doing with me, too.

"You make this painless for me," I whispered to her when the conversation in our circle moved away from us.

"When you get started on hydronic heating and those roof gardens, you're unstoppable," she laughed.

Pulling her away from the crowd, I folded her into my arms and kissed her forehead. "How do you feel about Arizona?"

"Dry heat. Grand Canyon. Cactus. I haven't spent much time formulating opinions," she said, smirking. "Should I?"

"I'm going to tell you what I'm thinking right now, and I don't want you to freak on me. Okay?"

Her eyes scanned the room. "If you're thinking about ripping off my skivvies, you're going to need somewhere more private."

"I want you to come to Arizona with me next month," I said. If I acknowledged that comment about her panties, I'd also want to touch them. It snowballed from there. "There's a sustainable design conference in Scottsdale, and I'm presenting on something. Think about it—warm weather, nice resort, alone time. I want alone time with you."

She started to respond, but more people approached us. Everyone was fired up about a waiver approved by the area zoning commission for a high-rise mega-development. That shit was my bread and butter, and no one enjoyed a good 'Boston likes paving over its history' circle jerk more than I did, but I was struggling to care.

Turning my head toward Tiel, I whispered, "Arizona?"

She brought her drink to her lips, an attempt to hide her smile from the broader conversation. "That's who we are now? The people who take fancy winter vacations?"

I tightened my grip on her waist, nodding, and pretended to listen to the discussion about filing injunctions against the development. "Those are good people to be," I mouthed.

"You're spoiling me," she said.

"Just wait until we get to Arizona," I said under my breath.

After the director of the Back Bay Preservation Commission stepped away and the debate dissolved, I spotted Matt and Lauren at the bar. Tiel followed my gaze, sucking in a breath the moment she recognized them. "You didn't mention anything about that," she murmured.

Turning her closer to me, I said, "She's really nice. She might be one of the nicest people I've ever met." Tiel gave me one of those wiggle-shake-shrugs that were more amusing to observe than interpret. "Trust me on this. She is dying to come over here and apologize, and I'm willing to bet she'll make you do some tequila shots with her."

"She doesn't have to apologize," Tiel murmured. "I was kind of demonic."

"Lauren loves everyone. *Everyone*." I nodded toward the bar, hoping she'd take the step on her own, but she didn't move. Lowering my mouth to her ear, I said, "Hurry up. My pocket feels empty without your panties and my hand is actually itching to slap your ass."

On a squeal, she marched to the bar while Matt headed in my direction.

We watched, side by side, as they talked. Somewhere along the way, I realized that I needed my family to accept Tiel the same way they accepted Lauren and Andy. I'd managed their disdain with my hook-ups for years, and ultimately, it didn't matter what they thought about those women because I didn't remember them long enough to form opinions.

But Tiel was different. She never lived in the hook-up category. If I was being painfully honest, I didn't know where I'd slot Tiel—girlfriend? Lover? The keeper of my existence?—but I knew I needed my siblings with me on this one. It wasn't about approval so much as it was their willingness to accept my choices without hesitation. We argued and bickered, and sometimes we held long, ugly grudges, but in the end we always had each other's backs.

Andy and Patrick came up beside me, and he nudged my shoulder. He said, "What's going on here?"

Tiel was staring at Lauren like she was describing her most recent serial murder spree, and I could tell by her quick, tight nodding that she wasn't enjoying the conversation yet.

Grabbing Andy's elbow, I pushed her toward the bar. "Go tell her cute stories about me."

"I don't *have* cute stories about you," Andy said, shaking off my grip. "I only have smarmy asshole stories and creative tyrant stories."

"Creative tyrant works," I said. "That shit's golden."

Andy joined them, and I could read Tiel's tension from thirty thousand feet. She was hating this, and after watching from a distance for several minutes, I knew I had to put a stop to it quickly. Just as I stepped away from Matt and Patrick, Lauren gestured toward us, rolling her eyes, and Tiel laughed. It was an honest, rolling laugh, and I saw her eyes brighten with pleasure.

"Whatever just happened over there," Patrick said, pointing with his beer bottle, "was at your expense, my friend."

"That works for me," I said. They shared more laughs, and Lauren eventually called for shots.

"Right, so now that they're best friends for life, can I take my wife home?" Matt asked. "We leave for Mexico next weekend, and I want to be with Miss Honey without worrying about her father finding me on his daughter and him making my body disappear."

"Yeah, I hate these things." Patrick downed his beer. "And Andy's dress is practically falling off. It's ready for me to finish the job."

I glared at them. "Would it kill you to keep that information to yourself? Is nothing sacred in your relationships?"

"Oh so you *don't* talk about fucking everything that moves anymore?" Patrick asked.

"How the mighty manwhore has fallen," Matt laughed. "I wouldn't have believed it if I hadn't heard it for myself."

He smacked my back and headed toward the bar, and I realized I wasn't looking for them to accept Tiel.

I wanted them to accept me.

Nineteen

TIEL

"CAN I ASK YOU SOMETHING?"

Sam looked over his shoulder, watching my fingers as they traced the designs inked into his back. It was dark, but moonlight poured in through the windows, illuminating the fierce lines against his light skin. My dress from the architecture party stood in the doorway like a taffeta tumbleweed, and though I should have ripped my gaze away from his skin long enough to admire his house, I couldn't. Those tattoos screamed with meaning and emotion, and I wanted to know everything about them. About him.

Nodding, he said, "Of course."

"Here's what I don't understand about you. You're always so cute and spiffy, and it's obvious you like things to be clean and tidy, but…" I followed the knotted shape on his shoulder, dropping a kiss there. "But you're all badass with these gnarly tattoos, and you have sex in bathrooms and that's totally gross."

In a flash, I was flat on my back and pinned beneath Sam. "Don't do that, Tiel. Just don't go there. Please, let it be in the past."

"Which part?" He gave me a hard stare, clearly disinterested in this topic. "The sex or the tattoos? I'd kind of like to hear about both."

Sam dropped his head between my breasts, groaning against my skin. "Pick one."

It would have been easier to select which arm I wanted removed.

This was what drove me crazy about Sam: the unknowns. I thought we knew everything about each other, but then there was still so much to learn. I wanted him to tell me everything, put it all out there—the ugly, the awful, the painful—and I'd do the same.

There was a desperate need boiling inside me to define *this*, and I needed to understand his past relationships to do that, but I was terrified to hear what he'd say. I didn't want to hear about the women who came before and all the things he did with them but never seemed to want with me, but I still needed to know.

Just not tonight.

"What do these mean?" I asked, nodding toward the tattoos on his chest and shoulders.

He released my wrists and sat back, completely comfortable in his nudity. By itself, that was a win. He didn't stay covered until the last moment, and he didn't reach for the sheets the second we parted anymore. He'd even started telling me where his pump was located before I could ask. It was small, so small, but he'd let me in.

He pointed to his arm. "Obviously, this is a fishhook. I like fishing."

"How have you never mentioned this?" I asked. "Where do you fish? When? How is that something you enjoy, with all the cold, floppy fish?"

Sam leaned back, laughing. "It's nice to get out on the water, be alone. It's a good time to think." He absently dragged his fingers along my legs, leaving me wiggling and wanting more.

"I've been thinking about buying a cabin in Vermont. Maybe Maine."

"Okay, wow. See? This is why we need to have these little talks," I said. "How else would I know that you're going to run off to fish in Maine one of these days?"

"I'm not running off. Shannon would come find me, and drag me back." He dropped down beside me and pulled me into his arms.

I'd heard a lot about Shannon. I'd heard about all of Sam's family, but Shannon stood out. I couldn't make sense of her level of involvement in his life.

I'd seen the sticky notes she left in his car, reminding him about appointments or calls he was due to return. I'd noticed his phone blowing up with texts from her at random hours. He'd mentioned her delivering his dry cleaning or occasionally doing his grocery shopping. He'd also shared the contentious battles they had at the office and the epic grudges she held. And one night, when we'd fallen into bed together after incredible live music and hours of dancing, he'd confided his suspicion that she was hiding something huge from him. More than anything else, he'd hated that she chose to exclude him.

It was obvious that they had a complex relationship, and on most days, his reactions to her were not positive. I didn't usually understand the velocity of his annoyance with her, but I knew I didn't like her on account of the stress she was inflicting upon him.

"Tell me about this one." I pointed to the circle beneath his collarbone.

"Divine geometry," he said.

Yeah, as if I was supposed to know what that meant.

He noticed my raised eyebrows and said, "There are patterns in everything. When you look closely, you realize it's the same shapes, repeated over and over, everywhere. When you look even closer, it's the Pythagorean theorem. Everything in nature, right down to the quantum mechanics of the universe, exists within the bounds of that theorem."

"Like octave equivalency?"

"Yup." He ran his hand down my thigh and back up, over my back. "Actually, I figured you'd have some ink. Lyrics or notes, or something special to you."

"Yeah, I don't know," I said. "It just seems so...permanent. What happens when I find a new favorite song? I can't imagine loving something enough right now to want it in thirty years."

He stared at me for a long moment, his gaze heavy and indecipherable. "Never?"

"I don't think so," I said. "Once, I thought about getting an eyebrow ring. Ellie has two and they look so good on her, but I decided against it. I didn't want to be left with a scar if I ever took it out."

"That kind of scar would be nearly invisible," he said. "Aren't most scars worth the stories associated with them?"

"Yeah," I conceded. "I don't know. Even if it was tiny, I'd always see it, and I'd regret it."

"Okay, Sunshine," he murmured. Yawning, he tucked me into his side and kissed my shoulder. "We'll talk about the rest tomorrow."

We fell asleep quickly, and though I slept soundly, early rays of sunlight had me stirring from Sam's iron grip on my waist.

Looking around, the first thing I noticed was the shortage of walls. What I'd thought of as a bedroom last night was actually wide, open space with a row of brick arches running down the center. They created the illusion of doorways, and in certain spots, Sam filled the arches with shelves or furniture.

I grabbed his discarded tank and pulled it on before fetching some sweats from my overnight bag. The house was quiet and I tiptoed from Sam's room into a cavernous kitchen, stopping to count the number of seats at the long table. Eighteen. When I looked closer, I realized it was a single slab of wood, irregular on the sides and finished to a lustrous shine to bring out the rings.

There was an area outfitted with a sectional and television, and a garage packed with tools and wood. Sam always talked about using real wood for his projects, but it was still startling to see actual branches, stumps, and segments of tree trunks lining the brick walls.

Another turn brought me to a spacious bank of open-air showers, just like the ones from my high school locker rooms. Morning sun streamed in from tall, ocean-facing windows along the ceiling line. I stepped to the center of the room and tested my pitch. The acoustics were perfect, and I dashed back to Sam's room to grab my instrument.

I'd basically packed my entire life when Sam told me to bring what I'd need for the weekend, and that always included Jezebel.

He was still asleep, and after drawing the blankets around his shoulders, I returned to the showers. I'd been wrestling with several pieces, and stood there, waving my bow back and forth until I could decide which to work on this morning.

Instead of playing any of them, I decided to experiment with 'Moondance,' an old Van Morrison tune I'd been lusting after for months. While I firmly believed that damn near anything could be adapted for strings, some Van Morrison songs weren't the easiest matches.

I hadn't brought any sheet music with me, and since I hadn't intended to attack this song, I was going from memory alone. I ran through it in my head several times, getting tempo and movement down, and then lifted my instrument.

The first couple of attempts were objectively terrible, but somewhere around the eleventh take, it started sounding less like an electrocuted cat and more like the jazzy sway I wanted. I kept going, scratching away for another thirteen iterations until I felt the notes coming together, bending, softening, melting.

Nodding in moderate satisfaction, I opened my eyes and

saw Sam seated against the faded yellow tiles, his arms folded over his bent knees.

"Oh my God, I can't believe you had to hear that," I said. I straightened my arms and shook out my wrists. "It was such crap. I actually thought to myself at one point, *this sounds like an electrocuted cat.* I'm sorry. I should have gone outside."

He tilted his head with that adorable, squinty expression he pulled whenever he was particularly amused and perplexed. Like most things he did, I wanted to throw myself on him and savor every morsel.

"You're kidding, right? Tell me you're kidding, because that was the most extraordinary thing I've ever seen," he said.

I lifted a shoulder and offered a noncommittal sound while I set my instrument back in the case. "It needs work."

Sam popped to his feet and approached me, his head shaking. "I'm my own toughest critic, too, but believe me when I say that was remarkable. I could watch you for hours."

"I'm sorry I woke you up. I really should have gone outside," I said.

"It's December. It's twenty fucking degrees," he said. "Don't even joke about doing that."

"I used do it all the time," I said. "My family could not stand listening to me practice, so I cleared out a section of the garage. I probably lost some brain cells to huffing gas fumes, and the acoustics were shameful, but it worked for me."

"Don't care." He glanced at me before yanking me toward him. "Why does my wrinkled shirt look so fucking good on you?"

"I'd argue it looks decent on you, too," I said. "But I have to tell you—this room has the most incredible acoustics *and* sunlight. I don't feel like I'm playing in a dungeon. I've never been so happy in my life."

Sam laughed, shaking his head at me. "Consider it yours."

What the fuck did he just offer?

"What?"

His lips moved over my shoulder, kissing, teeth scraping, sighing, and he said, "Riley and I didn't know what to do with this space. He wanted to rent it out for porn shoots, but I vetoed that one. If it works for you, it's yours. Come anytime. Stay. Stay as long as you want. Stay…forever."

I glanced up expecting to see a glimmer of humor in his eyes, some indication that he was joking, but I couldn't find it.

"You wouldn't have to book pre-dawn studio time," he said, his hand sliding under my sweats and over my ass. "You could keep your instruments here, and not have to cart them all over town. We could paint or…do whatever you wanted."

"Did you just ask me to move in with you?" The words ran out in a screechy rush.

"Um, I don't know." Sam's brow furrowed and he released a tight, self-conscious laugh. "Do you *want* to move in with me?"

He was being nice. This was his version of generosity, and he simply failed to think about what he was saying.

"We're all good," I said, patting his chest. "Don't worry about it."

He had an empty room that matched my needs, and he was being a gentleman by offering it up. Nothing more.

"Didn't you say there was a fireman's pole around here somewhere? That's something I have to see."

IF I COULD HAVE DESTROYED my phone with some evil glares, I would have. I knew the call was coming, and as always, ignoring it only delayed the discomfort.

"Tiel, hello," my father said.

"Hi, Dad." I hated the fake tint in my voice, the impatient cadence that refused—even after all these years—to stop wondering how I became irrelevant and expendable to my own parents. "How are you?"

"Such a busy time," he said. "Always busy, and we're happy to be busy."

"Well that's good," I murmured.

"And you?"

"All good," I said. "The semester is nearly finished, and I'm up to my eyeballs with grading this week. I was actually reviewing some term papers just now..."

We did this dance every December. He'd call, tell me I should visit for the holidays to meet my cousin's fiancé or congratulate my sister on her new home, and I'd dance around the request with some semi-legitimate reasons to stay in Boston.

Last year, I teamed up with a bunch of friends and college students to visit the area hospitals and nursing homes to play

Christmas carols. The year before that, Ellie and I went to Disney World. One of my first holidays in Boston, I was working with a particularly challenged kiddo, and his parents asked me to join them on their ski trip to Killington.

I knew Sam's family was having a get-together on Christmas Eve, but he was careful to mention it casually and never attach expectations to it.

"You should know we think this might be Yaya's last Christmas," he said, sighing. "She'll be ninety-seven next summer, and she hasn't been healthy. Her heart is giving her trouble, and she can't get around well."

I always wished I could be one of those people who cut negative things from their lives and didn't look back, but I never learned how to make that cut, not all the way. My family wasn't good for me; they didn't respect my choices or values, and though my father was attempting to broker some peace, that didn't alter their opinions of me. But I couldn't stop caring about them.

"The least you can do is see her at Christmas," he said. "I know Yaya would appreciate it."

"I need to look at my schedule," I said. "I'll let you know."

"You should be able to do this, Tiel," he said. "It's important. You'll regret it if she passes and you didn't say goodbye. For once, think about someone other than yourself."

My eyes squeezed shut, I took a deep breath and convinced myself it wasn't worth getting into an argument. It was easier to deal with this now than pretend I needed to consult some jam-packed schedule, only to call back later and agree to visit. Because of course I was going; I would always love my family, and I wouldn't let my grandmother go without a proper goodbye. "I can take the train down on Christmas Eve."

It was the right thing to do even if it was the most uncomfortable option available, and I groused my way through the week on that point of frustration. I shopped for Christmas gifts (angrily), graded exams (no generosity to be found), practiced (only the ranty tunes), and dreamt up (bitchy) ways to handle the barrage of questions I'd get when I arrived in Jersey.

The saving grace was my time spent with Seraphina and Lucas. She was getting good with her One Direction acoustic guitar, and she consistently said 'hi.' I didn't know the trauma that caused her selective mutism, and I probably wouldn't. My sessions only provided an outlet to manage her emotions and express herself through a medium that made sense to her. That she could find solace in songs was the win.

Lucas and I worked through complex pieces, attempted some new approaches, and sampled some holiday music. It was something of a breakthrough, considering he preferred the hard lines of Beethoven, Bach, and Tchaikovsky. He didn't smile when we played 'Rudolph, the Red-Nosed Reindeer' but he didn't immediately revert to the Fifth Symphony either, and that was progress for us.

His mother, Beth, even texted me this morning to say she'd overheard him playing 'Jingle Bells' before she got out of bed.

I was meeting Sam for dinner tonight at a tiny organic bistro near Porter Square, and I was determined to end all complaining. It was the first time we'd managed to connect in several days. He'd been tied up with unexpected issues on some of his projects, and I missed him.

We still talked and texted, and when I'd asked one too many times whether he was actually working and not blowing me off for a swanky club, he sent me a picture of himself in a hard hat with a dozen contractors poring over blueprints behind him. He'd been sending selfies with his texts ever since. Some were funny: his annoyed expressions when things weren't going the way he wanted at jobsites, Riley's coffee-stained pants, vague images from the Turlan project captioned "top secret." Others made me want to run across town and throw my arms around him: his groggy, adorable face when he first woke up, his reflection in the mirror with a question about whether he was adequately spiffy for my tastes, his frown when he had to report he'd be needed for another late night.

He knew I was going home for the holiday, and he knew I wasn't thrilled about it. We hadn't gotten much beyond those points.

Sam was running late again, and I sat alone in the bistro, waiting with my glass of wine. It felt oddly sophisticated to be sitting in a *bistro* and drinking *wine*, but I wasn't about to fight Sam on restaurants. He was particular about food, and I'd eat just about anything put in front of me.

He waved from the door, quickly shaking out of his coat and scarf before heading toward our table. Bending, he placed a kiss on my lips and sighed, his forehead leaning against mine. "Hi, Tiel."

"Hi, Sam," I whispered, edging forward for another kiss.

His finger traced the neck of my sweater dress, and I felt him smile against my lips. "You are so fucking gorgeous. What are you wearing under this?"

"Not much," I murmured. He growled, his fingers pressing against me in a sharp, urgent manner. My hands on his chest, I pushed him toward his seat. "So which crisis were you solving tonight?"

He sat across from me but made a small production of adjusting himself in the process. "No crises tonight, actually," he said. "I was at Lauren's board meeting, and it ran a couple minutes over."

"You were *where*?"

The words flew out and I watched as they cracked over him, the unintended anger and betrayal in my voice obvious as his eyes turned from playfully aroused to confused. "I'm on the board of directors for Lauren's school," he said. "I think I've told you about that."

"You have *not*," I said, powerless to rein in my tone. I looked away, desperate to find some of the affection I had for Sam under the irrational jealousy I was feeling right now.

"I *have* mentioned that she's very happily married to my brother." He shook out his napkin and draped it over his lap, focused on the place setting in front of him. "To me, she is a friend. Her, Andy...they're the women in my brothers' lives."

"I understand that," I said. "I do. I really do. But...it's hard for me to figure out this whole family thing for you."

We ordered and Sam gazed at me after the waitress left our table. He was quiet and cool, and I could almost hear him drawing down his words and placing them in a strategic order. "This isn't about me, and I don't think it's about my family either. It's just a convenient argument because the other explanation is a tad more complex."

He reached across the table, his fingers circling my wrist. Our freckles lined up when his thumb stroked my palm, those big brown splotches, and I smiled.

"You might be right," I said.

"You're pretty cute when you're feverishly jealous," he said. "You're all 'I'll cut a bitch' and I just want to get you naked and lick your nipples and fuck you for five or six hours."

I snorted, choking on my wine and laughing until tears streamed down my face. Sam shifted his seat closer, his hand moving up and down my back in large, serene circles while I recovered.

"Are we pretending that isn't what's happening right now?" he asked as I dried my eyes with his handkerchief. "Is that who we are tonight?"

I shook my head and tapped a fast, frantic segment of Paganini's Caprice Number Twenty-Four on the table. "I didn't mean to snap like that," I said.

Our entrees arrived but Sam stayed beside me with his arm over the back of my chair. "You know I won't do that, right?"

I nodded, but I didn't know what to think. There was always this lingering doubt, the suspicion that he'd quickly discover I wasn't as amusing or sexy or adorable as he once thought, and this would end. He'd be the next in a terribly long line of people who cut me loose over the years, and I'd survive like I always did.

He shared his recent construction woes while we ate, offhandedly mentioning a small, methodological difference of opinion that catalyzed a debate between him and his brothers. Then he rattled off a list of restaurants he wanted us to try when we visited Arizona next month, and it was quite possible I'd never seen him so excited about food before.

"So when do you leave?" he asked, edging the assortment of French macarons the waitress delivered with his coffee toward me.

I lifted the mint green cookie and ran my tongue along the middle where chocolaty cream peeked out. "Friday morning. Christmas Eve trains will either be packed tight or totally empty, but it will give me a chance to clean up my syllabus for the spring semester."

"And you're good with spending the holiday there?"

I wasn't—not even close—but I needed to see my grand-mother. "It'll be fine," I said. "It's just…ugh, I don't know how to talk about this."

"Start small. Explain why you don't want to visit," he said.

"I've told you—my family doesn't like me," I said. "And before you interrupt because I see you trying, please know that I'm not exaggerating. They refuse to accept that life exists beyond the family industrial complex."

Sam chuckled and stirred his coffee. "I don't know that I'm supposed to laugh at that, but you have me envisioning some kind of gyro factory run by children."

"And that wouldn't be inaccurate," I said. "When my sister got married, she had fourteen bridesmaids, but I wasn't one of them."

"Shannon and Erin haven't talked in—hmm." He glanced at the ceiling. "I want to say six or seven years. Erin did some… some terrible things, and Shannon retaliated, and I often wonder whether there's enough salt in the world to thaw that ice. But I know for a fact that Shannon would drop everything if Erin ever truly needed her, and Erin would do the same."

"Yeah, no," I laughed. "That isn't even close to the case with my family. Sam, they're *embarrassed* by me, and not just the stupid teenage marriage thing. I'm convinced they believe I play on subway platforms and survive on the loose change I earn there."

"And you know that's bullshit, right?" he asked. "Families don't make for the most objective witnesses."

"I just have to survive a few days," I said. Sam folded the napkin in half, then folded it again, leaving it in a smooth rectangle on his thigh.

He gestured toward me, confused. "I still don't understand why you don't call it out. Put it all on the table."

"Because it won't solve anything, Sam. It's just standard family dysfunction, and there's no sense stirring up drama."

"I'm all for conflict avoidance," he said. "But I really believe you should try to work it out. You have two living parents, and it might not seem like a blessing when they're openly intolerant of your choices, but I know there are a lot of things I'd say to mine if I could spend the holiday with them."

The crumbs wiped from my fingers, I reached for another macaron. "I understand that. Really. But their passive rejection is easier to handle."

He watched as I tasted the cookie. "I'm not trying to make it worse."

"You know that saying, 'you can never go home again'? There are times when I realize how frighteningly accurate it is. Whatever home once was, it can't be that anymore, and it makes me wonder if it was ever there to start with."

Sam nodded, his gaze still trained on my mouth. "There's a Welsh word for that," he said. He reached for his coffee, his expression moving between pain and pleasure with each sip. "You know, I'm trying to be mature and have a fucking conversation with you but you're sitting there, licking that thing like it's the head of my cock. I swear to you, I'm going blow in the next minute if you don't stop."

I glanced at the cookie and smiled. Sam and I enjoyed a lot of sex, but he stopped me every time I moved to taste his cock. There was always a mediocre excuse—he wanted to be inside me, he wanted to come on my breasts, he wanted to lick me—and he'd gone so far as to bind my wrists to the headboard after I tried to wake him up that way.

I had to wonder whether there was a bigger reason for the oral lockout. Maybe he only liked blowjobs when they came from random girls in semi-private settings. Or, despite his commentary, he wasn't excited about getting head from me. I wanted to know, and if eating these cookies forced his hand on the topic, I was going to keep on licking.

"A Welsh word? I thought you only tossed around archaic English."

"*Hiraeth*," he said. "It's the homesickness you feel for places of the past."

"Yeah. That," I said, and reached for the last cookie. "So now you just know random Welsh words?"

"I saw it a few years ago, one of those paintings with typography overlaid. It just summed up everything I was going through, and I contemplated getting it inked somewhere."

I thought about all his other tattoos. The assortment of Celtic knots. The doves. Those shapes that related to some equation. The cluster of trees just below his waist. The Iron Man helmet under his watchband. "Really? You don't have any other words."

"Hmmm, yeah." He handed his credit card to the waitress without looking at the bill. I'd stopped offering since he got so pissy whenever I reached for my wallet, but it niggled at all my righteous values. He'd also told me he appreciated my values, but he'd still be paying. "I haven't found any I like better than shapes."

Dragging my lip between my teeth, I nodded. I didn't want

him tattooing any homesickness. I didn't care that it was a cool word. He was already carrying enough reminders of the things he'd lost. "Like I was saying. I've changed, I know that, and it makes sense that I can't experience home the same way I did when I was younger, but it doesn't make it any less sad."

"You want me to go with you?" I sent him an aggravated glare. "What?"

"I don't think bringing an Irish boy home with me is going to solve any of my family problems," I said. Sam being successful and sexy and generally perfect wasn't changing anything; my family's issues were with me.

"I'll be here when you get back."

"I know," I said, sighing. "And I'll probably text you the entire time I'm gone and you'll be trying to get rid of me again."

Sam blew a breath out and the sound transitioned into a groan and then a growl, and his expression was dark, thunderous.

"All right, Tiel. This has been more than enough. Keep doing that," he rumbled, gesturing toward the macaron I was licking. "But don't be surprised if you find my cock in your mouth very soon."

I winked, and licked the rest of the filling.

Twenty-One

SAM

HOW I KNEW I'd officially lost it: I was moping at a party.

Perhaps moping wasn't the right word, but I was staring into my gin and tonic, too disinterested to bother drinking it. Riley, in his professional capacity as bartender for this event, also managed to pour a blindingly strong drink. This thing had the capacity to knock me into next year.

There was a great crowd at Patrick and Andy's apartment for their Chrismukkah shindig, and it really should have been amusing. But I hadn't been in a social situation without Tiel since the summer, and I didn't know what to do with myself. The temptation to text her was high, but I didn't want to interfere with her family's plans.

I also didn't want to be a needy little fuck.

"If you're going to sit in a corner, why don't you watch the rice while you're at it?" Andy asked.

She pointed to the cast iron pot on the stove, waving me off the kitchen island barstool. Following her direction, I grabbed a wooden spoon and stirred the spicy rice.

"I take it Tiel's out of town?" I nodded. "And she still hates me?"

"I don't think she's chromosomally capable of hate," I

laughed. "She's uncomfortable in big families. Her own is a rotting bag of dicks, and we fail to acknowledge that we're an intimidating bunch."

"That you are," she murmured. "It took me three weeks to keep you all straight, and there are still times when I don't know what the hell you're all talking about."

Whirling around, I almost knocked the salad bowl from Andy's hands. "Would you tell her that? Tiel?"

She leaned over the pot on the stove, breathing in the aroma and taking the spoon from my hand to add seasoning. "No problem. I don't get the impression she has any interest in talking to me, ever, but I can try."

I threw my arms around her shoulders and squeezed. "Oh God, thank you, Andy."

She patted my arm and said, "You're in rough shape."

"I'm fine," I said, careful not to spit the words out with the frustration I felt. "Wanting Tiel to feel welcome—"

"No, no, no. You're missing me," she said. She draped her arm around my shoulder, smiling. "It's nice to see you caring about someone, even if it's torturing the shit out of you right now."

"Um, yes," Patrick mumbled, coming up behind me. He elbowed me away from Andy and folded her against his chest. "Let's not be doing that, please. You do not need to be touching her."

"I was just thanking Andy for helping me," I said.

"Right, and you can do that with words," he said. "Keep your fucking hands to yourself."

I spent most of the night helping Andy with the food, and once that was handled I washed the dishes. It was a good distraction from missing Tiel, and it saved me from engaging in stupid conversations about snow predictions and the college bowl series.

When the night started winding down and only Patrick,

Andy, Shannon, Riley, Nick, and I were left, Riley took to mixing Irish coffees.

"Ri, this is strong enough to tranquilize a rhino," I said. Everyone was settled in the living room, and promptly sampled their coffees.

"It really isn't," Nick said.

"Dude, if you get hammered and piss on my wall, I'll kill you," Patrick said.

"Your tolerance is off," Riley murmured. "You haven't been hard drunk in months."

Maybe he was right. Tiel and I always had a few drinks when we went out, but never as many as before. My goal wasn't numb oblivion.

"That's positive," Shannon said. "Is that something you're working on now?"

"Shannon, can you do us all a favor and not talk to him like he's five?" Nick asked. "So his lady has some fire-breathing dragon moments. So do you. Oddly enough, no one's tried to run you off."

Her head turned toward him in extreme slow motion, unblinking, and I was concerned her glare would actually decapitate him. "I don't recall asking your opinion, so why don't *you* do *me* a favor and tuck it away with your little dick. Okay? Thanks."

"Does anyone remember the year we changed all the labels on the presents?" Patrick asked. "For the life of me, I can't figure out when that was, but we managed to peel all the tags off and rearranged them."

We glanced at each other, perplexed.

"At first Mom was really confused but then she was *pissed*," he continued. "She figured it out within a few minutes and she was steaming mad." He pointed at Shannon. "She gave us that exact look, that awful face-melting look you just gave Nick, and stared us down until we cracked."

"It was Matt's idea," I said. "But he blamed it on me."

"Yes," Patrick laughed, pointing at me. "And he did it because he knew Mom was going to beat his ass with a wooden spoon but she'd never get mad at you."

"Do you remember when we hollowed out the cake?" Shannon asked. Her voice was quiet, absent of the sharp tone she aimed at Nick minutes ago. "It was this big, beautiful layer cake that she made for one of those holiday parties we always had, and we cut a little piece and then scooped out the inside. We filled it with something—what was that?"

"Leftover stuffing," I said as they laughed. "Even at seven, Matt was very concerned about preserving the structural integrity."

"Such a fucking nerd," Patrick muttered. "But God, when Mom cut into that cake and realized what we'd done...shit, we'd never run so fast in our lives."

"Why do I remember none of this?" Riley asked. He got up to pour another round of drinks but I waved him off.

"You were two or three," Shannon said. "You were a baby. You wouldn't have remembered."

For a second, I felt the impact of Riley growing up without knowing these rare, happy moments, but that meant he didn't have the horrible moments either. He didn't have nightmares about Mom's death and he wouldn't remember the way Angus dropped into an angry, evil spiral from that point forward.

As I wondered whether I'd be better off erasing all the memories, I didn't notice Patrick leaning toward me.

"Can I give you some advice?"

I glanced at him and the apartment, surprised to find Nick and Shannon had left. "I get the impression you'll be giving it regardless of whether I want it or not."

"That's accurate." He shrugged and propped his feet on the ottoman, crossing his ankles. "Don't keep Shannon out of the loop. She'll turn into a fucking howler monkey if you try to shut her out, and she'll do crazy shit like sending you to a shrink because your girlfriend is a beast."

"Please do *not* say that," I ground out. "She needs time to warm up to everyone."

"You know what I mean," he said. "She seems like a handful."

My mind went straight to Tiel's naked body. My hands on her breasts. Her thighs. Her ass. Between her legs. "Something like that."

Patrick edged closer and knocked his glass against mine. "It's amazing what the right woman can do to you, isn't it?"

That was an understatement.

LAST NIGHT'S storytelling dredged an armload of holiday memories, and when I woke up, I stared out at the Fort Point Channel reliving them. Before my mother died, Christmas was a big deal. She went hog wild. The twenty-foot tree in the front foyer, miles of lights, garland covering every surface, wreaths and ribbons everywhere. There were even holiday towels in the bathrooms.

We never managed to resurrect any of those traditions when she was gone, and suddenly, I realized how much I missed them. Drinking beer and watching basketball at Shannon's apartment on Christmas used to be enough for me, but there was something missing. Something big.

I devoted the morning to finishing the chairs for Riley's office—finally—and constructing some small tables. One of them was destined to replace the particle board crap in Tiel's apartment, but I couldn't decide which.

I'd been thinking about her nonstop since she left for Jersey. I was worried about her. I didn't like the idea of her spending time with people who found it so easy to turn their backs on her for years. I could also admit I didn't like being separated from her. Even before we fell into bed, we'd been joined at the hip, and this distance was jarring.

It got heavier for me when I thought about Patrick's advice. *The right woman.*

He was too right.

She existed in a different stratosphere, a place where friendship and sex and affection were unsullied by anything I'd done before—at least for me.

Glancing at my phone, I decided to text her.

Sam: Merry Christmas

Sam: How's it going?

Tiel: omfg

Tiel: My grandmother keeps calling me Elena and has not a fucking clue who I am, and I actually feel pretty terrible about that but she's the only one who gets a pass

Tiel: I'm not sure this was ever home at all. My sister acts like I've been living on Mars.

Tiel: She introduced me to her husband as if I hadn't been at their damn wedding

Sam: I'm sorry.

Tiel: They've been telling people I'm a kindergarten music teacher…apparently that's more acceptable?

Tiel: I'd love it if someone could define for me why I'm such a fucking disappointment. They realize I'm not one of Snoop Dogg's groupies, right?

Sam: Allow me to remind you that you're the most talented, accomplished person I've ever met

Sam: (and this is coming from the guy who hears how talented and accomplished he is all the damn time)

Tiel: I just wish I had regular people in my life. Regular, non-ridiculous people who don't act like my entire existence is too weird for words.

Tiel: Normal family. All I'm asking.

Sam: You can have mine.

Of course it took her ten minutes to contend with that comment.

Tiel: hmmmm
Tiel: Not sure they want me either
Sam: They do and so do I
Tiel: It's not too early to start drinking, right? It is a holiday. People are supposed to be drunk on holidays.
Sam: You need a shoulder massage, a dry martini, and some dirty sex.
Tiel: Well, yeah, of course. I always need that.
Sam: I can give you all 3. You pick the order.
Tiel: lol. perv.
Tiel: At first I thought you were all preppy and gentlemanly, and now I know you're just a freak.
Sam: I'm still a gentleman. That doesn't mean I won't bend you over and fuck you, and then pour you a drink.
Tiel: Would it be wrong for me to get on a train tomorrow morning, and be drunk and bent over by noon?
Sam: I'd love that, and I'd be waiting for you at South Station.
Sam: And I know this isn't what you want to hear and it's not in my cock's best interest, but you should spend time with your family. I am getting you for an uninterrupted week in Scottsdale, after all.
Tiel: ugghhh. shut up
Sam: At the very least, you can tell them about me. I'm pretty great.
Tiel: And what would you like me to tell them, Samuel?
Sam: Whatever you want, although I'd omit the spanking. That is not elemental to the story as it pertains to them.

When she didn't respond for a few minutes, I dashed into the shower to wash away the dust and grime from woodworking. I didn't worry, figuring she got pulled into a conversation or started playing with a niece or nephew.

I left my phone nearby to listen for a new message, but nothing came through until I was dried off and stepping into a pair of jeans.

Tiel: And that's what makes me sad.

Tiel: I know you're going to have some smart ass remark like I should mention that I like a good spanking but that's not what I mean

Tiel: I don't know where I stand with you sometimes. That's probably super random to you right now but I can't stop thinking about it

Tiel: Are we friends or more than friends or just a game that you're playing or a weird part of your life where you figure shit out. Or some quick thing that's going to blow over in a few weeks. Or more. Or nothing.

Tiel: I don't know what I mean to you, if I mean anything.

Tiel: And I hate all of that, and I hate saying this.

Tiel: I hate being that needy girl who has to know what's going on but I'm here and you want me to tell my parents about you but I don't know what we are

Swallowing back the tension rising in my throat, I started responding to Tiel's messages but knew I couldn't get it into a text. Deleting it all, I tapped the icon beside her picture—the one from September, where she was sitting on the grass, wearing that smile that always brought out mine—and called her.

"Please don't freak out," she said. "I'm sorry. I can't remember who I am when I'm here, and all I want is some definition and structure. I'm in a terrible mood and being bratty. Rant, over."

"How long have you been ruminating on that?" I asked. She made a non-committal sound and I heard a screen door bang shut. "Just tell me."

"I don't know. Maybe since always?"

Aggravation bit at my nerves, but I pushed it all down. She managed to unleash every thought in her head on most occasions, but never mentioned the one thing that was truly bothering her. "Why didn't you say anything?"

There was wind rustling in the background and I caught an occasional hum or murmur, but minutes passed before she responded. "Because you're a weirdo and I like that shit. You're my friend, one of my best friends, and if nothing else, I didn't want to push away my best friend because I needed to know what it meant now that we're sleeping together. I've always wanted a lot more than you did, but I didn't want to tell you that and ruin things."

Well, shit.

I'd been operating under the assumption Tiel wanted casual. Everything about her was casual, all the time, and she eschewed every other label under the sun. She'd even told me she didn't necessarily like the term 'violinist' because she played 'a little bit of everything.'

And she'd wanted a lot more than I did? Yeah, I would have appreciated hearing about that much sooner. She freaked out when I offered to convert the showers to her practice space. She thought I wanted her to move in with me—it didn't sound like a bad idea, but it wasn't what I'd intended to say—and promptly dove into panic mode. If she wanted more of me, I wasn't averse to offering. "Can I tell you what I'm thinking?"

"Can't you always?" she asked.

If I had known…shit. I probably would have fucked it up somehow.

Simply put, she was unlike any other woman I'd ever met. Sure, I picked up the generalities, but there were so many more quirks I was only beginning to understand. It was obvious that this—the definition of us—was her cornerstone, and until it was square, we couldn't build anything else. And I was the asshole who hadn't put those pieces together until now.

But it killed me that she didn't mention it the other night at dinner when I straight-up told her I wouldn't be a lying dick like her ex-husband. There were a lot of names I'd willingly accept, but cheater wasn't one of them. Instead, she waited until she was seven hours away, and the best I could do was talk her down while I thought about spanking her and begging her to love me for eternity.

"More," I said, pressing my palm to my crotch to alleviate the pressure there.

"More?" She sniffled and blew out a breath. "More what?"

More of my cock inside you, fucking this silliness away and promising our forever, I thought. Probably not the right thing to say. There was honesty and then there was word vomit, and I needed to keep a handle on the latter.

"We're more than friends, and I don't want this to blow over," I said. "I want this to last. Believe me when I say that, Tiel. We have no idea what we're doing and we're probably going to screw up along the way, but...we can figure that all out. I want us to be the people who figure it out."

"Last for a little while?" she asked. "Or last for a long while?"

I'll last as long as you want me, I thought. Also, not the right thing to say.

"A long while," I said. "If that's what you want."

Let me tell you what you want right now: you want to be spread out on my bed and you don't want to think again until we've made love and you've come for me at least three times.

"You mean that? Don't give me the manwhore boilerplate, Sam, because I really cannot handle that today."

"Of course I mean that," I said. I wasn't addressing the player comment. It was intended to get a reaction out of me, and the only reaction that seemed to make a damned bit of difference on that topic was spanking her. And, *fuck*, I wanted my hand on that round ass. "Unless you want something different."

"I want to hang out with you," she said simply. "And have ridiculous arguments about irrelevant things, and long talks about random stuff, and laugh with you all the time. I want you staring at my boobs and saying pervy things, and then doing all those pervy things."

"Yeah, I get the sense we're good on the sex side of this," I laughed. I was going to need another shower. It would either be very long or very cold. Or both. "But you have to tell me when something's bothering you, Sunshine."

"I know, I know," she said. "I'm sorry. I just fall apart when I'm here and it magnifies everything else. It's like, I'm not good enough for my family, and maybe I'm not really good enough for you."

I'd thought of Tiel as my life raft since the day in the elevator, but it was possible we'd been keeping each other afloat this whole time.

"I'm here whenever you need me, and you're definitely good enough for me. Never doubt that, not for a second."

She sighed. "Okay. I have to confess…I've been checking out tomorrow's train schedules."

Yes, I thought. *Come back to me. Stay with me. Stay with me* always. *Let me bury myself in you for hours and say all the things I don't want to say without your skin beneath me. Come home and let me give you everything, all of me.*

"I've never doubted you," I said. "Go do the family thing, and then get your ass back here. I'm not letting you out of the bedroom until next year."

A HAPPY GLOW heating my cheeks and the tingle of Sam's affection zipping through my muscles, I headed down the street and up my parents' driveway.

I can do this, I thought. *Get through this day and get home to Sam.*

As I reached out to open the door to the back porch near the kitchen, I froze, some sixth sense holding me in place.

"It's just so sad." My mother's voice. "She has nothing. *Nothing*," she whispered. "My heart breaks for her, it really does. But how is she going to meet a nice boy? Or have a family? I doubt she has health insurance. What if she gets sick? What if she's in an accident? I live in constant fear that I'll get a call in the middle of the night that something awful has happened."

"You and Vikram should help her out." My aunt, Daphne. "You can spare some money. We helped Alex for a few years until he got on his feet, and he's doing well now. But you have to be patient. Sometimes it takes them longer to find their way."

"She'll be thirty, Daph." She sighed and I thought I heard her eyes rolling, too. "We never should have let her go away to school. She didn't have the maturity for that, and she's still paying for it. At what point do we stop trying to help? When do we go to her apartment, pack her things, and move her back home? Like an intervention."

I had to cover my mouth to keep from laughing out loud. It was hysterical in an outrageous, painful way.

"Didn't you say she's still in school?" Daphne asked.

My mother made a dismissive noise. "She claims she finished one program and started another, but that sounds like another one of her lies. How many degrees does someone need? It's just *music*. If she wanted to give private lessons, she could have stayed right here and gone to community college. But no one can tell Tiel anything. She does whatever she pleases, and she always has."

"Well it was nice that she came home," Daphne said. "We haven't seen her in so long, and she's grown into a lovely woman. I always knew she'd be pretty."

"I just hope she doesn't do anything to embarrass herself this time," my mother huffed. "I couldn't believe the scene she made at Agapi's wedding."

And by 'scene' she was referring to me hanging out at the bar during the reception, and not waiting on my sister hand and foot. Given that I didn't get one of the ugly blue bridesmaid dresses, I didn't see it as my responsibility.

Their conversation turned to the food, and I braced myself to walk through the kitchen. They stopped what they were doing when they saw me, staring for a long, tense moment, and then lapsing into rapid-fire Greek. I'd given up on learning more than the basics after my confirmation, and with nearly fifteen years separating me from regular practice, I didn't understand a word they were saying.

"What is it you're studying these days?" Daphne asked.

My mother watched as I poured a glass of wine, her stare communicating plenty of disapproval. She didn't come out and say it—not this time—but she harbored concerns about whether I enjoyed a hard-partying, rock'n'roll lifestyle complete with drugs and blacked-out drunkenness.

So I filled the glass all the way to the top. "Music therapy. My dissertation is focused on the role of musical performance on the emotional, social, and cognitive needs of children on the autism spectrum. I've published several journal articles on the power of early therapeutic interventions for children living with autism."

"Oh," Daphne murmured. Her face registered a slight hint of shock, but then an impressed gleam sparkled in her eye. This was the first time I'd come out and clarified my work, and it was pleasant to see some reaction, even if I'd polished up the situation a bit. "Good luck with all that."

"So you plan on staying in college forever?" my mother asked.

I glanced between her and Daphne while sipping my wine. "I'll be finished with my research in a few months. I haven't decided whether I want to pursue full professorship or clinical fellowships once I have my doctorate. Or perhaps I'll devote my time to private practice. I do have many more consultation requests than I can handle," I said, my tone intentionally contemplative.

I returned to the wine bottle and topped off my glass, my mother tracking my every move. "A little early, don't you think?" she asked.

Smiling, I moved toward the living room. "No," I said. "Not at all."

I settled in to watch Christmas Day parades with my grand-mother. She was thrilled to see me, and insisted on a tight hug.

She also thought I was someone else, so it fit with the theme of this trip.

I WANDERED THROUGH MY WORKSHOP, still bleary-eyed from one too many beers at Shannon's Christmas dinner last night, and I studied the raw wood ready for transformation. I'd been itching to build something for weeks, and since the office was closed until after New Year's and Tiel wouldn't be back until Monday, I had some time on my hands. I just didn't know where to start. I continued pacing, stopping every couple of minutes to examine a branch or stump.

I sketched a few things, nothing particularly interesting, and eventually went back to my tree ring tile project. I'd been thinking about ripping out the flooring in the bathroom on my side of the house—we didn't exactly have rooms since I blew out most of the walls when I moved in—and putting down finely planed wood. It was going to be a pain in the ass but it also had the potential to be tremendously cool. With the branches measured out, I started making the hundreds of cuts necessary.

It was tedious work but I enjoyed it. I'd always loved imagining ways to give trees new lives, and went out of my way to find the right ones. It was the one thing I'd learned from my father that wasn't coated in hate and pain.

It was also splendidly distracting. I could hone in on precise cuts, quieting all thoughts of Tiel and the way her words clung to me long after our call ended yesterday.

I did want this to last, and that was a foreign concept to me. I'd always operated with one hand on the escape hatch, but now I was too busy keeping both hands on Tiel to think about going anywhere.

I didn't know what it meant for something to *last*, but I wanted to find out.

"Hey," Riley called, banging his fist on the door to get my attention over the saw. "Punky Brewster's here."

Shoving the safety glasses onto my head, I said, "Who?"

He chuckled and shook his head. "Go see for yourself."

I followed him out of the workshop and found Tiel in the middle of my kitchen. She must have taken the first train out of Newark—just like she threatened. Smiling, I shoved my gloves in my back pocket.

Seeing me, she turned, and her eyes widened to saucers. She looked me up and down, drinking in the worn jeans hanging low on my hips and my navy blue tank, and beckoned me closer. "This is a *good* look for you."

Her hands landed on my chest and moved down over my stomach to grip my belt. A noise rumbled in the back of her throat, and it was decidedly predatory. Plenty of women had admired my body before, but this felt fucking lascivious. Her hand moved lower, cupping me, and I surged into her.

"I have missed you so fucking much," I hissed. "Do you have any idea how many wet dreams you've given me?"

"And on that cheerful note, I'll be going out for the afternoon," Riley called. "We might want to start investing in walls and doors around here, Sam."

Much to my relief, Tiel laughed and continued stroking. She didn't mind Riley, and she was better when she took my family in small doses. Who could blame her?

"I've missed you too," she said. "Going home is always

torture, but doing it without you was the worst. You're coming with me next time, and you're going to do filthy things to me in my childhood bedroom."

"Of course I will." I backed her toward my bed, slowly stripping off her clothes as we went. The notion of meeting her family lodged in the back of my mind, slowly dissolving into a cozy idea about me taking her there and showing her off, proving once and for all that she was a treasure.

"I've been thinking about tasting you right"—her mouth dipped to the hollow at the base of my throat, and she kissed and nipped that tender spot until the back of her legs hit the bed—"here. I've been thinking about that since I left."

"You love me in a perverted and shameless way. It's almost a problem, Tiel."

"I really do." She attacked my belt, tearing it from its loops as if it had insulted her, and my jeans were on the ground in a heartbeat. "Do you love *me* in a perverted and lustful way?"

These were real words, and they were dangerously close to real meaning, too. Suddenly, we weren't exchanging the same teasing barbs we liked to throw at each other.

I love you because you're the only person who can consume eight cappuccinos in a single day and still form syllables.

I love you because you're still under the impression we haven't seen 21 Jump Street *at least four times.*

I love you because you wear red dresses with pink shoes and manage to make it work.

I love you because you refuse to drink coconut water on account of its 'sploogy' taste.

I love you because you never stop announcing why you love me.

I love you because you've saved me from myself.

I flicked open her bra and filled my hands with her breasts, my thumbs passing over her nipples until they tightened and she leaned into my touch. "Let's be honest, sweetheart, I've loved you since you said an olive tasted like a briny ball sack. You stole my heart, and maybe my balls, that night."

"I win," she said. "I've loved you since you were knocked out in the elevator."

Pushing her down to the bed, I pulled off her jeans and grabbed her panties, twisting the simple green fabric in my hands and tearing. She gasped—it was an innocent sound that begged for something dirty—and I held them up for her to see with a pointed nod. Her lips parted, and she knew exactly what I had in mind.

I snatched a condom from the shelf alongside the bed, rolling it down as I edged toward Tiel. She was spread out before me, exactly as I envisioned yesterday, and her body told all the stories. There were no straight lines, no right angles. Just soft, rolling curves. Paths that were as much fun to explore as the destination was to reach.

"I *love you* love you," she whispered as my eyes caressed her.

I had her panties balled in my hand, waiting, holding back on the off-chance she'd say those words again. I just needed to hear it one more time. I wrapped her legs around my waist and thrust into her and that bliss rolled up my spine and straight into each lobe of my brain. It was peace and pleasure, and different than it was only a couple of days ago.

My hips snapped, moving in her urgently, and she threw her head back with a wail that echoed through the firehouse. "Oh, fuck, Sam," she groaned. "I *need* you."

"I know, Sunshine, and now you're going to do as you're told."

Smiling, I slipped her panties between her teeth, brought my hand to the small of her back, and drove into her. She was everything *I* needed, and as I angled her hips to hit that deep, soft spot that made her eyes roll back in her head, she trembled around me. It was light and gentle, but quickly robbed me of all senses.

And there was more: words forming in my chest like little waves, rising up then splashing down only to build bigger, stronger, until they were catching me, dragging me under. They deserved voice, and they seeped into me, claiming territory on my bones and vital organs.

"Tiel," I whispered, my fingers tangled with hers, squeezing. "I *love you* love you, too."

She hummed, nodding, and wrapped her hands around my neck. We came together, hard and fast, yet it lingered, zapping us with aftershocks and spasms as we rocked into each other. When I gathered the strength to lift my head, I wiped the sweat from her brow and tossed the panties to the ground. I tucked Tiel under the covers and left to deal with the condom, returning with fruit, juice, and nuts.

She snuggled into my side, her head cushioned on my chest, and said, "I meant what I said."

I had a quip about fucking her in a girly bedroom decorated with unicorns and flowers on my tongue, but I swallowed it when she glanced up at me with big, vulnerable eyes. This wasn't like my slick comments about her tits or my unending requests for blowjobs. This was just a bit of what it meant to *last*.

"So did I, Tiel."

Twenty-Four

I'D ALWAYS KNOWN that Sam's world was a touch different from mine, but this—the swanky Scottsdale resort, unending spa treatments, elaborate cocktail parties and dinners —this proved it.

And the hotel sex was pretty incredible too.

We had one more night in Arizona. I intended to laze by the pool while he attended sessions and participated in panel discussions this afternoon, and January pool lazing was something I could get used to. Tonight was the conference's closing celebration at Taliesin West, famed architect Frank Lloyd Wright's home and architecture school, and Sam was delivering the address.

"What are you getting?" he asked while he scanned the menu.

I could also get used to fancy restaurant breakfasts each morning. "Probably something with wheat. Did you want to share?"

"No," he murmured. "Enjoy your wheat."

Laughing, I reached for my coffee. He was so freaking cute with his quirks and food allergies and sexy growls. Those growls. They were like the opening chords of 'Back in Black,' and they drove me wild, possessing me, every time.

I ordered Belgian waffles and, as usual, Sam engaged in a detailed discussion of his order with the waiter. "Could I get an egg white omelet with steamed spinach and tomatoes? Not sautéed, just steamed. And no butter. Not for the vegetables or the eggs."

"Yeah, seriously with the butter," I said. "It makes him sneeze, and you can see how that can get really annoying, right? Just imagine him sitting here, sneezing for ten minutes straight."

"I'll tell the chef," the waiter said. He wasn't especially effective in concealing the these-people-are-really-fucking-strange look he gave his notepad before leaving our table.

"Thanks for that, sweetheart," Sam said, smirking.

"Anytime," I said.

And there it was: our perfect little love bubble. Perfect was easy when it came with delicious food, maid service, poolside margaritas, and hotel sex, and I was enjoying every last second of it. It wouldn't be this easy when we were back in Boston. Our lives were more complicated when work and family and life were involved—*we* were more complicated—but this was a gorgeous reprieve from it all.

And I did like being spoiled, just a little.

Sam gestured to my tote bag. "What are you reading today?"

I'd worked my way through Keith Richards' memoir and Arnold Steinhardt's account of his experience as the first violinist with the Guarneri String Quartet this week. There was one more I wanted to read, and I'd been carrying it around for months, waiting for the right mood.

"It's part biography of Johnny Cash," I said, holding up the paperback. "And part his love letters to June Carter Cash. I've been waiting to read this one. It's an intense, messy story. This sort of thing does a number on me. I mean, I cried like a baby when I watched *Immortal Beloved*. That scene—when she realizes? Oh my God." I pressed my hand to my mouth and shook my head. The tears were already prickling my eyes. "It wrecked me. I think of it every time I play Beethoven."

Sam frowned and plucked the book from my fingers. He paged through it, stopping occasionally to skim the images of handwritten letters. "Sunshine...I don't want you to be upset. Why don't you save that one for another day?"

"It's not that I'm upset," I said, digging into my waffle. "It's that they go through some pretty heavy shit and find a way to love each other in the end, and that gives me all the feels."

He lifted an eyebrow. "I thought that was my job."

"Different feels," I said, but that eyebrow didn't budge. "Enough with the faces. Eat your omelet."

NOW THAT I knew the drill, selecting outfits for Sam's events was much easier. I'd borrowed another fifties-styled retro cocktail dress from Ellie's closet, paired it with some shiny red flats, and twirled in front of the bathroom mirror. The full skirt lifted from my legs, briefly exposing the scrap of satin underneath.

I'd been saving all my rare pieces of lingerie for Sam to ruin.

"We don't have to go anywhere," he murmured as he caught me around the waist. "We can stay right here."

"Oh no," I said. "Not after I spent ten minutes on the smoky eye."

"All right," he grumbled. He stared at my reflection in the mirror, his brows furrowed. "Is this a little low cut?"

"And that's suddenly a problem for you because...?"

He turned, walking me back to the vanity until I was seated on the cool marble. Pushing my legs open, he leaned into me, his hands on my hips and his mouth on my neck. "Because sometimes I get possessive, too."

His hands moved under my dress until they connected with my panties. He traced the silky edge, back and forth over my center until I was panting for more friction. He gripped the fabric at my hips, and when I expected him to tear, he inched my panties down my legs instead.

"Let's leave these here," he said.

"You don't want to hang onto them?" I asked, already half drunk off the idea of attending a posh party without my skivvies. I couldn't explain why, but that sent me straight into hyper-aroused territory every time, and Sam knew it.

"I have to *speak* in front of two hundred people, Tiel," he said. "I'm not capable of doing that with panties in my pocket. I might not be able to do it just knowing you're sitting there, bare-assed."

Somehow, he managed. He discussed the role of sustainable preservation in keeping history and culture alive, and methods to approach the craft in a way that honored the original builders while also evolving to incorporate high-value technological advancements.

I tried my damnedest to listen but every time Sam's eyes met mine across the room, I felt electrified. No one else seemed to notice that his glances were scorching and filled with promise, or that I wanted to part my legs and show him exactly how much he'd turned me on.

He kept his hand on my thigh through dinner, and that was a new brand of torture. He smiled at me, fully aware that his fingers were awfully close to the hot zone.

When the plates were cleared, I draped my arm over his back and urged him toward me. "Hey," I said, and he grinned in response. "You mentioned on the ride over here that you were really jazzed to see this place. So I'm wondering, do you have a huge architectural boner right now?"

"Would you like to find out?"

"Actually, yeah. I'd also like to rip your clothes off and ride your cock until I see stars and lose the power of speech, if that's okay with you."

He barked a surprised laugh and squeezed my leg. "That's a

really sweet idea," he said. "But you're only doing that if I tell you to."

"Maybe I don't want to take orders anymore," I said, pouting.

"But you do," he said, his eyes twinkling. "Let's see if we can get out of here without anyone noticing."

Of course, someone noticed. An older gentleman struck up a conversation with Sam, and as it became obvious they'd be chatting for awhile, I stepped away to get a drink. It allowed me to watch him from a distance, observe the way he used precise gestures when he was talking about his work and twisted the ring on his thumb when he was thinking. He didn't acknowledge the purposeful glances women sent him as they wandered past, but he did scan the room every couple of minutes, and he smiled when our eyes met.

I could tell he was attempting to wrap up the conversation, without much luck. When he looked at me again, he sent me a frustrated stare, and I sucked my martini's olives off the spear to distract him.

Except one of those olives missed my mouth and landed right between my boobs, and he observed the whole thing. My eyes wide with shock, I saw Sam abruptly excuse himself and rush toward me.

He grabbed my elbow and dragged me away from the event. He led me into a small office with tall windows facing the McDowell Mountains. "What was that?" he asked.

"Rogue olive," I muttered. Inside the office, we looked at each other, smiling wildly, and broke into laughter.

"There's only one solution," Sam said, eyeing my cleavage. "If you'd like."

I gestured to my chest. "There's an olive trapped in my boobs. Clearly, this requires an architect."

"I don't know about that," he said as he slipped out of his suit coat and folded it over the back of the desk chair. "There're a couple hundred architects out there, and none of them are touching you." He traced the edge of my dress, his finger following the rise and fall of my breasts. "Can you be quiet?"

"What is it you think you're doing?"

He pressed his finger to my lips. "Shush."

That finger shifted until his entire hand covered my mouth, and he gave me a slow, solemn nod. He kissed along my throat and chest, and pulled my dress down, exposing my bra. He dragged his lips over my breasts and then between, his tongue sliding against the curves.

Sam straightened, a lopsided grin splitting his face as he chewed the olive. "You still want to rip my clothes off?" I nodded. Of course I did. "I think I'm going to let you."

And then I threw him against the door and tore his trousers open. A button snapped off and his belt smacked me in the face, but I was on my knees and pumping his cock before he had any idea what was going on.

It was better this way. A little desperate, a little frantic, and too quick to think about what was happening. No excuses, no arguments. I wanted this, and I knew he did, too.

My tongue wrapped over his head, sweeping up the bead of fluid leaking out and taking him into my mouth. He groaned, and the sound reverberated around us, heightening my own arousal.

"Tiel," he warned. "You don't have to…"

"I want to."

His hands fisted in my hair, and the muscles in his legs flexed as he pumped into me, fast and greedy. He swore—long and loud and wonderfully profane. It was rough, and I nearly gagged a few times, but it was exactly how I wanted him.

"I'm not coming in your mouth," he said, his body going stiff. "Not this time."

Sam grabbed my biceps and hauled me up, shifting to back me against the door. He widened his stance and placed my hand on his cock, guiding me to stroke him.

"You're wet, aren't you?" I looked up with a devious smile,

and he trailed a finger up my thigh to brush over my folds. "Really wet."

I wiggled my lip between my teeth, sighing as his finger slipped inside me. He growled, low and menacing, and his mouth crashed against mine. He hiked my dress around my waist, hooked my leg over his thigh, and was inside me before the moan vibrated in my throat. "I think this qualifies as having sex in public," I sighed.

"And if you think you're getting two cocks any time soon, I can guarantee you one of them will be rubber," he growled. "No one else is touching you. Not now. Not *ever*."

My fingernails dug into his hips, scoring his skin and demanding more. This was the wild side of Sam that I adored, the one that allowed desire to reign over technique. He knew his way around the female body, that was a given, but I loved it when he didn't focus on me, when he surrendered to the electricity that arced between us.

"Won't last," he murmured. I nodded, whimpering against his lips as he pounded into me. I was close; not close enough to come in the next couple of seconds, but this time was all for him. He thrust deeply, and we groaned together as his orgasm barreled through him.

Sam sighed my name as he rested his head on my shoulder, and for those throbbing minutes, it was perfect. We were sweating, panting, and in various states of undress in a random office that boasted an enormous window for anyone to observe our coupling, and my heart completely and totally belonged to him. "I love you," I sighed.

"Sweetheart," he whispered, his voice heavy from the exertion. "We didn't use anything." I squinted at him, not understanding. "I came inside you."

"Oh," I said, and the single syllable revealed a stilted quality in my voice. I'd never encountered this issue before. He knew I wasn't on the pill—I couldn't remember that kind of thing, and didn't enjoy the idea of pumping chemicals into my body—and

I knew he had regular blood work done and was clean as a whistle. "It's fine."

"Are you sure?"

"Um, maybe?" I was terrible at keeping track of these things. I only knew I was fairly regular, and the precise details never found a home in my brain. "Don't worry."

"Are you *sure*?"

"Yes," I said, and that sounded like the right answer to me. What were the odds anything would come of this one unprotected moment?

He kissed my neck—I was concerned about my sweating, but he went right on kissing—and brought his hand between my legs, rubbing my clit. He was still inside me, pulsing, and he brought me right to the edge. I was gasping and moaning when I exploded on his fingers, and I sank my teeth into his arm to stifle my scream.

Sam straightened his clothing while I leaned against the door, recovering. I was still hazy, and all of my thoughts and reactions had to fight through that fog. He bent to collect the button I'd sent flying, and then knelt before me. I didn't understand what he was doing, and watched empty-headed as he lifted my skirt.

He stared at me—or, more precisely, he stared at my crotch —and I was starting to think he was looking at an ugly mole or ingrown hair. But then he ran his hand up my thigh, smiling, and said, "Do you have any idea how fucking sexy it is to see me all over you? How much I love that? How much I love *you*?"

Sam used his handkerchief to catch most of the fluid between my legs, and leaned forward, leaving a light kiss on my mound. He dragged his fingers over my slit, and then speared inside me. It skated a razor-fine line between pleasure and pain, and when I cried out, Sam's fingers retreated. As he stood, I grabbed his wrist and lifted his fingers to my mouth. I tasted the mix of *us* on him, and I released a tiny groan as I sucked him. He wiped his thumb over my lips and leaned in, kissing me with more heat and emotion than I could manage.

"Does that mean you'd like to do it again?"

"As soon as possible," he said.

He smoothed out my dress and we basically sprinted through the compound until we reached the parking lot. We spent the evening wrapped in each other, laughing and kissing and touching, and forgoing the condoms.

Everything seemed fine until the morning, when Sam left for the resort gym—he always invited me, but I only ran when chased—and I stood in the shower, my fingers turning to prunes. I forced myself to go back in time and date my last period, and yeah, I was right in the middle of my cycle.

Hello, fertility.

The realization sank in my stomach, and my brain went into hyper-spastic mode.

I didn't say more than a few words when Sam returned and we headed to the airport. It was like I was sleepwalking, and I couldn't form sounds that made sense. We shuffled through airport security, and Sam put a bagel and cappuccino in my hand while we waited to board our flight. I stared at them, too lost in my thoughts to eat.

"I could be pregnant. Like, actually pregnant," I whispered. No one was seated nearby, but giving voice to these thoughts made them all the more real.

He removed the lid from his tea, the steam rising and curling between us. "And you'd be unhappy about that?"

I stared at him, my mouth hanging open in shock. "Wouldn't you?"

"Actually...no," he said, lifting a shoulder. "I wouldn't. I thought about it last night. *All* night. You slept hard, Sunshine, but I spent the entire night thinking about putting a baby in you. I wouldn't be unhappy. I'd be thrilled, as long as it was what you wanted."

What *I* wanted.

"How the fuck am I supposed to know whether I want a baby? I haven't thought about having kids since ever. And holy *fuck*, Sam, a baby is one hell of a permanent commitment," I said. "I mean…shit. I don't even know what to say."

"I love you." He squeezed my hand until I met his eyes. "And you love me?" I nodded. "Then we'll figure it out."

"But, what would we do?" I wanted specific answers. I didn't care that I was taking all of Sam's obsessive-compulsive tendencies and wearing them as my own. "When would I finish my dissertation? What about the classes I'm teaching? And the kids I'm working with—how would I have sessions with them? Would I be able to do all that with a baby? Would the baby come to the college with me? What would it do all day? And where would we live? And my family—oh God, my parents will have such passive aggressive things to say. And kids are expensive and I don't understand anything about breastfeeding or vaccines. And *everything* about my life would change."

"Do me a favor and breathe."

"You breathe," I said. I was being loud and screechy, and though this section of the airport was relatively empty, I was certain everyone was watching my life crack open. "It's not your vagina that's going to do all the work."

Sam cringed and pulled me from my seat into his lap. "I haven't thought about kids before now, either," he said, his hand stroking my back. "But I've thought about you, and all the things I want with you. We can have our own family, Tiel. You and me and *our baby*, and I want that more than I can explain."

"Why are you being so calm?" I asked, but it came out in a shriek. "Hyperventilating is a collegiate sport for you. Where are you with the thermonuclear panic when I need it?"

"I'm not living down that one time on the sidewalk in Cambridge any time soon," he said, shifting me from his lap. He collected my untouched coffee and bagel, and hooked my tote bag over his shoulder.

"You're only doing that because you think I might be carrying your spawn," I said as we walked toward the gate.

"No," Sam replied. "I'm doing it because I love you, and the least I can do is grab your bag while you freak the fuck out."

Once we boarded the plane and got situated in our seats, he laced his fingers with mine and kissed the back of my hand.

"I can give you answers to all those questions, but I don't think you want any of that right now." I stared out the window, watching as the ground crew tossed one bag after another onto a conveyor belt. "I will support you no matter what, and I promise you can trust me."

"I just have a lot to think about," I said. "And we're probably blowing this out of proportion. I'm sure it's nothing."

When we were airborne, I unraveled my earbuds, handed one to Sam, and called up my playlist. I rested my head on his shoulder, closed my eyes, and let myself drown in the music while I tried to convince myself that everything was going to be fine.

Twenty-Five

SHANNON WAS A NOTORIOUSLY PICKY EATER. Unlike me, there was no philosophy or dietary rationale behind her food choices. Nothing was ever cooked the way she liked it, I could name at least forty things she refused to eat, and more often than not, she ate a slim fraction of the food on her plate.

Knowing that, I wasn't looking forward to meeting her for brunch at Aquitaine the day after getting back from Arizona. She liked to pretend she enjoyed French food when in reality she enjoyed drinking French champagne before noon, and while I'd managed to tolerate that previously, I wasn't in the mood for it now.

I knew it was time to sit down and hash it out with her, but it also took me away from Tiel. I left her in my bed with a promise to return soon but wouldn't be surprised to find her schlepping back to her apartment this morning.

As I waited for Shannon to join me, I started an email to myself noting the work required on the firehouse. I wanted to finally convert the old showers to a practice space for Tiel, and the bathrooms required updating, and we might be in need of a nursery very soon.

I couldn't begin to summarize how incredible that felt.

"Who is licking your ass this morning?"

I startled at Shannon's comment, and tucked my phone away as she sat across from me. "Excuse me?"

"You look like a kid on Christmas morning," she said. "I take it you enjoyed Scottsdale."

"It was fantastic," I said, but couldn't remember anything about the conference.

Turning my attention to the menu, I ignored Shannon's expectant gaze. She stared at me for a moment, then launched into a detailed account of her week. The Turlans' public relations people were keeping her busy with update requests and ever-changing press tour schedules, and that was on top of the work she did with the assortment of councils and committees around town.

Every neighborhood had their own advisory board, or so it seemed, and she was the first line of defense for them all. She pushed them to reconsider regulations against otherwise unsightly home sustainability features like solar panels and rain water catchment, and managed them through well-intentioned yet ridiculous remodeling and construction guidelines.

"I swung by on Thursday with some groceries," she said. "It looked like Riley had been surviving on spicy mustard and beer. I got a few quarts of that soup you like. They're in the freezer. Oh, and I sent my cleaning lady to your place, just so you didn't worry about that when you got home."

"You didn't have to do any of that," I said, careful to keep my tone even.

"I wanted to," she said, shrugging as she destroyed a plate of brioche French toast. "No big deal. So listen. Andy is leading a walk-through at Wellesley soon. She wants to discuss the progress and get some feedback on issues. I didn't want that to come as a shock, and you don't have to go if you're not feeling up to it."

"I don't mind," I said.

Shannon inclined her head toward me and frowned. "I don't understand. What is it you don't mind?"

"I don't mind going to the walk-through." I shrugged and picked some minced chives from my eggs. Shannon stood abruptly, and moved beside me to press her hand to my forehead.

"You don't feel hot," she murmured. "Did you pick up Valley Fever or something? What's going on with you?"

"Nothing is going on," I said. "I'm just not going to get hung up on the house, or any of it. I don't have time for that shit, and there's no sense reliving it every day. I'd rather not sit around, holding hands and talking about how great Angus was, but I'll take a look at the progress."

She leaned back in her chair, her champagne glass pinched between her fingers, studying me. "All right," she said eventually. "Let's do this."

"Now?" I said. I glanced around the busy restaurant. "Here?"

"Yep," she said. "We can be civilized."

"Fine. I'm with Tiel, and she's not going anywhere," I said. I stopped short of mentioning that we might be having a baby, and despite every urge to the contrary, I didn't ask whether she knew where Matt picked up Lauren's engagement ring. I was fighting this battle one hill at a time. "It would be nice if you'd respect that."

"I don't *dis*respect that, Sam—"

"You certainly aren't supportive," I said.

She rubbed her forehead and murmured something to herself. "Honestly, I just want what's best for you, and if she's it, I'm on board and I'll do anything I can to make her feel included. You look healthy and you seem happy, and that's fantastic, but I have no idea what's going on with you. I had to hear about this girl from *Andy*. Do you even understand how much that hurt me?"

I pushed my plate to the side. "And you, Shannon, you vanish for random weekends and can't manage to tell me where the fuck you've been?" I shook my head and gazed out the window. "You can hide your shit from a lot of people, but you can't hide it from me."

We stared at each other, waiting for the other to speak first. The waiter circled back to our table three times during this impasse, and Shannon finally snapped at him to take her plate and bring another mimosa.

"All right. Fine," she said. "I started something over the summer. It was…" She turned her eyes to the ceiling, pausing as she selected her words. "To put it mildly, a very bad idea, but there were some extenuating circumstances."

I accepted another glass of juice from the waiter, wiped the rim with my napkin, and sipped. "It's fascinating how you're very obviously talking about sex, and you've never before felt the need to censor yourself with me."

"Yes, well, shit happens," she murmured. "Anyway. It ended, and that was for the best, and that's all I'm going to say. I'd like to hear about Tiel."

"Right," I said. "You actually deserve the credit for this one." She shot me a confused frown and I smiled. "I was stuck in that elevator—the one at Comm Ave.—with her when you bailed on me."

"You're very welcome," she said. "So what's her story?"

"She's incredible, Shannon. Like, really fucking incredible." I told her about Tiel's YouTube following and her conservatory background, and I mentioned the loopy family issues because that was one thing Shannon could commiserate with, and how Tiel was reasonably cautious in family settings.

Somewhere in the middle of dumping all these details on Shannon, her skeptical expression softened. She started smiling, her eyes crinkling as I told stories about our adventures in Boston's music scene and lazy movie nights.

"When she's not around, it's like I'm missing an organ," I said. "She was in New Jersey for two and a half days, and I didn't know what the hell to do with myself."

"Okay, so you're not going to clubs or the cool parties anymore? You're not screwing lots of random chicks and drinking your weight every night?" I shook my head. "Don't you miss it? Those are your nuts and bolts."

"We go out a lot," I said. "It's different from my old scene, but I have a lot more fun with Tiel."

"You're all going to get married," Shannon sighed. "And I will be that crazy cat lady."

"I don't think she's interested in talking about marriage," I said. "Her first was absolute shit, and the guy was a douche, and I don't see that in the near future."

Though it was rather antiquated of me, I didn't like the idea of bringing a child into the world without marrying his mother first, but I didn't see Tiel going for that anytime soon. I could be fine with it so long as we lived together.

"Oh so you've thought about it," she said.

I lifted a shoulder and tried to wipe away all hint of my true desires. Shannon was an effective negotiator because she could read people as well as I read bluelines, but I wasn't in a spot to be fully transparent with her yet.

"I've thought about a lot of things," I said.

"Sure," she said. "Of course." She glanced to her phone and then back at me. "I'm meeting Lauren soon, but…promise you'll talk to me. I have to do a better job, you have to do a better job, and we have to stick together."

Nodding, I stood to hug her. "I'll work on it, but promise me you'll love her. No matter what, I need you to love her."

"Always," she said.

The drive back to the firehouse was quick, and I'd never been so excited to get home as I was knowing Tiel was there. I also felt better about things with Shannon, and that eased an entire lump of tension in my neck. We were in a better place—not great, but getting there—and we'd figure this out. We always did.

Arriving home, I watched from the doorway as Tiel and

Riley laughed together at the kitchen table. He was telling stories that probably shouldn't see the light of day, and she was giggling, her whole body rocking with the force. She looked damned adorable in those little running shorts and one of my long-sleeved t-shirts, and the baby anxiety wasn't weighing on her like it did yesterday.

"Would it kill you to put on some clothes?" I asked, gesturing to Riley's boxers. If history was any predictor, we'd be seeing his junk very soon.

They turned toward me, and Riley mumbled something about his bits and bobs needing room to breathe while he lumbered up the stairs.

"Don't believe anything he told you," I said, leaning down to kiss Tiel. She shifted, wrapping her arms around my neck. I heard Riley coming back down the stairs, still muttering, but I ignored him.

"It is no fun getting up without you," she said. "You spoiled me this week. Your wake-up calls are the best."

"It's interesting that you mention that now," I said. Grabbing her around the waist, I set her on the table and stepped between her legs. "What do you say we fix up the showers and get you a decent practice space? Or build a real bedroom for us?"

"Mmmhmm." She fisted my sweater and brought me closer until I was lowering her to the table. "As long as you don't put Riley on the street. He's kind of growing on me."

"Yeah, he's got a lot in common with foot fungus." I pinned her, squeezing both hands around the globes of her ass. "You're not wearing any underwear."

"Nope," she said, grinning.

"Hey," Riley called. He refilled his cereal bowl and threw an annoyed glance at us. "Could you not make any babies while I eat breakfast?"

"It might be too late for that," I said, gathering Tiel in my arms and hauling her off the table.

"What?" he yelled, his bowl clattering to the countertop and sending milk sloshing out the sides.

"Nothing, Riley. Nothing at all," Tiel said.

"WOW," I murmured, craning my neck to study the new floor joists. I hadn't been to the Turlan property in the ten days since returning from Arizona, and it was obvious Riley had taken my instructions to heart. "You were busy."

"The subtext," Riley said, gesturing to Magnolia, "is that I'm a slacker, and Sam's impressed we accomplished anything without his beautiful mind to guide us."

They tossed quips back and forth while I studied the completed work, noting the rapid progress on resolving the plumbing issues without ruining that unique penny drop tile, tearing off the roof and building the framework for a highly efficient exterior, and fixing the missing hardwood planks in the dining room. The bones of the home were being shored up with new beams—some wood, some steel—and every window was new.

"We haven't mentioned the electrical issue, though," she whispered. Her hands were shoved deep in the pockets of her fleece jacket, and she was standing closer to Riley than me, and I was content with that scenario.

"Fuuuuuck," Riley groaned. "You tell him."

"There was some latent water damage in here. It had been painted over, but when we busted into the ceiling to fix the hot and cold water returns, we found some rot. We followed it down, and then we found this." Magnolia led the way to the front parlor and pointed to the bare studs. "It's all black."

Confused, I knelt down, expecting to find mold or fire damage, but I was faced with electrical wires. "Shit," I murmured. No white, no red. Just black. "Everywhere?"

"Yeah," Riley said.

This system dated back to the earliest days of electricity in homes, before codes were fully standardized, regulated, and delineated with color. "We need to trace it all back," I said, sighing. "Replace it all."

"Yep," Riley said. "Let me add that to my list of fun conversations to have with my trades."

I paged through the plans while touching base with the general contractor about his timeline for the roof. We were battling the weather, and though January was no treat in terms of building in Boston, Magnolia's timeline was already tight. If she wasn't able to dive in, we'd be looking at several months of delays.

"So it looks good?" Riley asked. "Aside from the major fire hazard?"

"Excellent," I said. "You handled this well, and I should have paid closer attention to the electrical from the start."

He mumbled something under his breath and went off in search of the electrician. I still didn't understand his inability to acknowledge that he was competent. Riley preferred being the family failure who barely graduated high school, but he was secretly smart in plenty of areas. Somewhere along the line, it'd become easier for him to fuck up than succeed, and he'd claimed that as his niche.

Matt knew that Riley was capable of far more than he let on, but he also provided Riley with the cover necessary to learn, practice, screw up, and then grow from his mistakes. I didn't know how to bring out the best in others the way Matt did, but I was determined to edge Riley out of the nest soon. He needed to find his footing and grow on his own, and as soon as I found the right project for him, he'd be going at it solo.

"Do you guys want to get a drink?" Magnolia asked. "There's no football on tonight, and I don't know what to do with myself."

"That really depends on where you'd like to go," Riley said. "Your preferences might be a little down-market for the boss."

He nodded toward me but I ignored it. Magnolia was still casually affectionate—there was no dodging her hugs—but she wasn't overtly flirting with me. If anything, she was flirting with Riley and if I wasn't mistaken, he was reciprocating.

Interception completed.

"The Salty Pig," she suggested. "They have some insane drinks. You have to try their Bear Skin Rug."

"That sounds pleasantly homoerotic," he said. "Seems like something I'd enjoy."

"Obviously," she said. "That's why I mentioned it."

Maybe this didn't have to be difficult or tentative, at least not for me. I stepped away to text Tiel, knowing she'd love seeing these two going back and forth with each other.

Sam: Hey my sunshine. What's on the agenda tonight?

Life was good. Really good, but not without its own set of challenges. We were talking about her living at the firehouse, and she admitted it was difficult to give up her space and independence, but was warming up to the idea. We had a hearty debate about the right way to load a dishwasher last weekend, and though it didn't meet the strict definition of a fight, we enjoyed an evening of make-up sex nonetheless.

We stayed together most nights, and though I wanted to spend every moment of every day by her side, I was also working on giving her the space she craved.

The (potential) baby situation lingered on the back burner and I couldn't find the appropriate forum to open that discussion. It was her body and I respected her privacy and choices, but I also wanted to know what was going on. I didn't think it was a good idea to show up at her apartment with a pregnancy test and an awkward smile, and I didn't know whether it was acceptable for me to request status updates on her menstrual cycle. We were together enough for me to have a general idea, but coming out and asking seemed rather forward.

She'd tell me one way or another, I didn't doubt that, but I was inwardly quivering for more information. I was trying to find a smooth way to suggest she start taking prenatal vitamins or swapping out some coffee for juice, but as of yet, I hadn't located one. Every time we held each other in bed or snuggled on the sofa to watch a movie, my hand went straight to her belly. I could barely contain the excitement I experienced at the prospect of our child growing inside her, and it was completely overwhelming, too.

I didn't hear Angus's voice as much these days—Tiel babbled too much for me to hear much else—but part of me worried about replicating my DNA. I was born with a full slate of issues, and I didn't want to see my kid suffering through any of that.

By all accounts, I hadn't been an easy baby. The diabetes came first and then it was breathing problems and food allergies, and by the time I was two, I was a bundle of nerves and neuroses. I spent my entire childhood with my stress hormones on blast, and I was afraid of my own damn shadow.

It was horribly ironic to reflect on the full panic I worked myself into a few nights ago as I wondered whether our baby would inherit my allergies, my anxieties, my chronic diseases.

The one thing I didn't worry about was being a father, and that was shocking, considering I didn't have a decent role model. If anything, I was looking forward to it with more enthusiasm than I'd conjured in years. I wanted to do it well, and I wanted to give our kid something I'd never had, and I instantly saw our little family coming together.

Tiel: Haven't even thought that far ahead yet.
Tiel: But I am hungry and I might start eating these papers instead of grading them
Sam: Don't do that.
Sam: Meet me at the salty pig on Dartmouth.
Sam: Or I could pick you up. It's really cold with the wind chill.

Sam: Actually, yeah, I'm going to pick you up. I'll be wrapping up in here in about 15 minutes

I wasn't interested in the mother of my baby—possibly—trekking through the Back Bay in near zero temperatures. Someone would probably slap me upside the head for that and remind me women have been bearing children for thousands of years, and there was no need for me to hover, but that wasn't changing my perspective.

Tiel needed someone taking care of her. She'd been doing it all on her own since forever, and it was fucking admirable, but it didn't have to be that way. That, and I derived a foreign—although very fantastic—pleasure from spoiling her.

Tiel: Oh please. This is mild compared to last winter.
Sam: It's still cold
Sam: I don't mind, really. I'll swing by
Tiel: No. I need to finish a few more essays
Tiel: I want to get this done and I'll just meet you at your place when I'm done. I probably have 2 hrs more anyway
Sam: Are you sure?
Tiel: YES!
Sam: Ok but call me if you change your mind.

Magnolia, Riley, and I headed to the restaurant, and settled in with drinks and industry gossip. I used to think I was well-connected, but it was becoming obvious to me that Magnolia had me beat with at least one population. She could trace the family tree for damned near every contractor in town, knew who he dated in high school, and how he took his coffee. And she wasn't just a know-it-all; people liked her, myself included.

"I have some news, if this is a good time," she said when Riley went to the bar for details on the making of a Bear Skin Rug. "*Coastal* reached out to me this week. They're featuring a roof garden that I did in Marblehead. Full spread, at least four pages. It's in the June edition. Other than the magazine and Riley, you are the first to know."

That was huge for her. *Huge*. She'd been struggling to get her business off the ground for years, and as I knew all too well, the right publicity changed everything.

Not long after I finished grad school and started working at the firm, I was trolling the club scene and found myself talking with the head of a venture capital firm. I drew some rough sketches on cocktail napkins, mentioned some sexy sustainability buzzwords, and had myself a multi-million dollar project by the end of the night. He loved the work we did on his brownstone, but more than that, he loved finding an unknown talent and telling everyone about it. That renovation put me— and the firm—in the spotlight in a substantial way, and that was exactly what Magnolia needed.

"That's incredible. How did you not tell me the minute it happened?" I moved to her side of the table and folded her into a tight hug. "So proud of you."

She leaned away from me, gripping my forearms, and said, "You've been awesome for me. All the introductions you've made with some of your clients, talking through proposals and projects with me, bringing me in on Turlan, all of it. Thank you."

I squeezed my arms around her shoulders, laughing. "Anytime."

"But really," she said, her voice becoming soft. "Thank you." Magnolia tilted her head and before I understood what she was doing, her lips were pressed against mine. I knew it was wrong, *so wrong*, but I held her there while the wrongness of it all registered. Panic flooded my system, and it took a full five seconds of alarms blaring in my head and her tongue spearing past my tightly closed lips before my brain was able to react.

I leaned away, gasping, and ran the back of my hand over my mouth. A streak of rosy lipstick stained my skin. "What the fuck was that, Magnolia?"

Turning around, still panting and overwrought, I found

myself staring at Tiel. Her expression was fully murderous, and I had the distinct impression I'd be choking on my own intestines right now if she had her way.

She crossed her arms over her chest and pointed her chin at Magnolia. "And who is this?"

"OH. HI. I'M MAGNOLIA SANTILLIAN," she said, extending her hand with a bright smile.

I glared at her, ignoring her hand. The woman had her mouth on Sam a second ago and had the balls to *smile* at me, and all he could do was scrub the lipstick from his palm like he was Lady fucking Macbeth.

Ugly silence settled over us as I glanced between them, but I wasn't running away. Not yet.

"This is my *girlfriend*, Tiel," Sam finally said, stammering as he attempted to pretend this situation was really fucking innocent, and God, I wanted to believe there was an explanation. I'd always wondered whether Sam could handle monogamy, and even though the answer was staring me in the face at this moment, I wanted it to be a mistake. I wanted to believe the past three months weren't a figment of my imagination, but the way they looked at each other was too familiar to ignore. "It's not what you think."

Right. Sam—with all his personal space issues and unwillingness to touch a fucking salt shaker without first dipping it in bleach—was kissing a random chick and it wasn't what I thought.

"I had no idea you were seeing someone!" She made a show of looking horrified, maybe a little embarrassed, and it would have helped if she didn't then whack Sam on the elbow. She needed to keep her fucking hands to herself. "Why didn't you tell me?"

"Of course you didn't," I said.

"This is all my fault," she said, waving frantically. "Sam did *nothing* wrong. Seriously, Tiel, this was all me."

I couldn't believe this was happening. My entire body was shaking with a torrent of rage and hurt and confusion, and I was a breath away from losing it.

"Erroneous, Gigi," Riley said as he came up behind me. "It's always Sam's fault. He's the master of weaseling out of things." He paused, glancing between me, Sam, and that bitch. To her credit, she had backed away from Sam and was looking increasingly uncomfortable. "Uh, what is the crime in question?"

"Tiel, I am so, so, *so* sorry," she said. She stepped toward me, her hands spread in front of her, pleading. "Honestly, this is on me and I might actually die from humiliation now."

I pointed at Sam. "Can I speak to you outside?"

"We should let the grown-ups have a little chitchat, Gigi," Riley murmured. He brought his hands to her shoulders and steered her away.

I didn't wait for Sam's response, instead turning on my heel and storming through the restaurant. I burst through the door, sending it snapping back and clattering against the restaurant's front window.

"Goddamn it, Tiel, stop," he yelled. "Just stop."

He stepped in front of me, his hand on my elbow, and I promptly shook it off. "Don't," I said. "Tell me what's going on. Tell me *everything*, and please do not lie to me."

He sighed, shaking his head and gesturing frantically until the words sputtered out. "Tiel, I'm sorry, sweetheart. She's a friend and colleague, and I was congratulating her on a magazine feature, and she got the wrong idea. That's all." He dragged his hands through his hair, and he was all the way desperate. "Just a misunderstanding."

There was always a simple, pretty explanation.

"If it was such a misunderstanding, why didn't you stop her? Why didn't you say, 'Hey lady, get your tongue out of my mouth'?" I could buy that argument if I hadn't stood there, staring at them kissing while full seconds ticked by.

"I just...I don't know. I fucked up. I didn't realize she was into me, and I thought Riley was going to handle it. They started hanging out and going to football games together and it seemed like she was over it, but—"

"Wait," I interrupted, holding my hands up for silence. I couldn't keep up with this ridiculous story. "Wait. How long has this been going on with her?"

"We've been working on the Turlan project since October," he said. "But *nothing* is going on. Nothing happened."

All this time.

I couldn't believe I'd been so stupid, so fucking foolish. This was Sam after all, the man who made no illusions about what he wanted from a woman, the man who once told me that love and forever were nonexistent, bullshit notions.

That was probably the only true thing he'd ever said.

"Sam," I sighed, his name falling from my lips in a low sob.

I didn't know how else to explain that this was *destroying* me but there had to be something. I looked around, desperate to find the answer in the shop windows, the street, the curious eyes watching us from inside the restaurant, but my search turned up empty. There was nothing to stop the fracture growing between us, nowhere to hold on.

"But you didn't tell her about me. You didn't mention that you were seeing someone. I didn't matter enough—"

"*No*," he interrupted. "I fucked up and I'm so sorry, but please, let's go inside, you're freezing—"

"I'm not pregnant. Just so you know. That's why you're putting on this concerned act, I get that, and you can stop now."

His face fell, the hard lines of frustration dissolving, and he murmured a soft "Oh."

My period started last night, and I'd never had so many contradictory feelings about it before. The first reaction was disappointment, and that was rather infuriating. This wasn't the right time to get pregnant but over the past week, it became a happy eventuality. It was as if we'd conceded that I *was* pregnant and we were ensuring that confirmation by forgoing condoms altogether.

But then I was relieved. We weren't anywhere near ready, and this was an opportunity to spend more time enjoying each other before we complicated matters.

And now...now I knew it was a stay of execution.

"Listen to me. Nothing happened with Magnolia except for me being too in love with you to notice her flirting. I swear to you on my mother's grave that I never once entertained an unprofessional thought about her, and Riley will tell you the same thing. And you fucking matter. You're my everything and I'm taking you home," Sam said. "We'll talk about this there."

He was tender and sweet, and God help me, I wanted to believe him. I wanted to pretend this had never happened. I wanted to run into his arms and stay there until I felt my doubt and distrust slide away. I wanted to replace all my wounds with his love...but I knew better than that.

I crossed my arms over my chest and shook my head. "I'm not sure why I thought it would be different with you. I can't believe I didn't see it sooner."

"Tiel, there's nothing to see because I'm telling you the truth," he said, his hands fisted on his hips. "Can we take a moment to acknowledge this is really about your asshole ex-husband? That once again, *none* of this has anything to do with me or us?"

I knew I needed to stop and breathe, but I couldn't see beyond the icy betrayal in my gut. "Don't you dare put this on me," I said. "It isn't my fault that you kissed someone. I wasn't the one who hid this particular *friend* and I wasn't the one with my hands all over some slut."

"She's not a slut," he said, his voice low and quiet. "So you're saying you don't trust me at all?"

It was horribly cold, frigid wind was biting at my face, and my bag's strap was digging into my shoulder, but nothing outpaced the throbbing pain coursing through my body.

"I can't trust you because you tell me to, not when you've made it perfectly clear that you fuck everything with tits and a heartbeat."

"And *I* can't believe you just said that." He shook his head, his expression turning bitter. "You know that isn't true. You know that isn't how it is."

"I don't know how *anything* is anymore, Sam." I backed away, desperate for some breathing room. "Here's what I know. You have a lot of sex with a lot of women and none of it matters to you. This little experiment of ours? We've been sleeping together for less than three months and you're already kissing someone else. I would be an absolute idiot to assume you'd changed, and I never should have tried in the first place."

A bus stopped at the curb, and when the doors creaked open, a burst of passengers spilled onto the sidewalk. We stared at each other, ignoring the people moving around us, and the hurt and anger grew, multiplying until I barely recognized the eyes gazing back at me.

"Yeah," he said. I caught a flash of grief in his eyes, but the fight inside him died and his expression morphed into indifference. He hadn't moved but I sensed his resolve ebbing and him backing away from me, detaching. "You're probably right."

"I...I need some space. From all of this. I cannot even begin to process tonight. And these past few months. I need space," I repeated.

"Take all the time you need, sweetheart," he said, his voice nonchalant. He pulled on that shiny veneer, the superficially perfect smirk he showed the world when he was busy hiding his vulnerabilities, and it was the saddest, most hollow expression I'd ever seen. "Whatever. So it's over. Like you said, it's not like any of this matters to me."

He dragged his unimpressed gaze up and down my body, lifted a shoulder, and walked away.

I STUMBLED through the rest of the week in a foggy, confused state, aching to call Sam and forgive everything just to feel his arms around me again. I wanted him more than anything, but I still couldn't reconcile his words, his actions—his willingness to leave me standing on that sidewalk after I found him kissing another woman—with the man I thought I'd uncovered.

This was a mess. A gigantic, horrendous mess, and I wanted to assign blame to Sam…but I couldn't. There was more, something I couldn't understand.

We were this close to having it all figured out, to moving in together, to—*holy fuck*—starting a family. And then it was gone, sliding out of our hands before we could grasp the threads and fragments.

We loved each other. Actual, real, hot, messy, complicated, marrow-deep love but I was beginning to think it didn't matter how much you loved someone.

Some things weren't meant to last.

When my last class ended on Friday afternoon, I was in the mood for some late eighties Billy Joel. Something dark, like "The Downeaster 'Alexa.'"

Maybe U2. The angsty shit from "Joshua Tree" and "Achtung Baby."

The more I thought about it, the darker the playlist became. I could focus on moving tracks around as I waited on the Red Line platform, and I didn't have to think about anything Sam said or did. None of our sidewalk argument echoed in my mind so long as I kept The Used, Sia, and AFI pounding through my earbuds.

When I reached my apartment, I stripped out of my clothes and went straight for the shelf in my closet earmarked for Sam. I pulled on his flannel pajama pants and gray tank and called up my new playlist. Without a proper title, it defaulted to the first song I selected: 'Criminal' by Fiona Apple. I hadn't cried yet, but when I curled up on the sofa, my entire body submitted to heaving, sloppy sobs. The hurt I'd been pushing down for two days was uncorked and overflowing, and once it was out, I felt stunningly empty.

The music played for hours before circling back to the first track, and I drifted into intermittent fits of watery, hiccupping sleep. I lay there, replaying those songs until they blurred, mutating into one long aching sob.

Ellie called, and though I wasn't sure I could speak, let alone explain, I answered.

"I fucked up," I sniffled, not bothering with an introduction. "With the prepster. And he did too, but...I said awful, evil things to him. He screwed up but I wouldn't even listen, and I should have. I tore into him. I don't know what to do right now, Ell."

"Okay," she said. "Am I going to you, or are you coming to me?"

She was on a flight to Boston that night, and when I woke up the next morning, she was across from me, dozing in the slouchy blue chair. Ellie was the best kind of people, and aside from music, her friendship was the only real constant in my life. There weren't many things I kept around, but Ellie was one of them. She was a better sister to me than Agapi could ever be, and between us, we had created more family than either of ours could offer. We didn't need blood to bond us.

Four iced cappuccinos sat on the table, and a large paper sack from my favorite bagel shop. I downed half the coffee in one noisy gulp, and her eyes blinked open. She sat beside me on the sofa, draping her arm over my shoulder and pulling the blanket around us. "Thank you for coming. I know you're missing shows and...I'm sorry."

"Don't thank me and don't apologize. This is making the back-up fiddler incredibly happy," she said. "Tell me everything."

"I fell in love with him," I said simply. "And then we almost got pregnant and some overly zealous bitch tried to kiss him. I flipped out and basically told him he was a whore and that he'd never change, and that's where I was wrong." I ran my hand through my hair and shrugged. "I think I really fucked it all up, and it's the kind of fucked-up you can't fix."

"Okay, why don't you rewind this story and slow it down for me," she said.

We drank all the coffee and ate most of the bagels while I talked. Ellie listened, forcing me to repeat certain parts and asking questions in others, and she sat back, tapping her finger to her lips when I finally finished.

"Whatever it is," I said. "Just spit it out."

"Here's what we can agree on: you're sensitive about infidelity, he doesn't have the cleanest relationship boundaries, and this Maggie or Minnesota or whatever her name is, she's definitely overzealous. I'm tempted to believe her when she says it was her fault, but that doesn't excuse the heightened zeal."

"Right," I said. "What's up for debate?"

She went back to tapping her lips and I attacked another bagel.

"Is it possible that Sam proved why it didn't work with Dillon?" I turned to her, my mouth full, and lifted an eyebrow. "Hear me out. Yeah, Dillon cheated on you, but he also had no idea who you were. You two had that weird instalove shit going on, and you were so busy being in love with being in love that nothing else mattered. You weren't friends. You didn't truly know each other."

"And how does that prove anything?" I asked. "Aside from

the fact I was a shallow teenager with a low threshold for affection?"

"You were friends first, and it seems like you authentically cared about Sam," she said.

I nodded in confirmation.

"And...don't hate me when I say this, but it sounds like you were convinced Sam was just like Dillon, even from the start, and you made that fit the circumstances?"

The comments about his sex life. I was the one who instigated those conversations.

The questions about his whereabouts. I was the one who didn't accept his word.

The reactions to his relationships with Andy and Lauren. I was the one who couldn't handle it.

The refusal to hear him out even when what's-her-name admitted fault. I was the one who broke us up.

"Oh, fuck," I groaned, and buried my head in the sofa. If I stayed hidden there, I wouldn't have to acknowledge that I destroyed the most loving relationship of my life because I refused to believe someone was worth trusting.

"Let's say Dillon never cheated on you. It still wouldn't have worked out," she said. "You would have realized that you were wrong for each other eventually, and while I don't condone his methods, Dillon just figured it out sooner."

"Okay, but—" I stopped myself because I didn't have an argument to defend. Ellie was right.

"Again, don't hate me but... Your real issue is that you've never been loved the way you deserve, and I think Sam might have done that for you. And maybe you didn't know how to handle it. I don't think Dillon hurt you when he cheated. You didn't care enough to be hurt. He was just another in a long line of assholes who thought it was okay to fuck you over and abandon you." I peeked out from behind a pillow, glancing at her in question. "Yes, I'm talking about your family. They're assholes and you know it as well as I do."

I finished the other half of the bagel without responding because once again, Ellie was right.

"Will you tell me stories about the tour now?" I asked. Her accounts from the road were my preferred fairy tales, and though I never saw myself playing with a band and traveling from city to city, I loved the vicarious experience. It was a sweet little escape, and that was what I needed at this moment.

Later, I sat on the floor of the shower while water rushed over me. I felt hollow and fragile, like I'd snap if I moved the wrong way. The lighthearted joy that usually came so easily to me was buried deep below the surface, in a spot I couldn't access.

I wanted to find Sam, to explain everything, but I was all out of words...and there were too many old, tender wounds obscuring my thoughts. I needed the music to tell me what I was feeling, how to make sense of it all, how to go forward. This was the sort of thing I processed by myself, bleeding it out every time I brought my fingers back to the strings. I didn't know whether I was built that way or I made myself that way, but it was my operating system.

And I knew where I had to go.

Twenty-Seven

SAM

"ARE YOU COMING?"

Riley was standing in the doorway to my office, his fly unzipped and a coffee stain resembling Argentina down his leg.

"RISD. Put your dick away."

I was in rough shape after giving Tiel six days of 'space' and let's be honest: she hadn't been asking for a couple days of space. She never wanted to see me again.

I wasn't sleeping. I couldn't convince myself to eat much. I was hitting the treadmill in the dead of night, running for hours and pretending there was something normal about that.

"My bad, my bad," he mumbled as he righted his trousers. "As I was saying, are you coming?"

Irritated, I scrolled through my calendar but couldn't find an appointment. "Coming where? I'm free all morning, and I was looking forward to feeling sorry for myself during that time."

That last comment earned me a lifted eyebrow from Riley. He was squarely in the camp of me calling Tiel and groveling my ass off. I was more interested in hating the world for the foreseeable future and not making a fool of myself again. "It's the walk-through at Wellesley. Shannon said you wanted to be there."

Fuuuuck.

"Shannon, Patrick, and Andy are meeting us there. Matt's driving. You can come with us, or I can catch a ride with him if you're out."

"No," I groaned, and shoved my things into my messenger bag. "I'm not in the mood to talk to Shannon, and she's going to come in here, guns blazing, if I bail. I don't have the patience for her dramatics today."

I slumped in the back seat of Matt's car—an exact replica of mine—and ignored the conversation he carried on with Riley about basketball. The traffic was heavy this morning, and after another endless night spent jogging on a road to nowhere, I fell asleep as soon as we hit Storrow Drive.

The crunch of gravel under tires woke me, and as I set eyes on the one-hundred-and-thirty-year-old Arts and Crafts mansion for the first time in years, I knew I should have stayed at the office. There were only so many hits a man could take.

Cold lead sank in my stomach but I followed Matt and Riley up the circular drive. They were pointing out the work in progress, but I couldn't hear them over the pounding in my head.

We joined the group in the kitchen, and Shannon wasted no time offering her commentary. "I didn't believe you'd actually show up. Let's commemorate this moment," she said, gesturing toward me. "I'd suggest a selfie but you look like shit."

"Play nice, Shan," Riley warned. They made eye contact, but I was too miserable to care about their exchange of grimaces and eyebrows and stares.

"Right, so…let's get back to the agenda," Andy said.

While I should have been listening to the updates and dilemmas, I started wandering through the rooms. It looked different with protective tarps on the floors, and scaffolding and construction equipment everywhere. Almost sterile. With all the furniture and home goods removed, it was the same as any other jobsite.

Just about.

There were some memories that lingered even when everything else was gone.

The small linen closet beside the window seat where I'd hidden whenever Angus was on a bender and looking to unleash some rage.

The back staircase he threw Erin down when she was thirteen, breaking her arm in three places.

The alcove in Shannon's room where I'd camped when it was too scary to sleep alone.

The room where my mother died.

And because my brain enjoyed fucking with me, I found myself in the middle of the nursery, thinking about the child Tiel and I weren't expecting.

Of course she wasn't pregnant. It was my fault, that much I knew. I wasn't putting a baby in her any more than I was proving string theory. Either my sperm didn't swim or the ones that did were dysfunctional, or the universe knew I was too fucked up to reproduce.

Or maybe—probably—Angus was right all along. I was a mistake, an accident, a fucking mulligan. I shouldn't have been born, and the only course correction was ensuring my genetic material never poisoned another generation.

He was right, and so was Tiel. I couldn't fool anyone into thinking I was capable of keeping anything good.

There wasn't a single moment of my life that wasn't a fucking disaster. As an adult, I knew how to cover it up with trendy clothes and professional expertise, but when those pieces were stripped away, I was still the excessively anxious kid who couldn't go anywhere without a crate of prescriptions and medical supplies. I was wildly risk averse—I stuck to my playbook and kept everyone at a safe distance—and for years, I had been just fine.

Tiel was perhaps my one uncalculated risk. Those girls—the

ones at the bars? There was no risk there. I had enough emotional distance and condoms to guarantee it.

She was a gamble. A noisy, colorful, gorgeous gamble, and it was clear that I lost.

I lost it all.

I WAS on a mission to obliterate everything. That's what sitting in an empty nursery in the most haunted house in Massachusetts did to a guy. It made him want to erase memories and kill brain cells.

"You should not be here. This is a terrible choice, and you should not be here," Riley said from a few steps behind me. "Girls claim they want space, but they want you chasing them. Yeah, they want some time to cool off, but for the most part, they want to take a deep breath and see you right there—not here, but there, wherever she is—with chocolate and flowers and shit like that."

I ignored him. I was exactly where I needed to be, and it was long overdue. He'd been bitching at me since I announced I was hitting the bars when we got back from the visit to Wellesley but I'd had enough of his mother hen routine. I couldn't take a piss without him asking where I was going and offering to hold my dick, and of course he appointed himself as my chaperone tonight.

"Have you called her? Texted? Sent a carrier pigeon?"

Fuck space.

Fuck time.

Fuck room to breathe.

Fuck everything.

Heading toward my regular red velvet booth, I waved at Alibi's manager and gestured for drinks. I was swallowing whatever she brought my way. "No. Why? She told me to fuck off, or something like that."

Riley's hand landed on my shoulder, stopped me in my tracks, and spun me around. That kid was built like a tight end. I wouldn't put it past him to sack me, and part of me was hoping for it. I wanted to hit something, but more than that, I wanted something to hit me. I wanted to focus on a different form of pain.

"All right, grasshopper. Listen. Couples fight all the time. Like, constantly. Matt and Lauren spend more time debating things and making up than doing anything else, and trust me, I've witnessed all of it."

He rolled his eyes and shuddered.

"But here's the secret—it's always your fault. Whatever it is, your fault. Even if she's being an asshole, it's your fault. Just apologize and do nice things, and it's better."

He shrugged as if it was that fucking simple.

"Call her. Apologize. Say something sweet, and you'll have some good old-fashioned make-up sex all night."

The manager appeared with a gin martini, and I sent her a wink. "You remembered," I said. She shrugged as if she remembered everyone's drink orders, and tossed her wavy blonde hair over her shoulder. "Good girl."

As she turned to leave, I smacked her ass.

"No, no, no. That's enough. We are leaving now," Riley said. I knocked back the martini in one gulp. "You have lost your fucking mind, son."

"Yeah, I have." I crossed my arms over my chest and rocked back on my heels. "And I'm not interested in looking for it. What's the point?"

Riley brought his fingers to his temples in obvious frustration. "The point," he bit out, "is that you love Tiel, and you need to fix things with Tiel. You should not be here right now. You should not be inventing ways to self-destruct. Why is this so complicated for you to understand?"

I handed my glass to another blonde. I didn't think she worked at Alibi, but she took it nonetheless. She must have spent everything on the breast implants because those grape-fruits were busting out of her dress. She wasn't a natural blonde, either.

I doubted there was anything real about her.

"Gin martini and some shots. Get yourself something, sugar tits, and put it on my tab."

"Ignore him," Riley said. He grabbed my bicep and towed me toward the door. "We're going, and you're not leaving the house until you get your shit together."

"Would you just back the fuck off?"

I shook out of his hold and leaned against the wall inside one of the cells converted into a cozy drinking nook. This part of the jail once served as the drunk tank.

I deserved all of this misery. Every moment of every day of my miserable life should feel this horrible.

I was exactly where I belonged.

I glanced up, avoiding Riley's steely gaze, and watched people pouring in and out of the bars and restaurants. This was one of the features I loved about The Liberty Hotel: the catwalk ringing each floor. This was where it felt most like a repur-posed jail, where I could imagine guards patrolling the corridors.

"Let's get out of here," he said.

That was a great idea. Truly.

If I was even remotely concerned with self-preservation.

"Yeah, I'm gonna go fuck that blonde with the tits. Get me another drink, or four."

She was standing against the bar, pretending to be perfectly casual. Her eyes widened as I approached, and she gestured to the shot glasses lined up beside her. I downed two, and two more, and another two. I inclined my head toward the hall, and tipped back the last two shot glasses.

Precisely enough to feel nothing.

"You down?"

"I'm Melan—"

I pressed my finger to her lips and shook my head. "Even if I knew how to care, I wouldn't."

She narrowed her eyes at me for a moment, but grabbed my hand and led the way. She knew the drill.

The alcohol was moving through my system quickly, and my hold on the horizon loosened. She tightened her grip on my hand and yanked me through a doorway. She was small but that didn't stop her from slamming me against the wall, and promptly rubbing her silicon investments all over me. Her fingers were clammy and skeleton-thin, and they went straight to my crotch.

I closed my eyes, not wanting to remember anything about her.

This was the empty, soulless existence I deserved, the one that would never know love or happiness or hope. I wanted to lose myself in that. I wanted to fuck a random woman and not care, not feel an ounce of longing for Tiel. I wanted to cut myself off from the love she stitched into my cells and I wanted to prove that I didn't need that shit.

And because it wasn't enough to simply drown in my own self-loathing, I pulled out my phone and fired off several texts to Tiel.

Sam: If something is broken
Sam: You fix that shit
Sam: You don't throw it the fuck away
Tiel: I don't want to throw anything away.
Tiel: Where are you? can we talk?
Sam: I'm very busy needing space

I wanted to crawl back to her, promise that she was the one —the *only* one—and beg her to understand that I fucked up with Magnolia and it would never, ever happen again.

The fake blonde pulled at the front of my trousers with a fury, unconcerned with my dick's wholly flaccid state, and no part of me wanted this. I hated what I'd done, and if it were possible, I hated myself even more. There wasn't a shred of arousal in me, but she continued stroking and jerking over my clothes while whispering filthy clichés about being a naughty girl and deserving a punishment.

Then she called me Daddy, and it turned my stomach. I *had* to stop this.

The acidic burn of alcohol and carrot-celery-honey juice and misery bubbled up my throat as I pushed her away. I choked it back for a moment, but another wave hit, and I vomited all over her.

And I mean *all* over her.

The first spurt hit her hair, and then her head snapped up to take the next two on her chest and dress. When it finally stopped, she gazed at the wreckage, horrified, and muttered something about my pathetic whiskey dick. She ran out crying, and left me alone in a puddle of puke.

Amazingly, only my shoes took the hit, and though I'd never wear them again, I needed just a couple of minutes to clean up before stumbling down the hallway toward Riley.

He was seated in a deep leather chair, his ankle crossed over his knee while he tapped his beer bottle against the armrest. I dropped beside him and signaled to the waitress. Maybe she could find me some flat cola. Or ginger ale.

I still felt like shit and wanted to crawl into bed more than I wanted my next breath. Cold sweat was running down my back, and I swore my organs were rattling against my bones.

"You didn't fuck her," he snapped, tearing my phone from my hands and making a show of wiping it clean. "You might be the biggest asshole in the universe right now, but you didn't fuck her."

I ordered the ginger ale, and deserved every ounce of scorn the waitress aimed at me. "Don't be so sure," I said.

"You are so full of shit," he said, scrolling through my

messages. "That wasn't even five minutes, and you look like death. Your pants are covered in vomit, by the way."

I glanced down but couldn't see more than the vague outlines of my legs.

He busied himself with his phone while I sipped my ginger ale, but it wasn't long before the alarm sounded on my glucose monitor. I couldn't win. I knew my blood sugar was next to nothing, and I needed to force down some real food.

"I need to get out of here," I groaned, my head dropping against the chair.

"You think?" he asked, and hauled me up by the collar but I didn't have much strength to stand. "Son, you are scaring the shit out of me right now."

"No, no," I said, my tongue too heavy to form the words correctly. "I'm fucking *great*."

I puked a couple more times while we waited at the valet stand. I was bent over the bushes with Riley's hand gripping my shoulder when I realized he was talking.

"I think you owe me, dude," he said.

I turned my head to tell him I didn't owe him a goddamn thing, but I ended up spewing all over his shoes.

"Seriously, Nick, I need your help and I don't care what kind of doctor you are. I'm throwing him in the car and taking him to your ER."

"No," I groaned. "I just want to go home."

"You have lost the right to make decisions for yourself," Riley yelled, then he lowered his voice. "I promised I wouldn't tell anyone about you fucking my sister after Matt and Lauren's wedding, and you promised me a favor in return. I'm callin' it in, my friend."

I begged him to take me home and let me sleep it off, Riley went straight to the hospital. I was too disoriented to care when the nurses stabbed me with syringes and tore off my clothes, effectively ruining a two thousand dollar Burberry suit and my favorite Eton dress shirt.

I didn't remember much after that. There was more, maybe a lot more, but it lurked in an inaccessible part of my mind.

WHEN I WOKE UP, Nick and Riley were seated beside my bed.

My mouth tasted like pennies, and was desert dry. "Where am I?" They glanced at each other, and Riley shook his head. He looked exhausted, and more than a little furious. "What happened?"

Nick shuffled forward on a rolling stool, and crossed his legs. "You're at Mass General." He pointed to the logo on his scrubs. "And right now, we're not buddies."

It hurt to open my eyes, and squinting was the best I could manage. "What?"

"It means you need to shut up and listen," Riley hissed.

"Sam, you had a blood-alcohol level of point two when you were brought in. That by itself is pretty impressive. You were in extreme hypoglycemia. You seized before we could get your sugar under control. The fact you're not in a coma right now is…unexplainably positive."

Maybe that was why absolutely every muscle in my body ached.

"You know the rules of this game. You work out hard, you crash. You don't eat, you crash. You don't sleep, you crash. You hit the bar, you crash. You can't do all that and expect your body to keep going." He tapped his pen against the tablet balanced on his thigh. "You and your brothers? Y'all handle stress the exact same ways. You run your bodies into the ground and have the balls to be pissed off when you realize you're just as human as everyone else."

"That's not what happened," I said. There was more I wanted to say, but my throat was burning. It would have been easier to speak if I'd been chewing glass.

"I'm keeping you for observation, and the endocrinology team is coming in for rounds at seven, but listen to this. You need to get your ass in line."

"Don't tell anyone else about this. Don't call Shannon," I said to Riley as Nick rolled away.

"Dude," Riley sighed. "How is me telling *Shannon* your biggest concern right now? I watched you have a fucking *seizure*. Do you have any idea what that's like? I can't sit here while you destroy yourself anymore."

"That's not—"

"*No*, Sam. No." Riley pushed out of his chair, pacing along the length of the thin curtain separating us from other patients. "You basically took a razor blade into the bathtub tonight, and you damn near succeeded."

"I didn't want to die," I rasped.

"You need to work through your shit," he said. "And you need to ask for help sometimes. You have to tell people when it's bad, and not just wait until you're circling the drain."

He continued pacing, his fists propped on his hips.

"I don't want to be a dick but, seriously, Sam, you need to deal with this. Get help. Talk to someone. Anything."

"I know."

"If you know, you should fucking do it," he said.

There was something I wanted to say but it stuck in my throat and I couldn't push past the heavy throb in my head. I fell asleep, and though I knew doctors and nurses were checking my vitals and drawing blood, I couldn't force my eyes open.

Later, Riley tossed some clean clothes at me and instructed me to get dressed. We drove home in silence, and he marched me to my room. I was still exhausted and didn't need any help deciding to get into bed.

"Take the meeting with Turlan tomorrow," I said. Riley nodded, but didn't move. "And...the rest of my meetings. Tell them I have the flu, or whatever. I don't care what you say, but I don't want to see anyone."

I didn't get out of bed all week.

I lost track of the world beyond the firehouse, spending my days numb and trapped in the maze of my thoughts. They circled and closed in on themselves, and they turned darker as the week went on. I doubled and tripled the dose on my sleeping pills and spent the better portion of every night in a blank, dreamless space.

It didn't matter whether I woke up anymore.

I WAS THERE, but I wasn't.

I pushed away from the table while my siblings discussed their projects, and I stared out the window at the sun-drenched street below. People were going about their lives, walking to school and work, arguing about politics and sports, cursing the weather. For everyone out there, life continued.

For me, life was shattering.

Eight months ago, I thought I'd found my new low.

I was wrong.

I couldn't do this anymore. I couldn't pretend that after everything we'd been through together, I could survive Tiel walking away from me or the things I'd done.

There was only one option left for me. I sat there, arms crossed over my chest and my feet propped on the windowsill, and I built my plan.

There were many things to get in order, and if I was doing this today, I had to work quickly. For the first time in ages, my mind wasn't fixated on germs or Angus or my broken fucking heart, and I was able to construct my action plan while my siblings talked over me.

"Hey," Riley murmured, tapping my arm. "You want me to handle Turlan?"

I didn't have to look up to know every eye was trained on me. "Yeah," I said. "It's all yours."

He spoke but I didn't listen. There was a time when the Turlan project mattered to me; hell, there was a time when anything mattered. It was long gone.

The meeting eventually finished and I made my way back to my office. I didn't let myself think about anything but the plan, and dug into the arrangements. It took the entire day and I only stepped out of my office for quick trips to the bathroom and printer. I forwarded all calls to voicemail, and I debated turning off my phone but there was a sliver of hope that Tiel would call or text and I couldn't risk missing that.

Shannon and Patrick held a weekly five o'clock budget meeting in her office, and I knew I'd find them there once my plans were finalized. Not wanting to return to the office after speaking with them, I grabbed my suit coat and messenger bag, and carried them down the stairs with me.

I stood in the doorway while they hunched over a spread-sheet on Patrick's screen, and waited. Shannon noticed me first, and then elbowed Patrick. "Hey, what's up?" she asked. She settled into her chair and he sat on the edge of her desk.

"I can't be here anymore," I said.

Shannon and Patrick exchanged quick glances, and she grabbed a pen from the silver jar beside her laptop. She was a compulsive tapper; it was what she did when the silences turned uncomfortable.

"Would you care to explain that one?" she asked.

I shifted the bag to my other hand with a sigh. "I'd like to take some time off. I've finalized designs and detailed notes for all of my projects, and I've left them all for Riley. Everything is on my desk, and backed up on the server." Shifting again, I ran my hand through my hair and the motion immediately brought back every memory of Tiel's fingers sliding over my scalp. "I need to be away from here. Please."

Shannon and Patrick exchanged another glance, and spoke simultaneously.

"How long are we talking?" she said.

"Are you okay?" he asked.

Patrick sent her a scowl over his shoulder, and she murmured, "It's not an unreasonable question, Patrick."

"No, I'm not okay." It was good to get it out, give it voice. I'd been pretending to be all right for so long, it felt like a vindication to finally say it out loud. "I'm really fucked up, and I need to go. I'm not sure how long."

Shannon tossed her pen back in the jar. "But Riley—"

"Riley is more than capable. Matt trained him well, and we don't need to treat him like an idiot. He can do this, and he deserves the opportunity to succeed on his own. I've written a letter to the Turlans—it's on my desk—and they'll be happy with Riley's work. This project will make his career."

She clasped her hands on her desk and stared at them, nodding slowly.

"What do you need from us?" Patrick asked.

I shook my head. "Nothing. Just...time. Time to get my shit together."

"Where are you going?" he asked.

I rubbed the back of my neck and hesitated. I didn't want my well-intentioned siblings to show up and ruin the solitude I required, but I knew boxing them out wasn't fair either.

"I'm going camping. I'm thinking Acadia, but maybe the Kancamagus. I haven't decided, and I probably won't until I hit the road."

"You'll let us know if you need anything? If there's anything we can do?" he asked.

"There's nothing, Patrick. I just need to be alone."

The city was as empty as I felt, and the drive home was oddly quick. I went straight into packing mode. I kept all of my gear in one of the closets alongside the original fire truck bays, and soon I had everything loaded into the old pickup I reserved for these adventures.

I didn't need much else; some clothes, some books, enough medical supplies for several weeks. Maybe months.

I was tossing my rucksack into the truck when Riley walked in. He pointed to the equipment in the truck's bed. "What is happening here?"

I lifted a shoulder and shrugged into my fleece jacket. "I'm taking off."

"Oh no you're not," he laughed. "Go on. Tell me another silly story."

Leaning against the truck, I slipped on my wool socks and hiking boots. "I'm heading up north. I want to spend some time in the woods. Breathe some clean air. You're in charge of Turlan, and the rest of my projects. Keys to the Range Rover are on the kitchen table. Utilities are paid for the next—"

"Stop. Stop." He held up his hands and advanced on me. "This is crazy. Turlan is *your* baby, and Patrick will never go for me managing any project that important, and you were having a seizure in the fucking hospital one week ago, and if you'd just fucking listen to me, we could figure out how to fix things with Tiel."

"He already knows, and you can handle it." I turned away to tie down the gear.

"Sam," he said. "Are you even going to tell her?"

"No," I murmured. "She's better off without me. I think that's abundantly clear to everyone."

His shoulders dropped and he shook his head. He watched as I secured the truck and shut the closet, silent. "Do you have enough insulin? Glucose tablets? What about replacement parts, and those little batteries?"

"All set."

"What about food? Do you need cash?" He reached for his wallet and offered up sixty dollars. I refused, but he shoved it into my coat pocket anyway. "Do you have a phone charger?

You better fucking call me *every day*, or I'm going to find you and kick the snot out of you."

I smiled in spite of myself. "There's terrible reception up north. Most of Maine is a dead zone. I couldn't call you every day unless I was camping in downtown Portland, and I'd rather not talk to another person for at least two weeks."

He crossed his arms and glared at me. "Are you going into the woods to detox from Tiel, or are you going to do something stupid?"

The keys dangled from my fingers while I considered my response. I didn't know what was going to happen when I got in the truck, and I liked it that way. I just wanted to go and be gone. I'd figure out the rest later.

"I need to listen to the earth for a little bit," I said. I never understood what Tiel meant until I needed it, too. "That probably sounds really lame, but I need less noise. I need to understand some things, and I can't do that here."

He crawled into the bed of the truck, pawing through my gear. "Call me. Just fucking call me. I won't tell Shannon or anyone, but dude, you can't go all *Into the Wild* on me now."

"I won't," I said, and Riley pulled me into a bear hug. "Take care of my properties. I'll tear off your arm and beat you with it if you fuck up Turlan."

He smiled, clapping me on the back in a tight man-hug. He watched as I pulled out of the firehouse, waving from the curb.

I didn't know where I was going or how long I was staying there, but soon Boston was only a speck in my rearview mirror, and I was on my own.

This was different than eating lunch in the bathroom when my high school's cafeteria was hostile territory. It wasn't talking to my mother's tombstone. It wasn't watching a woman's lips cover my dick but feeling nothing at all.

I was completely, thoroughly, enormously alone for the first time in my life, and forcing myself to feel all my broken pieces was absolutely terrifying.

Twenty-Eight

TIEL

"THIS IS HIGHLY UNUSUAL."

I pulled my lip between my teeth while the Dean scanned my transcript. He had to say yes. It had to work out.

"It appears you have more than enough credits to finish ABD," he said, his pen roving over the words on the page. "In fact, you've had enough credits for two and a half years. You're only missing a dissertation defense."

"Yes. Right. I *know* I'm All But Dissertation. That's why I'm here," I said.

I was trying to keep my impatience in check, but this guy was not listening. He was the fourth person to completely misunderstand my request today, and now I was vibrating off my seat with edginess. I'd also had seven cappuccinos today, and that was on top of the ones I drank last night, and if I thought about it, I couldn't remember the last time I slept.

But it was fine. Really. Everything was fine. I was researching and writing, and playing until new blisters formed on my fingers on top of old blisters and then playing some more, and that was keeping me too busy to think about anything else.

Except coffee. But I was totally fine.

I was always worried about more coffee. I memorized all the twenty-four hour coffee shops in town. Somehow, I presumed there would be a greater degree of all-night coffee availability considering the volume of colleges in the area. Someone should do a study on that: the ratio of college students to twenty-four hour coffee in a given area.

"I just need to know if I can schedule my defense. I'm almost finished, and I can present as soon as next month. That's all I need to know."

"Well," he said, drawing the word out while my heel bounced against the chair leg. "That seems rather quick—"

"But I've been working on it all this time," I said. "All this extra coursework," I leaned over his desk and pointed to the transcript. "It's helped my research. I'm ready. I swear."

"I don't usually agree to last minute dissertation defenses." He reached for a leather-bound book and thumbed through the pages, stopping on each one to underline the dates with his finger as if he was unfamiliar with the sequential nature of time. I could have jogged to Baltimore and back in the time it took him to find the right page. "The committee meets again during the first week of May," he said, and then went back to the elaborate page-turning routine. "And then again the second week of July."

He glanced up in question.

"May," I said. That gave me two and a half months to pull together an entire dissertation. I was going to need more coffee —pronto. Maybe I could move in at Voltage Coffee & Art in Kendall Square. "May would be perfect."

Once the details were ironed out, I hurried down the stairwell—I didn't do elevators anymore—and onto the street. I was headed for the T station when I realized my phone was buzzing in my hand.

Not recognizing the number, I ignored the call. Within a few seconds, a text came through from the same number:

Unknown: You don't know me but I know Sam, and you need to hear about what's happened to him. I want to talk. Please meet me at Pavement on Newbury this afternoon. I'll be there until 5.

The fear came first, quickly followed by longing. I hadn't heard from him since his cryptic late night texts two weeks ago —fifteen days, but who was counting?—and something was wrong.

I only indulged in my feelings—the raw, thorny pain that lingered right below the surface—on selected occasions. I couldn't let myself get trapped underneath that while I was scrambling to finish my degree, and I couldn't let it take me down now, either.

Panicked, I turned in a circle, then started down Boylston toward the Prudential Center. I didn't want to meet this person, and I wasn't entirely certain why I was, but my legs were intent on carrying me to the quaint coffee shop.

When I stepped inside, flustered and breathless despite the quick walk, I didn't know where to look. I glanced at the door to confirm I was at the right place, and then reread the text as if it would offer some new information.

"Are you Tiel?"

I jerked my head up and found myself face-to-face with a beautiful redheaded pixie, the kind who required tailoring for her clothes because even size zero was too big. "Yes," I said slowly.

"I'm Shannon Walsh."

So this was the infamous Shannon. I expected the pricey suit, the chic accessories, the insane heels. I didn't expect her to be tiny, or look so tired.

"Thank you for meeting me," she said. She gestured over her shoulder toward a table. "Can we talk?"

"Can you just tell me what happened with Sam? Is he all right?"

She tucked her hair over her shoulder and paused. "Can we sit? Just for a few minutes?"

Hopefully she didn't bring me here to mention that Sam had chlamydia. That seemed like something he'd delegate to one of his many platonic lady friends.

I nodded and followed her to a table. She summoned the barista and ordered a latte and a sugar cookie for herself. Another cappuccino for me.

Shannon didn't say anything while our coffees were brewing, and once I stopped being annoyed at her manipulating me into meeting, I noticed she was nervous. She was gnawing on her lip and stealing quick glances at me, then started dismantling her cookie when it arrived on a rustic plate.

"Is Sam all right?"

Her fingers continued breaking the cookie into smaller and smaller pieces until a small pile of sand started forming on her plate. "No, he really isn't okay," she said, and tears sprang to her eyes. They spilled over, and ran down her perfectly applied makeup. There were freckles under all that foundation, and they were pretty.

I grabbed her wrist to slow the cookie decimation. "Honeybunch, you need to start talking."

She nodded and blotted her tears with a napkin. After a shuddering breath, she said, "He's abandoned all of his projects. He left town, and we aren't sure where he is, but he said he was going camping." She returned to the cookie. "I thought it would be a long weekend. I didn't think he was serious when he said he needed to be away from here."

He wasn't sick or injured, and he wasn't spreading the clap. For that, I could be thankful, but...I didn't think there was a place for me in his life anymore, regardless of whether I wanted one. "And you're telling me this because...?"

She held out her hands and sent me an aggravated look. "Because...because I want to know why! I want to know why he walked away from everything and what happened to make him so miserable."

Carefully setting the cappuccino on the table, I sat back and laced my fingers together. "You presume I had something to do with it?"

Her eyes widened as she stared at the cookie sand on her plate. "As a matter of fact, yes. I believe you were dating my brother at one point, and now that you're not, he finds it necessary to vanish into the woods."

Great. I was going to offend another Walsh today.

"Shannon, I'm not clear how that's any of your business. Sam is an adult and he does not need you or anyone else managing every one of the minute details of his life. Anything that transpired between us was just that—between *us*."

For a second, her eyes flashed with fury and I expected an authentic ginger tantrum, but it morphed into sadness. She held the crumpled napkin to her mouth and burst into tears. This was not what I expected from Shannon Walsh.

She cried for several minutes, and I waved off the coffee shop's staff every time they ventured toward us with concerned frowns. We were probably scaring away their regular clientele.

Eventually it came to a sniffling, gasping stop, and she excused herself to the ladies' room. When she returned, her eyes were puffy, her nose was reddened, her foundation wiped clean, but her seriousness was now mixed with a stripe of sad.

"My mother," she started. "She died when we were young." She motioned toward me with her coffee. "Did you know that?"

"Yes." I didn't mention that Sam shared it last summer, or that I knew exponentially more about her and her family than she knew about me.

"Right, of course."

She nodded to herself and ran her hand through her hair, ruffling the smooth, styled wave she had going. I liked it better messy, but that was my preference for most things.

"I raised my brothers and sister. I've been Head Bitch in

Charge since I was nine. All I have ever done is manage the minute details of their lives. When they were kids, I made sure they were bathed and wearing clean clothes. I sewed buttons and fixed hems because there was no one else to do it. I took care of them when they were sick. I signed their report cards and paid bills. I went to work selling houses when I was eighteen so they could go away to college. I got them *through* it. And now that we're adults? I'm still getting them through it. I schedule their doctors' appointments. I file their taxes. I register their cars. I can't remember a time when my life wasn't about taking care of them. I meddle in their lives because I have been a lot more than their sister for nearly twenty-four years."

I traced the edge of my cup as the minutes passed. I didn't know what to say. I only knew how to handle these situations with kids, and I usually had an instrument to fill the silence.

"They don't need me anymore, not the way they used to. I thought it was a good thing, but I can't find the balance between being there too much and not enough. I've been trying to focus on myself."

She laughed as if it was a ridiculous endeavor and twisted the skinny silver bracelets on her wrist.

"It began with online dating a few years back. That's pretty much the worst invention in the world." Shannon rolled her eyes and shuddered. "But then Matt started dating Lauren, and now she's my best friend. I didn't know how to be friends with girls before her, and Lauren taught me," she said quietly. "She says nice things about you."

"I bet she does," I murmured.

She ruffled her hair again, and now it was borderline wild. "I started seeing someone last summer. 'Seeing' probably isn't the right word. It's more like scheduled sex. Really, really incredible sex." She looked up, disoriented. "I can't believe I just said that out loud."

"Keep going," I said. If she could demand the details of my relationship, I could ask the same.

"So, this all has been occurring," she said primly. "And I've been trying to maintain everything else, but I haven't been able to. I keep thinking that I should have been there for Sam when your relationship ended, but instead I was six states away for scheduled sex. I was supposed to be ending it, but...that didn't go as planned."

"Do you swoop in when all your brothers' relationships end?"

She lifted a shoulder and sipped her coffee. "My brothers don't have many relationships. Patrick kept his a secret for months. Matt holds me at a distance. Riley's still a toddler in my eyes. And Sam...well, Sam changed this year, and I didn't notice. I wasn't paying attention, I wasn't there, and I let him down."

"But the sex? It was decent?"

She blushed—hard—and pressed her fist to her mouth to cover a huge smile. "I haven't been able to get on a bike for spin class since." She laughed, but the happiness was gone. "If I'm not taking care of my brothers, I don't know who I am anymore."

I drained my cappuccino and shifted in my seat, hoping I could make an exit. I didn't have the right words for her, and it wasn't like I'd ever see her again.

"May I ask what happened? With you and Sam?" Shannon said.

She cared about him, and I appreciated it deeply because I'd dedicated the past few months to disliking her. That didn't mean I was rehashing anything. "I hope he finds what he's looking for, wherever he is."

It sounded pretty and tidy that way, but in reality it was a gigantic fucking mess.

Shannon frowned, clearly hoping for more, and that was my cue to leave. I gathered my things and dropped some cash on the table.

"I'm sorry you're going through this," I said. "I know you're trying to do the right thing. I hope it gets easier."

I turned away from the table, and Shannon said, "When he figures it all out and comes back, give him a chance. Please don't turn him away. He's so much more sensitive than he likes us to believe."

I pivoted, staring at her for a long minute. "Shannon, I know exactly how sensitive he is. You don't need to tell me that."

And I know how to love him, I thought.

Twenty-Nine

A FEW DAYS—MAYBE even a week—alone was nice. Calming. Restful.

A month alone was a purge and cleanse.

Two months alone was the most arduous experience of my life. I fished and hiked and read, but through it all, I couldn't escape my thoughts.

My hurt quickly tripped over into anger, and from there, I lingered in rage for too many days to count. I yelled at the trees, chucked so many stones into the river that my shoulder ached for a week, stomped up snow-covered mountains until my legs felt like noodles, chopped enough wood to heat most of Nova Scotia for the winter.

It took a fish to pull me out of that rage.

It was a beautiful striped bass, and it bit on my line during the type of fiery sunrise that warned sailors back to the shore. When I had it secured in the ice chest, I powered up the outboard motor and steered the boat toward the bay. I was fifteen minutes from land when the skies opened, letting loose torrential freezing rain mixed with hail and thundersnow, and there was nothing for me to do but ride it out.

I was shivering and soaked when I docked, but if I didn't

prepare the bass soon, it would spoil. Despite the heavy, wet snow, I jogged to the cleaning station downstream from the cabin and set to gutting the fish. Lightning struck no more than fifty yards away, zapping a low bush and singeing everything within a narrow radius. I jolted and my concentration faltered, and instead of stripping the fish's innards, I drove my knife into my thigh.

Cold, wet, and bleeding, I dropped to the ground and cursed every corner of the universe. Sitting on that rocky Maine beach in early March, my hands wrapped around my leg, I hated *everything*. There was nothing left to celebrate, to love, to desire, and I was so fucking mad at the world.

I wanted it to be someone's fault. I wanted *everything* to be someone's fault and I wanted to forward my fury toward that person.

But all of that was futile.

Regardless of how much anger I was cultivating, I was still alone, bleeding all over myself while I cried in the snow, and nothing was going to change unless I dragged my ass off that beach. I was the only one who could release that rage and free myself from all of it. I was the only one who could clean up after my mess.

So I got up. It hurt like hell and I was certain I'd ground oyster shell shards and fish guts into my exposed flesh in the process, but I didn't let that panic slow me. I got up and I put one limping foot in front of the other.

I called out—it was probably closer to a prissy yelp—when hail struck my shoulder head-on. If I hadn't already scared off the area bears with my routine hollering, they would have been running for the hills.

The trek to the cabin felt like miles, and when I was finally out of the storm I shucked all of my clothes in a waterlogged pile and examined my self-inflicted stab wound. It wasn't deadly but there was no way it would heal without stitches.

I waited until the storm blew over to make my way into

town. As far as fishing villages went, Cutler was as authentic as they came. It was a stone's throw from the Canadian border, and in the right light you could see Nova Scotia across the Bay of Fundy. I hadn't set out for the easternmost village in the state when I left Boston, but I was glad this was where my truck decided to take me.

The people were pleasant; they were curious about a mid-winter newcomer without being nosy, and I appreciated that. The words to explain why I'd fled an otherwise charmed life escaped me, and my baggage didn't need a seat at the town diner. I only ventured that far from the cabin when I required more supplies or a cell signal to text Riley. There was a respectable barbershop beside the grocery store, but I hadn't been looking in the mirror with enough frequency to care about my hair.

The doctor chattered about snowfall totals and hockey while he patched me up, but my mind honed in on the sear and tug I experienced with each stitch. It was a reminder that I still felt, but it forced me to acknowledge that if I could feel pain, I was capable of feeling everything else, too.

I capitalized on that pain, and I grounded myself in it every day. I hiked the forests and craggy shoreline, and I made it my goal to bury another bucketful of resentment among the rocks and trees and waves.

At first, I thought it was Angus and God and asshole kids that I was trying to forgive, but as the days passed and my leg healed, I discovered I was the one who needed forgiving. There was so much—my mother's death, my father's abuse, childhood bullies, losing Tiel, my long-term self-destruction—and it was time to send all that guilt and loathing away.

I'd experienced terrible things, some of it at my own hand, and I was leaving it all behind.

More rocks were thrown, trees heard my screams, wood was chopped, and slowly—too slowly to notice when it happened—I started feeling better. With the constant supply of ocean-caught fish, I was eating well, and my daily anger exorcism excursions guaranteed I slept long and hard. My blood sugar still had a mind of its own, but I was paying enough attention to handle those swings properly.

On the rare evening when I had enough energy to keep my eyes open past sunset, I lay on the floor in front of the wood stove and listened to the playlist simply titled 'Tiel.'

The tracks sounded different without her humming and tapping the beat beside me. But those songs, *fuck*, they gutted me.

I read every morning, devouring my weathered and well-loved copies of *The Count of Monte Cristo*, *The Cask of Amontillado*, *Les Miserables*, *The Adventures of Sherlock Holmes*, and *The Lord of the Rings* trilogy. In my haste to get out of Boston, I'd accidentally tossed Tiel's copy of that Johnny Cash biography into my rucksack. One morning when my longing for her was a tangible being in this tiny cabin, I started reading it just to be close to her.

The life story was engaging, but it was the letters that grabbed my attention. Pages and pages of handwritten letters from Johnny Cash to June Carter Cash, and I remembered how Tiel described it: they went through intense, messy times but found a way to love each other.

And that was how I wanted this to end.

I dug through my bags until I found a small notebook with a five-year-old tide chart printed on the inside cover, and started writing everything I'd been storing up since I walked away from my life weeks ago.

I loved her, fully and completely, and she brought out the best version of me. She didn't save me; no, this was something I had to do for myself. But she did keep me afloat.

Tiel was broken in certain spots, and strong in others, and we fit together that way.

I learned a lot about myself during that time. About the choices I'd made in defining myself and what I valued, and their implications. About the things I wanted to create—an identity independent of club-hopping, blackout drinking, and hook-ups. But more importantly, I wanted a family of my own, and I wanted it with Tiel.

I wasn't that guy anymore, that angry manwhore who wanted to drown his feelings in sex and gin.

By the end of April, the notebook was full and the plan came together in my mind, and I couldn't get out of Cutler quickly enough.

It was time to go home to my girl.

I WAS GREETED at Tiel's door with shriek. "Holy shit, it's a Yeti!"

A short woman slammed the door in my face only to open it a crack and peek at me. Turning, I glanced down the hallway, confirming I was on the right floor before I said, "Hi. I'm looking for Tiel."

The door swung open. "Tiel isn't here right now. Is there something I can help you with?"

I rubbed my forehead, fighting back my frustration. I'd been rehearsing this goddamn speech for six hours straight, plus the past two weeks. Every one of the three hundred and thirty miles from Cutler filled me with optimistic tension, and I was ready to tear the door off its hinges. "I'm sorry, this is sensation-ally rude but who are you?"

"I'm Ellie—"

"Oh," I laughed. "Ellie, I've heard so much about you. I'm—"

"Sam the freckle twin," she said with a grim expression. "I didn't expect the beard...or, any of this."

She gestured toward me, and when I looked down, I laughed. I couldn't remember the last time I paid attention to my appearance. My primary concern in Maine was preventing frostbite, and I hadn't once shaved. I was still wearing flannel-lined jeans, beaten-to-shit hiking boots, and a thermal shirt, and my hair was a shaggy, overgrown mess. I hadn't accounted for the arrival of spring in Boston when I left the cabin.

"It's about time you showed up." She leaned against the door frame, her arms crossed and her eyebrow cocked, her chin jutting in my direction.

"You're right about that," I murmured. "When will Tiel be back?"

She frowned, humming, and shook her head. "I need some more information about your intentions."

Most days I pretended Tiel was better off without me, that she was happier and moving on with her life. That was the only way I could survive the distance we put between each other. I'd wanted to call so many times and tell her I missed her, I loved her, I needed her...but I wasn't ready until now. I couldn't give her the broken version of me again. I had to be whole first.

She hadn't called either, and every time I touched base with Riley, I scanned my texts, emails, and voicemails for any sign from her. I hadn't considered that she might not be ready for me.

"Is she all right? Where is she?"

"Here's the deal. Tiel's the nice one in this apartment. I'm the bulldog." She nodded emphatically. "You showing up here all impatient and lumberjacked is wonderful, but that doesn't address my issue with you falling off the face of the planet."

In that instant, I loved Ellie. As far as I knew, she was the only person who consistently protected Tiel, and even though she was aiming that bulldog bark at me, I appreciated it.

"I love her and I need her, and the only way I'm leaving is with a restraining order, Ellie, and my sister is an excellent attorney, so I doubt that will happen. I'm here to stay."

"All right. Let's talk."

Thirty

TIEL

I GAZED AT THE COMMITTEE, quaking minutely where I stood. They paged through my dissertation, murmuring and jotting notes, and I continued knotting and unknotting my fingers. My knuckles hurt—hell, *everything* hurt. If I wasn't writing, I was practicing, and it didn't matter how exhausted or sore I was because I had to keep going.

I'd fallen apart once. That was enough.

They asked questions and offered blank stares while I spoke, and when I was convinced they were going to haul out a giant 'idiot' stamp and slap it on every page of my research, the Dean said, "The committee agrees your work merits approval."

I smiled through a round of congratulations and discussion of my future plans. There were offers to join a residency program at Boston Children's Hospital, a research fellowship at McLean Hospital, a clinical position at a school specializing in the autism spectrum, but I couldn't do anything with that information right now. Forcing a smile, I promised to take it all into consideration, and then I got the fuck out of there.

"ARE YOU HAVING FUN?" Ellie asked.

She was altogether too eager for me right now. Sure, I should be thrilled that my work wasn't tossed in the shredder and I wasn't laughed out of the building, but it hardly mattered. It was one dissertation with some overly ambitious correlations based upon a narrow sample set. I wasn't proposing actionable solutions for peace in the Middle East.

But Ellie had been determined to get me out of the house, and I was starting to think she was trying to get me some action, too. She'd insisted on visiting this new bar in the South End, and though it was a strange choice for us, I didn't have the energy to disagree.

I was okay, sort of.

I managed to pull together a dissertation in two months and added forty-six tracks to my YouTube channel. It was all part of a strategic initiative aimed at keeping me from crying in bed, on the sofa, or anywhere else that reminded me of Sam, and it was only partially successful.

My musical tastes were a blend of depressed teenage girl and eclectic hipster. My recent playlist walked a convoluted course from dark and moody to angry to melancholy to emo-angsty, and my subscribers were hungry for something happy but I didn't have it in me. Not yet.

I was all U2 ('One'), The Rolling Stones ('Paint It Black'), Arctic Monkeys ('Do I Wanna Know?'), Dashboard Confessional ('Vindicated'), Muse ('Madness'), No Doubt ('Ex-Girlfriend'), REO Speedwagon ('Take It On the Run'), The Shins ('Caring is Creepy'), AFI ('Love Like Winter'), The Doors ('Riders on the Storm'), My Chemical Romance ('Famous Last Words'), Joseph Arthur ('Honey and the Moon'), Tegan and Sara ('Where Does the Good Go?'), and Taylor Swift ('Style,' 'Blank Space,' 'I Knew You Were Trouble,' and basically everything else she'd ever recorded).

"Your enthusiasm is a little high for me," I said, propping my elbows on the table. "I'd really appreciate it if we can admire my so-called accomplishments with a hot bath. Or better yet, a nap."

"I love how you suffer for your art," she said. "It's a nice throwback to the nineties."

"Seriously, Ell," I said, leaning down to suck my drink through the straw. "I'm not in the mood. I'm tired. I haven't slept since the vernal equinox and if you tapped my blood, it would be sixty percent cappuccino, and I want to sleep right now. I don't understand why I have to party tonight."

Ellie eyed me from across the booth. "You got a doctorate today. Be happy."

"I will, as soon as I recover."

"That's a little fatalistic," she murmured. She was focused on her phone, and didn't look up. It was odd—wonderful, but odd —having her back in the apartment again. She'd spent one weekend with me before flying back to the tour, and now she was only home for another two weeks before the European leg kicked off. I was trying to enjoy my time with her but very obviously failing.

I scanned the bar while she texted, estimating how much longer we'd have to stay. It wasn't even nine at night, but now that I'd successfully defended and spent four hours in the studio, I wanted to crawl into Sam's clothes—the ones that had lost his scent when I washed them—and sleep for days.

What I wouldn't do to go back in time. Do it all over again, and do it right. Say all the things I wanted to say, let myself experience big, scary feelings and deal with them like an adult, and then give him as much as he gave me.

Then I heard it. 'Anna Sun.'

One song about never wanting to grow up. That was all it took. One song and a thousand memories swirled around me, pulling me into the quicksand. I'd avoided that Walk the Moon tune and so many others attached to Sam. All the memories I'd worked so hard to manage were right there, howling for my attention and clogging my throat with tears.

"Are those tears of joy? As in, 'I'm no one's research bitch anymore' tears?" Ellie peered at me.

"This song," I said. "It just reminds me of Sam."

"Yeah. About him," she murmured. "Have you thought about calling him?"

I shook my head and edged my drink away. Much more of that and I'd be face-down on the table. "And say what? 'Hey, it's been months but I miss you and I feel like my heart has been ripped out through my belly button and I just want to explain why I was a horrible bitch to you'? I don't see that happening."

"Well…" She grabbed my drink and drained it. "Why not?"

I rolled my eyes. "Because…because he might not want to see me."

"And what if he does?"

I snorted. "Would you go back to someone who was awful to you?"

"Why can't you see him and tell him it's been long enough? Get those big girl panties and make shit happen for you. Now. Go. Find his ass and give him a talking-to."

"While that is a fantastic idea and all, don't you think I could get some sleep first?"

Ellie shook her head. "I don't think so."

Before I could argue, she nodded toward the bar, and Sam was standing there. Maybe he'd been there all along or maybe I was imagining him, but there he was, tanned, bearded, and rather scruffy. Ellie slipped out of the booth as he walked toward me, and I knew they'd planned this beautifully choreographed dance.

I stared at him, peering past all the changes to find the man I once knew. All the words were bubbling up inside me and I was shaky and shivering, as if I was somehow chilled on a hot day, and *fuck*, I just wanted to touch him and never, ever stop.

"Hi," he said. That voice. It was surprisingly deep, and he wasn't saying much but he was saying *everything*. "Your hair is longer." He reached out, fingering the strands spilling over my shoulders. I hadn't found the time to get it cut since before we went to Arizona, and he was here with me, touching my hair even after I'd convinced myself it would never happen. "God, you are so fucking gorgeous."

"What are you doing here?" I blurted, and those words sliced right through him. He winced, sucking in a breath as he looked away. "That's not how I meant it to come out. I just... I'm sorry but where the fuck have you been? I didn't think I'd see you again. I mean, I'm not saying you should leave, but I want to know why you dropped off the face of the planet and I don't know what to say so I'm just letting words fall out of my mouth and hoping they make sense."

Focus, Tiel.

"I've been chopping wood and hating the world and dealing with my issues," he said. "And that took a lot longer than I expected, but..." He reached into his pocket and produced a journal. "Here."

Part of me was too stunned to speak, and the other part was trying to figure out what was happening. Sam placed it in my hands, nodding, and I opened to an arbitrary page.

Tiel –

I'll never forget the sound of your voice when you say 'I love you.' It's different, like you're telling me a secret or speaking in a language that only we can hear.

I just hope I'll hear it again.

I don't know how to ask you to forgive me for the things I've done, and maybe I don't deserve your forgiveness, but I need you to know that I love you and there is no one in the universe I'll ever want but you. I've been yours since always, and always will be.

Tears blurred in my eyes, and I flipped to another page.

Tiel –

I was so mad at you this morning. I hate that you didn't believe me when I tried to explain what happened with Magnolia. I hate that you didn't trust me. I hate that you didn't believe I've changed, that everything had changed.

But I still love you…and I hope you still love me.

Then another.

Tiel –

There are some walks you have to take alone, and this is mine. I had to leave and I had to cut myself off from everyone and everything, and I had to stop blaming everyone else for my problems.

But I should have told you. Just like I should have told you about Magnolia and I should have gone to your apartment after that night at Hermit Crab when you shoved your hand in my pants.

I tried telling you everything I was thinking and that worked for a couple of months but it didn't fix me. I had to fix me. Not a day has gone by that I haven't wanted to hear your voice.

I hope you understand how much I needed this. How I had to get all my issues out and deal with my own reality, and I hope you see a path where you'd consider forgiving me for the awful things I've done and taking me back. I'll understand if you don't, and I'll survive if you don't…but Sunshine, I want to do it right this time.

And another.

Tiel –

I've read The Count of Monte Cristo *about 200 times, but now that I'm reading it again, there are parts that feel different to me, and I realized I'm different.*

There's a quote that I never understood:
"There is neither happiness nor misery in the world; there is only the comparison of one state with another, nothing more. He who has felt the deepest grief is best able to experience supreme happiness."

I always thought it was ridiculous. If someone experiences suffering, it would make sense that they wouldn't need more than a small amount of joy. All I ever wanted was that tiny taste of happiness because I believed I didn't want or need or deserve more.

But I was wrong. You showed me more. You showed me that I could have crazy, wild happiness, and we could make something incredible together.
I want something incredible with you. Something safe and forever and real, and know that I will never want it with anyone else, ever.

And one more.

Tiel –

I dreamed of you last night. You were on a beach somewhere, and you were wearing that long yellow skirt. You were walking along the shore and I tried to catch up to you, but I couldn't. You were just out of reach and I had to watch while you collected shells and dipped your feet in the water. I think it might have been a nightmare but...I got to see you again and that made everything better.

Maybe it means we'll always be apart. That you won't be able to forgive me. That I'm not forgivable.

Tears were streaming down my face when I looked up, and if there was ever a doubt about this man ruining me, it died the second he offered me his handkerchief.

"I went to your apartment," he said.

"I wasn't there. I was defending my dissertation," I sniffled.

"Ellie mentioned that," he said. "Congratulations, Dr. Desai." He folded his arms on the table, dipping his head to meet my eyes. "Can I tell you something?"

"Of course," I whispered. I couldn't believe those old patterns came back so quickly. "And *of course* you're forgivable."

"I…shit, this was so much easier to say in my head." He brought his hand to his face and rubbed his forehead, and without thinking, my fingers tangled in his free hand. He looked up, at once surprised and buoyant, and I squeezed. "I realized a few things. You and me? We're not normal people. We're weird, and have perverted minds, and there's no one else out there for us."

"Is that so?"

"There should be nothing surprising about the pervert part," he said. He gathered my hands in his, his expression sobering. "Let's be the people who figure it out. The ones who learn how to do it right."

"What does that mean?" I whispered.

He was here, talking to me, and he looked fucking incredible. He was nailing the lumberjack underwear model thing, and I couldn't stop wondering how that beard would feel against my inner thighs.

Focus.

"It means I spent more than two months away from you but can't get the words in order to tell you I love you and I missed you and I can't spend another day without you, so please put me out of my misery and come home with me now."

"I missed you too," I said. "And I worked like crazy to get my dissertation finished, and I hate all the awful things I said to you. I shouldn't have pushed you away."

He studied me, but I couldn't interpret the gleam in his eyes. "I needed to hear everything you said." He looked around the bar, frowning. "Can we get out of here?"

He slid out of the booth, and of course I followed. We walked in silence, and when our hands bumped, I slid my palm into his. I didn't pay attention to where we were going, and I didn't care that we were wandering the city without saying a word to each other. For all the distance and time we'd put between us, being here with him was all I needed right now. This was the walk we were taking together.

We stopped on a corner, and Sam pointed across the street. We were in front of the firehouse.

"Who are we going to be, Tiel?"

Smiling, I leaned into him, wrapping my arms around him for the first time in too long. "We're the ones who figure it out."

epilogue

SAM

Six months later

THERE WAS A BETTER way to do this. Something elaborate or quirky, the kind of experience we'd retell for years to come. But that ring had been burning a hole in my pocket all week, and we had enough stories in our arsenal.

And maybe this one was just for us.

The ring caught my eye when I walked past the Newbury Street jewelry shop, and I knew that pale pink stone belonged on Tiel's hand. It was a rare, old-fashioned cut and the thin antique band was studded with white diamonds, and it was too odd to pass up.

And now, on this sunny November morning with her asleep beside me, I was tired of waiting.

We'd spent the first two months going to shows, watching movies, and making new memories to replace those from our time apart. There were a lot of issues for us to get through; simply deciding that we wanted to be together didn't change the fact that I didn't make healthy decisions or set the clearest boundaries with the women in my life, or that her jealousy and abandonment triggers were quick. But we talked and worked at it, and we agreed we wouldn't walk away, even when it was difficult or frustrating.

We weren't walking away *ever*.

After celebrating the Fourth of July with a whirlwind tour of regional music festivals, Tiel announced she was tired of bouncing between my place and hers, and we'd decided an experiment in cohabitation was in order.

From there, we'd spent the summer learning how to live together, fighting and making up, and discovering new ways to love and challenge each other every day.

The firehouse was in decent shape, too. There were a couple new walls and the tree-ring tile project was finished, and a crew was wrapping up work on her studio next week.

At Tiel's request, I hadn't evicted Riley, but he was safely ensconced in his own wing these days. Unfortunately, that didn't improve his ability to zip his pants.

Tiel had accepted an associate professorship, and for the first time in years, didn't spend the summer at band camp. With all that free time, she eventually agreed to Lauren's invitation for margaritas and pedicures. The paint wasn't even dry on her toes when she'd texted me to say Lauren was hilarious and she was developing a crazy girl-crush on her.

Over Labor Day weekend on Martha's Vineyard, Tiel and Shannon ended up chatting for hours—there were a few bottles of wine involved—and now they regularly met up for drinks.

Despite our commitment to complete honesty, I wasn't going to call out Tiel's dramatic pivot in that situation.

I glanced at the ring again, smiling. The stone was big, bigger than Tiel would ever select for herself, but wasn't that the point?

The idea of marriage was a strange compulsion for me. I craved this, and not because I doubted any amount of our commitment to each other. I'd spent some time unwrapping this urge for weeks now, and though I knew I could be content with our relationship as it was, I wanted the official confirmation that we were legally, socially, spiritually bound and possessed by each other.

I wanted Tiel as mine, and I wanted to be hers.

And we were ready for this.

"Sweetheart," I murmured, brushing her hair aside and kissing her shoulder.

"Five more minutes," she whispered.

"I'd like a little bit longer than that," I said, curling my arm around her waist.

She nodded and burrowed into my chest, her eyes heavy with sleep. "It's Sunday, though," she said. "Let's have snuggletime."

"Let's get married," I said.

Her eyes fluttered open and she stared at me, quiet and assessing. "Yeah," she said, her smile hitting me like a blinding ray of sunshine. "We're going to have really cool kids."

"Of course," I said, laughing as I slipped the ring on her finger. "They'll be smart and the good kind of weird, talented and cute, and we should start making them right now."

"You're brilliant," she said, wrapping her legs around me. "And more than a little pervy."

"*You're* a little pervy," I murmured. "And I love it."

THANK you for reading *Necessary Restorations*! I hope you enjoyed Tiel and Sam. Their story continues with an emotional journey to the altar and beyond in *Restored*.

CAN A REFORMED *player ever truly play by someone else's rules?*

Sam Walsh has finally put an end to decades of self-destruction, turned over a healthy new leaf, and now he's ready to call himself a married man. But love and marriage are only the beginning, and life is about to get much more complicated.

WILL TYING the knot tie down a free spirit?

Tiel Desai never imagined herself getting married again, and before she can blink, she's swept up into the Walsh wedding whirlwind. If that chaos isn't enough, she's also busy winning over her future in-laws, grappling with a bumpy adjustment to her new job, and staying afloat when a string of disappointments hit.

THEY'RE BUILDING A FUTURE, but can they ever fully demolish the past?

Sam and Tiel beat back their demons and learned to love each other, but love might not be enough to solve every problem that crawls their way.

RESTORED IS AVAILABLE NOW!

IF YOU LOVE the Walsh family's sharp wit and steamy nights, you're going to adore Will and Shannon in *The Cornerstone.*

A TOUGH-AS-NAILS BUSINESSWOMAN. *An arrogant Navy SEAL. A power struggle with no end in sight.*

Some people hook-up at weddings. Others break a hotel room bed (and a table, and a desk, and some complimentary bathrobe belts) and discover they've been surviving on bargain basement orgasms their entire lives.

The last one? Yeah. That's all me.

She's driven and demanding...I wasn't always a bitch. There's a dirty little trick to succeeding in business: the sweet and innocent rarely survive. I fought my way up from nothing, and I don't bend for anyone.

Until Will Halsted ties me to a headboard and makes me his...for now.

One wild, filthy night turns into another, and then...we can't stop. Each time we're together is more addictive than the last, but it's nothing more than a sexy escape from reality.

Or is it?

He's never walked away from a challenge...

I wasn't always a warrior but now it's in my bones and blood. That's what years spent in the Special Forces does to a man. My entire life is classified: where I've been, what I've seen, what I've done, and there's no mission too dangerous.

Until I realize that falling for Shannon Walsh is like trying to swim against a riptide. She's going to tear me up and toss me to the shore, and I'll love every minute of it.

Every time I'm down range, I want her counting the hours until I'm back. Waiting for me. She's done it before; she'll do it again.

Or will she?

They're wrong for each other in every possible way...
Or are they?

THE CORNERSTONE **IS AVAILABLE NOW!**

JOIN *my newsletter for new release alerts, exclusive extended epilogues and bonus scenes, and more.*

. . .

IF NEWSLETTERS AREN'T *your thing, follow me on BookBub for preorder and new release alerts.*

VISIT MY PRIVATE READER GROUP, *Kate Canterbary's Tales, for exclusive giveaways, sneak previews of upcoming releases, and book talk.*

also by kate canterbary

Vital Signs

Before Girl — Cal and Stella
The Worst Guy — Sebastian Stremmel and Sara Shapiro

The Walsh Series

Underneath It All – Matt and Lauren
The Space Between – Patrick and Andy
Necessary Restorations – Sam and Tiel
The Cornerstone – Shannon and Will
Restored — Sam and Tiel
The Spire — Erin and Nick
Preservation — Riley and Alexandra
Thresholds — The Walsh Family
Foundations — Matt and Lauren

The Santillian Triplets

The Magnolia Chronicles — Magnolia
Boss in the Bedsheets — Ash and Zelda
The Belle and the Beard — Linden and Jasper-Anne

Talbott's Cove

Fresh Catch — Owen and Cole
Hard Pressed — Jackson and Annette
Far Cry — Brooke and JJ

Rough Sketch — Gus and Neera

Benchmarks Series

Professional Development — Drew and Tara

Orientation — Jory and Max

Brothers In Arms

Missing In Action — Wes and Tom

Coastal Elite — Jordan and April

Get exclusive sneak previews of upcoming releases through Kate's newsletter and private reader group, The Canterbary Tales, on Facebook.

About Kate

USA Today Bestseller Kate Canterbary writes smart, steamy contemporary romances loaded with heat, heart, and happy ever afters. Kate lives on the New England coast with her husband and daughter.

You can find Kate at www.katecanterbary.com

facebook.com/kcanterbary

twitter.com/kcanterbary

instagram.com/katecanterbary

amazon.com/Kate-Canterbary

bookbub.com/authors/kate-canterbary

goodreads.com/Kate_Canterbary

pinterest.com/katecanterbary

tiktok.com/@katecanterbary

CPSIA information can be obtained
at www.ICGtesting.com
Printed in the USA
BVHW041254140522
637051BV00004B/15

9 781946 352682